The Madi[illegible]

Mon Bein-Aimé

By: allie fisher

Title ID: 4149943
ISBN-13: 978-0988824928

Acknowledgments

*To my sisters Bennia & Pam,
my ambassadors of inspiration and motivation. I will never be able to thank you enough for knowing when to praise, critique and push me.*

Nikki, my real life Jenna. Without you there would be no her!

To my pocket editor and partner in crime Julia aka: "lil'bug." Without your positive attitude and perseverance this book would still be stuck in my flash drive!

Contents

Intro:

Is it right to feel like you can't breathe? Like you are dying slowly with every breath, so you try to not inhale to slow the process. Numbness slips over every part of you until there is only a dull ache. The life that once danced effortlessly across your face has turned into a distant vacant expression. Do you remain because it's the right thing to do, or do you run; run until you start to feel again, breathe again, become alive again?

There is a movie, Night of the Living Dead, and although it is fiction, there is such a thing as a life of the living dead. It happens when you settle for what is right for everyone else instead of what is right for you. When you place all your hopes and dreams into a box and tape it up tightly and put them somewhere dark and far away. When the most important thing in your life is pleasing everyone else and you make sure to never think about those hopes and dreams ever again.

How can thirteen years vaporize, like a mist, into nothing? You wake up to discover that when you look into the mirror, you see only a shell of the person you once were. I don't think it happens right away. I think it starts slowly by eating away one hope, one dream at a time until the nothingness lulls you into a slumber. There it can more easily rob you of yourself until all that is left is empty.

I try to feel, but I can't. My mind just shuts down until I can't remember why or what I was thinking. I guess in the end it's okay to just not feel. Maybe that's the good part of it because not only can you not feel the joy, it even dulls the ache.

You ask yourself, "Is this what your life amounts to? Is this right?"

I can't help but feel like there should be more, but I am torn with the effect my personal choices will have on those around me. It was always one of my strengths, but now it is my curse, to care what everyone around thinks and feels. I want to scream, but it is stuck, no, buried deep inside and I can't release it.
I have heard that when a person starts to become hypothermic they shut down and feel very tired. Their only desire is to sleep. Maybe I am as I was once called, "frozen" an ice cube, no feeling, no heart.
I do vaguely recall a young girl who was not like that at all. Is she lost forever?

Chapter One:
Life after Death

***

It seems like a bad idea now; going back after so many years. Maybe too impulsive; leaving right after the funeral, but I know how much it meant to Dad and how many great childhood memories Mom, Dad & I shared there. Besides, I don't think I could not go. The urge to leave is too strong. That, combined with the fact that the dreams have gotten worse, more frequent and I can't shake my feelings for him – this man I have never met and don't even know if he exists. My therapist says creating him was a way to create the perfect man without ever having to commit. Like a fifteen year old can decide to do that, right? Oh, and my personal favorite, "I am suppressing my creativity, by creating this fictional character it helps me find an outlet for my subconscious." That was therapist number two. I can't blame her though, she's the reason I changed majors. Twelve years of wasted money just to learn what I already know: I'm the only sane person in a crazy screwed up world. Maine was my only sanctuary left.

I remember the first time I saw him, well the first time I dreamt of him. I was fifteen. I went with Dad to the summer house (really just a glorified old farmhouse Dad had inherited from his uncle before I was born). It sits on five acres overlooking the St. Croix River. A beautiful two story Victorian painted a faded red color with whitewashed trim and a huge wrap-around porch that has a swing facing the water at one end. We never visited there after Labor Day, but Dad had wanted to check on the old caretaker, Jed Randall, and make sure he had winterized the house. He was getting on in years, but Dad would never have replaced him. They had a special bond. In the summers we spent up there, Dad always made time to let Jed take him fishing. They seemed to enjoy each other's company.

I think Dad always missed not having a father figure and Jed was like a father to everyone.

It was mid-October and already there was a sting in the air when we left the airport in Bangor. It was the first time I had ever been there that time of the year. My teeth where chattering by the time we walked to our rental car. I hadn't expected it to be this cold; I was only wearing a thin hooded sweatshirt and jeans. I had brought a coat with me, but it was in our luggage and I didn't want to have to try and squeeze the overstuffed bag shut again. My mother had insisted I would need the extra warm sweaters and socks. He looked over at me smiling.

"Are you sorry you didn't stay in Arizona with your mom now?" as he was talking he took off his denim jacket and handed it to me to put on.

"Your mom will never forgive me if I let you catch cold."

I put it on and immediately held the collar to my face, smelling it. I love the way my Dad smelled, it was like rain on a summer day, clean and soothing. Something about it made me feel safe.

He just laughed at me when he saw what I was doing. It embarrassed me that he had noticed, but I laughed too. It seemed routine to me back then, but now I would give anything to smell him again; feel safe again.

After loading the trunk with our bags we headed for Robbinston. It was about a four-hour ride from the airport, but I had my headphones and a pillow, which I planned to use to occupy the time. My dad had other plans; he would always sing songs and make up his own words to familiar tunes. I guess it was to help pass the time, but being fifteen, it totally and completely annoyed me.

As we pulled into the gravel drive, something looked off. Then it occurred to me, I had never been able to see the house from the street before.

But, the trees that were usually thick with leaves were almost bare and all that was left were the small pines Dad and I planted for "privacy," as he said, even though they were only four feet tall. The old red house seemed to be more vibrant against the deep blue autumn sky, not as aged as usual. As we rounded the back of the house near the garage, we saw Jed waiting for us. His short, stocky body and thick gray wavy hair in total disarray, as usual. He was pacing back and forth, looking anxious.

"Hey there Jed. How is everything going?" Dad said, trying to make small talk.

"Hello," I managed in a low voice.

I was still sulking a little over my dad's lovely rendition of "Hold My Hand" by Hootie and the Blowfish he had been singing for the last two hours.

"Hello Doc!"

Jed glared at me with disbelief and then with two steps he had me in a bear hug.

"Zoe girl, I almost didn't recognize you. You get prettier every time I see you. You'll have to come out one of these summers for a barbeque at my son's house and visit. My grand boys would love me if I ever brought Zoe to a family outing."

"Thanks Jed,"

He was either an excellent liar or he was blind because my hair was looking similar to something a rat would be nesting in after my failed attempt to sleep on the way up here. I had been forced to use my pillow as earplugs. After being released I decide to check out the water. Dad motioned that he would be right there and began talking to Jed about the latest town gossip. The bay was gorgeous. The contrast in colors was breathtaking, deep blue sky and every autumn color in the world painted onto the trees and bushes. I wondered how anything could look so beautiful and lonely at the same time. There was something about the water that had always drawn me to it.

Mom always said it was my love of swimming. I was like a fish. But it was more a deep curiosity for the unknown. The water seemed like a veil over layers and layers of secrets and the harder you looked, the more she concealed, as if you could get completely lost in it. There was almost a fear that consumed me as I looked down at the seemingly calm, restful water. I thought for a moment I saw a reflection. Not my own, but behind me. I couldn't move, squinting and straining my eyes to focus. My dad must have been in stealth mode, because I didn't even hear him when he approached me. I jumped and drew in a deep breath, startled. I must have been concentrating a little more than I thought.

"Sorry Zo."

"I swear I am going to put a bell on you Dad. You just gave me a heart attack."

"I thought I had made enough noise in the car, I was trying to give you a break," he said, looking at me remorsefully.

I couldn't argue with that. We stood there for what seemed to be an eternity, silent, just standing in awe at the beauty of the bay in front of us. The sun was starting to go down and the temperature was too.

"Let's go inside Zo. It's getting chilly."

I realized I still had the poor man's jacket on.

"Sorry Dad."

He just smiled and put his arm around me as we walked up the slate steps of the path toward the house. The house was warm. Jed's wife had sent us a care package of food and some goodies. We hadn't thought to stop and buy any groceries because we were only staying the weekend. Dad brought my suitcase in and I started to drag it up the stairs to my room.

"Don't take too long up there Zo, this food looks real good and there may not be any left."

"I won't be long Dad," my suitcase making a thumping sound as it struck each step.

As I opened the door to my room, I had forgotten that everything was cloaked in my mother's white dust covers. I quickly pulled the one over my bed off. The rest could stay, less I would have to do before I left. I quickly changed into my sweats, a large thick sweater and the thick socks I had sworn to my mother I would not need and headed down the stairs. As I reached the bottom, I flipped my mop of tousled hair into a ponytail and joined my dad in the kitchen.

After stuffing ourselves on homemade crab cakes and blueberry muffins, we crashed in the living room again. Everything was covered in white, except the overstuffed sofa in front of the fireplace. It was Dad's story telling couch, since we didn't have a television in the house - "Dad's Rules." He believed that when we went to the summer house, it was to be with each other, not watch other families be with each other. So, no TV. Dad loved stories even more than making up songs, but unlike his songs, I actually loved his stories. I even looked forward to them. He was gone a lot with work, being a surgeon was more than a full time job, and our summers were everything to us.

"Okay Zo what type of story should I tell tonight?" There was only one that really came to mind. He already knew by my expression which one.

"Oh Zo aren't you getting sick of that one yet?"

"Dad, you know it's my favorite, besides you owe me for the car ride, remember?"

It was the story of "The Haddy," she was a salvage schooner in the 1900's. But more than that, Her captain was a man named William Madison. He was a legend in his time for being driven, obsessed with his love of the sea. Once he had his sights on something, he never gave up – to his demise.

His ship went down in Passamaquaotty Bay on November 13, 1909, while trying to salvage The Acadia, a smaller vessel that was stranded on the outer banks just south of Calais. Captain Madison was almost finished with the salvage when a terrible storm hit. A ship nearby, a coastal steamer, collided with The Haddy, sinking both vessels almost instantly. The entire crew on The Haddy went down with Her. Eighteen men lost their lives, gone in just seconds, including both Captains.

But my favorite part of the story was that of Captain William Madison himself. He was the only son of a wealthy French Aristocrat turned Banker from right here in Robbinston, "old money," as my dad would say. William himself was a mystery. There was very little known about him personally. He was said to be strikingly handsome and at age thirty-three, he was considered one of the most eligible bachelors of his day. He had never married and never settled down. My dad was very descriptive in his story telling, but it wasn't until he took me to the Maritime Museum that I was hooked. There in the corner of the museum is a picture of Captain Madison. It's faded and very small. It was the kind of picture that forced you to look at it. You couldn't turn away. Not only because of how devastatingly handsome he was, but it was the feeling you got from the photograph. It was absolutely haunting. His wide shoulders, dark wavy hair and dark eyes that were distant and lonely.

His bone structure was well defined and muscular. His sailor's pea coat fit him well with his thick wool turtleneck and of course, his Captain's hat. Exactly how you would picture him if you heard my dad tell the story. His expression was one of authority, even though he looked so young. But, his eyes, that's what did it. They made you feel as if he was looking into you, as if they were searching for something lost.

As locals tell it, there were some people that did not want the Captain's name or picture to be remembered in the museum. They felt that he was to blame for the loss of life and that his arrogant pride had caused the sinking of The Haddy. He had fair warning of the storm but was cocky and refused to seek shelter until it blew over. He would not quit, to the detriment of his crew, his vessel and himself. But money won out, his father paid off the right people and they agreed to allow his son into the museum, but only a small plaque that read:

> *"Cursed be the man who betrays himself and trusts the Sea, She never gives back her own. For a man to die doing what he loved 'tis a true cure for death. But for a man to die deprived of that which is love is the true curse. Sometimes, one must first be cursed to truly appreciate the cure."*
>
> *Captain William A. Madison Aug. 18, 1877 - Nov. 13, 1909*

Above it hung the small picture. I must have fallen asleep on the couch in the middle of the story, I felt Dad scoop me up and carry me to my room. He only bumped my head twice and apologized both times. I woke up thinking about William Madison. I wondered why I was so drawn to his story, to him. Was it the sad way he met his end, never having known love, blamed and condemned for the death of his crew? Or was it something else? Maybe those eyes, not frightening at all, but something in them reminded me of the water from earlier that day; veiled with layers as deep as the ocean itself and as dark as its depths.

I reluctantly climbed out of bed and walked over to the window. I peered out, checking the weather; gray and overcast. Not like the day before at all. I decided since we were leaving early the next morning that today was my day. I might as well make the best of it and go for a walk down the shoreline.

Knowing that it was probably as chilly as it looked, I opted for jeans, my turtleneck, jacket, and hiking boots. I did a quick mirror check, taking my hair out of the ponytail. I decided to leave it down and only pulled back the front with a large barrette. I knew my ears would freeze if I wore it completely up. As I reached the bottom of the steps, I could hear my dad singing. I chuckled to myself shaking my head and continued into the kitchen.

"There's slim pickings this morning Zoe. You have your choice of a muffin or a muffin."

"Well then I guess I'll have to say, a muffin it is."

"I promise we'll go to town for lunch, Zoe."

I was fine with the muffin. They were still moist with blueberries and Dad had warmed them up.

"I was thinking Dad."

"Yes Zoe?"

"Well I was thinking of walking down to Red Beach today to try out my new camera. Is that okay?"

"I guess so Zoe, but stay away from the water's edge."

"You're by yourself this time of year out here and I don't want you falling in that far from home. If you want to wait I will go with you, after Jed and I finish up here this morning."

It was only about four miles north of us but he and I both knew Mom would have never let me do it by myself, which is why I wanted to.

"No, that's okay Dad. I think I can handle it."

"And Zoe, stick to the bank of the river and don't wander off into the woods. It's too overcast today and you might lose your way. Agreed?"

"No problem Dad."

My steps were quick and full of purpose as I ran out the kitchen door to the porch. I needed to leave before he changed his mind or Mom called to check on us. I stopped at the car only long enough to grab my camera. I took the slate steps down toward the water's edge and began there following it. I couldn't believe how many things were visible to the naked eye this time of year. With all the under brush and leaves gone, the tree line was dotted with rock outcroppings. The air was filled with the smell of burning leaves and there was a chill in the air, but thankfully, it was not too windy.

As I followed the line of trees around The Pointe, I spotted the top of a large building that sat on a large stone outcropping surrounded by huge towering pines. The angle that it sat at would have made it completely impossible to see in the warmer months. As I moved closer, I wondered what it could be. The building was similar to the top of the city library back home. The size was monstrous. It couldn't be a home, could it? The view didn't improve the farther north I traveled, too many trees. I had to go higher.

Dad would never know I strayed from the path just a little. I began to climb the rocks just west of the large building. As I climbed higher, I realized it was bigger than I thought. The other half had been obscured by the angle I was at from the ground. It had six chimneys protruding up from a reddish brown slate top roof. The sides were stone, almost like a castle and I could just see the top of a window if I tiptoed. This was a house; it had to be. There were no museums or libraries out here, there were no roads to get to them. Now I was on a mission.

I had to see it closer; see what it was. I decided to let reason have a break and walk through the wooded area straight through to The Pointe. If anyone asked, I just got lost, turned around, and didn't realize there was anything out here.

The rocks were a bit slick from the damp air, but I managed. My heart began to thump hard from excitement, but why? This was probably just some old church. Still, I loved a good mystery. I reached a clearing, but as I drew near, I could see a tall black wrought iron fence jetting up from the ground like something from a Vincent Price movie. The view was better from here though and worth the danger. The hedges that surrounded this old mansion had to be as old as the house. They were huge. The windows on the south side of the house were as tall as our house, lined with what looked like heavy draperies. The side that faced the water had large stone steps like the White House, but more gothic. Large stone columns held up a porch above them.

My heart had slowed, but only a little. Then a noise, it was a rustling sound and then a low growling followed by barking. Dogs! More than one, I couldn't see them, but I could hear them. I turned to run, but the rocks around the fence were damp and slick.

It was hard to get my footing. Coming down was much easier than going back up. The barking grew closer now and it was fierce. The dense pines obliterated the sky make hard to see where to place my feet. I found a foothold and began to make my way up the rocks. I didn't look back, too afraid to see what was coming for me. I clawed my hands up the steep ledges and then heard a loud crash against the fence behind me. I fought myself to turn around. As I did, I caught a glimpse of the dogs. Four huge guard dogs! Rottweilers, I think. They were looking for a way out of the fence. I was terrified they would find one. As I reached the top of the outcrop, I heard a voice, low and commanding, calling the dogs. I stood for a moment, frozen by the voice as if it spoke to me. I strained to hear it again through the barking, but then the barking stopped.

I could make out only a dark figure moving towards me from the distance. I slid to my knees. The dogs had every intention of ripping me to shreds. Curiosity killed the cat, they say. An overwhelming sense of relief was quickly consumed by the overwhelming fear of how much trouble I was going to be in.

I turned and struggled back up the rocks. I began to walk as fast as I was able. The rocks were still very slick and I had already slipped several times. My leg was throbbing. Paranoia set in as I kept looking back.

I continued on toward home. I felt as if I was being watched the rest of the way. I am sure it was nothing, but the hair stood up on the back of my neck as I imagined who or what lived in that house.

There was another sigh of relief as I saw my own house's roof through the trees and walked faster now. It was getting darker out, more overcast and I had that feeling you get when you are walking up stairs after watching a scary movie, like something might grab you just as you reach safety. I took the slate steps two at a time up the path to the porch.

As I neared the kitchen door, I heard voices. It was Dad and Jed. I opened the door, afraid to stand outside at the moment. I stepped in and Jed's mouth fell open. Dad turned his face, losing its expression.

"Zoe what happened? You are covered in mud and leaves! You're bleeding!"

I looked down to notice a large spot of deep red blood near a large tear in my jeans, just below the knee.

"Oh, I slipped, I guess," I said, afraid to tell the truth.

"You are as white as your mom's dust covers here," Jed handed me a kitchen chair.

"Sit down here girl, let's have a look at you."

"I'll get my bag, stay with her Jed."

My dad always tended to overreact. Jed watched as my dad left the room, his face turned serious now.

"What were you doing when yah fell, Zoe?"

"Just walking," I said.

"Hmmmmm," His eyes searched mine to see if I was going to fess up, which I wasn't.

"Jed, do you know who lives in the big house near Red Beach?"

"What big house are you talking about, Zoe?"

I could tell he knew which big house I meant. How many were there? Now who was lying?

"The big house that juts out off The Pointe, and looks like a museum."

"Ohh that house?" His tone changed and he moved in close enough to whisper, his eyes furrowed.

"Now you listen to me Zoe girl, just you don't go there no more. I'm thinking that's what you were up to when you fell. What did you see out there?"

"Nothing," I mumbled.

My body shuttered thinking about what could have happened.

"Well you just forget about that. Nothing good can come from being anywhere near that house so you just stay clear of it."

"But, Jed...."

"No 'buts' Missy, you just stick to your yard here and you'll be okay."

If possible, I was a little more afraid now than I had been before. Something in the pit of my stomach verified everything he just said. Just then, Dad came in with his bag.

"Zoe honey, give me your leg."

"Dad, I am fine. Really. It's just a scratch."

"Let me be the judge of that, humor me."

He pulled up the leg of my jeans and wiped the debris and dirt away from the wound. It started to sting a little.

"Well, I don't think you need any stitches, but you'll have a lovely little scar. Go change and get cleaned up.

I'll put a bandage on it when you're all done. Can you make it up the stairs honey?"

"Dad, I am fine."

I walked as normal as I could pull off. Thank God they couldn't see me wincing up the stairs. Every bone in my body was aching. The shower felt good and I felt human again. I slid some comfortable clothes on and did my hair. I could hear dad coming up the stairs. A gentle quiet rap on my door,

"Zo, you in there?"

"Come in."

"Are you ready for your Band-Aid?"

"Sure, will it hurt?" I said as I batted my eyes humorously at him.

"Only if you don't stay still," he said, his face smiling as he placed the Band-Aid on, he looked up, his expression serious this time.

"Zo, Jed told me where you went." My eyes rolled.

"No Zoe, this is serious. He doesn't get this way without reason. Do me a favor; never go there again. Understand?"

I could not tell him no, he was so worried.

"Alright, I won't go there again."

And you would think I wouldn't want to after all that, but I did. For some strange reason, I wanted to see the face of the deep mysterious voice.

We went into town and grabbed lunch and something to take home for dinner, and of course, a bag of Oreos. When we got back, Dad put on his Van Morrison and played it while we spent the day finishing the work he and Jed had started. I mostly got in the way, but they were tolerant and made me feel helpful. After Jed left, Dad had gone into his study to do some reading. I retired to my room to read. I grabbed my skeleton crew off the bookcase and headed up the stairs. I fell asleep lying across my bed, reading The Mist. My mind raced as I fought to sleep.

I never had a problem sleeping before. In fact, I had never dreamed, at least not that I could remember. No one ever believed me, but I had never had one dream that I could remember. I sat up feeling out of sorts and went to the window. I opened it a bit to let some cool air in. I realized I still had on my jeans and sweater, so I grabbed my bag and took out a large scrub top Dad had gotten me from the hospital and put it on. I returned to my bed and lay down again, determined to sleep. I pulled up the down-filled comforter and drew in deep breaths until I felt relaxed and closed my eyes.

I was standing near the edge of a platform, surrounded by railings. It was like the railing of a lighthouse. I was looking out over the still water. I felt an overwhelming urge to let go, just step off. I heard in my head, "Don't be afraid, it's your destiny."

I held on, gripping tightly, and then felt him gripping me tightly. I gasped as I clung to him. He saved me. I looked up needing to see him, dark eyes and his face so beautiful.

"William?"

As I spoke his name, I felt peace wash over me, as if I had been looking for him. He looked down at me as if he would speak. And then I felt myself torn from him, my chest filled with pain. I gasped again, but no breath came. Darkness was all around me.

I woke grabbing my chest, gasping for air and crying like someone had died, like I had lost someone. If this was what dreaming felt like, I never wanted to do it again.

I got up and walked over to the window, it was morning. I felt like I hadn't even slept. I closed the window and got dressed, not able to shake my dream. It was lingering, the feeling of loneliness, being separated from him.

I heard Dad coming up the stairs and tried to tidy up and replace the white dust covers. He knocked and came in.

"Ready Zo?"

"Yeah, I think so."

He grabbed my bag as I flung the white dust cover back over my bed.
I didn't know then how much that weekend would alter my life and stick in my memories as one of the best times with my Dad.
I wonder if it will still feel like going home or just as empty and lonely as it does here in Arizona. It doesn't matter. I have nothing to go back to now, now that they are both gone. I never thought in a million years I would be moving to Maine, let alone Robbinston. It was always great for the summer, but winter gets very lonely and very cold and I have never been there without my parents.

Chapter Two:
Alone

***

The car ride was not as relaxing as I had thought it would be, three thousand miles with just me and Bailey, whose bladder is the size of a pea. But, I love him because my dad loved him. Dad bought Bailey for me eight years ago for my twentieth birthday. He hated to see me alone. So, he brought home this cute little black and white Am-staff puppy with one black eye, just like Petie from The Little Rascals. I never really owned him; he was always Dad's. Ninety-five pounds later, he is lazy and can't go two hundred miles without a pit stop. Did I mention he hates men? I mean, besides my dad. This was going to be really helpful if and when I ever decide to date. I was glad he was coming with me though. I could have never left him behind. That, Dad would have never forgiven.

As night approached, I was extremely glad I had brought all my CD's in the front seat with me, although Bailey wasn't thrilled to share the seat. Most of my things had been shipped to Robbinston already. I had only my personal stuff I would need for the trip, photos, and things that I didn't trust to anyone, consequences of being an only child.

I liked being an only child, though I was lonely sometimes, I never minded. And, I had my Aunt Kate and her kids. She was my aunt from my mother's side, whom I am sure would be calling in another hour to check on me, as she had for the last six hundred miles. I love her, but she can be a little high strung and mothering, especially since Mom died. She worried and fretted over Dad and me until she nearly suffocated both of us. But, she was with us every step of the way through Mom's cancer. Mom battled for over two years with it before it took her from us. She was such a fighter; never giving up, always positive, always supporting us, even more than we supported her.

She was our rock we anchored to. Dad and I were the dreamers. Mom was the one who made it all happen for us in all the little things she did for us, sacrifices she made. She was there for me when Dad and I had our little falling out, the year I decided to drop out of medical school and decided to go into photography. Dad thought I was wasting my talents; that I was too smart to settle. It killed me to disappoint him, but my heart was not in medicine.

Over time we patched things up, with Mom's persistence. But, I don't think he ever really got over my decision or losing her. She was only 54 years old when she died. He threw himself into his work after that and stopped taking care of himself. He became solemn.

Bailey and I were the only ones he communicated with after Mom died. It made me feel as helpless watching him give up as Mom's death had made him feel.

I tried to keep him going, but it was only three years after Mom died that I lost him too.

I was starting to get tired now; it was getting late. Aunt Kate had already called three times and I was running on a caffeine high that had begun to wear off over a half an hour ago. I would have to stop soon, maybe somewhere in Oklahoma.

"How does that sound Bailey, my little partner in crime?"

Okay, now I know I'm tired. The dog is looking at me like I've lost my mind. The next sign that came into view was a Comfort Inn. Although it did not look that comforting, I had to remind myself that beggars can't be choosers. If they were willing to let Bailey stay, it would have to do. After giving Bailey his pit stop at the doggie run, I let him back into the car and I walked to the front where a bright neon yellow and green sign said: "Office." Just inside was a long counter with a small shiny silver bell on it that said: "RING FOR SERVICE."

It was too much of a temptation for me. I was sure someone had heard the loud ringing sound the door made as I came in. The urge to ring it was overwhelming. I had to. That's what it's there for anyway, right? Right as I slapped my hand down, I looked up to see this scrawny head pop around the corner, the bell's chime cutting of his voice.

"How may I help you?"

My eyes batted a few times in disbelief. I had succumbed to my weakness. It was so loud; it had to be the caffeine. Rephrasing his prior question to me,

"My name is Kyle, what can I do for you this morning?" his voice almost as high pitched as the bells' ring.

He was my height and about five feet six inches with a slim build. His red curly hair cut short against his head and his eyes were very green. Every inch of him was covered in freckles. His plaid shirt and striped tie were almost as distracting as his appearance.

Embarrassed by my reaction to the bell and his voice, I managed to get out the all-important question:

"Do you allow dogs?"

"We sure do," he said with a smile.

I had to hand it to him, it was two o'clock in the morning and he was perkier than I was after three Red Bulls. I pulled out my credit card and handed it to him.

"I'll need one room please."

"And how many will be staying in the room?" he asked.

"Just one, I'm alone."

The words brought a whole new feeling of pain to my collection.

"Check out is a noon Miss Dossin, have a great stay."

As I placed my credit card in my wallet, I noticed the picture of Dad and I that he always kept in his wallet.

It was taken at the summer house and Dad was pushing me on the swing attached to the old willow tree out back. I had forgotten that was in there. As my eyes started to get moist, I quickly signed my receipt, grabbed my key and walked to the car before I could think about it. Bailey met me with his whole body wagging and shaking. The once black Range Rover was now frosted with the dust from the last eight hundred miles. I hopped in and pulled around back. It really wasn't that bad. The outside had been freshly painted and the interior of the room although bland in color, was also freshly painted and clean.

Two full sized beds sat in the center of the square room, separated by a nightstand. The bathroom was clean, but small. It was plenty big enough for Bailey and I to share though. He was a gourmet when it came to toilet water. I dropped my bags and flopped onto the bed as Bailey claimed the other bed for himself.

I lay there for what seemed like only a few seconds, feeling like I was now so tired I couldn't sleep. But, the minute my body stopped, I was out.

And of course, it came again. I was used to it now. Since the funeral, it had become a nightly thing. The dream, the same dream I had had for thirteen years off and on. But lately, I had them more on than off.

I felt the sun warm on my face. I awoke to Bailey snoring and then the realization that I had forgotten to close the curtains last night. I had slept there all night with them wide open. I wondered how many passers by had enjoyed watching me toss and turn in my sleep. I cringed to think about the scrawny night clerk peering in at me and was instantly creeped out. Putting that out of my mind as quickly as possible, I jumped up, closed the curtains and headed for the bathroom. As I held my face under the water in the shower, it hit me: I'm alone, really alone for the first time since my dad died it had become real.

Tears began to freely flow down my face and it seemed like there would be no end. I was in Oklahoma having a breakdown by myself because I was by myself. What irony.

As the hot water ran out, I decided to take my breakdown into the other room, seeing that Bailey's bladder was calling again. I grabbed my shorts, tears slowing only a fraction as I put Bailey's leash on him and headed out the door.

I jumped when my cell phone rang, not realizing I had it in my hand. I already knew who it was.

"Yes, Aunt Kate. I have been brutally raped and am as we speak lying dead in a ditch," Frustration building in my voice.

"I'm sorry, is this Miss Dossin?"

This was not my Aunt Kate, unless she had suddenly become a young man.

"Hello, I'm sorry, who is this?" my voice cracking from the tears and dry mouth.

"It's Justin"

"Justin? Justin who?"

"Just Randall, Jed Randall's grandson."

"Oh yeah, I mean yes, yes. I am so sorry."

I am sure I was bright red now, trying to regain my composure, wiping off the last remnants of tears and clear my voice as quietly as possible.

"How can I help you Mr. Randall?"

"Oh no, call me Justin, please. Are you alright Miss Dossin?"

He had one of those voices where you just knew he was amazing looking, self-assured.

"Please, call me Zoe and yes, I am. I'm fine."

I was trying to convince myself more than him at this point, saying it with a controlled tone.

"I was told to call you and double check when your arrival in Robbinston would be."

Shoot, I had forgotten to call the real estate agency that handled the maintenance of the house to confirm.

"I am so sorry I forgot to call and confirm. I will be there on Friday evening, August fourth. Thank you so much for calling to check."

"No problem, I just want to make sure everything is set for your arrival. I know how much my grandfather liked your family and he would want it to be perfect. If
you have any questions, you can call me at this number. It's my cell. The real estate offices will be closed Friday through Monday for the Blueberry Festival. So, if you need anything, call me, okay?"

"Yes, thank you so much, I appreciate your call."

"Are you sure you are alright?"

Again, his voice was that of concern and sincerity. My voice must have still had that "I've been crying" tone to it.

"I assure you that I am fine, Mr. Randall, I mean, Justin. Thank you for your concern. I'll see you Friday."

"I look forward to it, Zoe."

I am an idiot. Nice way to greet someone you've never met. He probably thinks I'm nuts. The entire population of Robbinston will know Dr. Dossin's little girl has lost her mind. And what did he mean by, 'I look forward to it?' Who says that? He doesn't even know me. Obviously I am in no shape for someone to look forward to seeing me.

My ranting came to an abrupt halt as I realized Bailey was done and sitting at my side, looking up at me. A man and his wife walking their Yorkies stood watching me tell myself how crazy I am with wet hair, no shoes, an inside-out pajama top and shorts on.

Today just keeps getting better and better. Smiling lightly at them, I made my exit and quickly closed my room door behind me.

Once in my room, I packed my things and looked in the mirror. My eyes were abnormally green, from the crying spell earlier I guessed. I ran my fingers through my partially dried curly hair. Mom always said I was lucky I had such thick curly hair, but I didn't see it that way. It really needed to be cut. The long layers were starting to grow out, making my hair thick and heavy. My usually dark auburn hair was now slightly highlighted from being in the hot Arizona sun too much. But, it usually stayed up in a clip anyway because as of late, there was no one to impress.

Sticking to my routine, I grabbed my favorite hair clip and I was good to go. I checked out of the hotel with relief that Kyle's shift was over. In his place was a petite, dark-haired girl named Pam. She wasn't quite as anxious as Kyle and she quickly checked me out.

One last pit stop for Bailey and we were in the car. I drove to the closest fast food restaurant and grabbed a bite. I popped my Evanescence CD in and was on the road sharing my breakfast burrito with Bailey, which I am sure I will regret later.

The miles flew by, stopping every once in a while to allow Bailey his relief. I hadn't realized how many hours had passed since we had eaten, but my stomach was letting me know I was suddenly hungry, although I really didn't feel like stopping. It was only fair though. I knew I if I was hungry, Bailey had to be too. Not wanting to leave him in the car, I found a small Mom and Pop restaurant and grabbed a sandwich, chips and water.

I found a shady spot under a large tree at a nearby rest stop and Bailey and I sat down to eat our lunch. Bailey wasn't very interested in his dry food I put out.

I guess he felt like since we weren't home, he should get to eat fast food too. I couldn't resist his charms and he finished off the other half of my sandwich.

The trip would have been unbearable without him. He was a good distraction. I had been so used to caring for Dad, that my need to care for something, someone was dire. Bailey seemed to like the extra attention of course. I was going to have to start running him if he continued to eat like this.

I stayed longer than I should have at the small rest stop. The weather was beginning to change. The once blue sky and white, billowy clouds were becoming gray and overcast. The air smelled of rain and I quickly grabbed our things and headed for the car. Just as I closed the door, a downpour of rain came and for the rest of the day, we drove through the rain, stopping only to get gas and walk Bailey.

I managed to drive fourteen hours before stopping for the night. I had never driven that far and I was a little proud of myself. 'I can do this,' played through my head. Bailey and I were getting our routine down and I was making great time. I seemed to sleep better last night and was able to shower without the additional water works. I was certain I would make it to Robbinston by noon on Friday.

I felt a little scared by that thought. Could I really do this? I already felt completely alone and now I was purposely driving three thousand miles, leaving any shred of company and relatives behind me. My Aunt Kate's last words to me began to ring in my ears.

"Running away won't bring him back. He won't be there Zoe."

Her words cut me even deeper than before. Was I running away from it or trying to run to it? I don't know why I felt such a need to be there. I hadn't been there in over ten years. Life had become too busy to break away. The last time we were there together was for Jed's funeral. That was the first time I ever saw my dad cry. It bothered me to see it, but not in a normal way.

I had always pictured my dad as a super hero, never accepting defeat. And him crying made him seem very human to me. Death to him was losing. I imagined in his profession, he fought death often. This trip was stirring up so many memories; it was almost unbearable. The tears came again and I was getting good at driving while I cried.

I didn't know what I was looking for, but I had to go. There was no way around it. The pull was stronger than anything else. I would either do this or stop breathing. The last two hundred miles of the trip were a blur. I don't even remember turning on my exit.

Chapter Three:
Coming Home

***

The sun was shining and I felt the end of my trek nearing. It was around three in the afternoon when I came to the small sign that said, 'Welcome to Robbinston.' My heart skipped a little and I drew in a deep breath.

You can do this Zoe. But, can I? Why was I really here? Was it for him? He wasn't real. I spent a lot of money to come to the understanding that he wasn't real. How can you love someone that you've never met and isn't alive?

Traffic was heavy. There were some roads closed, probably due to this weekend's Blueberry Festival, I assumed. I made my way through the main drag and took a less traveled route to the house. I would run to the small store nearer to the house for groceries and supplies later, after I got settled in.

My car seemed like it was at a crawl as I turned onto our road. The house was barely visible to the road. The pines Dad and I had planted had grown and become what Dad always said they would be: great privacy.

I pulled into the gravel driveway and there it was, just as I had remembered it, same faded red color with white trim. I was taken back to all the wonderful times we had there. It was like a flood that washed over me. I already felt safer somehow.

I pulled around back and parked in front of the carriage house that had been converted into a garage before we inherited the house. I was earlier than expected and Jed's grandson, Justin, had not yet arrived.

Bailey was out of the car as soon as the door opened. I'm sure he was as relieved the long trip was over as I was. We walked down toward the slate path and headed for the waters' edge. I didn't have to worry about Bailey going into the water; he hated it.

He never could swim. He fell in our pool when he was young and sank like a stone, straight to bottom. Dad had to jump in and pull him out. Since then, he won't go near water.

It was as lovely as ever and I was surprised at how good I felt to be there. I thought for sure I would have a melt down as soon as I got the first glimpse of it, but there was an overwhelming sense that this is where I belonged.

A voice broke the silence and Bailey growled. I grabbed him by his collar and started up the steps. By the time I reached the top, Bailey was in a full out barking frenzy.

There was a well-built young man in jeans and a tight fitting tee shirt. His hair was thick and blonde. His skin tan from the sun only exaggerated his huge smile full of snow-white teeth. He looked to be in his twenties.

"Hello, Zoe?"

"Hi, excuse me for just a moment. I just need to put him in the house."

Bailey was making such a scene, I wanted to kill him as I scrambled for the keys to the house. The gentleman had already started to unlock the door for me.

"Thanks."

I quickly stuffed Bailey in the house where he could pitch his tantrum in peace.

"Sorry about that."

"I don't think he likes me. I'm Justin by the way, Justin Randall," he said as he stretched his hand out to greet me.

"Hello, nice to finally meet you," I replied, taking his hand to shake it.

His hands were large and calloused, but not too badly. He obviously worked with them and his dimples made you want to pinch his cheeks. With his blonde hair and blue eyes, he looked more like he belonged in California than Maine.

"I'm sorry about that," I said, pointing to Bailey, still in his frenzied state.

"He has a problem with men."

"Well, don't be too hard on him. If I were him, I wouldn't want strange men around you either."

His comment threw me off. Was he flirting with me?

"Well Justin, I really don't know what to say to that."

He thought for a moment and then let out a deep laugh.

"Let me help you with your things, Zoe."

"So, do you live here year round, Justin?" I asked, trying to make small talk.

"Yes, my family does."

"Oh that's right, your dad is a fisherman."

"All of us boys are."

"How many siblings do you have?"

"There are six of us, five boys and my sister. I'm the youngest."

"Wow! That's a lot of kids."

"Yeah, Dad wanted a lot of kids."

"So, how do you have time to run maintenance for the real estate business then?"

"We take turns; usually it's myself or Mason, my brother, The older ones usually work for my dad fishing. Is he going to let me in eventually?" he said, looking at Bailey, watching him intently through the window.

"He's all bark and a big bluff. Here, let me show you a trick." I reached in my pocked and handed him a small bag of treats.

"Just give him one when we go in and you'll be fine."

"Bribery, huh?"

"You can try it without the bribery if you want."

"No, no. I'm not above bribing someone to get what I want."

"You're very shy aren't you?" my tone purposely sarcastic.

"You noticed?" he said with a half smile.

We unloaded my things and walked toward the house, Bailey looking warily at him. I opened the door and walked past him. Justin followed; his hand held low and out. Bailey sniffed it once and then took the bait. Although after that, he followed poor Justin everywhere in the house wanting more.

The house was bright and open. Someone had come in and taken all the white dust covers off the furniture and cleaned. There was a beautiful basket of fresh flowers on the table.

"Did you do this Justin?"

"No, my sister Jenna did. Oh, that reminds me. I have something for you in the truck. I'll be right back."

He turned to go, but stopped and looked at me again.

"He'll let me back in right?"

"Still have the bait don't you?"

"Right! I'll be right back."

I set my things down in the parlor and walked into the living room. There was Dad's couch, as if everything were the same. But, it was never going to be the same. That was the thought that terrified me. My life would never be the same without them.

Alas, the meltdown I was planning on had arrived. Tears burned down my face and I wanted to run, throw myself on the couch and bury my face in it to see if I could still smell him there.

A low growl interrupted my thoughts and then the door. I turned and there was Justin. In his arms a familiar large basket, a checkered cloth in it twisted around its contents.

"Zoe, did something happen? Is everything okay?" his face looking like he had done something wrong.

"Fine," was all I could manage without losing it again.

"It's just the first time I've been back since my parents died."

Setting the basket on the table, he stepped towards me and hugged me.

"I'm sorry, I didn't know. No one from the real estate office told us. This must be really tough for you."

As much as I tried, I could not hold back. It just kept coming. The tears shook me. I was probably scaring the crap out of poor Justin, who I am sure, was just trying to be nice and did not need someone he barely knew falling apart on him like this. He patted my back and held me until I was ready to let go.

"I'm sorry. I don't know what came over me. I'm not crazy, really."

"Here, sit down," he said, handing me a chair.

"I know you're not crazy. My grandfather talked often of your dad. Your family meant a lot to him and I just feel terrible that we weren't told of his passing. Stay put, I'll get you some tissues."

He brought back the whole box. Although I think my meltdown was retreating.

"What's in the basket?" I asked, trying to change the subject.

"Oh, my sister made you a care package."

"Your grandma used to do the same thing for us. That's so nice. Please thank her for me."

"Oh! That reminds me, all the boxes you had shipped we put in the extra room upstairs, except for the things marked for your room. We guessed which one was yours; hope we were right. If not, just let me know and I'll move them for you. I noticed you don't have any TV or Internet here. Did you want me to talk to anyone about that for you?"

"Oh thanks. I will want to get the Internet, but no TV for now."

"I'll have the agent give you a call Monday then. No TV huh?" his eyebrows wrinkled.

"Gets awful lonely out here in the cold months."

"So I have heard, but I'll manage."

"Well, I have to get going, are you sure you're okay? I can come back later if you'd like?"

"No, you have done enough. I'm fine now, a little embarrassed, but fine. Really."

"They're calling for storms tomorrow evening. I'll come back before it hits and help you close the storm shutters."

"Thank you for everything, Justin."

"Anytime. Call if you need anything. Guess I'll see you tomorrow."

And he was gone. This was the first day. It would of course be the hardest, right? Not wanting to think too long about that, I unpacked Bailey's things for him and gave him fresh food and water. He seemed excited when I unpacked the large rawhide bone I had decided not to bring in the car with us.

I walked upstairs to my room at the end of the hall. The double doors to my parents' room stared at me. No way was I going to put myself through that today. I would save it for a time when I felt braver.

They had guessed right. All my boxes were neatly tucked in the far corner of my room. I had forgotten how cozy my room was here. It was light and airy, a pale blue color with white wash trim around the doors and windows. Across the room from my bed was my favorite spot: the window seat. Mom had covered fluffy cushions with soft white cotton fabric. The four-post bed was white washed in color with soft white voile fabric draped across it and gathered at each post. Caramel colored sheets peeked out of a thick white down comforter. I always loved pillows, so there were about eight on my bed, varying in color from caramel to blue and white. The kind of bed you want to curl up in and never wake up.

I flopped on my bed and lay there on my side looking out the large window at the trees and water.

I must have dozed off because when I woke up, it was dusk. I looked at my phone to see what time it was. Eight p.m.! I had missed two calls, both Aunt Kate. She would call the National Guard if I didn't call her and let her know I was fine.

After reassuring her I was fine, I changed into my jeans and a tee shirt. I went downstairs and noticed I hadn't seen or heard Bailey. I called, but no answer. I looked all over the house. Finally, I went in the living room and there he was, sprawled out on the large sofa. He must have loved the way Dad smelled as much as me.

"Come on, Bailey. Let's go for a walk!"

I grabbed my camera bag and we headed outside. The sky was streaked in tones of orange and pink across the water. I snapped a few shots of the back of the house and Bailey as we walked north down the beach.

I wasn't paying attention to where we were until I realized how far we walked. I looked up and there was The Pointe. Though the house wasn't visible, I felt its presence. A jolt of fear and excitement raced through me. I grabbed my zoom lens out of my bag and snapped it in place, focusing on where the house should be. The trees were dense; I couldn't see anything. The sun was going down and it was getting late; we needed to head back.

On the walk home, I decided I would maybe have to take a walk to Red Beach tomorrow and take some pictures and if I happen to take a small detour in the area of The Pointe, well maybe I would snap a few shots. I was a grown woman. I didn't have to answer to anyone and it was foolish to be afraid. I was a girl last time. Houses can't hurt you.

It was almost dark when we got back and Bailey was tired, his tongue was dragging the ground. He was so glad to not be cooped up in the car that he had been running back and forth in front of me the entire walk.

I took a deep breath, pausing before I walked back up the path.

Knowing there was no one waiting for me inside was almost unbearable.

I rummaged through the basket of goodies and found what I wanted. I opened the refrigerator to discover a new half gallon of milk, some bottled water and a plate of food. Justin must have brought it back for me. He was either really nice or he thought the bribe thing might work on me too.

I popped the plate in the microwave and got myself some milk while I wanted for it to heat up. I grabbed my food and sat at the island in the middle of the room. I flipped through some junk mail on the counter while I ate, distracting myself from the emptiness of the house.

I spent the rest of the evening unpacking the boxes in my room. As I got up to take some boxes downstairs, I passed my full-length pedestal mirror. I saw how different I looked compared to the last time I stood in front of it. My hair was the same, a little longer now, but my body and face were more mature. I filled out my tee shirt a lot better, that's for sure. I can remember standing for hours in front of that mirror, looking at myself, wishing my hair was straight and blonde or that I was taller.

My life was so different the last time I gazed into it. I was still so naïve, naïve enough to think my parents would live forever. Why was death so final? Is that why I dreamed almost every night of a dead man?

Jed's death had not made me think of the reality that your life, no matter how old you are, has no guarantee of time. If it had, I would have treasured each moment with them more.Picking the boxes back up, I headed for the garage. As I stepped out, Bailey scrambled past me to go relieve himself again I was sure, but I was glad to have the company. It was brighter than it should be out.

Looking up through the trees I could see the moon was full and it cast an eerie glow onto everything. I dumped the boxes into the large can and replaced the lid.

Turning to look for Bailey, I walked down the slate steps to see where he went. The moon was even brighter at the waters' edge. My pale blue tee shirt looked as though it was under a black light. The soft sound of waves breaking at the shore was hypnotic.

I suddenly had that same feeling of being watched from so many years ago. The hair stood up on the back of my neck. My mind raced and I heard a low growl. I froze in place.

"Bailey, come," my voice broke as I called his name.

He came to my side, but still looking back, his growl low, rumbling in his large chest. I grabbed his collar and pulled him closer, backing back up the steps. When we reached the top, I broke into a sprint with him for the door.

Once we were both in, I closed the door and flipped the dead bolt. I stood there, my mind going in a million directions, trying to catch my breath. It was a raccoon, that's what it was, an animal coming to check out the new neighbors. It's nothing to freak out about Zoe, just your stupid imagination.

But, Bailey was at the window peering out, his hair still raised on his back and that same low growl. I tried to think of my options if something/someone did try to get in. What would I do? I ran back to the study and opened the closet; my hand was frantically searching for a specific object that had to be here, Hah! Found it! I pulled it from the back, a large wooden bat we used to play ball with when I was younger.

I turned and went back to the kitchen. Bailey had stopped growling but was still at the window, sitting like he was waiting for something.

"You're freaking me out Bailey, knock it off!"

Then I did something I wish I had not done. I flipped off the light so I could see outside better.

As my eyes adjusted, I saw it, only for a moment: a dark figure at the bottom of the porch. And then, it was gone. Did Bailey not see it? Was it only my imagination out of control? I gasped and stumbled back. My thoughts racing, I remembered: the front door! I ran for it and bolted it quickly. Now Bailey was back on alert. He followed me from room to room as I checked windows and doors.

I stood in between the living room and kitchen at the bottom of the steps, breathing faster than I thought possible; too fast in fact. I put my hands on my knees praying not to pass out.

I jumped when I heard the grandfather clock in the parlor chime. It was already midnight. Not knowing what to do, I grabbed Bailey and the bat and sat in the floor, my back to the wall between the two rooms. Not able to move or think, I just sat. Finally, the breathing slowed and I reassured myself everything was okay.

I stood, the blood pouring into my legs like pins and needles. I waited to listen; nothing, no sound. This is what happens when you don't have a TV. Your mind goes crazy and you start to hear and see things. I was done being scared for tonight. This was my house! If someone was trying to scare me, they can forget it. Fun is over.

I marched into the kitchen and flipped on the light. And then I did what any other woman in my position would do. I took a bottle of red merlot from the pantry, my Dad's private stash, and opened it. I also stopped at the drawer near the stove and pulled out a malicious looking knife and headed for my room, my bat, drink, knife and dog in tow.

I woke up on the floor of my room, the empty bottle in one hand and the bat in the other. Bailey was on the bed, snoring as usual. I sat up, my head in protest. The room took a slow spin and I lay back down for a moment.

I never drink like that, maybe an occasional glass with dinner or on a special occasion, and now I remember why my head was exploding. I lay there now wishing I had met my end last night. Did it really happen?

One thing I managed to do was drown my dream. I either couldn't remember having it, or it didn't happen. My head was so thick; I needed coffee – badly.

I stood up, this time successful and dragged myself into the bathroom. The hot water felt good and I thought for a brief moment, I might survive this. I looked out the window of the bathroom.

The sun was trying to peek through, but it was still a little cloudy. It was supposed to storm later, but still be pretty hot during the day. So, I got my tan cargo shorts and pink tank top out to wear. After dressing, I combed out my hair and scrunched it. It had been a long time since I had done my hair. It felt good to have it down for a change. I even decided a little makeup might be nice too. I wasn't a big makeup person, but the older I got, the more I appreciated its effects.

As I finished, there was a knock and barking. I ran downstairs to see who it was.

Chapter Four:
A New Friend

***

Through the French doors, I could see him and motioned him in.

"Hey, Justin."

His hand was held low and out, he remembered the treats for Bailey.

"Works like a charm," his tan face looking up at me.

"You look like you slept well. Feeling better?"

Ah, the power of makeup. Because I should have looked like I passed out on the floor of my room last night.

"Yes, very sound."

It really wasn't a lie.

"I would offer you some coffee, but I haven't been to a store yet."

"Well, actually, I was coming to see if you wanted to go into town with me and get some breakfast. And after, maybe go to the Blueberry Festival? Unless you have other plans?"

I remembered the walk I had planned, but his idea sounded like a safer outing after last night. And, I would always have this afternoon to go for my stroll.

"Sounds like fun, let me get Bailey out."

"I can do that for you," as he patted his leg to call Bailey.

"You go grab a jacket, it might be cold later."

I wondered how long he planned on being out.

"Will we be back in time to let Bailey out in a few hours?" I asked, really just wanting to see what his answer would be.

"We can swing by and let him out, sure."

"Are you being vague on purpose?"

"No. I just don't want you to say you can't go."

I'm sure he was used to never being told "no" with that smile.

"How's this, I'll bring you back whenever you're ready to come home?"

"Good answer," a hint of praise in my voice.

I ran to get my sweatshirt. We put Bailey in the house and made sure to lock it. He was asleep before we hit the bottom step, too much excitement for him last night.

"My truck is over here."

And he walked me to the door and helped me up into it. His hands on my hips, he easily lifted my weight. It was a large truck with over-sized tires, the kind you take off road. The color was vague because of the dirt, but I think it was silver.

"Sorry, I should have had it washed, but I didn't have time. I was afraid if I came any later, you might be gone again."

"Again?"

"Last night. I brought you something to eat, but you weren't here. Where did you go? Your car was here."

"Oh yes, thank you for the food. That was a life saver."

"And?"

"Oh, I went for a walk, just to clear my head," my body shifting to ease the bumpy ride.

"Hope you don't mind that I let myself in, but I didn't want the food to spoil. I left you a note. Did you get it?"

"No. I didn't. Where did you leave it?"

"On the counter."

"It must have blown off, I didn't see it. Sorry."

"You shouldn't leave your doors unlocked either. That's not a good idea."

"I don't. I locked the doors. Are you sure it was unlocked?"

"Yea, I wouldn't have gotten in if not. I left my keys at my house."

"Well, I'm glad you left the food. So where are you taking me to eat?"

"Dinty's. It's a dinner style restaurant. Mostly locals, non-tourists. But, they have a great food."

"Sounds perfect!"

I actually was hungry considering the drinking binge I had last night.

"So, how old are you Justin?"

"Twenty-six. And you?"

He looked over for my response, running his fingers through his tousled blonde hair.

"Twenty-eight," my voice more assertive now.

"Is that a problem for you Zoe?"

"Why would it be Justin?" trying to pretend I didn't know what he was getting at.

"Well, some women like older men, that's all. What do you like?"

"Justin, we really have to get you out of that shell."

"It's really a burden to be this shy," batting his eyelashes at me.

I was glad he didn't make me answer his question.

"So why aren't you working today Justin?"

"I am. I told you. I'm the caretaker right now."

"And what are you taking care of today?"

"You."

"Me?"

"So you taking me out, is that part of your job?"

"Not exactly, no. But, it would be a great job."

"Are you always this forward?"

"I always say what I feel – yes. Do you always care about what everyone thinks Zoe?"

"Yeah, pretty much. I am not quite as honest as you. Aren't you afraid of what they will think?"

"Sometimes. But I am still going to be honest. Why beat around the bush when you can get right to it?"

"Why that comment shocks me is a surprise Justin."

We both laughed. Over breakfast, the conversation was lighter. He was talking about his family and it hit me.

"Justin, you were raised here in Robbinston weren't you?"

"All my life."

"Tell me something."

"Anything," he said with a smile leaning in.

"What do you know about the big house South of Red Beach?"

"What house?" the color left his face and he sat up straight.

"The house the size of a public library off The Pointe."

"How do you know about that house?"

"I don't. That's why I'm asking."

"I mean, how do you know it's there? Who told you?"

"Nobody. I saw it."

He was getting irritated now. Which strangely enough, made me a little happy to see him thrown off.

"When did you see it?"

"When I was fifteen. What's the big mystery?"

"You shouldn't go near that house," his voice raised slightly, his neck muscles tightening.

"Ever!"

"But why? Who lives there? I know someone lives there."

He looked around the restaurant, grabbed the check, left the money and escorted me out in a hurry, his hand holding me above the elbow.

"This is really great for effect, but not necessary. Justin, where are you taking me?"

We walked a few more feet and made a quick turn into the courtyard of the City Bank, his hand still holding my arm. Looking around again, his voice low,

"You can't just go around asking about that house. It's not a good subject."

I pulled my arm free.

"Who lives there, Justin?"

His eyes stared off.

"Fine, I'll just go ask them myself."

His face now locked on mine, clenching his teeth, his jaw tight.

"Don't even think about it Zoe. It's a bad place."

"Then tell me Justin," I leaned closer to him and give him the innocent look.

"Fine. But not here," he nodded his head toward the grassy area.

We walked over to the bench near the park and sat down.

"Okay, spill," my interest was a little more than peaked.

"That house belongs to the Madison family. Have you ever heard of them before?"

I wanted to laugh when he asked me. I was more than aware of who they were. I hadn't had a serious relationship because of William Madison. I was in fact, in love with him. Somehow I knew telling him that would almost surely change his mind that I was crazy. Play dumb Zoe, the small voice inside my head told me.

"William Madison?"

"Yeah. You know about the story."

"Just a yarn my dad used to tell me. And I have visited the Maritime Museum."

"Really?"

"Yes really. Why?"

"I don't know. I didn't peg you for a history buff Zoe."

"There is a lot you don't know about me Justin. Just finish the story."

"Okay. Well, there was bad blood between the Madison family and the families of the other men who died," stopping for a moment, his face confused and worried.

"Some of this is going to sound weird, Zoe and I don't believe it all, but there is always some truth to old stories. And this I know, that house and all in it are under a curse."

I had trouble swallowing the fact that that had been his house. My mind whirled as I tried to reel it in.

"Curse? What kind of curse?"

"It's been said that the Madison family is cursed. Old man Madison had lost his wife the year before to TB. When his only son died, he couldn't accept it. He vanished for a year and a half after his son died. No one knew where he went. And then, he just appeared again. His grief drove him to drinking and then madness. Right after his son's death, he had insisted they put his picture up in the museum. Made a huge deal of it, he even spent a lot of money bribing the right people. Two years after his death, he started claiming he found a way to bring him back. And then, after he returned, he wanted it taken down because he said his son wasn't dead. They refused of course. He was obviously crazy, but soon after, he died."

"Who lives there now?"

Again, he leaned in as if people were listening.

"That's the strange part. Right after old man Madison's death, his nephew from Europe, who no one ever heard of before, arrived with a hand full of servants. None of them spoke English. I guess his descendants live there now."

"What do you mean 'guess'?"

"No one has ever seen them. His servants only come in at night to pick up shipments and groceries."

Now I leaned in. We were like two children on the playground telling secrets.

"And none of them say anything?"

"No. They don't speak to anyone."

"So that makes the house cursed?"
"No, it's not just that Zoe. People have seen strange things."
"What people?"
"Ships, mostly coming from St. Croix. You can see the house better from the water. They say they've seen a strange blue light coming from the house. But, it's only visible when it's colder. The trees block the view of the house in the warmer months."
"So what do you think the light is Justin?"
"I don't know. But you've been there Zoe. I know you felt it."

I swallowed hard, hoping he wouldn't notice.
"Felt what?"

His eyes narrowed and pulled back.
"The evil coming from that house. I was never allowed to go near there as a child. My grandfather would have killed me if he found out, but my friend and I snuck
out one day in the fall and hiked to the rock wall. We stopped there because of the noise coming from the house. It was like someone was being tortured. I had nightmares for months."
"And no one ever goes or comes from there?"
"No. no one is ever seen coming or going besides the servants. Just promise me you'll stay away, okay Zoe? I hate that you are out there so close to it all by yourself."
"Thanks, now so do I," my face smiling as I rolled my eyes.

His arm stretched around me and pulled me up,
"How about I take you for some ice cream and we forget all about our little conversation?"

I pretended to be wooed by his smile.
"Deal."

But, I could never forget about that story.

That house, that person had changed my life and I had to get some answers. If nothing else, I wanted my life back. After ice cream, we walked some more through the various tents at the festival, talking about favorite music, favorite foods; the conversation was light. I really did enjoy being with him. It was fun and a challenge. He kept me on my toes with the banter back and forth, but I felt a strong urge to go home. I needed to be close to that house again, see if it felt different somehow now that I knew who had lived there.

"Do you think we could stop by the store now? I really need to get back to Bailey soon."

He looked a little disappointed.

"Aren't you having a good time?"

"Yes. It's been great, but I'm still a little tired from that long trip and I have so much to still get done."

The store was almost empty. Everyone was at the festival. I grabbed just what I had to have for the next few days, telling myself I would return Monday to finish. We loaded up the grocery bags in the back of his truck and I managed to get in on my own before Justin could get to my side. He seemed a bit upset by it.

The festival traffic was a little lighter and the ride home seemed like it was half the time. It was around four when we arrived and Justin took the grocery bags in while I let Bailey out.

"Looks like storms rolling in. I better help you get those shutters closed."

He motioned towards the Southeast,

"Yes, do you mind?"

"Course not."

He had them all closed and locked before I finished one.

"You've done this before?"

"Caretaker, remember?"

As much as I wanted to go explore, I hated the thoughts of being alone in that storm tonight.

I had to weight my options: stay alone in a bad thunderstorm or ask hot nice guy to dinner?

"Did you want to come in for a while? I could fix some supper."

His eyes flashed with excitement and he was on the porch holding the door open.

"After you Miss," his grin creeping up one side of his face, exposing only one of his dimples.

"Thank you. Make yourself at home Justin, I'll go start dinner."

"How about some help?" coming from behind me and placing his hands on my hips as we walked into the kitchen.

"I see, caretaker and cook huh?"

"Well, I don't like to brag but..."

"Yeah, I believe that," rolling my eyes.

"I'll be right back, Justin," running into the den, I grabbed one of Dad's CDs and hurried back.

"Mind popping this in?"

I pointed to the stereo system at the end of the other room.

"Sure, Van Morrison?"

"You don't like him?"

"Love him."

I wasn't sure if he was being nice or if he really loved him. While I was gone, he had opened the bottle of wine purchased at the store. Having not learned my lesson from the night before, he poured it into two glasses.

"Hope you don't mind. I opened it."

I grabbed the glass while shaking my head "no."

"Here," I handed him the pasta.

"Can you boil water?"

"Cute, Zoe, very cute. Why yes, I think I can manage it. What are we making?"

"Pasta!" I said, smiling back at him.

This was getting fun.

"With?"

"How about tomatoes, basil and a little garlic?"

"Sounds like a plan."

I put on the sauce to simmer and he grabbed the fresh loaf of French bread and sliced off two pieces. It was so easy being with him; he made himself at home. Although knowing his way around my house helped. It didn't hurt that he was good looking and as my cousin, Abbey, would say, "ripped."

We sat down and enjoyed our dinner with more light conversation with little thought of our earlier conversation. As we cleared the dishes, the first of the storm hit and knocked out the lights. Justin grabbed the flashlight plugged into the wall and we began lighting candles through the two main rooms. The thunder rumbled, still a ways off, but the strobes of lightening were consistent.

I borrowed the flashlight and excused myself for a moment, going upstairs to check my smile. I was worried I might have a piece of basil in my teeth. I brushed them and gargled to make sure not to offend him with my garlic breath. I was glad I wasn't alone; he made it easier to forget.

I headed back downstairs. He was sitting in the living room on the couch, looking relaxed, his arm stretched out on the top of the sofa, his tan arms defined by the candlelight. He had brought the bottle of wine in from the kitchen and our glasses.

"Justin Randall, are you trying to get me drunk?"

That crooked smile of his and dimples – trying to bail him out of trouble.

"I would never even think that way Zoe."

I sat on the chair opposite him, which removed the grin from his face briefly.

"How long is it supposed to last? The storm I mean."

"Just tonight."

Just as he finished his sentence, a huge crash came from the front yard, sending Bailey into a barking frenzy. We both jumped up, almost bumping heads.

"What was that?"

"You're asking me? You're the caretaker."

He headed for the front door and Bailey followed. The mammoth oak that bordered our property had broken in half and was resting on the split rail fence that ran the length of the property.

"No worries. We'll get a crew out here tomorrow to cut it down."

He turned faster than I thought. I had been right behind him peering through the glass in the door. I couldn't back up for Bailey. He caught me before I fell and pulled me into him, looking at me for a moment, and then slowly moving forward. My heart pounding, his soft, full lips melted against mine, his hand softly caressing my face and neck, then tracing my neck with his lips, my entire body warm with his embrace. We stepped back toward the living room, never breaking the hold he had on me, my hands still pinned to his chest. As we reached the sofa, he stopped and looked at me again for a long moment and took a deep breath.

"I don't want you to think this has to go anywhere, Zoe. I know you've been through a lot. You're just so beautiful. I swore I wasn't going to do this."

I had to admit, I had pegged him for the kind of guy who would do this, but, as always, he surprised me with this honesty.

"I'm not beautiful Justin. You're just surrounded by a lot of men all the time. And, I am a big girl and know how to say no, so don't feel bad. If I didn't want you to kiss me, you wouldn't have."

"So you're not mad at me?"

"For what? Kissing me?"

"Well, yes!"

I placed my arms around his neck and pulled myself to him, pressing my lips on his. His breath hot on my neck, I could feel his heart pounding out of his chest and his hand gripped mine, pulling them down around his waist, his other hand sliding the strap of my tank top off my shoulder, tracking my collarbone and neck with his fingers.

My breath was deep and steady with his. I wanted this, but for the wrong reason: to prove that I was able to? I had had too much wine and this was happening fast, too fast.

"Stop, please. I'm sorry, stop."

His lips resting on my neck, he drew a deep breath.

"I'm sorry. I'm just not... I can't do this."

His eyes met mine, sincere.

"It's fine Zoe, there's time. No rush here."

His voice still passionate and low, making me want him more. It was like saying no to chocolate. You wanted it badly, but you would regret it later. The storm outside was dying down and it was almost eleven o'clock.

"I should probably go. I've stayed too late and you said you were tired earlier," his eyes melting me with his concern.

"Thank you Justin."

"For what?"

"For everything. You're a great guy."

"You're pretty great yourself, Zoe Dossin. And thank you for going with me today and that wonderful dinner. I'll send a crew out tomorrow to take care of the tree."

"You won't be with them?"

His face smiled again, with satisfaction that I sounded disappointed. And I was. He was an even better distraction than Bailey, more dangerous, but better.

"No. I have real work tomorrow. But, I'll send Jenna over to check on things."

"That's not necessary. I'll be fine. But when will you be back?" My face showing my disappointment again.

"Few days. Don't miss me too badly," leaving me with a gentle warm kiss on my forehead.

"Take care of her Bailey. No strange men around while I'm gone," patting Bailey on the head, he turned running into the rain toward his truck.

"Try and stay out of trouble Zoe," his voice rising above the rain.

I locked the door and stood there for a moment, collecting my thoughts. The day seemed to flood through my mind. It was only one day, yet it seemed much longer. I had decided not to test fate and let Bailey out the front door instead of the back. He didn't like the rain and was back inside in seconds. He followed me through the house, checking every door twice.

Chapter Five:
Dreams & Distractions

***

I was tired. I hurried and put the rest of our glasses and wine away and went upstairs. The rain had all but stopped and the moon was bright through my window. I opened both of my windows, letting in the cool night air. The sound of the water was tranquil.

I slipped out of my clothes and into my nightgown. The bed felt wonderful as I slipped between the covers. The air was cool and the weight of the down comforter made me feel not so alone. I should have felt giddy and warm from the evening I had with Justin, but instead, just more questions and the ever-present guilt I had felt anytime I tried to be intimate with a guy.

What was I thinking? I was not the one-nightstand type. I needed more than that and I wasn't able to deal with a messy relationship right now. My heart was missing right now. I still felt physical needs, but they pale in comparison to the mess my emotional state was in.

My mind raced back to our conversation in the park earlier. What caused such a response from Justin? And why was everyone so hell bent on making this house and it's contents so mysterious. Did people really think any of that could be true? People don't come back from the dead, no matter how much money your father has or how much you wish it to be true.

Still, I couldn't get William's face out of my mind. It didn't seem to fit the monster they painted him to be. Those stories couldn't be true. I wanted it not to be true. What was it that drew me to him? I had never met him or even heard more than a few words about him, but he had been with me for 13 years, almost every night, haunting me. He was dead for God's sake. What was I thinking? I had a live man downstairs an hour ago and sent him away.

And now I'm lying in my room, wondering about a hundred year old dead guy. I am a mess. Was I going mad? No, if anything, I was already there.

I couldn't deny that even if it was fantasy or making him someone he wasn't, it was just easier for me to create this fantasy. That way, I wouldn't have to commit to a real person. Was it the sympathy that I felt for William, his marred legacy he left behind or his terrible death? Or was it simply his face, the sadness there?

I drifted in and out of sleep, my mind on him, wondering what his last thoughts were. Did he have regrets? Regrets of being alone, not sharing his life with someone? Did he struggle? Or just let death come quickly?

Screaming, I sat up in my bed, sweat pouring off my body, my hair wet with it. I was sobbing and the feeling of loss was overwhelming. I pulled my knees to my chest. All I could do was rock back and forth. I have never had such strong emotions before. I had never had this dream before, never. This was so real, like I lived it. I couldn't catch my breath. The tears were bursting down my face and my chest hurt like someone had driven a hot red poker through it.

His face kept running through my mind, darkness all around, and the water burning my lungs with each breath. I felt my body struggle and then a strange peace wash over me, followed by the burning in my chest again. I reached down to feel it, to see if I had been struck by something. There was nothing. My body was intact. Faces flashed before me, faces I had never seen. I tried to focus, but they were coming quickly, then, a blue light, dim at first, then bright. The burning in my chest returned now, with more intensity and I had stopped trying to breathe. My body wrenched with pain and then stillness, weightlessness.

I suddenly felt drawn to go to my window; everything in me was pulling me to it.

I looked out through the now clear night sky; my eyes adjusting to the moon's glow, looking out over the water, scanning it, searching. My hand was still on my chest as if the pain might return.

There by the waters' edge was the dark figure, illuminated by the moon. I wasn't afraid. I had expected this. It's what I had been searching for in the darkness. It was facing my direction and seemed to know I would be there. I stood for what seemed like a long time, waiting. When I opened my eyes, I was in my bed laying down, still covered up. I felt my face to see if it was still wet from the tears. There was nothing. My chest was fine; no burning, no marks. Daylight was breaking through the windows. I lay there trying to figure out if I was losing my mind.

I decided to get up and clear my head. Without thinking, I put on my running shorts and a tee shirt, pulled my hair back into a ponytail and went downstairs. I grabbed my Ipod off the counter and slipped on my running shoes. Bailey recognized this and was on my heels. We ran almost every morning back in Arizona before Dad died. I tied my hoodie around my waist and put Bailey's leash around my neck.

I started down the slate path and headed south. This time, the beach was too full of rocks to the North and I needed to clear my head, not tempt fate. Running felt good, my body missed the free feeling that came with it. The sunrise over the water was breathtaking. "Dawn: the sign of a new day, rebirth," the music from my Ipod was helping me to release the total frustration of the past two weeks that I felt. I ran hard now, faster. Bailey kept up alongside me.

I needed this. I needed to run, run away from all the confusion and hurt. Life was unfair. It was hard, too hard. Was I supposed to be alone?

Was the empty feeling always going to be there where my heart once was?

I felt hollow, like there was a piece of me cut out and missing. Was I doing this to myself? The words came back to me again, "Running won't bring him back Zoe. He won't be there." What was I running from now? Life? Fate? All the dark feelings buried in me deep, the ones I was afraid to think. Was death that bad?

Pushing myself, I ran faster, turning back to the house now. My thoughts came as quickly as my feet left the ground. My dad and I playing chess, mom teaching me piano, the last time I saw my dad, our last words to each other. I missed them so badly. I couldn't breath. I had to stop. My tears made it hard to see. My side ached with a sharp pain that comes from cold muscles. Why was this all happening to me? My life was not supposed to be this way.

I walked the rest of the way back to the house, my muscles feeling tight now from the run. I opened the refrigerator and took out a bottle of orange juice. I drank it straight from the carton, not caring about manners at this point. Catching breaths between gulps, I tried not to think about what just happened or the thoughts that were emerging.

I went up to take a shower and change, hoping to erase all those thoughts for now. I ate cereal out on the porch, enjoying the sunshine while Bailey napped. I had decided while showering to decompress today. To relax, not think at all, about anything. No decisions would be made today. I heard several cars pull up and got up to investigate, putting Bailey inside first, of course.

There was a large truck that had "Jim's Tree Service," on the side and two guys. The other car was a red convertible and there was a blonde female, tan and dressed too nicely to be working for a tree service.

I walked out to greet them. The woman spoke first.

"You must be Zoe? He's right. You are pretty. Sorry, I'm Jenna Randall, Justin's sister."

Her smile gave her away, same white teeth, same dimples.

"Right! Nice to meet you. Yes, I am Zoe."

"These two gentlemen are here to get rid of that tree for you. Is it okay if they get started?"

"Yes. Great. I mean, that would be wonderful. Please come in Jenna."

"Okay boys, you heard her. Get to work!"

She followed me into the house.

"Is this the puppy Justin was afraid of? Hey baby, you're a good dog. Yes, you are."

Bailey loved women as much as he hated men.

"Yes, but in Justin's defense, he's putting on a show for you. He's not like this with men."

Bailey was on his back; feet in the air, letting her rub his pink belly.

"Can I get you something to drink: water, coffee, Red Bull?"

"Red Bull, please."

I like this girl already.

"I wanted to thank you for the basket of food. That was very nice of you to take the time."

"I'm glad you liked it. So, Justin tells me you're a photographer."

"That's right. I shoot mostly landscapes, historical sites, some wildlife."

"No people?"

"Nope. No people. Not interesting enough and they complain too much."

"Wow. That's really great. How exciting."

"Well, not really. There's not as much recognition in shooting landscapes as shooting people. But, it's what I love."

"Have you always wanted to be a photographer?"

I was starting to see more than a physical resemblance between Justin and Jenna.

"Actually, yes and no. I went to college for pre-med, got accepted into med school and dropped out."

I can't believe I just blurted that out so matter-of-factly. I must still be numb from this morning.

"I feel so insignificant now. All I do is work for the real estate office and my dad's fishing company. You win, you have the cooler job."

She smiled and it made me feel good to talk to her like she was an old friend. I didn't have very many girlfriends. This might be nice.

"So, what are your plans for the day? I have orders from Justin to keep you out of trouble!"

My face was blushing from her comment.

"Well, I hadn't thought about it. What would you suggest?"

"Well, we could go get facials, a manicure and a pedicure, get lunch, then shopping and then after, go to the last night of the festival? All you can eat crab legs and beer," her lines delivered flawlessly.

I'm sure Justin had practiced each line with her.

"I hate beer, but the rest sounds great, just what I need. Are you sure you don't mind?"

"Are you kidding me? You're the most interesting person I've spoken to in a month. I have five brothers, remember?"

"Let me just let Bailey out and we can go."

"Take your time Zoe, we have all day."

My perfect distraction, even though he wasn't here, he was working his magic. The ride into town was fantastic. The sun was warm, the music energizing and for a moment, I had forgotten everything.

Jenna had called ahead and booked our day of beauty while she was waiting for me. We got to sit by each other during our pedicures and manicures and talk. I felt like old friends talking to her.

We discussed life, college, guys we dated – although she had more experience in that department than me. I had only had two real boyfriends, one in high school that was more like a crush and for a year in college, I dated a self-absorbed guy in his second year of med school to make my parents think therapy was working. I was miserable, even Dad didn't like him. I had never found anyone who was a match, but I was okay with that. I watched girls in college date the wrong people because it was expected, but that's not enough for me. It has to be right.
Jenna, on the other hand, was just as honest as her brother. She liked having a good time and didn't really expect to meet Mr. Right. She was having too much fun with her Mr. Wrongs.

"Zoe, you've got to loosen up. Life is too short to wait for it to fall in your lap. You have to get out there and have some fun," her voice confident and careless.

"You know something Jenna, I think you have enough fun for both of us."

We left feeling revived and refreshed. Jenna even talked the girl into doing our makeup for us. It was a little more than I usually wore, but it looked great. We headed for lunch next, she had picked out a nice sidewalk café in the middle of town where she flirted with our waiter until I was sure he gave her his number. We had great service though and a nice lunch. She knew how to handle people. I could tell the years of manipulating five brothers had paid off for her, she knew the male psyche inside and out. Shopping was my thing; I had always loved clothes, shoes. Mom and I would go for hours. Jenna and I were well matched for this. Her taste a little more risqué than mine, but that made it even more fun.

"You are trying this on Zoe, I won't take no for an answer. Go!"

She pointed towards the fitting rooms, holding out a beautiful red dress that wrapped in the front. I never really wore red much, I was always afraid it would clash with my hair, but she was so persistent. So in I went. I slipped on the silky dress over my head and tied it on the side. Standing, looking in the mirror, I could not believe it was me. I felt embarrassed at the amount of cleavage the dress revealed and how great it really looked.

"Let's see it Zoe. When you get it on, come out!"

"I don't think so Jenna."

"Fine – I'll come in," and she pushed the door open.

"Oh my! Where were you hiding that figure? Whoa! Smokin'!" she said shaking her hands.

"Stop! I can't be seen in this. It's obscene."

"Exactly. You're buying it."

It was beautiful. And on her, she could pull it off. But, I was not used to my body being exposed. I had decided to humor her and buy it, telling myself I would bring it back when she wasn't with me.

"Now you have to have the perfect shoes to go with that dress."

"Jenna, where exactly am I going to wear that dress?"

"I don't know Zoe, maybe some hunky guy will ask you out to dinner."

I could only assume by her smirk that by 'hunky guy,' she was referring to her brother. After talking me into a pair of black heels that tied around my ankle, we hit the festival. The last day of the festival was always crowded, but fun. The music was everywhere.

Chapter Six:
Gypsy

***

Not following the crowd, we turned off the main drag, taking a short cut. There was a psychic's tent set up in the small alley entrance, for effect, I'm sure.

"Hey Zoe, ever been to one of those?"

"No."

"Let's go, it'll be fun."

She said as she dragged me into the dimly lit tent, it was just like the movies; a small table covered in various drab colored fabrics, the walls draped with more of the same and only a few candles for light, to set the mood. Out from behind a curtain stepped an attractive dark haired woman, looking like a gypsy from an old movie.

"Good evening, Ladies. Please, sit."

She pointed to two chairs. Her voice had an accent, almost French or Italian, but not quite.

"Who wants to go first?"

"Oh, I don't want to go. Jenna will go," I said as I pushed Jenna forward.

She smiled and laughed at me,

"Scaredy-cat!"

The woman told her generic things about making lots of money, finding a man, etc... When they were done and we were leaving, she grabbed my arm.

"Stay child. There is much to be said."

Jenna motioned for me to sit down. I hesitated, but eventually sat. Just then, Jenna's phone rang.

"Sorry Zoe. I'll wait out here. It will just take a second; I have to take this call."

Looking back at the woman, her expression was different, serious. She grabbed my hands and looked into my palms, then my eyes. Her eyes flashed, her voice low and quiet.

"Something troubles your sleep my child. But, it is not what you think that brings you this sadness.

You have had thoughts of the dark one lately, have you not?"

My face went blank as if all the blood had run from it. My chest heaved. I couldn't speak; she didn't wait for my answer.

"Your soul is pure and your heart is in a good place, but darkness preys on the innocent. Beware of its pull. It will consume you, if you let it. It draws strength from you – don't give in to it! You have been given a gift, a second sight. Learn to trust it."

The fear was all consuming. Now it ran through me; the hair on my arms stood up.

"There is one who will become the air you breathe – your other half, one who you've waited for. He is your destiny, your fate. There will be a time when you will need to be brave and follow your heart instead of what makes sense in your mind. I see many choices you will have to make and much heart break."

Her grip tightened on my hands as she drew near, her voice, a light whisper.

"We make our paths. They are not set. Find your path Zoe and don't be tempted to stray from it. You have a gift; you are more insightful than you yet know. It will come to you."

Her hands released mine and I began to breathe again. I jumped when Jenna's head popped back in the tent.

"What did I miss?"

The woman smiled.

"She is very fortunate to have such a good friend."

Jenna grabbed my arm and tugged.

"Come, Zoe. Night's still young. Come on."

I didn't look back. I couldn't. I just let Jenna pull me through the crowd. We finally stopped and she turned to look at me.

"Are you alright Zoe? You look like you've seen a ghost!"

"Yeah, I'm fine."

"What did she say to you back there? Did she upset you?"

"No, no, just the same old mumbo jumbo. You'll meet your true love kind of thing, you know? I think I'm just hungry."

No – I just had someone tell me something about myself I didn't want anyone to know and that I will potentially be tempted by some dark, evil force, but I'm fine. Ignore the twitching. I'm just going mad.

"Let's get you some food then."

We went to a friend of Jenna's food tent and hung out there. They had live music and dancing. Jenna was up dancing and I was glad she didn't ask any more about the gypsy. I had lost the celebration feeling I had had earlier and just wanted to go home.

After we ate, I used the excuse I wasn't feeling well and Jenna was a trooper and left early to drive me home. She came in only briefly and then left after I assured her I would be fine after some sleep. I did however let her stay until I had let Bailey back in.

The house was empty, silent as usual, but I didn't seem to care. I couldn't get a clear thought, too many things in my head. I needed some sleep. I made myself some hot black currant tea and headed upstairs. Not even the sight of my bed brought me comfort tonight.

I put on my pj's, pulled my hair back in a loose braid and washed the makeup off my face. It felt good to have the air on my face instead of the two inches of makeup. I slid beneath the covers and prayed for sleep that would not come. The events of the day whirled in my head until they made me feel dizzy. I decided to get some air. I crossed the room to open my windows, opening the smaller one first and then sitting in my window seat.

I looked out across the water. Tonight wasn't as bright as it had been and a thin patch of fog rolled in from across the bay.

There was no man in black watching me tonight, just the sound of my breathing and the low hum of the water.
I had to look at myself now. What was I doing? Tormenting myself with this memory that wasn't even real. I had let it become real and now it was driving me mad. I can hear what my Aunt Kate would say right now, "Always running Zoe, you need to face it." She would be right, but I couldn't face it. It was too terrifying; even more so than the black figure. I was in a downward spiral and I was just letting it happen.
Maybe I should have stayed in Arizona like Aunt Kate said. My eyes began to get heavy and I felt sleep wash over me. I grabbed my throw and stayed looking out the window. His deep voice called to me through the mist, my name like honey from his lips. I would have had no choice but to follow it. It commanded my every move, like I was in a trance. I wanted to be closer to it, listening to where it was coming from, the darkness and mist concealing its owner.
The voice was closer now, from behind me. I closed my eyes awaiting his arrival, his hands on my shoulders holding me in place, running down the length of my arm until they reached my hands. Warm breath caressed the back of my neck, making my body alive to every beat of his heart. My breathing increased steadily, his breath following my shoulder around to my face. My eyes were still closed. Why couldn't I open them? His body, now in front of me; I could sense his face, close to mine, his cheek pressing against mine. He held me there in his embrace.
I awoke to the sound of birds chirping and a lawn mower. My body was stiff from lying in the window all night. I stretched to work out some of the kinks. And then suddenly, I remembered my dream and was a little embarrassed by it.

It shared only one thing in common with my other dream, it seemed too real, as if closing my eyes right now; I could almost feel his touch. Why could I not see the face? Who it was my heart longed for so desperately. I needed a shower, a cold shower. And I Also needed to go to town to get some supplies for the next week. I made my list, let Bailey out and locked up the house. It was nice out today. I thought about what I would make for dinner and if Justin would be back tomorrow.
Before stopping at the market, I stopped into the local cable company to order my Internet. I would need to be able to send my work in. The clerk was helpful and I was done in moments. He said it would be installed no later than Thursday. I would have to get started on my photos soon.
The grocery store took longer. I spent twenty minutes in the pets' aisle getting Bailey some new toys and food. I probably bought enough for four people, but I was hungry when I went in and that was always a bad idea. I would probably come out of this whole ordeal a hundred pounds heavier.
I ran into Jenna out in front of the store. She seemed glad she saw me.

"Hey, what time did you leave the house this morning? I tried to call you and there was no answer."

"Oh, I left early to get some stuff taken care of," pointing to my cart.

"Well I wanted to invite you over for dinner tomorrow. My father and brothers are coming back and we are having a barbeque at our house. Want to come?"

"Are you sure you want me to come?"

"Don't be silly Zoe, Justin would kill me if I didn't make sure you were there."

"Well, in that case, I had better come. What can I bring?"

"Just yourself. About four-thirty okay?"

"Yes and Jenna, thank you for everything yesterday. I had a lot of fun."

"I enjoyed it too Zoe, besides, we need to stick together. Us girls, you know?" Taking her glasses down, I could see the sincerity in her eyes.

"Call me later when you get home, I would love to talk some more."

"Sure thing Zoe," her phone rang and she nodded as she answered and drove away.

I loaded my car and pulled out of the parking lot. The traffic was all but gone; the small town had almost gone back to normal. The Blueberry Festival was over and the only sign it ever existed was the banner still up in a barbershop window. It was so peaceful here, homey. Why would you not love living here?

I took the long way home to soak up more of the sun. After unloading the groceries, I decided to change into my bathing suit and lay out. It would probably only be a few more weeks and I would be wearing sweaters, so I took advantage of it. Besides, my tan was already fading. I took my chase lounge and Ipod and set them up on the patio closest to the water. I felt so relaxed lying in the sun. It warmed my sore muscles. Between yesterday's run and sleeping in a window last night, I needed it. I must have fallen asleep because the sun had gotten lower in the sky. I squinted to see the time on my phone. It was already two p.m. I was hungry and I'm sure Bailey was. Bailey followed me inside. I ran upstairs just long enough to slip on a pair of shorts and grab some CDs. I thought since I was going to be alone, I would have to get used to it.

Music helps. I couldn't help it; I had to listen to my Bob Marley CD first. I poured some of Bailey's dried food into his bowl and mixed some beef broth in it for a little treat. He loved it.

Next was my food, I made myself a gourmet peanut butter and jelly sandwich; extra crunch peanut butter and a glass of milk.

It felt a little unnerving at first, but not as bad as I thought. I went over in my mind how I wanted to convert the back den into my workroom. I would need help from Justin to move the small sofa and furniture that was in there now to storage. I think I'll go shopping this evening and buy a new desk and worktable, some lighting - yeah. I even think I'll paint it. That would keep me busy. I needed to not think about any of the events that have transpired over the last three days.

The desire to investigate "the house" was still very strong, but I needed to pace myself. That would have to wait until I could shake the fear that has, as of late, been consuming me every time I think of the house or its contents.

After finishing lunch, I went into the back den, boxes in hand and began to go through all the drawers and bookshelves. I managed to do it without thinking. I just packed all of it except for the photo albums, which I did not even open. I just took them to the living room entertainment center and stashed them away. I didn't want to be sad today, not with "I Shot the Sheriff" booming in the house. It felt good to kind of take charge. I taped up the boxes and labeled them so that when I could lure Justin over to help me, they would be ready to go.

He was a really good distraction for me. I was looking forward to seeing him again tomorrow. The whole meet the family thing, I'm not so sure about, but I'll manage. Plus with Jenna there, it would be easier for me.

The windows in the den were quite large and took up the whole back wall, letting in diffused light, perfect for viewing my shots. It would have been impossible to have this much natural light in Arizona; you would have fried yourself.

I took down the draperies but left the plantation shutters, the window looked even bigger now. I love it. I think I will even have enough room to set up my painting easel. With all the natural light in and a view of the bay, it will be a great room for it.
It was getting to be about dusk and I decided to take Bailey for a run. I desperately needed to burn off some extra energy I had from drinking Red Bull and listening to Bob Marley all day. I ran up, changed and grabbed Bailey. I stopped at the end of the path looking towards the North end of the river. Come on Zoe, you don't need the drama tonight. The South end of the beach is just lovely, I told myself. Don't ruin this day with your stupidity and curiosity.
I turned before I could change my mind and headed South, running so fast so I could get further down the beach, the whole time arguing with myself that I was being smart. The run was short and my heart wasn't in it. After twenty minutes, I headed back towards home. Bailey was not upset about the short run. He was getting used to the treats he got when we got back home, and that was all the motivation he needed to get home.
For dinner, another gourmet meal: a microwave dinner; quick and simple, no dishes. I locked up and went to my room to take a shower before I went to bed. I made it through an entire day by myself and I didn't even cry, not once. I can do this. But something in the back of my mind, a small voice, said 'the night's not over.'
I toweled off and got dressed, aggravated at the small voice for raining on my victory. I will not cry and I'm not thinking negative! I will just think about Justin, my beautiful distraction. I would have to figure out what to wear tomorrow and I... Ugh! This was not working! No. I can do this! I closed my eyes and tried picturing Justin with his brothers fishing; his muscles flexing, skin a glossy tan color. Nope. Still not working. I couldn't focus.

Thoughts of the gypsy kept invading my wonderful vision.
How did she know about me and why couldn't I have the nice fortune, like Jenna? No. I have to get the "you're doomed" fortune. I don't believe in that stuff anyway I kept trying to remind myself, but it's difficult when it happens to you and what she says makes you know there is no way she could have guessed that.
I needed to sleep. I had a big day tomorrow and I would have time to mull this over later. I found a position in bed that was comfortable and drifted off. I was back in the tent where the gypsy had been looking down into a cup of dark liquid. I imagined it was tea. It clouded over and then I saw him, his sculpted body and broad shoulders, his dark hair, so familiar to me. His hand was at his forehead, gripping it as if his head was hurting. I wanted to comfort him, needing to take him in my arms and console the pain away. I looked closer, trying to see the face I knew but couldn't picture. The dark liquid swirled, making it hard to see and then calmed again. A single white lily lay on a stone table. I could smell the pungent aroma of it all around. I tried to see the stone table. It wasn't a table at all. There on the front of the stone, beneath the beautiful white lily was a name: Zoe Elizabeth Dossin. It was a tombstone, my tombstone!
I shook my head to clear my thoughts. The dark liquid swirled again and it was him again, this time on his knees in front of the dark stone. What was my name doing on that stone? I'm not dead. I'm not dead. I kept saying it over and over. I'm not dead.
I woke up reaching for him. I hated this dreaming. I was lucky to have never remembered my dreams before. I felt like it was so real, so disturbing to think of being dead.

Chapter Seven: The Randalls

***

I lay back down, trying to clear my thoughts. I must have fallen asleep because the next time I woke up, it was Bailey nudging me to be let out. I looked at the alarm clock. It was ten-thirty am. I haven't slept that late since I was in high school.

I hurried downstairs to let Bailey out. There was a strange feeling that hovered over me, and I couldn't shake it. I made some coffee and poured myself a cup. So much for a good night's sleep. I still felt tired like I hadn't slept at all, my cell phone rang, and it was Aunt Kate. I didn't feel like talking to her, but I answered so I could get it over with. Otherwise she would call me all day until I answered.

She was surprisingly agreeable and seemed to be glad I was getting along so well; of course, it's only been five days. As we hung up, she reminded me that she expected me home for the holidays. That reminder sent a chill down my entire body. What would it be like this year? My very first Christmas alone. I made up the excuse that the cable guy was at the door. She let me go for now, but promised to call me in a few days. I love her, but she is so controlling. My phone rang again, and I was sure she had forgotten to tell me to put on clean underwear.

"What now Aunt Kate?" I said with an attitude.

"I'm starting to sense some animosity towards this Aunt Kate," his voice sounded as charming as ever.

"Justin? God, I'm sorry. I keep doing that."

"Yeah, I'm starting to get a complex."

"You're back?" my voice a little less reserved than I had hoped.

"Yeah, we just got back and a little bird told me I would be graced with your presence this evening. I wanted to know what time you want me to pick you up?"

"Oh that won't be necessary, I can drive myself."

"Zoe please, I want to. Besides, I don't want you going into that house after dark by yourself. So, what time?"

"Well actually, I kind of have some errands to run. I was hoping you might want to come with me. That is, if you're not too tired."

"Sure, I would love to. Where are we going?"

"I have a proposition for you, but you have to be here so I can show you."

I was getting better at this flirting thing.

"When do you want me there? I can be ready in forty-five minutes. Is that enough time?"

"I can't wait, see you in forty-five minutes then!"

I ran upstairs to freshen up. I had showered last night, so I just fixed my hair and put on some makeup. I would have to come back and change before I could go to his house for dinner tonight, I still wanted to look nice. After all, I was going to try and talk him into helping me fix up the den. So, I thought my white shorts with my powder blue tank top would be perfect. Not only did it show off my tan my dad always said my best color was blue.

I got downstairs just in time to meet him at the door. Bailey, obviously not used to Justin quite yet, was barking. He held up both hands as a sign to show me he had forgotten his bribe. I opened the door and Bailey started wagging his tail and sniffing him for his treats. I handed him the biscuit and he gave it to Bailey.

"I thought he would be cool with me by now."

"If barking got you what you wanted, would you stop?"

His face wrinkled as if thinking hard and then he said,

"Definitely not. Whatever works."

His eyes sparkled as he leaned in closely to my face and in a deep, almost whisper said,

"You have something to show me?"

Our lips almost touching, my heart was beating a mile a minute. I admit he was better at the flirting thing. My face went blank for a moment,

"Yes, I do as a matter of fact. Would you like to see it?" Speaking in the same low tone with our faces still close.

"That's what I'm here for, to see your proposition."

"Okay," I said, being the first to back up.

"You win, it's back here. Follow me."

His face was gloating.

"Too intense for you, huh?" his voice sounding confident.

"No, just running out of time."

"Ouch! Be nice, you'll hurt my ego."

"Not a chance, Justin."

I led him to the den.

"I want to go buy some new furniture for in here. I would like to set this room up as my studio and I need a few things."

"And you want me to help you pick out furniture?"

"Well, yes. I would also like to hire you to move the old furniture out and maybe help me paint it."

I didn't look up. I was waiting for his reaction.

"So basically, you just want my muscle and not my brains, huh?"

"No. I want both."

As it came out, I felt my face get warm.

"I didn't mean it that way and you know it."

"Are you blushing Zoe? It's nothing to be ashamed of. A lot of girls want me for my brains and muscle. I am a good looking guy," he said, raising one eyebrow while striking a body builder's pose.

"Oh stop Justin! Will you help me or not?"

"Yes, I think I will, but only because you asked so nice."

I led him to the back den and he took time carefully measuring the room.

He was very patient with me as I described the look I was wanting for my workspace. He seemed genuinely interested in the whole project.

He took me to the local furniture store and I found a few pieces that would work perfectly. I wasn't as put out this time about his truck. It came in handy for all the bulky items. We went to the hardware store next and he helped me with the paint. I really didn't know exactly what I was looking for. I would know it when I saw it.

"What do you think of this one Zoe?" a voice called from the opposite side of the color kiosk.

He was holding a swatch of blue tones. The one he pointed to was called Cloudy Day.

"Wow Justin. I wasn't really thinking blue, but I really like it. I'm surprised you found it."

"Well thanks a lot Zoe. I thought you look so good in blue that it only makes sense," his face looking a little like the wind was taken out of his sails.

"I didn't mean it that way, I'm just surprised that I didn't think of it. Oh, forget it. I really like it, I didn't know you were so multi-talented. Is that better?"

"I think so."

He ordered the paint and we went to get lunch. He took me to the same place that Jenna did. I feel like I've been spied on. It's like he sent her to pick my brain and I don't have anyone to be my cohort. But, I think I'm up to the challenge.

"So, Justin. I know this is a little late, but are you seeing anyone?"

"Wow Zoe, that's a tough question."

"Why is that a tough question?"

"Well see, there is this one girl I really like, but it's hard because she's different."

"Different? Like she's deformed?"

"No. She's really smart and complicated. Not my usual type."

"So she's ugly?"
"No, she's beautiful, but hard to figure out. Complicated."
"So have you made your intentions known to her?"
"Not exactly, but I think she has an idea."
"Do you think she is interested in you?"
"I hope so, but like I said. She's a challenge."
"Is she worth all that trouble?"
"That's my favorite part. She makes me work harder and I'm all for a challenge. I have a plan though, to even the playing field a little."
"And what would that be?"

He looked in all directions as though he were afraid someone might be listening.

"My family. I'm going to let her fall in love with my family and then, it's over."
"That's your plan? What if you scare her off?"

His face was confused for a moment and then worried.

"I hadn't thought about that."
"Well, good luck with that strategy."

He leaned in close, sending my pulse flying.

"Well, if all else fails, I'll just do this," he said, placing his hand gently around my neck and pulling me into him across the table.

He kissed me, his lips warm and soft. The effect was a success. My mind was in too many places to respond.

"Yeah. I thought that might work," he said smugly as he put his hands behind his head.
"Okay, so I'll let you have that one. It doesn't mean you won. Do you mind driving me back to the house so I can change before we go over to your house? That way we can drop off all my things too."
"Yeah. I don't have anywhere to be right now. That's fine."

We unloaded the items from the truck, well actually, Justin did.

I just kind of got in the way. He is so strong and healthy, really healthy. I need to stop thinking like that. It's not nice to ogle him like that, but it's his own fault for looking that way.

"I'll be right back, make yourself at home Justin," I yelled as I went upstairs to shower and change.

I had a sun dress that I had never worn, pale blue with spaghetti straps. I wasn't playing fair using the information he unwittingly had given me earlier, but I had no cohort like he did. It showed off my tan perfectly, I did my hair again so it was now starting to become a habit. I had all but forgotten my clips. I put on my small silver locket my dad had bought me for my eighteenth birthday. I slid my sandals on and went down for inspection.

He had fallen asleep on the couch, poor thing. I felt so bad, I wore him out. He had just come home from working forty-eight hours and he spent the day shopping with me. I had to give it to him; he was a trooper. I cleared my throat and said his name softly,

"Justin?"

"What? I'm sorry. I must have dozed off. Wow! You look..."

"What? Don't you like it?"

"I love it. You look beautiful. Wow!"

"Thank you."

Mission accomplished.

"Did you let Bailey out?"

"Yes, but we're taking him with us," Justin said.

"We are? Do you think that's a good idea?"

"Yeah. He'll be fine. My family loves dogs and I figure he'll learn to appreciate me after he meets my brothers."

I have to admit, I feel a little nervous going over to his house with his whole family there.

He must have sense it because he made the excuse that Bailey should ride by the door so he could stick his head out the window, making me sit next to him. He grabbed my hand and held it.

"Will everyone from your family be there?"

"I think so. They are all really looking forward to meeting you."

"They are? Why?"

Now I really was nervous.

"Look Zoe, you have nothing to be nervous about. They will love you.

"Tell me your brothers names again."

"There's Colton, the oldest. He's thirty-four and he's married with two little girls. His wife's name is Maggie. Then Aaron, he's thirty-two but he's not married. Then there's Lucas and Mason, the twins, they're thirty. Lucas is married to Taylor, but has no kids and Mason has a girlfriend he's been dating for four years. Her name is Tiffany. Jenna, whom you've met is twenty-eight and me of course; twenty-six."

"Your mom stayed very busy."

"Always, and still is. Four of us still live at home."

His information didn't help my nerves much, but it had kept me from noticing we had arrived.

The house was pale yellow, soapbox style with dark green shutters. The porch was enormous and painted white with a sprawling green lawn that was beautifully landscaped; the long driveway was full of cars making my stomach flip.

"Are you sure Bailey won't be in the way?"

"He's fine, and so are you Zoe. Don't worry so much."

He helped me out of the truck, taking Bailey's leash from me and taking my hand.

We walked around to the backyard and there they were, all of them, more than when my family had a reunion with aunts and uncles included. Breathe Zoe, just breathe.

Jenna was the first to come over and loudly tell me how fabulous I looked. I am sure the color of red my face turned complimented the dress. Then they all made their way over. Bailey greeted each one first, then me. His brothers were almost as good looking as he and Jenna, but out of the six, Justin and Jenna looked the most alike, even more than the twins. They were all very nice and I noticed his brother Aaron giving him a sly grin of approval, at least I could only hope that's what it was.

"Where are Mom and Dad?"

Jenna piped in,

"Mom's in the kitchen and Dad's burning the food on the grill. Come on Zoe, I want you to meet everyone else."

She grabbed me away from Justin, but not before he shot her a look that she conveniently ignored.

"I'll bring her back – selfish."

And she continued through the crowd, introducing me to each face. Maggie, Colton's wife, was sweet and their little girls with their blonde curls were adorable and pleasant. Mason and Tiffany were well suited, she was brunette and tall, about five foot eight, with large brown eyes. Her skin was beautiful and she was thin. Mason was the darker haired one in the family, but still good-looking. His eyes were blue like Jenna
and Justin's but he was a little stockier than Justin. Jenna took me to her dad, J.J. Randall, first who bore a striking resemblance to Jed and even sounded like him. He was friendly with his coarse voice and rough sense of humor. I could see that every one of the boys listened to him intently when he would speak to them.

Jenna was a little different.

You could tell that she was daddy's girl and probably had him and the rest of the boys wrapped around her little finger.

She took me inside next to meet their mom, Rebecca Randall. She was stunning for her age and had a perfect little figure. She was about five foot four and couldn't have weighed more than one hundred and twenty pounds. How could such a tiny thing be responsible for all those huge boys? Her smile reminded me of Justin's with his big dimples and perfectly white teeth.

"So nice to finally meet you dear," she said sweetly. "We were sure sorry to hear about your folks. They were good people. Jed just loved them. Hope you're hungry, we have an awful lot of food."

"Yes, it smells great."

There were platters of lobsters, mussels, corn, steak, baked potatoes, rolls, salad and every kind of dessert you could imagine. They had music playing and lights hanging from everything outside. The tables were dressed in white cloths with silver galvanized buckets and citronella candles on each one.

Justin finally got tired of Jenna monopolizing my time and came to steal me back. I was glad; I felt better when he was closer. He put his arm around my waist and leaned down asking me if I was okay, lightly kissing my hair.

"I'm fine really. This is wonderful. Do you do this a lot?"

"Almost every weekend we are all home."

I couldn't imagine ever feeling alone with all these people, so close and loving. You could tell they cared for each other.

"Can you play?" he asked, looking toward the horseshoe pit.

"I manage."

I was being modest, I was really good at horseshoes.

My dad and I played all the time back home with Uncle Steve. Most of the boys were playing horseshoes while Tiffany watched.

"Well, think we can take them Zoe? How about Mason and Tiffany against you and me?"

"Let's give it a shot, shall we?"

It took a moment to warm up and then it was like riding a bike. We beat them four games and then of course we had to play the rest of them, until Jenna and Aaron finally beat us. Only because my arm felt like a noodle after so many games.

I sat between Mason and Justin at dinner. Jenna was across from me. Mason was assuring Tiffany that he was just not on his game today and that's why Justin and I beat them. They all started picking on Mason after that. It was fun to see how much they like to pick on each other. I never had that growing up. It's hard to fight with yourself. Somehow, you're always right.

"So Zoe, you live right off Lakeshore Road right?"

Aaron was down at the end of the table slightly raising his voice over the rest of the conversations that were going on.

"Yes I do."

I felt bad having to raise my voice to answer back.

"You know she does Aaron, why are you asking?"

Justin's tone was slightly impatient.

"Well I'm just saying, I'm surprised you can get Justin over there at all."

"Why would Justin not come to my house?"

Justin was looking at Aaron like he was going to strangle him.

"Well you see, my little bro here has always been afraid of that area, since he was a little guy. Isn't that right Mason?"

"Yeah, Yeah. He would never go over near Red Beach."

The story came back to me now. What Justin had told me about the house and when he was little and all the nightmares it caused him. Justin's face was looking down now.

"Oh, you mean because of the Madison house right? Yes, Justin filled me in on that."

All eyes were on me now. All conversation had stopped.

"Have you ever been down there Aaron?"

"No, not exactly. Have you?" his voice gloating now.

"As a matter of fact, I have."

Justin looked up at me now with a look of surprise.

"When I was fifteen, I stood just outside the house at the gate."

"You went that close to it? Are you nuts?" Justin said with his voice breaking a little.

"It's very intimidating, but it's just a house."

"It's not the house you have to worry about," J.J., Justin's dad, joined in the conversation.

"It's what's in it you should stay away from," he said, sounding so much like Jed when he said it that I wanted to cry.

"I'm sure she isn't interested in your boogie man stories Dad," Jenna piped in.

"Besides, everyone knows some rich mob guy lives there and it's probably some drug front."

Mason and Aaron began to laugh at what she'd said and began talking like they were Al Pacino.

"Thanks," Justin said in a low voice to me.

"But I don't want to hear that you have gone anywhere near that place again. Understand?"

I had decided to let this go for now and agreed with him.

"Yes, never again. Got it."

Dinner was great, I ate too much. I hope he doesn't think I eat like that all the time, but I had been eating PB & J's for the past week and this really hit the spot.

Justin grabbed a quilt from the house and guided me to a beautiful spot under the giant willow tree at the back of the yard. It was just past dusk now and the sky was barely pink with streaks of orange. He laid the blanket down and we sat looking out over the water. Bailey seemed to appreciate the blanket as he sprawled out at the bottom of it.

"Well, do you think I scared her too badly?" Justin asked.

"No." I said.

"I think your plan may be working after all."

"So you think she might be interested yet?" he said as my eyes were still looking out at the water.

I looked up at his blue eyes melting me with his stare. I leaned in this time, closing my eyes and kissed him. He pulled me closer to him and kept his arm around my waist.

"I'll take that as a yes," he chuckled.

I felt guilty being so carefree with this. I should take it slowly. I was in a bad place right now to try and make emotional decision. I just wanted something, anything, to fill the chasm that had been left by my loss.

We stayed until it got dark, just looking at the beautiful colors. We went back up to the house to help cleanup and pack up the leftovers. His brother, Mason, was still upset that we beat him at horseshoes and was trying to schedule a re-match. Tiffany was on the quiet side, but seemed pleasant. She was a better loser than Mason.

"We are so glad you could come today Zoe. We love having you here, you're like family. You have to promise to come back next weekend. We'll make Mason behave himself, I promise."

"Mom, I'm telling you, Justin brought home a ringer. She's like a pro. I'm not even kidding you, it's unnatural how good she is."

"Mason Andrew Randall, she's our guest. You be polite and act like you have some manners."

His Mom was less than amused with his poor sportsmanship. I can only assume she didn't see Justin behind her egging him on. Colton and Maggie were leaving now and they each gave me a hug, even Madeline and Macy, their little girls. Colton was a lot like his dad, more reserved, not as silly as Mason, Aaron and Jenna were. Lucas was more like Colton. His wife was not there tonight. I had heard someone say she was under the weather. Rebecca packed a plate for him to take home to her and whispered something in his ear and hugged him. He nodded and then left. I wondered if everything was okay, but I was quickly distracted by Aaron and Mason arm wrestling in the kitchen.

"You boys knock it off now. I mean it!"

They looked up and Mason mouthed to Aaron,

"I'll beat you later."

But, they immediatcly broke it up, no arguing.

Justin was laughing and razzing Mason. I could tell out of all of them, Aaron, Mason, Justin and Jenna were the closest. Jenna walked up to me and nudged me with her arms.

"So what do you think of this "motley crew"?"

"I think you are very lucky to have such a loving family Jenna. You should never take them for granted."

She looked at me and smiled as if to agree.

"What do you think of my brother?"

I couldn't tell if she was asking for herself or for Justin.

"I think he's lucky too."

"That's not what I meant Zoe and you know it!"

"I care a lot about him and he's a great guy Jenna, if you're going to be my friend and want the juicy gossip from me, you need to choose sides, because I'm not going to give you all my secrets just so you can run and tell him."

"That's not fair Zoe! He's my favorite brother," she said, whispering now.

"And he trusts me."

"Well how about you only give him the information we agree he should have?"

"That I can live with."

She laughed as she walked through the pack of boys getting Justin's attention.

"What was she laughing at? What did you tell her?"

"We have an understanding, that's all."

"What do you mean understanding? Jenna get back here! What kind of understanding?"

"No more using her to do your dirty work. You'll just have to fend for yourself,' I informed him.

"Oh no you don't Jenna! We're flesh and blood. You can't do that!" he said, yelling so she could hear.

All could hear was devilish laughter from the other room as she must have let Aaron in on our arrangement.

"We'll talk about this later Jenna!" his face flustered.

"Well, I should probably take you home before they give you my room and boot me to the curb."

"She's welcome to your room anytime bro!"

Justin shot Aaron a glace through the doorway of the kitchen.

"Yeah, I'm sure Aaron that has nothing to do with the fact that we share a room does it?"

Aaron just laughed from the other room.

"Okay, I don't want to come between you two, so I'll keep my own room at my own house."

"Well Zoe, we certainly have shown ourselves to you tonight, haven't we?" Mrs. Randell said shaking her head.

"Oh Mom, she knows we're just kidding."

Aaron stepped into the room, his face looking guilty.

"She's probably not going to want to come back now Mom," Justin said with a smirk on his face only Aaron could see.

"It's fine, I really have enjoyed myself."

"See Mom, she's cool with it. She's not freaking out like a little girl like Justin is."

Justin stepped toward Aaron.

"Boys! Aaron, I need you outside to help me, and Justin, I think Zoe here would probably like to get home sometime tonight. Poor girl's had her arms full for twenty minutes while you two play patty cake." Mrs. Randall said sternly.

"Sorry Zoe, I forgot you had that in your hands."
He was obviously embarrassed by his dad's insight.

"Now you don't mind these boys Zoe, you come back to see us real soon."

"I will. Thank you Mr. Randall."

"Mr. Randall was my dad, call me J.J."

"Goodnight sweetheart, now if you ever get scared up there in that big house by yourself, you let us know. You're welcome to come stay here. Jenna has plenty of space in her room for you," his mom said, looking carefully at Justin as she made that last comment.

"Well, I'll be back in a while."
Justin took my goodies from my arms and I put Bailey's leash on him, pulling to wake him up.
The ride home was quiet; I could tell he was in deep thought.

"Do you want to come in for a bit?"

"Do you mind?"

"I wouldn't have asked if I didn't want you to. Besides, it's kind of dark. I forgot to leave any lights on."
He came around, took Bailey from me and let him off his leash so he could relieve himself. Coming back for me, he helped me out of the truck, his arms tighter around me than necessary, and then grabbed the food.

"I have my keys in here somewhere," I said as I rummaged through my purse.

"No need. It's unlocked," he said as he pushed the door open.

"Okay. I know I locked that. You saw me lock that!" I was beginning to get really worried.

"You're probably just turning the key the wrong way Zoe. I'll check the lock before I leave, I promise. Don't get upset."

I walked through the door and turned and locked it behind me, hearing the deadbolt click into place.

"I know how to lock a door Justin," my voice a little more frantic now.

"I didn't mean that you didn't, but these old doors don't always latch properly. I'll take care of it. If I have to, I'll put a new lock on it tomorrow."

I couldn't believe what I was about to ask, but I was desperate.

"Would you be able to stay tonight?"

Chapter Eight:
Visitor

***

His face had a look of surprise and intrigue in it.

"I'm just a little freaked out about being here alone with the locks potentially not working. There are extra beds upstairs, you wouldn't have to sleep on the couch."

"I guess I could. Sure."

"Your mom will probably think I'm terrible for letting you stay, huh?"

"No, I'll have Jenna cover for me."

"Is that something she does often for you?"

"Are you accusing me of being promiscuous Zoe? That hurts. Here I am just trying to be nice and you insult me like that," he said, unable to contain his laughter through the last few words.

"Okay, very funny. Laugh at the scared girl, but you're the one who made me scared in the first place: 'I hate the thoughts of you out there by yourself, so close to that house.' Remember?"

"Yes I do hate that, which is why I am staying with you even though it goes against all my morals. I will sacrifice them tonight to be here for you." His smile curled until it made his dimples visible.

"Well thank you for the sacrifice Father Randall," I said sarcastically. "I'm going to go change, do you want me to bring you a pair of sweatpants or something?"

"I hardly think I'll fit into your sweatpants Zoe."

"No silly, I think my dad has some extra clothes still upstairs for an emergency. I'll be right back."

I hoped that the guest room would have something in it, but there was nothing. I had to go into their bedroom. I could do it if I just didn't think about it. I stood outside their door for a few minutes and then pushed it open slowly.

I reached for the light switch, it was just as I remembered it. I walked straight to the walk-in closet and flipped on the light. There on the top shelf were two stacks of clothes. I dug through and found a pair of gray sweatpants and a white t-shirt.
I left the room quickly and turned off the lights. I went to my room, still not allowing what I had just done to sink in. I grabbed my PJ bottoms and a tank top and went back downstairs.

"Here you go, they should fit. You can change in the bathroom down the hall if you want."

"Thanks, I'll be right back."

"How about some popcorn?"

"Sounds good," his voice getting quieter as he walked.

I popped some popcorn and got a couple of bottled waters out of the refrigerator. No wine tonight. I wasn't doing that again. He was probably already reading way more into this than he should.

"Well how much smaller than me was your dad?"
The t-shirt fit tightly. He was a lot more muscular than Dad, but about the same height. The sweatpants fit him well though.

"What? You look good," trying to hold back my giggles.

"Okay, enough gawking at the poor homeless guy."

"Awe, I really think you're very cute in that, really."
I think he actually blushed a little, but I had harassed him enough and I didn't want him to leave tonight. I didn't want to think about the kind of dreams I would have if in the back of my mind, I thought something could just open my door and come in.

"Let's go into the living room and eat this. How are you at Rummy?" I asked.

"Good enough to kick your butt."

"Well would you like to make a wager?"

"Okay Zoe. What's it going to be?"

"Loser has to cook dinner for the winner tomorrow night."

"I just want you to know that I really love Mexican food Zoe. I hope you don't disappoint me."

"You are so going down Justin Randall. Just deal."

I handed him the deck of cards. At first I was in it to win, but I quickly started to get tired. The score was now 4-3, but there was no fight left in me.

"Well, I guess I'll be cooking tomorrow. What kind of Mexican do you like?"

"Why don't we discuss it tomorrow?" His eyes gleamed with victory.

"Before we turn in there was something I wanted to ask you. It's none of my business, I know. But, I was wondering what is going on with Lucas' wife. Is she seriously ill?"

"Oh. It's not exactly that. She's sick, but..." his face looked a little sad. "Well, they have been trying for a long time to have a baby, about three years now, and she just had another miscarriage. She's taking it pretty hard. She was with her mom tonight. That's why she wasn't there. I think it bothers her to be around the other kids."

"I'm sorry. I didn't mean to pry. I just thought, I don't know, I just felt bad for him tonight."

"Zoe, please stop apologizing. It's not your fault, things just happen. It doesn't change how lucky they are to have each other."

A feeling of guilt came over me. I felt like I had misjudged him. I always pegged him for a "macho man" kind of guy, seeing this side of him was really surprising.

"I want to have a family. Don't get me wrong, but I'll just be thankful if I can talk the right girl into marrying me. What about you Zoe?"

"You mean, do I want to have a family?"

I almost spit my water that was in my mouth at him.

"I don't know, I never really thought that much about it."

"What do you think about marriage then?" He looked a little disappointed in my first answer.

"I don't know. I guess if I was in love with someone and he asked, but its hard to answer because I've never been with anyone I would consider."

"Wow. Really? I thought that's all you girls did was conspire on how to wrangle men into commitment. I have to say, I figured you for the type of woman that would want to settle down and have a family."

"I didn't say I didn't want to get married or not have a family. I've just never really thought about it. So since you have thought so much about this subject, how many kids do you want Justin?"

"I have always thought a big family would be nice. I'm not saying I want enough for a football team, but three or four would be good."

I was hoping the thoughts I was thinking weren't apparent on my face.

"You never cease to amaze me. I really didn't see that coming from you. I figured you for the permanent bachelor type, playing the field, never settling down."

"Really? Then I guess we have our work cut out for us. We can't assume anything with each other, can we?"

"I guess not."

Bailey saved me from the uncomfortable silence that had occurred from our intense conversation. He had to go out.

"Justin, could you let Bailey out while I go upstairs and straighten up the guest room for you?"

"Sure. But I can just crash on the sofa Zoe. It's fine. I've slept on worse, trust me."

"No, don't be silly. There are two extra beds upstairs. It's no big deal. I wouldn't be able to sleep if I knew you were squished on the sofa."

I turned and bolted up the stairs before he could argue with my any more. The guest room was very warm and relaxing. The bed was probably the most comfortable in the house. It had a down pillow top on it that you could just sink into. My mother had such a knack for decorating, so the room felt very comfortable. She paid attention to every little detail there was. There was little to do in the room to prepare for someone to sleep there. Jenna had already changed the linens and put fresh ones on the beds. I turned it down and fluffed the pillows for him, just like Mom would have if she were living.

She was the kind of person that would get up and cook at two am if she thought you were hungry. She was a people pleaser, always putting others before herself. I missed her soothing voice so much, always knowing the rights words to say to make me feel like I was going to be okay. I had to stop. I had allowed that terrible lonely feeling to invade my thoughts. I hated it more than the dark figure that haunted me. I could hear footsteps coming down the hall.

"I'm in here Justin," I raised my voice a little louder than necessary. I didn't realize he was already outside the door, Bailey right behind him.

"Hey, it looks very comfortable. Maybe I'll just move in and live here, all this special treatment and pampering. Do I get tucked in too?"

"Well Mr. Randall, the tuck in service is extra, but there is a lovely continental breakfast at nine am that is complimentary," trying to use my best stewardess voice.

"Well, I am disappointed. I think I'll call the concierge and see if I can renegotiate my perks."

"Okay. Enough. Seriously, is there anything else I can get or that you need?"

A devilish grin began on one side of his face and crawled across to the other side, his dimples deep in his cheeks.

"You know what, I should have known better than to give you that much rope. I do, however, appreciate you staying here and sacrificing your reputation."

"Already taken care of. I called Jenna while I was letting Bailey out and she is covering for me. But she did make me promise to behave myself tonight. Luckily... I crossed my fingers."

"I am sure you will be a gentleman and keep your promise, seeing as how you've managed to surprise me at every turn this evening."

"Why did you have to go and say that? Now I have to be all noble and courteous. You take the fun out of everything Zoe."

His grin turned to a pouting frown like an eight year-old boy would have if told he couldn't have candy.

"Thank you again for staying."

He was now a few inches from me, looking down at me, his blue eyes sparkling. I am sure in the past this maneuver had worked like a charm. My heart was speeding up now and my head not so clear. I knew I should to not let this happen tonight; I needed to slow down because I didn't want to hurt him and I was a mess emotionally. Right now I am not in any condition to have this relationship happening.

He gently placed his hand beneath my chin to raise it up so I would have to stare directing into his eyes, something I had been trying to avoid.

"If you need anything, you call me. I'll be right here. Sleep well Zoe," his lips gently caressed mine and then, he let go of me.

I couldn't believe it. I stood there in shock. How could he just stop?

What a total let down. I mean, I planned on being strong and stopping him after a few minutes, but this was too short. What a tease! And they say women are bad!
His face looked sweet and innocent with a slight edge of smugness. I tried to regain my composure.

"Thank you Justin," I turned, thinking he had maybe changed his mind.

"You can leave the door cracked if you want so I can hear you if you need me."

Ooh, what a tease! He was like a Jedi at this!

"Goodnight Justin."

As I pulled the door shut, I felt a little more in control. I just hoped I wouldn't regret it later. The house was a little chilly. I started to think maybe I should tell Justin where the extra blankets were, just in case he should get cold. But, on second thought, I was not going back in there to be humiliated again. I was going to have to step up my game. I couldn't stand that feeling that he beat me at the whole physical restraint thing. I really am way too competitive. I think I need therapy for it, among a million other things that I don't want to think about right now.

I slid under the cool covers in my bed and tried to coax Bailey on the bed to keep my feet warm, but he was already sound asleep in his bed. I lay there thinking about all the things that had transpired in just the six short days I had been back. Which seemed much longer. I was glad I had met the Randall's. They were all so nice, especially Justin and Jenna. I was very lucky to have befriended them. I don't know what I would have done without them. My mind was tracking the evening back through every step, replaying it like a movie, that bickering that went on between Justin, Aaron and Jenna and how much fun they had. They seemed to love each other, even when they disagreed. I was now feeling like I had been cheated in some way by not having siblings.

If Mom and Dad would have had more children, I would not be alone right now. But I am and there's nothing anyone can do about that now. I will have to learn to cope like everyone else who doesn't have a large happy family does.

I started to wonder if Justin's presence would keep me from having the dreams that had been consuming my sleep. I was almost curious to see what it would be tonight. No strange events had occurred to make me have any dark thoughts. I hadn't seen any imaginary figures looming about outside, although technically, I hadn't been outside alone after dark today. So I didn't have the opportunity to freak myself out. I wonder if this is a sign of total hysteria? I'm seeing things that aren't there like imaginary dark figures, strange gypsy women, and your own headstone. I was probably having a nervous breakdown of some kind that would inevitably land me in the psych ward at some hospital. Maybe I will just start collecting a ton of cats, become a recluse and people will overlook the craziness.

I will just embrace the dreams and give in. Still, I couldn't be too crazy. Justin seemed to like me and he's normal enough. I had already decided before I even started playing cards with him that nothing was going to happen tonight. Then he goes and acts all cool and collected, a pillar of strength. I hope he knows he didn't stand a chance anyway. I wasn't going to allow it or get carried away again.

I had even prepared a speech about how things are going too fast and I'm not emotionally ready to have a complicated relationship right now, but he goes and acts all prudish and superior. Why was this bothering me so bad? Is it because I was upset he didn't try or that nothing happened? Okay, enough of that thinking. He was just playing his guy games. He was probably very good at reading women and just waiting to catch me off guard.

Yea he knew I was expecting the romance thing tonight and is watching to catch me off my guard. Ha! I knew it. He's not better than me. I would say that we are pretty equally matched. This is going to be fun.
I lie there, waiting for sleep to find me, but was unable to get completely relaxed. My muscles were tight and my mind very alert. I did what most people do when they can't sleep; I tiptoed out of my room and down the stairs to the kitchen to sneak a little snack. I grabbed the bag of Oreo's and poured myself a glass of milk. I felt like I needed to be quiet so no one would hear me. This would be terrible to get caught eating cookies and milk at two am. I was on my fourth cookie when I suddenly felt like I was not alone.
Why had I sat with my back to the glass doors? I was going to have to turn around to look. I couldn't look I was frozen, my breaths coming faster now. I still had the half eaten cookie in my hand. I thought about whistling for Bailey to see if I could call him down without waking Justin and looking like a total baby. I knew he would start barking if I made any strange noises or possibly not hear me at all. There is something so unsettling about there only being a thin piece of glass between you and what scares you.
This had all the makings of a bad horror flick. Stupid girl comes down and eats right in front of creepy scary mass murderer and isn't aware until it's too late. I was never a sissy like this before, why was I turning into one now? Of course, I never saw dark figures lurking outside of my house before either. I put down the cookie and slowly slid my stool away from the island and stood pretending I was stretching. As I raised my arms, I tried to peek under my right arm to see if I could catch a glimpse of anything, but I couldn't see a thing. I still couldn't bring myself to turn around.

So like the chicken I had become, I walked through the hall towards the stairs, putting more space between the back doors and myself. I flipped the light switch off like I was leaving the room and turned halfway into the hall, looking briefly at the doors. I drew in a huge breath and blew it out. There was nothing there, at least not now. The hair on the back of my neck was standing up. I know I shouldn't eat before bed, it's not good. I already have a problem with reality lately and the sugar just amplifies it. I hurried up the stairs to my room, closing the door behind me and jumped into bed. My heart was still pounding. Bailey was snoring loud enough to wake the dead. I suddenly felt very much like sleeping. It didn't take long for sleep to find me this time. I think I was out as soon as my head hit the pillow.

The smell of bacon and coffee was wafting in the air as I woke up. I had forgotten Justin was here, he must already be awake. I washed my face and pulled back my hair. He was going to eventually have to see me without makeup, now was as good a time as ever. I wasn't going to be able to pull off the "well-put together girl" thing very much longer anyway. This is who I was. I did refrain from going down in my PJ's though. I slipped on some yoga pants and a t-shirt and headed downstairs.

Justin was humming to himself at the stove cooking breakfast.

"You should have woke me up."

"You were sleeping sound, I didn't want to bother you."

I suddenly noticed that Bailey was already downstairs.

"Umm, Justin, how did Bailey get out of my room?"

"I don't know. He slept in my room last night. He came and got in bed with me at around three am and just stayed. Is that okay?"

"Of course, I just don't remember letting him out of my room,"

“Oh and you really need to watch leaving these doors unlocked. I know it’s rural here, but you still get transient people from time to time.”

“Those doors?” I was pointing to the glass French doors that faced the back.

“Yeah. They were unlocked when I came down this morning to let Bailey out.”

I felt like I wanted to faint and felt all the color leave my face, as my knees were getting wobbly.

“Zoe, are you alright? You look like you just saw a ghost. Here sit.” He quickly handed me a chair and sat me in it.

“I’m fine, I think I just got up too fast, that’s all. I just need to drink some juice.”

“Sit. I’ll get you some juice. Does this happen often to you?”

I wanted to tell him only recently, since I started seeing things.

“No, I am fine. I’m just a little light headed is all. I think I’ll go back upstairs for a minute and lay down to get my bearings if that’s okay? I’m sorry.”

“Zoe, breakfast won’t be ready for about fifteen more minutes. Take your time. Do you need help?”

“No, I think I can manage just fine.”

I went back upstairs, my hands shaking as they grabbed the doorknob to my room. The thought that someone had touched it, someone I didn’t know, made a shiver go down my spine. I threw myself back on my bed. Bailey was in my room last night. I know he was. He never even woke up when I went down to raid the kitchen.

I saw him when I came back into my room. He never even moved.

So how did he get through the closed door into Justin’s room? And how did those doors in the kitchen get unlocked? I wasn’t able to think of what my heart knew was right. My mind wouldn’t wrap itself around it.

He was here in the house the dark figure my undoing.

He was here while I slept how did he get past Bailey? I was almost hyperventilating it couldn't be true this just doesn't happen in real life only in movies. What was he a demon or some kind of strange stalker? Maybe Justin was right maybe it was a transient like he said just looking for an empty house or some food. But I knew down deep like I know myself I knew it was more much, much more than that.

"Knock, knock are you feeling better?"

Peeking his head around the corner with a white tray in his hand.

"Oh Justin you didn't have to bring it up here I could have come back down. I'm the one who lost last night remember?"

"I wanted to do this besides we have a lot of work to do today on that room and the quicker you feel better the sooner we can get started."

"You don't have to work again today?"

"Later I have to go check on some houses near Calais but you have me for a while."

"Good will you join me then?"

"Are you inviting me onto your bed Zoe Dossin?" He said batting his eyes innocently

"Actually I thought we could have a picnic in the floor. Justin will you come eat breakfast with me on the floor?"

I batted my eyes this time. He had such a calming effect on me I was already relaxing and my breathing had improved greatly.

"Well if you put it that way. Okay, move over I just don't want you to get the wrong idea about me. I mean I'm not some easy local you know."

His smile was boyish and cheesy.

"I would never presume that you are easy. I mean after last night I think just the opposite."

"What does that mean?"

"Nothing."

His face looked a little blank. Finally I felt vindicated about his total power trip last night. Breakfast was good he was becoming very useful and a fun to be around. We worked on the back room for the next three days in between Justin's work it was nice to forget about all the disturbing unexplained happenings. He was nice enough to stay in the guest room although I never told him about anything he seemed to know I was a chicken. He was a total gentleman on his best behavior but he did beat me at Rummy, scrabble, and monopoly to where I owe him about twenty dinners. I'm starting to think my dad used to let me win all the time. Justin was just finishing up the bookshelves he made for me and we would be done. The room was just as I had pictured it I couldn't wait to get started. My internet was installed and all I had to do was download my program and I was back in business. I missed working I had a lot of ideas for areas I wanted to shoot but I was a little disappointed Justin was leaving tomorrow to go out with his dad and Brothers again. He would be gone for a least a few weeks I didn't know what I would do without him helping to keep my mind off of everything. But I would have my work to keep me busy and Jenna promised to check in on me from time to time, as Justin had insisted. He put the last bookcase in and we both stood back in awe it looked great. The dark wood floors, white trim around the windows and the silky blue paint color went perfect together.

"Wow, we did good!"

"No we did great! Well you did great, thank you for working so hard I love it! Are you sure you have to go?"

"I don't want to but yeah I have to I'll hurry back I promise. I looked at the locks on the doors too Zoe, they are all fine just double check yourself."

"I'll be fine don't you worry. I'll have this room full of pictures by the time you get back."

"Well don't work to hard you have plenty of time to take pictures. Any ideas of where you'll start?"

"Nope, I'm doing research tonight and scouting out some places tomorrow. I'll be busy all weekend! Oh and I promised my Aunt Kate I would visit her she's not feeling well and she is going in for a few tests Tuesday, so I thought I would fly in to see her."

"What about Bailey what will you do with him?"

"Oh there's a great kennel in Calais I thought I would board him for the three days he doesn't like to fly."

"Do me a favor, leave a note of where you'll be and how long you'll be gone okay? I will have Jenna check on the house while your gone and that way she'll know when to expect you back."

He was trying to be professional about it but I could clearly see he was concerned and wanted to keep tabs on me. It felt weird to have him be so concerned but nice.

"At least let me make good on one of the dinners I owe you before you leave."

"I would love to but I have a lot of packing to do and we have to leave early in the morning to get to the boat by 5am."

"Wow I think I'm going to miss you."

"Don't sound so surprised of course your going to miss me handy man, security guard and cook."

"Don't forget entertainment. I mean with the card games and all."

"I think I'm going to miss you just a little too."

He was standing in front of me now looking down at me with his perfect smile and deep blue eyes. I didn't want to seem so needy but I really was not ready for him to leave. He had become my new roommate and I was going to have to get used to being alone in the house again. His hand pulled me to him and held me for a long time placing his lips on my head he gave a deep sigh.

"I don't know why, but you have to promise me you're going to be careful while I'm gone. I don't want you being a daredevil while I'm away. Can you promise me you'll be super careful?"

"Me of course, my middle name is super careful."

"Yeah well, just the same Zoe Super careful Dossin, stay clear of that Madison house."

I tried to pretend like the mention of that house didn't send me into a curiosity frenzy I had put the thoughts of investigating that house completely on the back burner because of my distraction but he was leaving and it was beginning to creep back in. I was going to have to lie and lie well.

"I won't do anything unsafe or risky while you are gone I promise"

"And …."

"What?"

Trying to look as innocent as I could. Lying wasn't my strong suit.

"You won't go near that house."

"Fine I won't go near the house."

He pulled me back to look at my face I was confident in my promise because I planned to keep it and investigate too.

"There's nothing up there Zoe and remember you are alone out here right now I don't want you playing detective."

I really stink at this.

"Do you want it in blood?"

"No, I just want you to be here when I get back so we can …"

"Play house some more?"

"Something like that. If you'll promise to behave while I'm gone I have somewhere I want to take you when I get back."

"You aren't going to tell me where that is are you? How can you do that to me, you could be gone weeks."

"Or only one, but yes, I'm not going to tell you it will have to be a surprise."

"I'll just have to behave then won't I?"

He put his hands on either side of my face and bent down his lips gently separating mine I pulled him closer not wanting him to leave he would be so far away. My breathing was coming harder and faster as was his. His hands pulling at my shoulders then sliding down my back. His kiss was softer and slower as he began to pull away. He was ridiculous with the self-control thing It was becoming annoying. He gave a sigh and put his forehead on my lips.

"For you I will wait and do this right."

His voice was full of conviction and determination.

"I really am going to miss you. One week?"

"I'll try I promise."

He kissed me softly one last time brushing my cheek with his thumb.

"Bailey buddy, she's all yours again take care of her for me."

He rubbed Bailey's chest and headed for the door. I followed after him and watched him get in his truck and pull away. I don't know how or why we had gotten so close so fast. Maybe it was because I needed someone to keep me from feeling so alone and he is just an amazing guy who knew that. I have never believed in the fairy tale stories of boy meets girl, they fall in love immediately, and live happy forever. I knew it wasn't like that but Justin was helping fill an emptiness I had and I wasn't going to question that right now. I had never been able to give myself emotionally or physically to anyone.

My fixation, as Dr. Landon my 2nd therapist called it, with William Madison had taken care of that. This was the most I had felt for any real person besides immediate family and I did care for Justin. He would be back and I would be fine alone for now. I went to the kitchen fixed a bite to eat before I plunged into my work. The most difficult thing to do when you are alone is eat. Especially without a television, I was starting to rethink the whole TV issue. It might have been a good reason when my parents were still alive but I would like to at least hear someone else talking even if it's Stewie Griffin. I put a large note on the message board call and get Cable hook up for TV and buy a TV. I would wait of course until Justin returned so he could help me get it home. I decided to get in some research so I headed for my new studio AKA the den. Two hours later and two calls to tech support my software was installed. I needed a break and so did Bailey it was cooling off so I grabbed my jacket and his leash I wanted to get some fresh air just as I was walking out the door the phone rang it was Jenna he hadn't even been gone 4 hours and he had her checking on me.

"Hey Zoe, it's Jenna, sorry to bother you but Justin tells me that you are going away. When are you leaving?"

"Hi Jenna, I am leaving in the morning after I drop Bailey off, why?"

"Oh are you driving to the air port?"

"I'm not sure, I might have the airport shuttle pick me up so I don't have to drive so far."

"If you need me to drive you I would."

"No that's crazy it's to far. The shuttle service is very reasonable and I might even decide to drive. But thank you for the offer tell Justin I'll be fine."

"Call me Zoe, if you need anything okay?"

"I will and I'll call you when I get back I promise Jenna. Okay Bailey, let's go."

Chapter Nine: The Familiar

***

I made sure to take my keys hiding my purse in the pantry in case some transient wandered by as Justin would say. And I double-checked the doors to make sure they where locked Bailey's patients were running out and he was now pulling me away from the house. He walked down the path and I followed he normally stayed at my side but for some reason he was highly motivated to get down the steps we entered the clearing we both stopped. Bailey because nature called and me because I noticed the clouds were getting really gray it wasn't supposed to storm but it looked like it. I had decided we would go for a short walk so I went toward the darker clouds so I could keep an eye on them. I was thinking about my trip back to Arizona and hoping my Aunt didn't think I was going to be coming home for a visit every two weeks. I also hoped she would be alright it was just a routine check when mom got diagnosed with her cancer. I was not ready to have to see my Aunt go through that. I was making a mental note to call her and tell her I was going to come after all. When she first asked me I didn't want to go so I told her I would have to see if I could board Bailey somewhere. But after I thought about how great she was with mom and us through everything I decided I needed to go. I knew she would be so excited. I started thinking about our shopping trips together Aunt Kate, my cousins Abbey & Erica, Mom and me. All the lunches and laughing I missed it so much. Bailey was pulling harder now he must have caught the scent of something. I hadn't really been paying attention to how far we were walking and we had gotten farther than I wanted to from the house.

It started to sprinkle and I was pulling hard on Bailey now to turn him around this storm was coming up fast.

The temperature had dropped significantly and the wind was picking up. I tried to stay under the tree line to keep us out of the rain but the rocks were getting slippery. I couldn't believe how stupid I had been to not pay closer attention. I was cold and wanting to get out of the rain I tried to pick up the pace but I was losing my footing. I felt I was losing my balance and tried to correct myself. I heard a cracking noise and felt a sharp pain on my side as I went down I watched the light get dim as I passed out. I could hear Bailey barking and growling I tried to call to him but I couldn't get anything to work not even my voice. Then there was a new sound, a voice I had heard before deep and familiar Bailey instantly stopped barking. I was straining to open my eyes but all I could see was red. I felt another sharp pain and then the feeling I was being carried. There was a distinct smell of betadine, I recognized it from all the times dad had stitched me up. My head felt thick like I had been drugged. I was able to see a very bright light and felt a pulling sensation at right my side where the pain was earlier. I could hear mumbling and then nothing. The feeling of pain came again and I opened my eyes; I was alone in a dimly lit room. The bed I was in was enormous and draped with heavy fabric. My head still felt very thick and the pain in my side matched the pain in my head. I tried to make sense of what happened. Where was Bailey? I tried to get up but pain sent me backwards I lifted the covers to find I was in a white cotton gown. I lifted it to see the extent of my injury, there was a compression bandage placed around me and under that white gauze. I couldn't see anything. I gently let my hand follow my hairline until I could feel another bandage about ¼ inch from my hairline above my right eye. I noticed my hair had been pulled back into a braid. I tried to get up again this time I managed to just sit up. My eyes panned the room trying to adjust to the lack of light. I heard the doorknob turn and laid back into the pillows. It was a small woman.

"Hello?"

There was no response as if she didn't hear me.

"Where am I?"

Again nothing she seemed to ignoring me.

"Did you find me?"

She looked startled and began speaking in a foreign language that I didn't recognize. She put her finger up to motion me to wait and she left again, I hoped to find someone who spoke English, so I could find out where I was and what had happened to Bailey. My head was pounding now I could hear my heart beat and it was like a drum in my head. I had definitely been given some type of painkiller and it was wearing off fast. The door opened again this time it was a larger figure, a man, he stayed purposefully out of the light following the darker shadows of the room. His build was tall and muscular I caught a glimpse of his dark thick hair but his face was just out of sight.

"Hello can you tell me were I am?"

There was a moment of silence.

"I had a dog with me please, is he okay?"

My voice began to crack as I felt tears welling up in my eyes at the thought of loosing Bailey like that. It was stupid of me to get so distracted. He spoke, his voice again deep and familiar.

"You are safe and so is your dog. He is being kept in another room so you could rest. How is your pain?"

"My head and my side are sore, what happened."

"You broke at least three ribs and had quite a large puncture wound on your right side. You have some stitches there and on your forehead as well. I will get you something for the pain."

"Please wait tell me were I am, and who you are?"

"You are safe and very near your home. I will send in something for pain."

He was not going to tell me his name so I didn't want to push the issue.

"How long have I been here?"

"It's been about eighteen hours."

"I need to get home."

I started to get up pulling back the covers and putting my feet over the side, which instantly caused pain to shoot from my side and head. I drew in a deep breath which only made the pain in my side worse. He stepped out of the shadow keeping his head down so all I could see was his dark hair. He placed me back into the bed.

"You aren't going home right now you need to rest."

He commanded as he pulled back away from the light, drawing in a deep breath.

"I'll be back in a moment."

He said sounding only slightly more composed than before. Was I being held captive? I started to panic, no one would know where I was and I had taken Bailey with me. My purse was hidden, for all Jenna knew I was in Arizona, no one would even look for me for a week. I tried to rationalize the situation. If he had wanted to kill me he would have done so already. Why would he fix me to turn around and kill me? My eyes began to search the room again. The curtains that covered the windows were very tall. The room itself felt large. The ceiling of the room had to be tall because the canopy of the bed was about 9 feet. My heart stopped as I realized were I was. There was only one house on this beach that was big enough to have a room this size. I must have bumped my head pretty hard because I was definitely hallucinating. This could not be happening. The saying be careful what you wish for came to mind. The door opened again and the small woman came in with a glass of water and a white pill.

"Where is the gentleman that was here?"

I said it slowly to see if that would help her understand.

She only shook her head and gave me the same gesture as before and retreated. Ah! This was starting to get me mad I was entitled to know where I was. I wanted to see Bailey, to make sure he was okay. I looked at the pill in my hand and wandered if I should take it. The door opened again this time it was Him.

"Is there something wrong? Do you need anything?"

He seemed agitated.

"What are giving me?"

"You need to take that it will help with the pain."

"I don't want to sleep again."

"That is what your body needs right now to heal."

His voice had a condescending tone, why was he so mad at me?

"I don't mean to sound ungrateful but I really would like to know were I am."

"Why don't you take the medicine and we will discuss that later."

"Because I don't want to wait until after I take it to discuss were I am, why won't you just tell me?"

Now I was starting to get angry.

"You need your rest and it is complicated so please just take the medicine and lie back down."

He was being so persistent! My red headed temper was starting to surface and I knew I dare not open my mouth. I just stared at him with an equally stern gaze and shook my head no.

"Why must you be so difficult?"

He spoke through clenched teeth then taking a deep breath as if to compose himself again.

"Take the medicine and I will tell you what you wish to know."

His voice made me want to do as he said not from fear but something different. There was something that was almost hypnotic and familiar to his voice.

I paused for a moment I had a feeling I was going to take the medicine one way or another so I popped it into my mouth and took a drink of water.

"Now you where saying?"

I said smugly with my best poker face.

Although I could not see his face I could hear him breathing, it was heavy at first but suddenly got slower and more even.

"You are in Robbinston Maine near Red Beach a guest in my home."

My mouth was agape he had managed to answer my question but not disclose my location at the same time. I was going to have to help him.

"You mean I am a guest in the Madison family home?"

His breathing had stopped for a moment after my question.

"You're not from here, how do you know of the Madison's?"

He seemed confounded by my reply.

"I don't, I only know of the house."

I didn't feel telling him what I had heard would go over to well.

"Yes, you are in the Madison home."

"And you are?"

"You may call me William. I will leave so you can get some rest."

I felt my face get warm as he spoke the name William. I desperately wanted to see his face.

"No wait, please can I see my dog?"

"I can get him for you and then will you rest?"

"Yes, I promise I will rest after I see him."

"I will have Darlei bring you something to eat you must be hungry. I will return with your dog after you have eaten."

I felt like I was a child being bribed to do as I was told, but I played along with him grateful I would see Bailey soon. He retreated still making sure his face would not be seen. I wondered if he was terribly disfigured or possibly did not want me to remember what he looked like so I could not describe him to anyone. Justin's words from the park that day came back to me.

"No one but the servants come and go from that house."

Why all the secrecy? The pain in my head and side began to dull and I was feeling a little drowsy when the small woman he called Darlei brought in a tray of food. The smell of warm bread and soup filled the room. I ate quickly trying to make sure I could stay awake long enough to see Bailey. When I was done she removed the tray and was leaving the room when I heard voices in the hall. I couldn't make out what they were talking about but I could clearly hear His voice and another male voice speaking in that same unrecognizable language. It sounded as if he was reprimanding the other man. He kept his promise and brought Bailey in to see me. I don't know who was happier me or Bailey. Bailey was very well behaved, in fact better than he has ever behaved, he was not on a leash when he entered the room and yet he never jumped on me once.

"Thank you for letting me see him and taking care of him."

"You are welcome, I will let you visit with each other and return for him in a little while."

"Could he stay here with me tonight? It would make me feel better to know he is close."

"I guess that would be alright as long as you promise to rest. You can't be moving around so much your injuries are quite severe."

"I promise I will rest. Thank you William for your kindness."

“I will leave you then if you need anything just pull the tassel on your left and Darlei will see to your needs.”

His mood had seemed to change from angry and confounded to tolerant and composed.

“Thank you William.”

I was having trouble keeping my eyes open I decided to take his advice and rest. I wasn’t going anywhere in the shape I was in, for now anyway. Bailey jumped up after William left and laid at my feet whimpering quietly like he used to when my father would leave. I wondered why he had not tried to eat William, he certainly looked like a man and Bailey usually hated men, especially tall men. My medicine was winning the battle so I closed my eyes and sank down into the covers. I woke to the smell of hot black current tea with mint, and warm cranberry scones. Darlei was back again with the tray of food. She sat the tray on the table near my bed and opened the curtains it was slightly overcast but the sun was trying to peek through the gray clouds. Bailey was not in the room. I knew it was no use to try and talk to her again she obviously spoke no English. Just then she turned to me and said,

“Master William will be in soon.”

I don’t think she even knew what she was saying, as if she had rehearsed the sentence and was simply repeating it back. She simply nodded and left. The tea was soothing and the scones were delicious. I had my appetite back that was a good sign.

I really did need to get up to use the little girls’ room I pulled back the covers and tried to slide my legs over the side. My side and head opposed my movements. I sat for a moment and then stood to my feet the room spun and I felt my legs go wobbly.

Before I could catch myself his arms were around me and lifting me like I was a porcelain doll gently placing me back on the bed.

"Are you trying to tear your stitches out or puncture a lung?"

His voice had lost the tolerance and it's composure from last night and was replaced with a controlling, contemptuous disposition.

"No I'm sorry I had to..."

"Had to what, prove that you are super human? You are still recuperating you can't go on the fly out of the bed."

"I had to use the lady's room if you must know and I was trying to get someone to show me where it was."

"The tassel is right next to you try to use it next time."

"Why are you so angry with me?"

"I'm sorry, I didn't mean to get angry I just don't think you realize how extensive your injuries are."

"Then why didn't you call an ambulance when you found me?"

There was a long silence and then his voice was softer.

"I didn't want you to have to be in pain that long. The ride to the hospital in Bangor would have been two hours at the very least."

"Are you a doctor William?"

"Not a formal doctor but I have studied medicine for a long time."

"I appreciate your concern but I still need to visit the little girls' room."

"Oh yes, one moment."

He pulled the tassel never letting me see his face directly but I could tell he was not disfigured in fact he looked handsome. Darlei was back, he spoke very quickly to her and then turned to me.

"Darlei will help you get a robe on and I will carry you to the lady's room."

"That's not really necessary I can manage on my own."

I feel like I had been arguing with this man since I woke up.

“Again with the stubbornness, why must you be so difficult?”

“You are used to getting your way are you Mr. Madison? “

“That’s beside the point. I won’t allow you to just go walking around with broken ribs and a possible concussion. Although if you like I could have Darlei bring you an alternative.”

Pointing to something that resembled a bedpan.
Although I could not see his face I sense a smirk rising on his face.

“I’m thinking no. Fine you can help me get to the bathroom.”

The small woman gently helped me with a beautiful robe and then he stepped in head still down and scooped me up handling me again as if I might break.

”Let me know if I am hurting you.”

I shook my head. I suddenly felt like I was five again after I got my tonsils out and dad carried me from the car to the house. We stepped out of the big room and into the corridor, down the long hallway. I felt bad that he had to carry me but he wasn’t even out of breath when we stopped at a door. He gently let me down keeping his arms around me. He smelled wonderful like something so familiar I couldn’t place it.

“I think I can take it from here.”

“Oh yes, Darlei is right here if you need anything. I’ll wait out here.”

He didn’t argue with me about it this time. The bathroom was ornate like the rest of the house. I washed my face I didn’t look as bad as I had expected.
I checked my head lifting the small bandage there were four small stitches like a surgeon had placed them.

I inspected my side also this was harder just lifting my arm made me want to pass out I peeked under the gauze, my side was blotchy black, blue, green and yellow the stitches again were perfectly placed. I heard a rap on the door.

"Yes I'm fine, I'll be right out."

I replaced the compression bandage and walked slowly to the door. He looked relieved when I stepped out.

"Did you think I tried to climb out the window?"

"No although I would not put it passed you. I was worried you passed out again."

"Well thank you, but technically I never really passed out earlier."

"Again we agree to disagree. Truly you are tiring, do you ever go along with anything?"

"For some reason no, not with you. Is there a reason why you won't let me see your face?"

He laughed a deep laugh it rolled down the hallway and then abruptly stopped.

"Do you always say what you are thinking?"

"No, well not usually but you are so secretive and again you didn't answer my question."

"I merely wish to stay anonymous."

"Well then, you should not have brought me home with you and patched me up."

"Yes, you keep telling me that. I'm sure the best thing would have been to leave you broken on the rocks but as you can see I chose not to. You must be getting tired I'll take you back to your room."

"I think I can walk, really."

His jaw tightened and he let out a low growl and scooped me up.

"Or not, you could carry me back I guess that's fine too."

He didn't talk all the way back to my room I could still smell him, taking in deep breaths was hard but I so wanted to remember where I had smelled that before.

He placed me on the bed and started to leave.

"No wait please, when will I be able to go home?"

"Is it so terrible here that you would rather be home, alone with no one to take care of you?"

"How did you know I live alone?"

There was a long silence.

"And how did you know I like Black currant tea? Or where I live?"

My voice was getting higher with each question.

"I have upset you, I'll go."

He said quickly turning to leave the room.

"Upset? Upset? Are you kidding me?"

I felt my side protesting my rapid breathing.

"It's been you outside and inside my house, hasn't it? Have you been watching me?"

My mind flew a million miles a minute racing through the events that had recently been plaguing my sleep.

"You are getting yourself upset, I'm sorry you are mad I didn't mean to frighten you."

"Frightened? I thought I was going crazy. I thought I was seeing things and you tell me don't get upset that some strange man is stalking me and scaring me to death!"

I could hardly breathe. Transient my butt Justin, I was right. My side felt like it would tear open at any moment.

"Please lay down, I am sorry, I never meant for you to see me. I didn't know I was scaring you. I tried to stay out of sight. It's really your fault you know."

"What? You are blaming me for this?"

"You visited me first. I saw you on the outcropping and I needed to find out who you where. I thought you were a reporter or someone fishing for a story."

He said obviously trying to place the blame elsewhere.

"I didn't come to stalk you. I was just curious about the house, I am a photographer and the old architecture of this house intrigued me."

"Of course, it had nothing to do with the stories of monsters and curses right?"

"Why did you come to my house William? Do I know you, I feel like I know you?"

He was slowly moving towards the door as if the conversation made him uncomfortable.

"Please you are tired and you need to rest. We can talk about this later after you have rested. I will bring in Bailey so you can see him."

He was gone. I still had not seen his face but I could tell I was starting to wear on his better nature his voice had moments where it was not entirely human and a little dark. I felt a chill run down my entire body thinking of it. I felt ashamed of thinking that way about him, his privacy was obviously very important to him and he had been so gracious as to take care of me. I was surprised that I wasn't more creeped out. The dark hovering image that had basically been stalking me and even been in my house was holding me captive for all I knew. Why wasn't I scared right now? I didn't buy the whole I thought you were a reporter story.

There was something about him I couldn't put my finger on it. I had made up my mind when he came back in I would apologize to him and thank him for his generosity. Maybe if I made him feel more comfortable he would divulge more information. I was starting to get restless I needed to get up and move around but my body felt differently, the pain was still very intense.

Still, I couldn't wrap my brain around the fact that it was him all along. I should be terrified but somehow I wasn't, I was just the opposite. In fact I felt a huge amount of relief that he is human flesh and blood not some creature or devil but just a man.

I needed to see him. I needed to put a face to his voice it was so smooth but dangerous at the same time, it was familiar to me but it shouldn't be at all.

I couldn't help but think about the first time I had heard it some thirteen years ago when I first saw the house. I know now it was him who saved me from the dogs. But how? He doesn't seem that much older than my self and that voice could never belong to a teenager. I was only fifteen when I heard it the first time; it had to be his father, right? My head was starting to hurt from thinking to much I needed to relax and think of how I was going to explain this to Jenna and Justin. I'm sure they will notice the bandages. There was a faint knock and then the door opened before I could say anything.

"Bailey, hey buddy. Thank you for bringing him back."

"I figured I had to or you might start going room to room searching."

"Was that an attempt at humor William? No, you know what don't even answer that I am sorry. I have behaved very badly and I don't want you to think I don't appreciate what you have done for me. I am grateful that you found me and you were gracious enough to bring me into your home and take care of Bailey and me. Thank you."

"You are very welcome Miss Dossin."

"Please call me Zoe."

"Zoe, as I was saying you are very welcome to stay as long as you need to. I should probably apologize to you as well, I tend to come off a little gruff and I'm sorry for that. I don't entertain guest usually and I am a bit out of practice on my manners."

I was shocked at his remorseful disposition. It was such a contrast from his earlier mood.

"William would it be okay, I mean is there any way, I could possibly freshen up and maybe walk around a little later. I feel like I am going to go stir crazy and I know I need to rest but could I just even walk down the hall or something?"

There was a moment of silence, I could tell he was reluctant to answer me.

"If you are feeling up to it, I can have Darlei bring some things in for you to freshen up with and I'll escort you on a walk but it's not going to be a long one you really shouldn't be walking a lot."

"I promise it can be short, thank you. Has Bailey been a big inconvenience to you?"

"No actually he is a very bright animal, he is extremely obedient."

"Bailey? Are you sure you didn't fall down? Bailey never listens to anyone and he hates men. How did you get him to let you near me?"

"I have a way with dogs, I have a few of my own. You have to be confident. They are very smart they can judge people better than we give them credit for."

"Have you lived here long William?"

"Yes all my life. But you, you have lived somewhere else haven't you?"

"Yes this was only our summer home, my father inherited it from his uncle. I spent every summer of my life here pretty much. We lived in Arizona the rest of the time, my dad was a surgeon there. I have an Aunt and her family that still live there which reminds me did you find my cell phone? It was in my pocket when I fell?"

"Yes, but I am afraid it was broken."

"Do you have a phone I could use? My Aunt, she was going to have a test done
and I was supposed to fly there and go with her. I feel terrible that I didn't make
it. She'll be worried when she can't get through to me."

"I understand, yes I have a phone. I will have Darlei bring it to you but I would ask a favor in return.

"I would very much appreciate it if you didn't mention where you are or who found you. I prefer to be anonymous if you don't mind."

"I won't tell her I promise. Thank you again William."

I can't believe I just blurted that out like half my life story right there. It must be the pain meds. He pulled the tassel and Darlei was there within seconds, he spoke quietly and in the same strange language. She left the room quickly.

"She will bring you a phone and some things you'll need to freshen up but don't get your stitches wet they need to stay dry, I'll come in when your through and put clean dressings on your wounds and then we'll have our walk if you feel up to it."

"Yes that would be lovely, thank you."

She returned with the phone, Aunt Kate was all done with her tests and relieved that two of the test had come back negative. She bought the whole I have the flu story I had cooked up. I hated to lie to her but if I had told her the truth she would have been knocking on the Madison door before I could warn them. When I was through I pulled the tassel and Darlei came back in. She had brought a large basin of hot water, fresh towels, a change of new under garments, which I have no idea how they knew my size or where they came from, a beautiful nightgown and robe. The pale blue color of the layers of chiffon and silk where bordered by ivory lace. There was also a beautiful pair of Ivory slippers that matched the gown.

She sat the Basin near a dressing table and placed a chair for me to sit in when she was finished setting it up she motioned for me to stay and pulled the tassel.

I was wondering who she was calling but before I could invent someone it was William who came through the door.

"You must have something more important you should be taking care of."

"No, you are proving to be a full time job. I don't mind really."

This time he asked my permission before he scoped me up. He was getting more comfortable when he was near me, I actually caught a glimpse of his face this time, it was quick but he is defiantly not the hunchback from Notre Dame.

"I will wait outside until you are finished and then I will check your bandages. I'll be just outside if you need me Zoe."

There was something about the way he said my name that made a flutter run through me. Darlei helped me to the dressing table across the room it was as ornate as the rest of the furniture but it was gorgeous. The mirror was carved out of a deep, cherry wood, I could imagine the lady of the house sitting here to get ready.

Sitting on the stool and looking in the mirror made me think of my mother and how I used to sit at her dressing table back home when she was getting ready and she would let me put on her lipstick. Darlei helped me get partially undressed and handed me the soaps and bathing supplies as I needed them. She also pulled my hair back for me but just on top letting the rest fall around my shoulders. As she brushed my hair she hummed a beautiful but eerie tune, it sounded so familiar but I know I had never heard it. I slipped into the new clothes and I felt like a princess, a princess that fell out a window but a princess all the same.

The gown fit like it was made for me. The sweetheart neckline was trimmed with lace as was the empire waist, the entire hem about five inches wide was also lace. I put on the matching robe grimacing as I put each arm through. I held to the chair and made myself stand. She went to the hall to get him.

He stood for a moment and didn't move still staying in the darkest part of the room. I tried to not look directly at him it seemed to make him more comfortable when I wasn't trying to see his face.

"Is something wrong?"

"No, no nothing, everything is - perfect." His voice almost doting.

"Thank you for the clothes they are beautiful you shouldn't have, really but thank you."

"May I?"

He gestured to help me to the bed I nodded walking was painful but I didn't want him to know if he knew there would be no walk and I would be out of my mind with boredom. He laid me on the bed gently he had obviously mastered keeping his face out of sight.

"I need you to lift your gown on your right side so I can change the bandage if you don't mind."

He turned his back to me and I lifted it and pulled up the sheet to cover my legs and lower torso.

"Okay ready Doc."

He chuckled and leaned in not realizing I could see the side of his face still not able to make out his complete features but what I did see well I think I hit my head to hard because he looked remarkably like someone familiar. I quickly shook it off. He worked like he knew exactly what he was doing.

"Well everything looks like it's healing well."

"Does that mean we get to take that walk now?"

"I was hoping you had forgotten that but a promise is a promise I guess. It will be a short one and if I see you are getting tired-"

"I promise I will tell you if I am feeling anything but well."

He helped me off the bed and put his arm around my waist for support.

I caught myself closing my eyes and trying to breathe as deeply as my broken body would allow me to smell him it was intoxicating how wonderful he smelled.

"Please let me know if I am walking too fast."

"I will, I am just so glad to get out of that bed."

"Is the bed not comfortable enough?"

" No the bed is lovely but what I mean is I can't stand to feel cooped up and just
laying drugged in a bed, no matter how beautiful it is drives me out of my mind."

"Good then, I am glad I could save you from the torment."

"Was that an attempt on humor again William?"

"Are you insinuating that I lack a sense of humor Miss Dossin?"

"I am not saying you lack one, I just haven't had the privilege of experiencing it first hand."

He let out a deep chuckle and we continued down the long hallway. At the end it opened up into the huge staircase I'm sure he saw my color change when I realized how many steps there were.

"If its okay with you I have something I would like to show you but its downstairs. Would it be alright if I carried you?"

It was now that I regretted all those late night Oreo binges. I looked up to answer him and I realized that I could see his face, His entire face! I tried to calm my breathing that was steadily getting faster I couldn't believe it, not even a slight difference he was the spitting image of his great uncle. He was standing holding me, the very image that had haunted my dreams for well, too long. I felt a little faint as my mind tried to slow down my bodies reaction to his face.

"Are you alright Zoe? You look pale."

He touched his face with his hand realizing that I could see him he turned away like someone who was disfigured as if he was embarrassed by his appearance

"You didn't want me to see you?"
"No" he shook his head and looked down."
"Why? You act like you are some savage beast."
"It's just not the best idea. It's dangerous to be around you Zoe"
"Dangerous, me?"
"Yes because I forget who I am when I am with you and that's dangerous."
"Well it's too late now. I guess you will have to kill me or make me your prisoner."

I saw his smile for the first time his dark eyes and hair I couldn't turn away. He started down the stairs holding me like I was a small doll.

"I guess we've come this far might as well do this."
"You said you had something you wanted to show me?"
"Yes, it's just down here."

He turned at the bottom of the stairs and we headed down the next hall.

"Oh I'm sorry you wanted to walk didn't you."

He gently placed me back on my feet. He was very tall. Taller than Justin and even my dad, I think. He placed his hands on my waist and walked beside me down the hall. The rooms off the hall where beautiful and at the were huge double doors of dark mahogany. He pushed through the one and held it open for me. It was a brightly lit room even for such an overcast day and the walls were lined with paintings and drawings.

"Oh William this is wonderful. Who is the artist? I don't recognize these paintings."
"Well most of them my mother painted, she love to paint. Some are charcoals she did when she was young. She loved this room because of the natural light, I figured you would also like it since you like to take photographs."
"Your parents, do they live here too?"
"No, my parents are both deceased."

"I'm sorry, I didn't mean to just be so rude."

"They have been gone for a very long time. And you why do you live alone? Where are your parents?"

"My parents are both gone. My dad just about a month ago and my mom a couple years."

"Do you have any siblings?"

"Nope just me."

"I'm an only child also my mother wasn't able to have anymore children after me. Do you miss not having any brothers or sisters?"

"Sometimes but growing up I never really thought about it. My parents always made me feel so special I never got lonely, and I had my cousins to fight with. Did you miss not having any siblings? I mean a huge house like this would have been a blast to play hide-and-seek in."

"I actually have always wanted to play hide-and-seek in here with all the lights off."

"Well when I am better we'll have to make that happen for you. It's the least I can do to repay you."

"We will see about that. Are you getting tired come and sit down, I will have Darlei bring you some tea."

He led me to a sofa in the middle of the room and walked across the room to ring for her. His dark sweater was tightly fitted and his pants were tailored perfectly to him. He was back and sat across from me in a large chair. He seemed so interested in everything about me we talked about medical school, my dad and how he wanted me to continue with my courses which I think William agreed with him on. He even had me talking about my mom and her illness.

"How exactly did you meet the young Randall boy?"

"Oh Justin, well his grandfather was the caretaker for our house here and I guess since his death the family has continued to take care of his business. How did you know I knew him?"

His color changed and he got a little red, he seemed uncomfortable with the question.

"I have seen him there a lot lately and I was just curious."

"Well to be honest, I have had him staying with me because I was a little freaked out. Some dark figure has been stalking me and I thought I might be killed in my sleep so I asked him to hang around."

"Well, now that you know that's not the case you won't have to be bothering the poor boy anymore."

I detected a little hostility in his voice as he spoke about Justin.

"I guess not but I still haven't heard anything about you. What do you do when you aren't saving people?"

"I do research and I study medicine."

"That's it? You don't do anything else? I have told you my life story and you give me that?"

"You are probably getting tired we should head back."

He was immediately on guard again.

"I'm sorry I didn't mean to press I just feel like you are at an advantage. Please don't be angry you have been so nice to me and-"

He placed his finger over my lips.

"Shh Zoe its fine trust me there's nothing there you would want to know. I'm not that interesting. Another time I will explain. Let's get you back so you can get some rest."

He gestured with his arm for the door. It was quiet all the way back to my room. I wanted to say something but I couldn't think of anything that wasn't a question.

I hated that I had said something to bother him.

He seemed distant like he was concentrating on something. As we reached my room he opened the door Bailey was there waiting for me, as I bent down to pet him I felt a hot sharp pain in my side and then warm liquid. I looked down at the same time he did.

"Zoe what have you done!"

He scooped me up and placed me in the bed. I couldn't understand why he was mad at me again.

"Oh no I have ruined it! I am so sorry."

Blood was seeping through my bandage and had soaked through my beautiful gown.

"You must have torn the sutures."

I went to stand up and he pressed me back down.

"What are you doing? Are you trying to do more damage?"

"I don't want to get it on the sheets. I've already ruined my gown."

He looked at me like I had just told him I see dead people.

"The gown? You are worried about some stupid gown? Stay still I'll be right back. Do not move, understand?" His voice was deep and stern.

"Yes I won't move."

The pain was starting to get stronger. Why did it have to happen? I ruined an absolutely gorgeous gown and managed to re-injure myself. He was back with a black case and Darlei was at his side, she had some blue paper pads in her arms.

"I am going to have to get this gown off you I am afraid you have torn those sutures loose. Darlei will help you. Be very careful when you lift your right arm if we have to I can cut it off."

"Over my dead body! You are not cutting this gown, I'll get it off. If you help me back up it would be a lot easier to pull off."

He very carefully lifted me and helped me stand.

He turned his back as she helped me remove the beautiful garment. All I had on was my bra and panties I convinced myself that it was as much cover as when I wore my bikini in public.

"Okay it's off."

He turned to help me back into the bed, making sure to keep his eyes on my face. He spoke to Darlei and she quickly left the room. He still would not look directly at me.

"Here let me put you in the bed and you can cover up. I'm sorry she didn't bring you anything else to wear."

The bandage was completely saturated with blood when he tucked the blue pad underneath me and pulled the lamp closer as he started removing the bandages.

"This is going to sting a little but I have to pull the tape off."

He worked gently removing the tape; I could feel the heat from his hand even through his latex gloves.

I tried to hide the effects his touch on my skin was having on me but inside butterflies flipped in my stomach with excitement.

"I am going to numb this up a little so you won't feel me suture it you'll feel a little poke okay?" His voice was like velvet catching me off guard and pulling me from my gaze.

"That's fine did I rip it loose?"

I was trying to see what he was doing.

"Please Zoe quit moving you have to stay still."

He numbed it in three spots and then began to clean the area.

"Are you sure you never went to a formal school for this? You're very good you know."

"No but I have a feeling if I had you around long enough I would get as much hands on training as if I did go to school.

Only two came loose, you tore some of the tissue, I'll have to clean it up a little better and re-suture it again. Can you feel this?"

"No, I think it's numb."

He was finished in no time and gave me a new bandage.

"This new compression bandage should work a little better it's smaller and should hold you better. I shouldn't have let you walk so far today you over did it."

"Really William, I did it when I bent over to pet Bailey, I just bent to far that's all. It was my fault not yours, I feel terrible that I ruined the gown and that you had to do all of this. Are you ready to get rid of me now?"

Darlei came back in the room with a white cotton gown in her arms.

"If you want I will help you back off the bed, I won't look, I promise."

He was seemed genuinely embarrassed to see me in my underwear. He sat me down and Darlei helped me with the new gown. It wasn't as elegant but it was soft and very comfortable.

"Okay I'm decent."

He turned and lifted me back into bed.

"I should leave you would probably like to rest. I am going to have Darlei bring you some lunch up here and then something that will take the pain away. Don't look so surprised Zoe, I know you are in pain from that."

"Oh, well I'm sure you're eager to get away from my graceful presence."

"Yes you do probably need to wear a helmet or some type of protective gear if you are going to keep getting injured."

"So you are eager to be rid of me huh?"

"Not quite, now get some rest. I'll let Bailey stay and keep you company in here for a while and I'll be back soon to check on you. Ring if you need me and let Darlei know if you have any requests she does understand a little English, she just doesn't speak it fluently."

"William?"

He turned and looked at me with his dark eyes.

"Thank you again for everything I appreciate it."

"You're welcome Zoe. Now stop worrying and get some rest."

I had so many questions I wanted to ask him. He always seems to dance around every question I ask. There is something about him that makes me feel protected. I can't understand the connection but I know deep inside there is one. Why have I dreamed about someone I have never met? I needed to talk more to him. There was something in me that needed to know who he really is, as if it would help me understand myself better. What were these feelings I had for him and why were they so intense? I had, basically known him for 13 years, every night I spent with him. They were dreams, I knew it wasn't real but here he is flesh and blood the image of the man who had haunted me. I wanted to hug him, feel his touch, I longed for it like nothing I had ever desired before.

To make sure he is real but he's not the William in my dreams, not the same William who loved and adored me, who caressed me and longed for me. I needed to not think of these things it would only get me in deeper and I'd end up making a fool out of myself. I had spent the better part of my adolescence learning he didn't really exist, why go backwards now?

I decided to spend the rest of the afternoon thinking back on everything that had happened.

My parents, the move to Maine, Justin and how he would be livid if he knew where I was and somehow blame himself for me getting hurt. We haven't known each other very long but in the few weeks we have spent together I can tell that he is the kind of person you can always count on. I feel torn, even though I should want to leave and get home, I feet a sadness that eventually I would leave and go home and probably very soon.

I have a basic need or desire even to be near William and that is dangerous. Had the trauma from my injury caused some sort of hallucinations?

How does someone who has lived every moment of her life as a very independent person have the need to be in someone else's presence? It's the feeling I have when he is in the room, like it's hard to breath, I can't think about anything else. I must have fallen asleep after lunch my pain medicine did its job, I woke up to the sun going down.

Bailey was getting a little restless so I decided to ring for Darlei.

I still couldn't wrap my head around the whole pulling the tassel thing it felt strange. She must be very close by waiting for me to ring it because she was literally in the room in less than a minute. It was a little creepy having someone who is at your beckon call.

"Darlei, I think Bailey needs to go outside. Could you get someone to take him out?"

She nodded and motioned for me to wait. Somehow I knew he would be the one to come get Bailey, at least I hoped it would be him.

"How are you feeling? Did you have a good rest?" He asked as he walked into the room.

"Yes thank you, isn't there anyone else who could take him out? I feel terrible that I have dragged you away from what you were doing."

"I know how much he means to you, I don't mind taking care of it really. I'll be back when he's done."

"I would like to speak with you about something when you return."

His expression was more than concerned. I knew I didn't want to but I needed to go home. I was getting too involved in this mystery and I needed to separate myself from it to be able to see it clearly. He was gone for what seemed like only minutes probably eager to hear what I wanted to discuss with him.

"That was fast."

"Yes, well Bailey wanted to run a little so we left him out on the grounds to get a little exercise. There was something you wished to speak to me about?"

"Yes, William you have been very kind and generous to me. I don't want you to think I am ungrateful but we need to discuss me going home."

"Is something wrong? Did Darlei do something because I can have someone else-"

"No, no nothing like that."

"Is it me? Have I offended you or said something?"

"No, I just can't stay here forever and I have things I need to take care of and people that will be very worried about me. You have been very accommodating to my every need but at some point I will have to leave."

"By people do you mean Mr. Randall?"

There was a definite distaste for Justin in his tone.

"Yes, him among others. Please don't take this as me not enjoying your company I have very much enjoyed meeting you."

"But you would rather go home and have someone else take care of you or be alone instead of here? You are not my prisoner I would never make you stay where you do not wish to be. When were you thinking you would like to leave?"

His voice sounded hurt but his face showed it more. I felt horrible that I had insulted him and hurt him.

"Well, if it's alright with you I was thinking tomorrow."

"If that is what you want I will make arrangements for transportation for you."

"William it was not my intention to insult your hospitality. I have very much enjoyed being here out side of the whole injury thing and you have been a perfect host the whole time I have been here. Truth is I am a little afraid I could get used to this. Will you at least have dinner with me this evening so we can visit some more?"

"I will see what I can do. I have some things I need to attend to."

I felt a sharp pain in my chest but it was nothing from my injuries it was the fact that I had hurt him and made him feel like I was ungrateful.

"If that is all Miss Dossin I will have them bring Bailey back in for you."

I simply nodded my head in reply. I felt tears building but I kept telling myself to hold it until he was gone. That was terrible I couldn't have handled that any worse. I kept telling myself that I barley knew him. Why should I feel bad but there was such a feeling of loneliness in his voice that I recognized all to well, I couldn't let this feeling get the best of me. I needed to be thinking clearly now and that was impossible with him around, there was something about his very presence that made it impossible for me to have a clear thought.

I can't explain it; I felt such a strong desire to be with him, something much more than physical attraction.

The door opened and Bailey was let into the room. Where was he, where was William? He always brought Bailey, but not this time he was simply let into the room by an anonymous person

I couldn't see. As Bailey jumped up on the bed I felt the warm tears spill over my cheeks. Why did it hurt me so badly? I simply stated the obvious, did he think I was going to stay forever? Contrary to popular belief I do have a life, empty as it may appear it is there. Still the thought of not having him close made me not be able to breathe.

This is stupid, I'm just being emotional, probably due to the medication I've been taking.

Justin would be home in a week or two and life would go back to normal without the mystery of this house. It's just a house, no more, case closed. Okay, so why do I still feel like there is a lot more? I needed to snap out of this I felt like I was standing out side my body watching everything take place, like I had no control. I started to pull the tassel and call for him to come and finish the conversation so I could make him understand. I couldn't do it, I knew I would only succeed in hurting him more and I was not in the right frame of mind for that.

I decided to relax, meditate on being calm, I would get my thoughts together and discuss it with him later after we both had time to think. There was some commotion outside my room that woke me up. Bailey was off the bed and standing near the door a low growl grew in his chest. It was the man's voice I had heard earlier speaking with William. The voices were muffled but I could tell they were in disagreement. I sat up and decided to try and get closer so I could make out what was being said. I put my feet over the edge of the bed this time successful, although the pain shot up and down my side but my head was better. I slowly stood and walked toward the door they were speaking in that other language again. I strained to hear what was being said but I couldn't. I pulled Bailey back and motioned for him to sit and stay, unbelievably he did.

I did make out my name several times, Miss Dossin, why did they have to be speaking in another language besides English? They stopped and I heard footsteps outside my door I scrambled to get to the bed but they stopped just outside and waited for a moment. I was anticipating the door opening but they simply turned and disappeared down the hall. My heart was pounding out of my chest. Why didn't he come in? There was a gentle rap on the door it was Darlei she had clothes in her hands and a white envelope. She placed them on the bed and motioned for me to open the envelope.

Zoe,

Something has come up that needs my immediate attention. I am sorry I will not be able to say goodbye in person but I have left instructions with Darlei and my staff to make you as comfortable as possible. They will make sure you arrive home tomorrow safely and have everything you need. If there is anything you desire, you need only ask, my staff is at your disposal. I regret that we could not spend more time together. I hope you will accept this gift from me I would like you to have it.

William

I shook the envelope and a small silver heart shaped locket fell out into my hand. It was detailed and very beautiful. Inside was a small grain of what looked like salt. My mouth fell open and I just stood there holding onto the bed. Tears filling my eyes why did he leave? I had a feeling it had nothing to do with his work but everything to do with my request to leave.

Darlei placed her hand on my back and as if to comfort me. As I looked at her, I saw a look of concern on her face.

"I would like to go home tonight if possible. Do you understand me? Home tonight."

She nodded and motioned for me to wait. While she was gone I decided to get dressed I unfolded a beautiful sundress and sandals. Again everything fit me perfectly. I walked over to the dressing table and sat down I placed the locket around my neck and pulled my hair back. I used some of the lotion that was on the table it felt good on my arms and legs.

I could hardly face myself, I felt guilty and sad. Sad because he was gone and I could feel it. I don't know how but the room felt very empty now. There was a familiar rap and the door opened again there was Darlei and a younger gentleman. She motioned him over to where I was.

"Miss Dossin, I am Andoe, I speak a little English. Darlei thinks you wish to go home tonight instead of tomorrow is that right?"

He looked to be around twenty his dark skin and complexion was perfect.

"Yes, she is correct. I do wish to leave tonight if possible."

"Master William had said you would be leaving tomorrow is everything okay?"

"Yes, I would just like to be home tonight there is nothing wrong."

But there was something wrong, I couldn't bear being there and knowing he wasn't.

"Master William said anything you wanted so I will make it happen for you. It will take me about an hour if that's okay? I will make sure you are safe and home tonight."

"Thank you Andoe that will be fine."

Every time he says William's name I feel a sharp pain in my chest. I will be glad to go home and get back to normal. I sat on the small chase lounge at the far end of the room and looked out the enormous window onto the water and the grounds. It was breathtaking in the moonlight, even though there was no full moon its light settled onto everything.

I began to wonder where he was, what he was thinking, was he thinking of me? Why did he get so hurt when I wanted to leave? Does he feel like I do when we aren't together? I hadn't thought about Justin this whole time, what did that mean? I know I like him and yes it's only been a few weeks but still I felt a huge wave of guilt over the feelings I was having for William. I didn't even know him but somehow I did, deep down I knew him like I know myself. It didn't matter because I had probably hurt him so bad he would never want to see me again. So why do I feel so guilty about Justin? This is crazy as much as I like Justin, I can't get William out of my mind. I have to get out of here I'll be more focused at home and able to sort this all out. I just want to wake up and have everything be back to normal. There was a knock this time and then Andoe entered

"Miss Dossin I have made the necessary arrangements for you when you are ready the car is waiting."

"Great, I'm ready now if that's okay."

"Very well follow me, I'll escort you to the car."

I took one last look at the room and felt I would miss it somehow. I turned and followed him out the large doorway. Suddenly I remembered the stairs and the long way down them, we slowly walked as I deliberated how I would manage them without William. We finally came to the end of the hall where it opened up into the staircase where there was a very large gentleman waiting. Andoe turned and smiled as he said,

"Miss Dossin this is Ryson, he will help you down the stairs."

He must have seen the expression on my face as the huge gentleman stepped from behind the doorway.

"Master William made it clear you were not to walk down them alone. He is very sturdy he will not drop you, I assure you."

It must have been the mention of his name that made me feel better about being carried down the steps because I didn't feel comfortable with it at first.

"Well then I don't want to get you in trouble."

He was much larger than William but lifting me was not as easy for him as it was with William. He didn't smell as good either. We made it to the bottom and Darlei was there with a sweater in her arms for me, she gave me a hug and motioned for me to put it on. Andoe opened the large front doors and walked Bailey and I to the large black car waiting. To my surprise Darlei and Andoe both got into the car with us and closed the door. He handed me a small card with writing on it. It was a phone number and the writing simply said in case of an emergency.

"Master William wanted you to have this, you can call it at any time should you need anything."

I turned and looked back at the house for a moment, I could swear I saw a dark figure looking out the large upstairs window but then it was gone.

Chapter Ten:
White Lies

***

It was a short ride to my house as we pulled up I noticed a red car in the drive. It was Jenna's my mind began to race trying to think of an excuse as to why I looked like I had fallen from a two story building and was being dropped off by a limousine to my house. All the lights were on in the house my mind was coming up blank.

"Miss Dossin, Master William has made all the arrangements please do not worry."

Jenna was on the porch as we started getting out.

"Zoe, oh my god honey are you alright? I couldn't believe it when I got the call from the hospital. I am so sorry I wasn't there with you but we didn't know, I guess no one did. Well at least your home now. Your Uncle called and made all the arrangements, is that the nurse he arranged to have stay with you? I fixed up the guest room for her the way he instructed. I offered to stay but I work and he was worried you wouldn't have enough help during the day."

Wow, he is good. I have to give him credit he covered the bases. I can't wait to hear what he told her about how it happened.

"Oh Jenna you didn't tell Justin did you?"

"No he hasn't called in yet today why?"

"Do me a favor, don't. I don't want him to worry for nothing I am fine."

"Let's just get you in and out of the night air."

"This is Darlei my nurse and Andoe the concierge from the hospital."

"Nice to meet you both, now let's get you inside."

Bailey ran past us and into the house.

"Your uncle had me open the house so they could bring in the groceries. I wanted to help put them away but they wouldn't let me. Well, you look better than I thought you would, what a terrible thing to have happen. I told you, you should have let me drive you to the airport those shuttle drivers are terrible drivers."

" Does it hurt much? He said you cracked some ribs."

"I'm fine now that I'm home, Andoe thank you so much and please tell William I said thank you."

"Please call if you need anything I will be back in a few days to see how you are doing if there is nothing else you need?"

"No everything is perfect."

"Jenna could you please show Darlei to her room and let her put her things away, she doesn't speak English but she understands a little."

"Sure this way Darlei let me help you with those bags."

My head was still reeling from the story that he had concocted. It made me feel hopeful that he wasn't to mad at me if he did all this. Still it was very presumptuous of him to take it upon himself to do all this but I did appreciate the story I would have never come up with one that believable. I hated lying to Jenna but it was for her own good, she would just stick her nose into the whole mess and make it worse. I wasn't crazy about the idea of Darlei staying there but it would be very helpful with letting Bailey out. It felt good to be home, I was ready to change into something comfortable and just decompress. I could hear Jenna coming back down and decided to catch her and see if I could talk her into helping me get changed. It was fun getting up the stairs but we managed, I grabbed a pair of sweats and a tee shirt and Jenna helped me get them on.

"Hey Zoe, where did you get that? It's different than the other one? I have never seen you wear it before."

She was looking at my locket.

"Oh just something my Uncle gave me."

I couldn't help but chuckle I was starting to get good at this. The phone rang and I hurried to answer it, I had a feeling it was Justin and I didn't want Jenna blowing things out of proportion.

"Hello, Hello"

There was a long moment of silence.

"Hello Zoe, I see you made it home alright is everything to your liking?"

"Yes Uncle William, everything is fine as a matter of fact I was wondering if I would get to speak with you again. I thought you might be angry that I left so soon."

"Is there someone with you?"

"Yes, Jenna is here and Darlei they are taking great care of me, thanks to all your planning which you really shouldn't have done."

"The story I came up with was acceptable then? I wanted to be there when you left but I couldn't as I said something very important came up. I will be gone for a few days but I will be home after that. Did Andoe give you the number?"

"Yes he did, and thank you for the lovely locket it's beautiful."

"I hoped you would like it. Well I'll let you get back to your company if you need anything don't hesitate to call that number. Goodnight Zoe."

"Goodnight Uncle William."

I could swear I heard him laugh before he hung up. I wished I could have talked to him longer.

"How's your Uncle Zoe?"

"He's fine just checking up on me."

"He sounds young is he married?"

"No he's not married."
"You should introduce us then he sounds hot."
"Oh, no he's not your type Jenna besides he's too old for you."
"Not my type, huh, what I'm not good enough for your family Zoe? Just kidding."
"Yeah sorry Jenna I'm a little off my game today. We should go check on Darlei and make sure she's okay."
"Yeah I have to hit the road soon I have to show two properties tomorrow but I'll call and check on you I promise."

Darlei was down stairs getting familiar with the kitchen, she had set out some milk and Oreo's and placed my pain meds on the counter. I don't want to know how she figured out I like Oreo's and milk.

"Thank you Darlei."
"You take your meds Master William says."
"Yes, I know he says, thank you."

Jenna just laughed and shook her head

"You're in good hands I can see Zoe, get some sleep I'll talk to you tomorrow. Come on Bailey I'll let you out for the ladies before I go."
"Thanks Jenna and remember mums the word to Justin, I mean it!"
"Yeah you want me to get killed when he gets home don't you."
"I mean it Jenna no sharing with Justin."

I took my milk and cookies into the living room and read a little until I got sleepy, Darlei joined me and sat quietly knitting. The next few days dragged by I dreamed both nights of the dark figure and although something scared me about him I was so utterly drawn to him I couldn't stop thinking about him.

I was awakened by the smell of bacon and coffee which was a little strange Darlei had been on her game about what I liked and had pretty much been making me a light breakfast. As I sat up in bed I realized my side was not bothering me like it had been and my head felt very clear. I was getting used to the dreams so I was able to go right back into deep sleep after I had them. I hurried and washed up careful not to get my stitches wet and got dressed. I heard music coming from the kitchen a man's voice singing along.

"Justin?"

It was my Bob Marley CD, I walked as fast as I could turning the corner I saw Darlei sitting with a disapproving look on her face and Justin cooking.

"Justin your back!"

He turned and smiled.

"Well sleeping beauty is finally awake! Hey kiddo how are you feeling? You should have called down we would have helped you."

He reached out to hug me and I stopped him pointing to my ribs. Mostly it was because I felt a little uncomfortable hugging him in front of Darlei. I gave him a nice pat on his back and a partial hug.

"Yah that's right I let you out of my sight for a few days and you go and practically put yourself in a body cast."

"Really it's not that bad, what are you doing home? you aren't supposed to be home for another two weeks Jenna said. She told you didn't she?"

"Yes and you better not blame her. I could tell something was up you didn't answer your cell phone."

"Oh yah I have to get a new one."

"Anyway, after she told me not to come home a hundred times because you would never speak to her again, I got off at the next port and hitched a ride home.

You only have me for a few days and then I have to go back, but I had to see you and make sure you're okay, really okay."

"Well here I am don't I look fine?"

"Except for the goose egg on your forehead outstanding!"

"Why are you making breakfast?"

"Because I thought a good hot breakfast would do you some good besides I was bored waiting for you to get up and I don't think your nurse likes me."

He lowered his voice to a whisper.

"Why do you say that?"

"She keeps giving me that look."

"What look would that be?"

"Like I just asked to see her naked."

"Oh that one."

"Breakfast is ready want to eat it on the deck?"

"Sure that would be fine can I help?"

"No, just go on out there I'll bring it out."

It was a cool morning but the sun made it feel warmer. The tones in the sky where breathtaking, it would have been a great morning to get some shots but I don't think I'll be going out on my own for a few more days.

"Here we go,"

He placed a tray of food on the table in front of me.

"Justin you really didn't have to but thanks it's lovely."

"Well like I said, bored and you need to eat to build up your strength."

He sat beside me and handed me my plate and juice. It was nice to see him but I had an uneasiness settling in me that was never there before with Justin. I felt like I was doing something wrong by being with him.

"What's up Zoe you look a little..."

"A little what?"

"Distracted or worried, different."

"Must be the meds Justin, I feel a little out of sorts not myself, but don't worry I'll be fine."

"What's up with that nurse she's a little creepy."

"Who Darlei? She's harmless, and she's been very good to me."

"I don't know, there is something about her that makes me think she doesn't like me."

"Not like you, Justin the Charmer? Never, everyone loves you Justin!"

He smiled and we both kind of giggled but he was right she did seem different when he was around. It made me wonder if William had given instruction to her to watch Justin.

"So you are here for a few days and then back out?"

"Yah well I might have to leave out tomorrow night depending on when my ride back is heading out and I know that you are in good hands with the drill sergeant nurse here I wont feel so bad about leaving I doubt even the boogy man could get past her. I had to practically give her a blood sample to get in and she would not let me go upstairs to check on you."

"Wow, I didn't realize she was like that sorry, but she is very nice to me."

I tried to play it off but I felt even more off after hearing him talk about Darlei's reaction to his presence.

"She will be leaving soon I am sure."

"Yes, Jenna said your Uncle William had arranged for her to be here. Is that your Aunt Kate's Husband? "

My mind was searching for a way to not have to lie to him, but not tell on myself or William.

"No he's just a family friend that helped me out."

"What happened with the accident I mean who's fault was it? Jenna just said your shuttle car was involved in an accident?"

"Well you know something Justin I don't really remember the accident, it's all a little blurry it must be the head injury, But I am feeling much better now."

I am glad that Darlei came to the door to bring me my medicine that I have already decided not to take. She was not happy about me not taking them and I swear I heard her say something about Master William not liking that but I can't be sure. The rest of the afternoon was peaceful I took a ride into town with Justin and we picked up the T.V. I had picked out prior to being in my "accident". He also managed to hook up the cable to it and although it went against everything in me to put the T.V. in the living room it was the most reasonable spot. We made popcorn and sat and watched T.V. until after midnight. I was beginning to worry that he was going to want to stay the night and how would I explain that. I had a feeling like I was being watched and as much as I would have hated that before I am strangely glad it made me feel closer to William, my not so creepy stalker.

"Well its getting late you really should be going to bed Zoe and I think Darlei is still up I hear her pacing upstairs. I need to go so you can get some rest."

"Are you sure? I will see you tomorrow before you go right?"

"Yeah, I'll swing by for a while before I have to leave."

He leaned in and kissed my forehead leaving his lips resting there for a moment his hands on either side of my face.

"You know I would stay but I don't want to get you in trouble with your Uncle and I think that nurse is a spy for him."

I had to laugh at the irony of his statement.

"Yes, I think so too. Thank you Justin."

"I'll see you tomorrow, you know I can be here in like 3 minutes if you need me."

"I know, I will call if I need you I promise."

"And Zoe, if you ever get hurt again and don't call me I will be very upset."

"I'm sorry Justin, I will, I promise."

"I will pick up your new phone on my way in tomorrow if you like?"

"That would be great."

He patted Bailey on the head and pulled the door together tightly making sure it locked behind him. I turned off the lights and headed up stairs. I am a little worn out from the activities today and am ready to pass out. I thought it would be easy to fall asleep but instead my mind played over the predicament I was in. On one hand I was so glad to see Justin and be with him but I felt like I am being unfaithful and that was just absurd. I didn't even know William and I am a grown woman I don't need his permission to have a friend, male or female. I do care about what he thought and I am glad that Justin would be gone again for a few weeks it would give me time to sort out how I am feeling and why. I can't wait to see William again, I have so many questions to ask him and I have decided that I would try to ask them in a way that didn't make him closed off or on guard. My mind finally shut down and I felt sleep come over me. I felt myself standing on the edge of a catwalk that over looked the water as I looked behind me I could see that the catwalk was attached to a lighthouse. The water was raging and the wind was blowing so that it was all I could do to hold on to the railing. I was looking for something, someone but who? I was confused now, I normally always looked for the dark figure but I was not sure this time I couldn't find a link to who I was supposed to search for or why my heart felt heavy and hopeless.

I felt myself getting overwhelmed with loss worse than when I lost my dad.

I couldn't breathe as I placed my foot over the rail, what was I doing? Then the other now my hands where gripping for dear life part of me wanting to let go, give in, the other holding on trying to reason. I felt my grip giving and the wind pelting my face with rain.
I awoke to the feeling of falling. It was quiet, peaceful then I opened my eyes I was in my parents' room laying on there bed. I jumped to my feet as quickly as my body would allow and left closing the door behind me. It was still dark out, how did I get into my parents room? Why was I in my parents' room?
I went into my bathroom and splashed my face with water as I looked into the mirror I noticed my forehead the wound was almost entirely healed you could only barely see the faint line of a scar. It should have still been red at the very least pink. As I rubbed my hand over it I couldn't believe my eyes. I quickly checked my side I carefully removed the bandage and again the scar was almost non recognizable there was very little soreness and no pink or redness to be found. How is this medically possible? Did I dream the accident or have I been asleep for 6 months because that's how long it would take any wound like I had to be that healed. I couldn't explain it. I will have to have a talk with William and get to the bottom of this. I felt tired and needed to lie down. I went back to my bed and lay there thinking of my life and how crazy it had become, did I try to fight it or roll with it? I wanted to speak with William, it would help to talk with him and find out why I felt this connection with him and put a rest to the mystery once and for all. I mean really every woman loves a mysterious man, maybe that's all this was, the mystery. I was done thinking for the night I needed to sleep. I woke up early, surprised, that I didn't feel tired after all the thinking and dreaming going on last night. I decided to shower and get dressed before Darlei could stop me, after all my wounds where all but healed.

As I finished getting dressed I heard Bailey barking. I knew exactly who it was and ran down to greet him as I turned the corner I saw Jenna standing there.

"What's up Jenna? Where is Justin?"

"Sorry Zoe, he had to leave out early this morning and didn't want to wake you. He sent me here to tell you how sorry he was, he didn't get to say goodbye. He promises to call just as soon as they reach another port."

My face must have shown my disappointment, I had wanted to tell him goodbye and wish him a safe trip.

"Are you okay? They shouldn't be gone more than a few more weeks."

"Yes I will be fine, just wish I could have told him thank you and goodbye."

"Thank you?"

"For helping me yesterday and coming all the way back just to see me. That was really sweet. He even cooked breakfast yesterday for me."

"Really? Wow, he must really like you if he cooked for you. They always make him cook when they're away and he rarely cooks here because he gets tired of it. In their defense he is the best cook."

"Now I feel really bad. And he is a really good cook."

"Well I wish I could stay but I have to leave for work do you need me to pick anything up for you I could drop it by after work?"

"Not that I can think of but if you feel like it call me when you leave work. If I think of anything I'll call and let you know."

"Sure take care and call if you need anything. He'll be back soon Zoe."

"I know, I'll live."

Chapter Eleven:
Answers and Enemies

***

Darlei was in the kitchen I could here her humming. I sat eating my cereal and reading an advertisement paper feeling sorry for myself that I was stuck with a person who barely spoke English and no one to hang out with. I had to come up with a game plan for the day I decided to try and paint a little, it would be relaxing and keep my mind off things. I hadn't painted since before my mom died but I settled in and started with what I thought was going to be an abstract piece but slowly became an outline of moonlight over water and the outline of the dark figure. It was coming so easy. Before I knew it Darlei knocked on the door to tell me it was time I ate something, as I looked at the clock it was 3:45 I had been in there all day, it felt like only a half hour. I hated to stop I asked her to bring me in a sandwich if she didn't mind and she was more than happy to oblige me. I assumed because she was worried if William found out she let me starve he would be upset. I took a few bites and went right back to it. As I painted I started to see it almost completely clear like I was looking right at it. My silence was broken by the sound of a familiar voice, I walked to the door to listen. As I placed my ear to it there was a knock that sent me backwards about 3 feet.

"Yes come in,"

As the door opened I saw his face I couldn't believe it.

"William!"

I attempted to run my fingers through my tangled hair, I suddenly remembered I had put it up in a clip and I was wearing old jean shorts and an old oxford shirt of my dads great!

"You look surprised? I can leave if you like?"

"No!" My voice sounding a little more desperate than I could contain.

"Darlei says you've been in here all day, are you alright?"

"Just working."

I stood in front of the easel covering it as best I could without looking conspicuous.

"May I see?"

"No please, it's not finished and I'm not that good it's just a hobby."

He peered over my shoulder.

"Really it's nothing."

I turned to cover it with my drop cloth.

" I promise when it's finished I will let you see it."

I made a mental note to paint some fruit or something later to show him.

"Very well I don't want to press. Have you eaten anything yet?"

"Well a sandwich earlier why?"

Sliding the plate with the half eaten sandwich behind the monitor on my desk.

"That's what I thought."

His eyes followed the movement of the plate.

"Well if you are up to it I thought we could go back to my house and have some dinner. There are some things I would like to talk about with you."

"Sure of course, can I have a few minutes to get ready? I just need to get freshened up."

"There are a few things I need to attend to at the house I will send the car back in about 20 minutes for you but please take your time I'll tell them dinner will be at about 7:00 if that's okay?"

"Sure, that will be fine."

Only problem was I had no Idea what time it was right now. I hurried and ran upstairs to find something to wear. What do you wear to dinner at a house like that? I knew the person to ask only I don't think Jenna would be real keen on giving me fashion advise so I could go eat with William Madison.

As I looked through my closet I began to get frustrated I decided to go shower and think about my options. I carefully inspected my injuries and was again amazed at how healed they where. I finished my hair and make up and couldn't procrastinate it any longer I had to find something appropriate. That's when I saw it hanging on the back of my bedroom door. The red dress Jenna made me buy that I had forgotten to take back. I couldn't, what would he think? It was over the top but I really didn't have anything that dressy in my closet so I decided to try it on one more time. As I stood in front of my full-length mirror all I could hear was Jenna's voice saying, there is no decision Zoe wear it. It wasn't as bad as I remembered I think the make up job I was wearing the night Jenna and I bought it made it look worse. I heard the car pull up and I was out of time it was this or nothing. I grabbed a sweater out of my closet to cover up with in case I got chilled or chickened out. I fixed my locket around my neck and realized I didn't have my locket my dad had given me. I hadn't noticed but I haven't seen it since the accident. I must have lost it when I fell or maybe William would know, maybe they had taken it off when the were patching me up. Darlei was at the door letting me know the car had arrived. I scrambled down stairs letting Bailey out to go to the bathroom; I had decided to leave him here. I was surprised to see William holding the door of a jet-black Mazerati open as Bailey walked straight toward him and sat in front of him. I couldn't believe he didn't even jump on him. William patted him and Bailey trotted off to finish his business. He looked amazing he was wearing a dark, tight fitting sweater and black slacks. Easy Zoe girl, I repeated in my head just stay composed on the outside.

"I thought you where sending a car back for me?" "I did you don't like this car? I can call for the other car if you would prefer it." "No I didn't realize you would be coming for me."

"Well I only came for you, Darlei is staying here to attend to Bailey."

As he walked towards me I felt my body get warm, like I was standing to close to the fireplace. He whistled and Bailey went straight inside. He nodded at Darlei who now stood in the doorway and she closed the door. I was wishing I had put on my sweater now instead of holding it I felt a little venerable with just the dress.

"Shall we?"

He held out his arm to me and I drew in a deep breath he smelled as good as ever. As I got closer to his car I realized all the windows were tinted something I had become accustom to living in Arizona so long but here it was hardly necessary the sun was never that hot. The car was a beautiful black spotless clean; the silver rims gleamed with the last of the day's sun. He held the door for me and slowly walked around the front of the car staring at me the whole time, but once in the car he kept his eyes on the road. It was silent for a few minutes but I suddenly realized we had turned the wrong way to go to his house.

"William shouldn't you have turned right out of my driveway?"

"I hope you don't mind I wanted to show you something I think you will enjoy its especially beautiful this time of year."

"Of course that's fine, what is it?"

"A surprise, you will just have to wait and see."

"Thank you for, well for everything. I don't know what I would have done with out you helping me like you have."

"The night has just started you should wait until it's over, how do you know you will like it?"

"You know what I mean, Darlei staying with me the whole accident story that you cooked up, which was genius by the way Uncle William."

"Well I hated to lie to your friends I don't like to lie but I can in a pinch."

"You got back quickly, I was surprised to see you so soon. I thought you would never talk to me again after our last conversation."

The car was quiet for a few seconds and I was frantically trying to think of something to say.

"Here we are."

He sounded almost relieved. It was a long driveway lined with trees on either side but you could see the dim sunset and water at the end as the tree line opened up, I saw it. It was a tall white lighthouse; I began to breathe a little fast as I realized it was the very lighthouse in my dream. The sunset was spectacular over the water the car came to a stop and he got out and came around to my side of the car to open the door. I tried to compose myself before he arrived on my side. He reached for my hand and helped me out. I quickly put my sweater on thinking it would help me feel more secure. He led me to the waters edge and we stood for a while just looking out over the water neither of us speaking. It was so calming and peaceful any anxiety I was feeling was all but gone.

"I've been coming here since I was a boy. I used to come with my mother. She knew the light keeper and his family; he would let us go up in the lighthouse. It's not open to the public anymore and there is no light keeper it's all automated now."

"Well it's beautiful I can see why you would come here. There is something about water that amazes me. It can be so calm and peaceful one minute and the next so violent and deadly."

"That is why you must always respect it. Never take the calm peaceful side for granted."

I turned to look at him and was unable to turn away. His features where amazing his broad shoulders and olive skin, were only matched by his dark hair and eyes.

Yes it was definitely his eyes that did me in, so deep and endless with his equally dark lashes that lined them perfectly. I had to make myself turn away.

"Thank you for showing me this William I love it! I would like to come back and shoot it sometime. We could bring a lunch."

"I thought you might like it. We should probably go get you some dinner. I did promise dinner, didn't I?"

"That you did and I have to say I am starving."

As we pulled into the drive I couldn't help but gasp at the enormity of his home. It was even bigger than I had imagined, I had only seen it from the side. We pulled around to the back and walked up the most beautiful stone steps.

"I would love to shoot your house sometime it's amazing."

"I think I could arrange that for you, I'll speak with the owner he and I are like

this." Making a gesture of his fingers crossed.

He took my arm and led me into the house this time getting a little closer to me than before. I didn't mind, it made it easier to breathe him in. We entered the dinning area and there was a long table in the middle big enough to seat about thirty people.

"Don't worry Zoe we aren't eating in here."

He smiled, as I am sure he saw the look of relief on my face as we reached the doorway at the other end, we where greeted by Andoe.

"May I take your wrap Miss Dossin?"

"Thank you Andoe."

As he helped me out of it I immediately realized what I had on and

wished I had said no. The look on William's face, I honestly thought I saw him blush.

"That will be all Andoe, Thank you."

Looking away for a moment he quickly regained his composure.

"That is quite a dress Zoe, you look beautiful. You will have to excuse me I am not used to being around such a beautiful woman I should have told you how lovely you looked when I picked you up. I warned you about my manners."

"Thank you William "

I could feel myself blushing everywhere.

"I didn't actually pick this out myself, a friend did and she is a little more daring than I am. I am afraid I got a little overzealous when I found out about coming to such a beautiful home for dinner."

He led me into the adjacent room where there was a smaller more intimate table

set for two. The lighting was dim and the table filled with candles and white roses. The candlelight danced off the silver on the table. He pulled out my chair for me to sit down.

"Would you care for some wine Zoe?"

"Yes, that would be great."

He poured me a glass of red wine and sat down.

"Aren't you going to have any William?"

"No, I don't drink."

"Anything?"

"No, I just don't drink alcohol. I find alcohol tends to intensify ones personality and mine does not need to be intensified. Please enjoy your wine, I'm no alcoholic, I choose to not drink it."

We had light conversation over dinner mostly about me again. Dinner was delicious, by the fourth course I was stuffed.

"Would you like to go out onto the terrace for coffee?"

"Yes I would love to."

He guided me through huge French doors out onto a stone balcony that over looked the water.

At one end was a fireplace with a roaring fire, an over stuffed sofa, and two chairs. The outdoor room was lined with sheer draperies that hung at all four corners of the balcony making it very cozy and again candles everywhere. It was dark out now and the moonlight was beautiful on the water. He escorted me to the couch that faced the fireplace and sat in a nearby chair that faced it.

"How lovely, I have trouble believing you aren't around any beautiful women you certainly have the house for entertaining. It's beautiful."

"I come out here alone sometimes, but never with anyone. It's a shame really this house was designed for entertaining. My mother, she really loved to entertain. She was always the life in this house."

His face seemed so sad.

"You are more like your father then?"

"Never, I bare no resemblance to his personality."

He seemed upset at first by my question but regained composure quickly.

"I was a terrible disappointment to him I'm afraid."

I wanted to hear more but his mood seemed to change when he spoke of them and I didn't want him to be upset so I decided to change the subject.

"You said you needed to speak with me about something?"

"And you said you wanted to speak with me?"

"William it's your house, you go first."

"What does that matter? Is that a rule I am unaware of?"

"Yes it is, now you have to go first."

"Well since it's my house, I make the rules and I was always taught that ladies should go first."

I could see we where getting nowhere he was so stubborn.

"Fine, I concede this time. Why don't you ever go out into town? And why don't you have beautiful women around?

You are very handsome, and what did you do to me to make me heal so fast?"

It came out like a blur, like if I didn't blurt it out he wouldn't have let me ask it. He sat for a moment and looked away. Then he stood up and walked over to the balcony.

"People in town don't like me. I try not to push myself on them, as for beautiful women see answer one."

"William people in town are afraid of the legend of this house not you, they fear what they don't understand."

"Yes and with good reason Zoe you don't know me, you trust to easily. How do you know I am not as they say, a monster is it? You don't, you would do well to listen to them and stay clear of me. It's selfish for me to be around you it's not good for you."

"Not good for me? What are you talking about are you a drug lord or something? Is that it? Are you involved with some kind of illegal trading? What? What is so dangerous about you William? Please tell me because I want to know what is so terrible? I'm not the one afraid of you, you are!"

"Your right, I am afraid of me and how I feel about you. Because you make me forget who I am and that is dangerous for you."

"Who are you William? What are you, you are in my thoughts, I haven't been able to get you out of my head since - I first got here and I hadn't even seen you yet."

I wanted to tell him I had been thinking of him since I was fifteen but I would definitely scare him then.

"I don't know you yet but I feel as though I have always known you like I know myself. How is that possible?"

We where both standing now he was still looking out over the water his hands clutching the cement railing and I looking at him.

"William what is going on here? What are you afraid to tell me?"

"I am afraid to tell you, I don't want to scare you away and I don't want to risk you getting hurt. I don't think I could be away from you; I tried to go away just for a few days to clear my head. The further I got the more I felt as though I would not be able to breath. I am not who you think I am, not in the sense that you think."

He turned to look at me his eyes intense and wild, it was hard not to look away but I couldn't as badly as I wanted to with everything in me I couldn't look away. I felt another presence in the room he quickly looked over me. There was a gentleman standing in the doorway of the house staring at us. Andoe entered the room and walked over to William and whispered to him. I never took my eyes off the man in the doorway. There was something about him that made me uneasy.

"Zoe something has come up, I am sorry but I need to attend to it I will have Andoe see you home."

Williams eyes where still intense but not the same.

"No that's not alright William, who is he? And why does he not want you to talk to me?"

"How do you know he doesn't want me to talk to you? Has someone said something to you?"

I honestly didn't know how I knew it but I could feel the hatred the man felt for me. The anger over William's affection towards me bombarded me.

"I just know, I can feel it. Please William you can't just send me away not like this."

He hesitated for a moment looking back at the man and then turning back to me.

"Wait here, I'll be right back."

He whispered to Andoe and they both headed towards the man in the doorway. They all stepped in the house. My head was reeling everything in me said run, but I couldn't I had to stay I because like him I couldn't breath when we are apart. Something about him made me lose myself and I was not the same as before I met him. Something in me had changed. I stood at the balcony and stared over the edge looking at the water, as chill ran through me, what was I doing? A few weeks ago I wasn't sure I could handle grocery shopping and look what I am trying to handle now. This was crazy I felt a hand on my waist I closed my eyes knowing I had missed my window to flee but it was my own doing. I chose to miss it there was no other choice to make I had to let this unfold.

"Is everything okay?"

I turned slowly he didn't move he was staring out over the black water. His eyes searched for what to say.

"I don't want it to be this way with you and I."

"What do you mean this way?"

His face turned down looking into my eyes and sadness replaced the intense look. He didn't have to answer I knew what he meant.

"I don't want this for you, you deserve to be happy and with that young Randle boy. Not with me, only I can't stand thinking of you with him or anyone for that matter."

"I really don't think you have a say in that choice William. What if I don't want that?"

His dark eyes were wild again his voice changing from sadness to anger.

"Then you aren't as smart as I thought you were."

Pushing away from me he turned and looked at the door where the man had been. I reached for his arm his body tensed as I touched him.

"Who is he William, why does he scare you?"

Something deep inside told me he was in danger from the man in the doorway, I wanted to keep pressing and have him give me my answers but again something inside told me to let it go for now. I was learning to listen to that voice. His body relaxed a little. His eyes still looking out towards the water.

"I'm glad you are feeling better,"

"I have a great doctor."

I would let him change the subject for now because I knew it was what was for the best for both of us. I walked over to the couch and sat down he followed quietly and sat beside me, taking the throw off the back of the coach and gently covering me. I wanted to scoot closer but I didn't want to push it after everything that had happened. He reached out and slid me closer to him still looking straight ahead as if looking at me would give him away. I slipped off my shoes as we lay back looking at the fire my head on his chest, hearing him breathe, he gently tucked the cover around us and it was silent but no words where necessary. I felt overwhelmed by my feelings for him. They were so strong I wanted to cry; I dreaded having to leave and be without him, this man I don't know. But that wasn't right either because I did know him for some completely unexplainable reason, I did know him.

I must have fallen asleep because when I awoke I was in the room I had stayed in before. I recognized it all to well. I was still in my red dress. I jumped to my feet and I headed for the door almost half expecting it to be locked but to my surprise it was unlocked.

I looked up and down both sides of the hallway no one was in sight. I gently closed the door behind me and tip towed down the hall being careful not to startle or wake anyone. It was not daylight yet but it had to be early in the morning.

I came to the end of the hall, I could either turn left and take it to the stairway where I knew what to expect or turn right and take it down to the huge doors at the end. I decided I had listened to that voice in my head enough for one night and I turned right. I could see a light under the large door at the end of the hall. As I came closer to the door I felt the urge to run again but my curiosity was overriding everything in me at the moment. I felt like I was going to wake everyone up with my breathing. I needed to relax, so I was in a big creepy house with some strange man running around who looked like he wanted to kill me ten different ways, no big deal I would just peek into the room and get it over with. It was probably just another ornate bedroom I stopped just outside the door preparing what I would say if someone should be in the room when I peek in. I could hear muffled voices, I didn't need to strain as I could hear clearly who it was I would know Williams voice anywhere. The other voice was Andoe's he was speaking broken English mostly answering William's directions.

> "He is not to go near her, I want you to watch her every move. She's not safe as long as he is here. He'll be going back soon we just have to be smart."
> "Why is Dr. Jared back so soon Master William? I thought he wasn't due back until October."
> "There have been some set backs and changes we have to work out in the processing of the serum. I will have to think this all through before we move forward. No matter what, I won't be responsible for any more people I care about dying. You're the only person I trust to watch her Andoe don't let me down."

Andoe's answer was a blur to me I stood there with my mouth agape. It was like a bad episode of Dark Shadows. What was going on here? What had I gotten into?
I was suddenly aware of where I was standing and the sound of footsteps approaching.

I scrambled trying to run quietly down the hall and popped into the first door available. The room was almost completely dark but I sensed there was someone else there. I turned and scanned the room.

"I don't think we have had the pleasure of an introduction Miss Dossin."

The voice came from the dimly lit corner. I was frozen, his voice matched his demeanor he was a medium build not unattractive but there was something about him that repulsed and terrified me. Of all rooms to pop into, perfect Zoe.

"No I don't think we have, Mr.?"

Trying to make my voice sound sane and rational not at all how I felt at this moment.

"Dr. Craig, Doctor Jared Craig."

He stood up to walk across the room my body language must have given me away I felt myself back up into the closed door.

"So jumpy Miss Dossin, it is a large old house isn't it? It makes me uneasy at times. I promise I mean you no harm. I couldn't sleep either."

He was standing directly in front of me now I had to pull it together.

"Yes it is I - I'm just a little disoriented, I thought this was my room. I couldn't find the restroom either."

I attempted a chuckle but my mouth was dry and my voice crackled.

"Well you are welcome to stay as long as you like in my room but I am sure William would never go for that. What do you think, Zoe is it? Is it alright that I call you Zoe or do you prefer Miss Dossin? I personally hate formality."

"Zoe is fine, I'm sure William would not have someone staying in his home he did not trust Dr. Craig is it?"

"Please call me Jared."

"Jared, as I was saying there is nothing to worry about I am sure, I'll just show myself out and find my room. I am sorry I bothered you."

"No bother but if there is nothing to worry about why are you trembling so? Do I scare you Zoe?"

My name off his lips made me shudder, his very continence was foul. He was too close now I tried not to look him in the eye, the distance between us was uncomfortable to say the least.

"You don't scare me Dr. Craig, I told you I'm just a little turned around I have my bearings now, I will be fine."

"Yes you are fine, I can see why he would be drawn to you and how you would be such a distraction to him. I can't say I am entirely happy about that. It's not good for him to be distracted right now from our work, but I can see how tempting it would be. You look like your healing quite nicely amazing isn't? It was such a nasty spill you took."

His face was beside mine now, bent down, his breath on my neck as he spoke, I stayed staring straight ahead. My chest pounding I tried to hide my fear by swallowing hard.

"Oh, have I gone and scared you again? I assure you that is not my intention."

"What exactly is your intention then if not to intimidate me? Because I am sure if you where trying to be a gentleman than you would keep your distance and not be standing against me."

He stepped back a few inches looking smugly crushed.

"I apologize if my manners are unbecoming to you I just think we should get to know each other so we can reach an understanding."

"What understanding would that be Dr. Craig?"

"One where you know your place and mine."

"My place?"

This time I moved to the side to get further away, my fear turning to anger.

"And what is it that you think is my place may, I ask?"

He stood looking not so smug and a little surprised at first but his face took on the look it had earlier in the night when I felt he wanted to kill me. The anger quickly left me and fear was back with a vengeance. I was now about three feet from the door he was the only thing between me and freedom.

"There is no need to get defensive I merely suggest that we, meaning you, know where I am coming from. William seems to need you around and for now I will tolerate it. What will not be tolerated is you poking your nose around where it doesn't belong. You want to play with fire be my guest but please make no mistake Miss Dossin, nothing is going to come between what William and I are doing. I wont let that happen. Are we clear with each other now?"

"I wonder Dr. Craig if William would be so keen on you setting me straight on our relationship? Something tells me you have already had this discussion with him. One can only assume that he did not receive it very well or it wouldn't be necessary for you to try and intimidate me. And I can assure you my nose will be nowhere near you and your business, whatever that may be. Not that this hasn't been enlightening but I would like to leave now."

"By all means, be my guest and Miss Dossin..."

He stepped aside and motioned with his arm for me to pass.

"There are scarier monsters than me in this house, you would be wise to remember that."

I tried my best to not run out the door.

The thought that kept running through my mind was how evil and cynical he was. I felt like I needed a shower just being near him. I fought to figure out where to go. I wanted to be far from here but I desperately wanted to talk to William also. I wanted to tell him how awful Jared was and how he spoke to me. I would have to pass by Jared's door again to get to William and I had tested the waters enough for one night. I quickly walked back to my room and closed the door behind me. As I paced back and forth I replayed the night in my head, this Jared character was smart, his words were burned into my brain. I also thought about what William had said not wanting anymore people he cared about dead who was he referring to? His voice sounded so desperate so worried. I needed to see him and know he was okay.

I turned to walk out and there it was my answer, the tassel. Would it still work with Darlei at my house? Who would come? I didn't care as long as it wasn't Dr. Jeckle.

I started to pull it and as I looked down I saw a shadow of feet under the door. I paused holding my breath thinking maybe I had pushed too many buttons with Jared, maybe he was coming to permanently put me in my place. Before I thought I said it, it just came out.

"William? Is that you?"

The door began to open I looked for something to fend off my attacker. I grabbed the small crystal bowl beside the bed and held it over my head as the door opened to my relief it was William.

"Zoe? Are you alright? What are you going to do with that?"

There was a few seconds of laughter in his voice I'm sure I looked ridiculous.

"William!"

I dropped the bowl and ran to him burying my head into his chest he wrapped his arms around me.

"What's wrong? Why are you trembling?"

My mind was moving a million miles a minute. I wanted to tell him everything but that voice inside told me better. What if telling him put his life in danger. William was obviously afraid of what Jared could do or he would never put up with him. I just shook my head trying to catch my breath.

"I'm fine, I just had a terrible dream and I woke up not knowing where I was that's all. What where you doing standing outside my door?"

"Just making sure you where okay, I know how much you like to explore. I got worried you might decide to go for a walk alone and tonight's not a good night for that."

I had to bite my tongue with that remark.

"Will you stay for a while? We don't have to talk."

He looked back at the door as if he might say no and then turned back to me and nodded.

"I can stay, if you would like?"

"Very much, please."

We sat on the Chaise near the window there was so much to say and ask but I was strangely glad for the silence. I watched him as he stared out over the grounds and water. I was amazed by his chiseled jaw line and dark features. The centerpiece of his handsome features were his thick, coal black eyelashes but there was a sadness that seemed to reside there behind them somehow. I tried to think what my dad would say about this situation I had gotten myself into.

Something Jared had mentioned as I was leaving the room was plaguing my thoughts, it's not that everything he said wasn't completely disturbing but the last dig he managed to spout out. 'I'm not the scariest monster in this house.' What did he mean by that? Was William protecting someone or something monstrous besides our lovely Doctor? He couldn't mean William, that's insanity. No it had to be something else.

William's breathing was steady and even, the white shirt he was wearing was unbuttoned revealing a his sculpted chest and olive skin. He had his sleeves cuffed up which was unusual he always seemed so polished and well put together always wearing long sleeves. As I admired how well put together he was I noticed bruising similar to what accompanies blood work or and injection site on the inside of his arm it was quiet large about the size of an orange. I traced it with my fingers he sat quietly at first and then noticing what I was tracing he pulled away.

"I'm sorry, did I hurt you?"

He laughed a strange laugh.

"Hurt me no, no you didn't hurt me."

He quickly un-cuffed his sleeves. I stared at him waiting for an explanation,

"What happened, how did you get that bruise?"

"It's nothing just a bruise."

He looked at me I could tell he wanted to tell me but for some reason he was holding back. What was he protecting me from?

"I'm a really good listener William, you can talk to me if you want. It's okay.

Are you ill is that the reason why Dr. Craig is here?
"

It came out before I could stop it or even realized I had said his name.

"Who told you he was a doctor?"

His expression changing the intense look returned and his breathing was rapid.

"Answer me Zoe, did he talk to you?"

I felt him grip the upper part of my arm. I searched for the right thing to say as I felt the tears pooling in my eyes.

"What did he say to you?"

His jaw clenched and his eyes glared he stood to his feet releasing me he paced back and forth like an animal his chest heaving.

"You have to leave you have to go back to Arizona, Zoe your not safe here close to me."

"No, I'm not going anywhere until you explain what is going on here? I have a right to know what is endangering me."

"You want to know what is putting you in danger. Me, I am, I was stupid and thought I could pull it off but I can't. I care to much for you and I won't be responsible for hurting you."

"Well it's a little late for that William, you don't think sending me away from you will hurt me?"

"You would be alive, it's not the same."

"You won't let him hurt me William, he's just a man."

"You think I'm afraid of him hurting you?"

His laugh was resonating almost maddening.

"It's not him that I'm worried about hurting you, it's me. I'm not what you think I am and I'll never be a normal man again. It was stupid of me to have that fantasy but now it's over and you are leaving like it or not!"

"You can't be serious, I am not leaving. I'm a grown woman and you can't just tell me what I am going to do. I'm not afraid."

My tears were making it hard for me to express how mad I was at his decision to just discard me.

"That's because you don't understand the danger."

"Then tell me if I'm going to die anyway, just tell me so I know what to expect because I'm not leaving you. Do you care so little for me that you can just send me away? Do you give up so easily? You know what, you're right I don't know you because I thought you cared about me, staring in my window all night, breaking in my house, saving my life. Yeah, I'm in real danger, from a broken heart thank you. Really I have to say you took the long way around to decide I'm just not worth it."

His face lost all expression he turned away from me his fists still clenched.

"Is that what you think of me? That I don't think you're worth it? I've never felt this way before about anyone Zoe, I've never loved anyone or put anyone above what I want. I couldn't live with myself if something happened to you. I tried to distance myself from you and keep you from this but it was somehow unavoidable. I might never be the man I once was but I have enough of my humanity left to not do this to you. You're going to have a long life, with a wonderful young man, have lots of babies, and never think of this again."

I stood there trying to hold back the complete break down that was building.

"Well William, seems your crystal ball left out the part about me not being able to have children, ever! So you think you know what's best for me and you have my life so neatly planned but I will never have a normal life not like you described. You know we are supposed to be with each other. I tried being with Justin, I did, and he means a lot to me but family means everything to him. I know he wants children, which means he would be giving that up for me. I couldn't do that to someone I'm not completely in love with. I've never even kissed you and I know that deep down we are supposed to be together. You don't think with every fiber of my being I don't want to run as far as I can away from this? But it's impossible. You're right it's unavoidable.

I can't stand seeing you pull away from me and putting up that wall you hide behind. Why can't you trust me enough to tell me the truth? You can't just send me away because you're scared. I deserve to know why we can't be together."

He turned to face me looking like he was about to speak but no words came out. He just stood there his face flushed and worried. I could feel the anger rising in me, as sorry as I felt for him and how torn and difficult this was for him. I couldn't help but feel hurt and mad that he didn't love me enough, or trust me enough, to tell me the truth. I needed to leave and clear my head. I didn't want to go but we were at an impasse and this was only causing him more pain.

"That's fine William, I can't say I understand because I don't, how can I? I have no idea what's going on but I know you aren't going to tell me what I need to know, I am leaving. When you decide to tell me the truth we can talk again. If this is what you want I love you enough to give you that."

"Will you be going back to Arizona then?"

"No William, my home is here in Robbinston not Arizona. I'm staying here."

"Zoe you can't! You need to be far from here."

"Well unfortunately like me, you will have to learn to live with disappointment. The whole your in danger thing, is crazy, and until you explain what it is exactly I am in danger of, I'll be down the road. Thank you for dinner and please tell Dr. Craig I said goodbye."

I walked quickly out of the room trying to wipe the onset of new tears from my eyes. I stormed down the hall breaking into a sprint near the stairway I took the steps two at a time until I neared the bottom where Andoe was waiting.

"Master William says you should wait here until he can escort you home properly."

"You can tell Master William I can find my own way home, thank you very much."

"Master William said to tell you, if you said that, to tell you please?"

I knew I should just keep running how long could it take really to run barefooted in the dark 4-6 miles? I couldn't say no to him.

"Is there a restroom down here Andoe?"

"Yes Miss Dossin, I'll show you."

He led me through the hall past the room William took me in before, the one where his mother's paintings were. I needed to wash my face I'm sure I was a mess and I felt like I had been hit by a bus and I looked that way too. I splashed my face with cold water and tried to rid myself of my raccoon mask of eyeliner and mascara as best I could. I was feeling so many things my head was spinning.

"Master William is bringing the car around, Miss Dossin if you are ready."

"Yes, thank you Andoe."

He handed me my shoes and a jacket

"Master William said you should put this on."

I through the jacket over my arm. Andoe shook his head in disagreement of my decision to not put the jacket on. As we walked out the door I could see the outline of the Black Maserati against the white crushed gravel of the driveway. I slipped my shoes on and slipped into the open door Andoe was holding for me.

I struggled to latch the seatbelt, the car was dark and I couldn't feel quite where it was. I felt his hand over mine latching it. My heart raced from his touch. We drove out of the driveway and onto the main road again turning the wrong way to go to my house. I wanted to know where we were headed but I did not want to be the one to break the silence first.

I tried looking out of the corner of my eye to see if he was looking at me. He was staring straight ahead into the dawn that was just starting to break. He reached without looking and turned on the heat in the car.

"Why are you so stubborn?"

His voice sounding frustrated by breaking the silence.

"How am I the one being stubborn?"

"You wouldn't even put the coat on I had Andoe give to you and I know you're cold."

I sat for a moment contemplating how I should respond to him. I didn't want to keep arguing but I wanted desperately to just not think about anything.

"Where are we going?"

My voice was ruff and broken from crying and talking so much.

"We need to discuss this situation and figure out what we are going to do."

"I told you, until you decide to tell me what is going on I was through talking."

"See, again with the stubbornness. You're going to make me do this aren't you?"

"Tell me the truth, yes. Why are you trying to protect me? You're only hurting me worse by not telling me."

"Are you not feeling well? Your voice sounds like your getting sick."

"I'm fine, just tired and it happens when I cry."

"I don't like it when you cry, especially when I'm the reason you're crying."

"Then stop making me cry."

The car made a quick turn and came to a sudden stop. It was a clearing, he put the car in park and turned it off.

"I don't know what else to tell you to make you trust me William, except that I love you."

He turned to me taking my face in his hand and wiping the tears that had re-emerged. His touch was firm and warm. He looked at me with such intensity it was almost more than I could stand. As he leaned in I felt every worry and concern I was feeling vaporize. I felt his face against mine, his hand still holding it, his lips softly passed by mine, caressing, them as if testing to see if I would let him kiss me, then pulling me harder into him.

His lips firm and powerful, his kiss was deep and unyielding. I gave in and kissed him back. I didn't want it to end, I wanted to stay here in his arms. I could feel his heart pounding through his chest even more than mine. He stopped quickly forcing me back. He grabbed the steering wheel with both hands gripping it until I could hear it making a popping noise. Looking at the ceiling of the car, he let out a loud growl that was not a human sound and got out of the car. He walked quickly away from it to the edge of the road. I jumped out and ran around to see if he was okay.

"William it's okay, I'm fine nothing's wrong."

"Everything is wrong don't you see?"

"No I don't see, I don't understand."

"I can't stop."

"But you just did."

"No, I can't make this feeling go away. I can't let you go. I wanted to, I tried getting mad, I tried making you hate me. I'm not strong enough no matter how much I love you. I can't give you up. I'm sorry, I'm so sorry. That is why you have to leave you have to make me go away."

"William are you afraid of the kiss?"

"Zoe I can't allow myself to get that lost in what I feel, I have to stay in control. I'm not..."

"Not what William?"

"I'm not who you think I am. I am not William Madison's nephew. I'm not a relative Zoe, I am William Madison."

There was along pause as if he where waiting for me to run or scream.

"That's impossible."

"I died along time ago, about hundred years ago to be exact."

"William if you are cooking up this story to scare me-"

"No Zoe, I am Captain William Armande Madison. I died almost a hundred years ago in a shipwreck. I'm not alive the way you are."

"I know the story of how William Madison died but it's physically impossible that you are Him. You are standing right in front of me breathing."

"Yes that's true, I am in a sense alive but not how you are alive. My father he went mad with grief after I died. He had just lost my mother, he and I weren't on speaking terms when I had my accident so when he found out I had died, he lost it. He went on a drinking binge and began reading any books he could find about death and resurrection. He came across a book written by S. Craig M.D. entitled 'Bringing The Dead Alive'. He began corresponding with the Author and decided to visit him while he was in Haiti.

The book spoke of a ritual the Haitians perform to resurrect the dead and how this Doctor believed there was something to the medicines the Shamans used. He convinced the Shaman to come to Maine and perform the ritual. It took him six months to prepare, get him here, and on the one year anniversary of my death they preformed the ritual. At first they didn't think it had worked but three days later my body washed up on shore about a hundred miles from where I drowned. A blind man and his dog found me, they found my name inside of the Silver amulet I wore, that my mother had given me, and contacted my father. But that was just the first part of the ritual in order to finish it they had to have my body. I didn't know who I was, where I was, or where I had been. They brought me home to finish the ritual, which is where I was first given the serum that stops the body from decaying. It is what makes the Dead stay alive, without it you would begin to decompose and turn back into dust but the side effects are to say the least horrifying.

The pain is terrible, your body's nervous system is completely altered even the slightest touch feels like hot knives, then comes the rage and hunger. Your most primal urges are brought to the surface, all your inhibitions; morals, which make us different from animals, are gone. You act on shear instinct for survival. I began having flashes of my life and family when I returned home but something dark began to happen. The Shaman had warned my father that the ritual was usually performed right after death occurred and the serum administered prior to death. They didn't know what to expect. My father didn't care all he wanted was me back. See the ritual only brings back the body my brain was damaged from well, being dead. I became something dark what they had feared most. The Serum has to be administered once a month. Every time they administered the serum I would go into a total rampage. My father and then a very young doctor and Author of the book named Samuel J. Craig, set out to find the true antidote for the original serum. My father promised to fund the doctor's research as long as he promised to keep searching for the 'Cure' as he called it. He took the plants and fish poison used in the final ritual and began running tests to see how they affected the brain. He had very little luck at first. I did recover most of my memories but it was difficult to control my urges, which made me very dangerous to be around. They had to keep me locked up for a nearly a year. I became very close to Sam, he was like a brother to me and the only one I trusted. I begged for them to kill me when I had my lucid moments. Sam had some progress in finding the rudimentary properties of the plants and began testing different Serums on me. They where only partially effective they helped my brain function but not the primal urges. The Serums had an effect on the healing and aging of the human body so after the first two years of taking the Serum I stopped aging. My father didn't live to see the effects of the final

Serum he died about 6 months after they brought me back. He died before I was human again. Samuel stayed with me and we continued the research together. We made an agreement, once we stabilized the serum to never allow it to fall into the wrong hands, it was too dangerous and could be misused. It was Sam's intention to find a cure for organ replacement and cures for diseases such as cancer, T.B., etc... As time went on Sam got older but I did not, he had a nephew Marcus that followed in his footsteps and began helping in our campaign. Along the way he got very ill, he had leukemia, his son was only 14 when he died it was difficult for him to take. All that research we had done and the serum had only a minimal effect on the disease. Sam was afraid to give Marcus a stronger dosage. He didn't want him to live with the symptoms I had to live with. We weren't able to save him. Samuel died a few years later leaving his great nephew Jared then seventeen alone. I took the boy in and put him through Medical school, he is brilliant. We have had several breakthroughs that are amazing but the serum is still not stable enough to be used by the living, not in a capacity that would be safe and without symptoms. Jared couldn't accept that and without my knowledge he began experimenting on himself. Driven to find a cure for death, because of the loss of his father, I would assume. He hasn't always been like he is now, he was once a bright and loving person. He suffers from some of the darker side effects of the serum. I wasn't aware he was taking the serum until it was too late. He, like myself, has to take it now or the more sinister side takes over. He has never forgiven me for his father dying, he feels in some way I let it happen. All this death, pain, and work and I will still never be able to release our research. There are too many people willing to exploit it without regard for its effects. The bad far outweighs the good that can come from the serum. It can't be allowed to fall into the wrong hands."

I stood staring at him trying to absorb the story he had just told me. I searched for his expression to see if there was anyway I had misunderstood what he had just shared. My mind was having trouble putting it into perspective but my heart believed him.

"You don't believe me do you?"

"I believe what you told me, I just can't wrap my head around it. It's medically impossible William."

"Yet here I am Zoe, I don't know what dark thing they called forth to bring me back from the dead but it happened."

"But the new serum, it keeps you from the urges you spoke of?"

"It curbs them but it really is mostly my ability to overcome those urges."

"What exactly are they, these urges?"

"The extreme levels of testosterone created from the serum causes uncontrollable feelings of jealousy, anger, and well, intensified sex drive. There is another side effect which I cannot explain."

"And what is that?"

His face turned away as if the shame from what he was about to tell me was too great to look at me when he said it.

"The craving of human flesh. Cannibalism."

The word echoed in my head, I felt a chill go through me and I shivered.

"The serum helps with that though right?"

"It does, but I have tried to keep those temptations away from me. That is why I try to keep human contact to a minimal. I have never had to control those urges as much as I have being around you. That is why you need to go far away from me."

"But you did it and here I am, not a scratch on me. How old are you then William?"

"This April I will celebrate my 131st year. I was 32 when I died and I don't think I can count the entire year I was dead."

He turned back and looked at me as if he was surprised I was still standing there. His face still beautiful but he looked tired or worried.

"How old is Jared William? Has he stopped aging to?"

"No, not stopped just slowed down, he is about forty five now."

"That is why he can't be trusted around you. Our agreement is I allow him to have his supply of serum and he continues the research in Haiti under supervision. Lately he has been behaving rather badly, unpredictable really. I am trying to figure out a way to save him from himself. He is supposed to be in Haiti until October but there is a problem with the processing. We have never been successful in growing the plants here or anywhere except a small area in Haiti. The original serum was made as I told you with poison taken from a fish and the extract taken from this plant. We have modified it to where we can now use some synthetic additives removing the need for the fish poison it's too unstable. The plants are becoming harder and harder to harvest. The Haitian government is becoming a problem as well as the exportation of the serum.

Money is not a problem, thanks to my father and uncles investments, but money can only go so far when dealing with a superstitious culture. I have enough serum in reserve to get by for a while, if it where just myself taking it but Jared's need is becoming more of a problem. I hate what I am, I have to monitor myself constantly. I still have the original effects from the Ritual but I have learned what triggers it and I control it."

"The hunger?"

My mind was not even able to comprehend the words coming out of my mouth.

"Yes the desire for human flesh is completely irresistible before the serum is administered. After it is taken it can be managed if you so desire."

I was speechless I didn't know how to absorb it all. It was like I had been watching a movie on Sci Fi channel.

"How can things like this really exist?"

"I don't know Zoe, I have asked myself that question over and over with no answer. I am an abomination. How can God allow me to live? That is why I need to perfect this serum, if I could turn it into something different something that would save instead of creating monsters then maybe I could redeem myself."

"Redeem yourself for what William? What could you have possibly done that would merit this punishment?"

"You didn't know me before Zoe, I was not a good person. I treated life with total disregard and those around me also. My thirst for making a name for myself and to prove my father wrong controlled everything. I am responsible for the lives of my men. There is a reason I was allowed to come back Zoe, there has to be, because what I am goes against everything in nature."

His eyes seemed not as dark as before, his face more boyish. I wished I could think of something to make him feel better, something to take this pain away.

"William you can't honestly believe this is some kind of punishment or test?"

"I don't know what it is Zoe but I won't be responsible for your death as well. I couldn't live with myself if anything happened to you."

"Did you give me the Serum William? Is that what made me heal so fast?"

"I didn't give you the Serum that Jared and I take no, I applied a derivative of it to your wounds in a very small dose. It has a remarkable effect on small wounds."
"Will it make me like Jared?"
"No not used like that, it has no permanent effect."
"Why did you have to stop kissing me?"
"Any time I am not 100% in control of my emotions I run the chance of losing control over the darker side. I'm not like Jared, he is still alive just altered almost like a drug addict. I'm not dead but not alive either something happens when you are separated from your soul, I don't think any ritual can bring that back. There are fragments of the man I once was, memories of a life past, but I am different than I was. It has taken me a long time to come to terms with that. The Haitians call what I am the walking dead -"Mache Mouri". I have tried to kill myself as many ways as I could imagine but my body just heals itself. I do feel pain especially after I have taken the serum, like I said it alters your nervous system causing your pain level to be exaggerated. As of yet I can't figure out a way to put an end to this. My biggest fear is that I will not have the Serum and become what is fighting to take control.
I wish I had never involved you in any of this it was selfish to try and take what I can never have."
"Jared told me that there is a monster worse than him in your house, did he mean you William?"
"Jared isn't dead, he can die he never had the ritual done to bring him back. He can be stopped."
"And you? You can't be stopped is that what he is saying?"
"Yes I guess, I guess that would be true. The difference is I fight to keep the darkness of this hidden and Jared he feeds it."

"William I don't understand everything but you are right there is a reason why you were brought back, I feel it.
This is probably going to sound crazy but I have dreamed about you every night since I was 15 years old. Since the first time I saw you. We have a bond, I know you feel it too. I can't explain it but it was so strong my parents thought I was going crazy. I was in therapy for years trying to decipher why I would be dreaming about a man that had been dead for years. I don't know how to not be with you now that I know you're alive, I have to be here."

He looked at me amazed but not surprised.

"You thought of me as well? I thought it was just me, your Auburn, hair those green eyes, every time you came I knew you were here. I sensed it and when you stopped coming it was terrible but I was happy for you because I thought you had maybe settled down and had a life with someone. I knew that was better than what I would give you and I knew if you never came back you would be safe."

I stepped back and sat on the cement wall near the edge of the road. My mind trying to process what was actually happening. I felt a euphoric feeling of relief I wasn't crazy or maybe I was but I wasn't alone. It was daylight and the chill of the dew settling was making me shiver.

"We need to get you home for now Zoe you're shivering. I shouldn't have told you any of this. It would have been better for you to have left while you could. "Will you stay with me, I mean tonight or this morning? I would feel safer."
"You are the only person I know that would feel safer having a flesh craving dead man stay with her."

He shook his head and opened the car door for me. His face seemed to soften somehow and his mood a little lighter.

Similar to how you feel when you just let a skeleton the size of an elephant out of your closet, I would guess. I had so many questions but I was exhausted. I know he needed a break from the insane night we had just shared. It had to be around 6am when we got back to the house and I headed upstairs he stopped for a moment at the bottom of the steps.

"What is it? Are you seriously going to pretend like you don't know your way around my house?"

"That's not it, I should stay down here on the couch."

"And why is that William? Never mind I guess you prefer spying on me after I've gone to sleep."

"That was below the belt, but deserved. You really are like the mouse jumping over the cheese-covered trap you know. If it would make you feel better I will come up."

I was surprised that Bailey hadn't come down to greet us when we came in but he was probably sound asleep upstairs with Darlei. He waited in my room while I quickly changed into some PJ's and brushed my teeth I was almost half expecting Andoe to be waiting for me in the room saying Master William had to leave but he was there sitting in the window seat looking out.

"Not as good of a view as your house, huh?"

"It's a lovely view."

He pulled the blinds closed, I jumped into the bed and slid over leaving a spot for him to lay down, he looked at me puzzled for a moment.

"I'll lie in the floor."

"William please, I won't bite I promise. Okay a poor choice of words I know, I'm tired but please just lay with me. I have dreamt about you every night for 13 years, I finally find you and you are going to be a prude? We will sleep I promise."

"You really like to test the water don't you?

Which is what worries me, one of us should have the sense to say no!"

I put on my most pitiful face I could muster. He slid his shoes off and walked over to where I was. He carefully covered me and then lay atop the covers. I guess beggars can't be choosers. I scooted closer to him laying my head on his arm, even after everything he still smelled great. I had so many things to think about but all I wanted to do was lie there with him and sleep. I didn't want that part to end. I feared for what was ahead of us, but I was glad he would not be leaving, now anyway. I drifted in and out of sleep, he laid so still watching my every move as if I might disappear from his sight if he blinked. I felt sleep coming regardless of how much I tried to fight it. I almost expected to have one of my dreams but to my surprise I didn't dream at all. I woke up and before I opened my eyes I reached beside me to see if he was still there, it was empty but I had already prepared myself for that. I rolled over and pressed my face into the pillow where he had laid breathing in, it still smelled like him. I made a mental note to never wash that pillow again and got up. I wondered if he had completely left or if he had just gone downstairs I opened my door and listened down the hall to see if I could hear any voices.

The house was quiet so I closed the door and headed for the bath room when I heard his voice outside.

I looked out the window to see him playing with Bailey throwing a stick near the porch. I quickly jumped in the shower, happy that he was still here. I was toweling off when I heard the knock at my door, I threw a towel around myself.

"Just a minute."

"Oh I'm sorry, I thought you said come in, I'm sorry."

His face was red and he wouldn't look at me at all but he didn't leave either he was frozen.

"William it's okay give me a second to put something on. It's fine, it's hard to hear from the bathroom to the hallway. Just wait here."

I turned and grabbed my clothes off my chair and headed for the bathroom.

"It is a big deal, I didn't mean to barge in here like that I thought you would still be sleeping. You're a young lady, gentlemen shouldn't be in your bedroom when you're not dressed."

"Yes dad, but I think since you've seen me in my underwear already that counts, you're like my doctor."

Although I couldn't see his face I could see him thinking about the day he had to re-suture my stitches.

"No comment? Wow, I guess I got you on that one huh? I have to say I was glad when I saw you were still here. When I woke up I really thought you would leave."

"Why would you think I would leave? That wouldn't have been very nice after the night I put you through, besides there are some things we need to discuss."

"William if it's about me leaving the answer is no! I won't go."

Trying to make my voice as firm as possible.

"Well that discussion can wait for now, there are other things I need to know."

"Okay what would you like to know?"

"Let's get you some breakfast and we'll talk."

My hair was still a little wet and curly from not being done but could never look as badly as I had last night and he kissed me so I think I'm safe with the damp hair. I grabbed a bowl of Banana Nut Crunch and a glass of juice,

"Did you eat already William?"

"Yes, I had coffee earlier before Darlei left. She'll be back but there was something I needed her to do for me and I thought we could use the privacy."

"Well I'm all yours."

"I like that."

His smile was sly and devilish.

"I meant, what did you want to ask me?"

"Yes I know, well last night you mentioned that you could not have children."

I would like very much to shoot myself for losing my temper and letting that fly out of my mouth right about now.

"Yes, I am not able to have children."

"If I may ask, why?"

His face was serious and focused.

"Well when I was born I was missing my Uterus and a kidney. You can live without both so I guess I'm fortunate in a way."

He sat studying my face for a moment.

"Its fine I have learned to deal with my short comings like you have with yours."

"Have you ever been married?"

"No, not even close."

I couldn't help but chuckle at the sincerity in his voice. He looked a little confused.

"You're not married and you're a lot older than I am."

"Well that's different I'm not what you would want to bring home to meet the parents."

"Well you're in luck because I have no parents to disapprove. Why all the questions about me?"

"I'm just trying to figure you out. You are taking everything I told you last night very well, most people would still be running. Why aren't you scared?"

"I am scared but not because of you, but I am afraid to lose you.

I have never felt this way about anyone. I can't leave, I told you. Why did you never marry before the accident?"

"I was a different person back then young and arrogant.

I thought I had all the time in the world for that. I did everything my father hated. He wanted me to be a businessman like him but that was never me. I love the sea, besides my mother it's the only thing I loved. I hated it when I was back on land. Now I never go out on the water. It's different, I'm different."

"Can you have children William? I mean is that part of you normal?"

He laughed like I had embarrassed him. He thought for a moment about how to answer my question.

"I'm not sure about the children thing. I don't think I would chance that, the outcome could be, well let's just say bizarre. That's not what you were asking is it?"

He must have noticed the disappointment on my face.

"Well let me rephrase that, can you be with a woman? Are you just like a normal man?"

His face turned red again,

"If you're asking if I can have sexual relations with someone, physically I am completely normal. As far as being with someone, you saw what happened when I kissed you last night. I don't know if I would have enough control of myself especially with you."

"Why especially with me?"

"My attraction to you is strong and it makes it dangerous because of the emotional feelings, I told you I forget what I am when I'm with you. I have never tried to suppress that type of primal urge, I haven't had to deal with that, it's new to me and I have to be careful,"

"Careful meaning you're not sending me away?"
"You would be wise to go and I should stop being selfish and make you go but I still have a little of the old me in here and unfortunately for you, I have never given up what I want."
"Well that makes me very happy. We can do this William, we can make it work, I will help you with whatever I can."
"You can start by wearing more clothing, it's really hard being around you when you are barley covered."
I was just wearing a tank top and shorts.
"You mean like how I am dressed now?"
"Well now and last night, you really put me to the test last night."
"Sorry, I'll keep that in mind."
In a weird way it made me feel good that he was physically attracted to me, I thought he didn't like the dress.
"I do need to know what Jared said to you last night. I think we both know you spoke to him, another one of your exploring moments."
"It's your fault you know, I was looking for you. You shouldn't have left me alone if you didn't want me to wonder around."
"I promise you won't be out of my sight again. Now what did he tell you?"
"He was just a little annoyed that I was distracting you and he wanted to make sure I knew that I was not to go snooping around and messing things up for you and him."
"That arrogant little snipe, he is really pushing my patients."
"Why do you tolerate him William?"
"I was very close with his father, it killed me that we were unable to save him.

The very reason he wouldn't take the serum, those horrific side effects have now become his sons curse. I don't know how to stop him without killing him. I can't stop giving him the Serum now it's too dangerous but if he continues to take it, it will completely alter him.

He is already barely human. He wants to sell the serum to the government to make money, he doesn't care how many people would be killed. I honestly think he's driven by pure instinct for power and money. He is staying here for a while until I can figure out how to back him off the dosage he is taking. I can keep an eye on him here better than if he goes back. We are going to have to keep an eye on you as well while he is here, power and money aren't the only things he has a lust for."

"Oh, you mean women?"

"Yes, you could say that, the drug causes increased testosterone levels. He doesn't have the desire to control himself he lets it rule him. We keep him away from anything that might tempt him."

"I'll keep that in mind as well."

It made me cringe to think how close I was to being his new love interest or snack last night.

"So should I go put a long sleeve shirt on then? I wouldn't want you to try and kiss me again."

"It's really not funny. I know you are getting a big kick out of that but only because you don't realize how great the danger is to you."

I stood up and gathered the dishes to take them into the kitchen, I heard him call to Bailey as I was walking in. I placed the dishes in the sink, Darlei had moved things around and I had to look for the dish soap as I stood up he was standing in front of me. I almost fell backward I wasn't expecting him to be that close. He grabbed me and held me up to him. He looked at me for a moment

"Sorry, I'm such a klutz."

He had a devilish smile never showing his teeth, his dark eyes sparkled.

"Just how brave are you?"

"Well I'm letting a dead guy hold me right now, what do you think?"

"Well technically I'm not dead just half dead."

"Is the temptation too difficult for you, should I go put some clothes on?"

"No I think I'll manage, would you mind if we try again?"

I placed my hand on his neck, I had to tip toe to reach him. He is a lot taller than Justin. He met me half way gripping my waist, there was a pause for a moment our lips almost touching.

Chapter Twelve:
Deadly Acquaintances

***

I heard the knock at the door and it opening.

"Hey Zoe, you home?"

It was Jenna, I pushed him away quickly my heart pounding.

"Yes, in here Jenna."

I gave him a quick look but it was too late she had to know someone was here his car was parked out front.

"Hello,"

"Jenna this is William. William, Jenna Randall."

"Very nice to meet you Miss Randall."

"Yes, Uncle William is it?"

Her face smiling from ear to ear.

"Zoe you didn't tell me your Uncle was so handsome. "

I looked down at the bag in her hand.

"Oh yeah, I brought your new Cell phone to you. I forgot I had picked it up yesterday. You look a lot better."

"Yes, I am feeling much better."

"Well I was going to see what you were doing later but if you have company I don't want to intrude."

"Oh well, Jenna actually, William and I haven't discussed how long he is staying here yet, can I get back to you on that in a little while?"

"Sure no problem, don't want to come between family. I'll call you in a couple of hours and find out what the plans are. Oh to bad Justin isn't home we could double. It was very nice meeting you William."

"Like wise Miss Randall."

"Please, call me Jenna."

She was pulling out all the stops, Jenna was a master at flirting.

This was going to be fun to explain to her the hot guy she is flirting with is the one I am breaking her brother's heart for.

"Yah, too bad call me and I'll let you know, thanks again for bringing me the phone. Are sure you won't stay and chat?"

I really hoped she would have somewhere to be right now but she had been so sweet I couldn't be rude to her.

"No, some of us have to actually leave home to go to work Zoe! But thanks for asking. Talk to you soon."

I walked her to the door and watched her pull away. William followed me and stood behind me. It was nice having him so close.

"What did she mean by double?"

It took me a minute to think over the previous conversation.

"Oh she meant that Justin and I, Jenna and you could go on a double date."

"Oh, well I hope I didn't give her the wrong impression, what is she going to think when you tell her I'm not your Uncle?"

"Well maybe I should leave that up to you, since you're the one who told her you were my uncle. Seriously I don't know, I feel terrible they have been wonderful to me since I moved here. I feel badly that I led Justin on like I did but I didn't mean to."

"Well maybe I should speak with him for you."

I wanted laugh at how absurd that remark was. That would be the test for him keeping his cool because when Justin finds out I've been within 100 feet of his house let alone I'm in love with William Madison. He will go crazy.

"No William, why don't you leave that up to me."

"Do you have feelings for him?"

"I care about him because he has been so nice to me but not like I care for you, it's not the same. Why are you jealous of Justin, William?"

"I would be a fool to say no, he can offer you much more than I can, you won't have to worry about him causing your death."

"Now where is the fun in that? On the other hand maybe you're right, maybe I'll have to wear that red dress for him and see how well he behaves."

I don't think he found that funny, his jaw tightened at the thought of someone else seeing me in that dress.

"That would not be wise Zoe, I might have to hurt someone if they didn't behave in a respectable manner."

"I was just joking, I will never wear that dress again I promise."

Crossing my heart with crossed fingers.

"Well I think I did pretty good under the circumstances."

"Yes, you behaved extremely well, I never had a clue you wanted to kill me."

"I never said I wanted to kill you, there are worse things than dying."

"Really, worse than dying huh?"

He came closer bending down his face next to mine his warm breath on my shoulder and neck. It was when he was close to me I felt the strongest connection to him. I could barely stand being still but I didn't want to make it harder on him, I'm beginning to understand his caution. I was having control issues of my own. My pulse rocketed as I closed my eyes breathing him in.

"You need to be careful playing with fire."

What he said made me instantly think of Jared, he said the same thing to me. I shivered thinking about him. My thoughts didn't stray long William had his hand on my waist the other pinning me against the wall.

I brushed my face against his; his skin was soft and warm. He pressed against me holding me tighter, leaning in even more my body tingled as he kissed me, I felt heat fill my face and neck, his lips gently caressing me behind my ear and following downward at my shoulder. He stopped and looked at me for a moment his eyes melting me with intensity. He pressed his lips on mine kissing me deeply. I could hardly breathe I started kissing him back holding him as tightly as I could. I wanted him to scoop me up and take me to my room when suddenly he stopped pushing me away again. His breathing heavy he held his hand up for me to wait and he walked away for a moment. I stayed against the wall my eyes closed reliving the moment that we had just had together. It was hard to imagine being with anyone else again. The feelings I have for him were so strong. I opened my eyes to see him standing in the doorway.

"I'm sorry, I will have to work on that."

I couldn't imagine improving on that but if he insisted I would comply.

"William I'm here, I'm not going anywhere."

"I think you should go with your friend this evening."

"Where is this coming from, you don't want me around?"

"I think it would be good for you to get out and I have some things to deal with. I would feel better knowing you were with someone."

"Will you be back later on tonight?"

"If you would like I can arrange to come back."

"If you can arrange that I will agree to go out with Jenna."

"Good it's settled. I will go take care of the business at hand and you make your arrangements with Jenna. I will expect you to be on your best behavior. No scouting young gentleman. Or should I have Andoe escort you?"

"You wouldn't dare? Don't you trust me?"

"I trust you, but you tend to help trouble find you. You and you're exploring."

"I promise no exploring tonight, just two girls going out, probably to the movies or something completely boring."

He looked at me in total disbelief that I could manage not getting into trouble. I hated him leaving but I knew that he needed to address the problem with Jared and maybe he would be able to help him. Besides I needed to have a heart to heart with Jenna and help her understand my relationship with William and Justin. After William left I called Jenna and set up a time to meet, she was picking me up about 6pm. We planned to go have dinner and go to the movie in the park night at the town hall. It was that or Karaoke and I don't think there is enough alcohol in Maine to get me to go with that girl to that. I sat on the porch staring out at the water rehearsing my conversation with Jenna knowing how much it would probably hurt Justin was killing me. He deserved so much more than me.

I would never want him to settle for someone who wasn't as in love with him as he was with them, and he deserved the chance to have a large family like he wanted. With my mind resolved on how the conversation would go I went up to start getting ready. I couldn't stop thinking about William, I wanted to call Jenna and tell her I suddenly got sick so I could be with William instead. I knew I couldn't do that she was too excited on the phone when I told her we were going out.

I had decided to go casual and wear jeans and a t-shirt, the less attention I drew to myself the better and I couldn't get what William said about covering up out of my head I felt a little bad now, thinking about him having to see me in my under wear when I tore my stitches.

I made sure my locket was fastened tightly, I didn't want to lose another one.

I did leave my hair down and put make up on, after all I would be seeing William later and I did want to look good for him. I wondered if my Mom and Dad would have liked him. I know my Mom would have approved outside the fact that he was dead and resurrected, oh and desired to eat my flesh, all that aside as long as I was happy she would be. My dad was a little pickier. He would have liked the fact that William was into research and medicine and probably would have had long conversations with William on how I am wasting my abilities on photography and how I should be in medicine. The fact that I didn't have them anymore was already a reality but times like this when I would love to talk to them was the hardest. Knowing he'll never give me away when I get married, share special things with my mom, girl things, will never happen. I know why Jared hates death so much. It robs you of everything important. I wondered if I had had the opportunity to bring my Mom or Dad back would I have chanced it knowing the risks. That would be a hard decision, one we are not supposed to have to make. I looked out my bedroom window over the water thinking about everything I had taken for granted. I made a decision to never let an opportunity pass me by to be with someone I love, no matter what the cost. I saw the red car pulling into the drive and figured I had been morbid enough for one day. Taking a deep breath I headed down stairs. Jenna never went anywhere that she didn't look fabulous and tonight was no exception she looked great!

"Come on in Jenna, looking great!"

Her outfit would have definitely sent William over the edge.

"Hey you look cute too."

"Thanks but I feel a little under dressed I thought we were just getting dinner and a movie?"

"Yah we are but I got excited about having a girl's night out you look fine besides I met a guy!

He's gorgeous and very mysterious. You are meeting him tonight I hope you don't mind but I told him to meet us at the movie and after we can go for drinks."

"Great can't wait to meet the mystery man. Let's get going."

I let Bailey out and we were on our way. Dinner was fun we ate at an outdoor café' with live music the conversation was pretty much all about Jenna and how she meet this hot guy and he wouldn't tell her his name he just came into the office asking for directions and he couldn't take his eyes off her. She was so excited and I was glad for her maybe now it wouldn't be so hard for her to except the news about William and me. We decided to walk over to the town hall instead of driving it would give us more time to talk.

"Have you heard from Justin at all?"

Trying to ease into my monolog.

"No but don't get worried it's rare that they get a signal that far out, only 12 more days and they'll be back. I know he'll call you as soon as he can Zoe. What about your uncle William huh? He's a hunk and a half! Why is that man not taken?"

I almost chuckled as I thought about the many reasons he would not be appealing to most women, top two being the potential for death and the fact that he was dead for a year.

"Well Jenna I'm glad you asked because there is something I want to tell you and I hope we are good enough friends for you to understand it."

"Sure Zoe, What is it?"

"Well you know how I told you we aren't related, he's not really my uncle."

"Yah you said he's a family friend."

"He's not exactly a family friend."

"Yah I got that Zoe, really is it that bad because you look like you're going to puke."

"Sorry I just don't want to hurt you. You and your family have been so wonderful to me I couldn't bare you being upset or hurt because of me."

"What is it? Is he a serial killer or something? What? Spill because you're killing me."

"Okay, He's not my uncle and he's not a family friend. I met him when I had my accident and I'm in love with him."

I waited for a response I didn't know what to expect.

"Wow, that was fast what about..."

"About Justin, I know it's complicated, I care a lot about your brother. I do, but this is different, I can't help the way I feel. I'm so sorry Jenna, I know how close you are to him and I know he likes me. I didn't mean to hurt him I would never do anything to hurt him."

"How do you know you love this guy you just met him right?"

I could tell she was more than disappointed, her face which was normally so full of life clearly showed her disapproval.

"Yes, I just met him but it feels like I have known him my whole life. There is something there I can't explain."

"Well I am more than a little surprised, I really can't say I saw this coming. I thought you and Justin were such a good fit. I know this will crush Justin but I know if you are happy that's all that will matter to him. Eventually he will get over it but it won't be easy for him. He doesn't ever fall like this it's always the other way around. You have time to think about it Zoe, feelings change Justin won't be back for 12 days that's time enough to ride this out and see if you are really in love with this guy."

She was acting like I had a slight crush but its so much more than a little crush.

Even now I want to be near him. I had hoped I would be a little more convincing about being in love with William. Doesn't it show how different I am? I wanted to shake her and make her understand but she was used to falling in and out of love a lot I think. I decided to go with it for now and let her have her fantasy that it was a crush.

"Thanks Jenna, now where is this gentleman meeting us?"

"Over near the Gazebo, I hope he didn't get lost he said he's not from around here."

We waited for a while looking at everyone who passed but he hadn't shown up we decided to sit near the Gazebo thinking maybe he had gotten lost. The movie began and I could tell she was disappointed that he hadn't come. I had just started watching the movie when I felt Jenna tap me.

"I have to go to the bathroom I'll be right back."

"You shouldn't go by yourself hold on I'll go with you."

"Don't be silly we will lose our seats, just stay put I'll be right back."

She wasn't gone too long when I felt a tap again on my shoulder. I turned to see a pair of feet standing behind me. I stood to get a look at who they belonged to as I stood I could clearly see who it was.

"Jared! What are you doing here? Where is William?"

I looked frantically to see if William was near.

"I haven't seen him. I needed to get out I was bored with my surroundings. I'm sure you understand."

I saw Jenna approaching and tried to think of a way to get him out of here before she saw him.

"Hey, did you two meet? You found it."

"Yes, a little late but I'm here. Jenna you look good enough to eat."

His eyes pierced through me as he spoke goading me for a response.

It made me sick to think this is Jenna's mystery man. Jenna ate up his remark thinking he was being smooth when in fact he was being literal. I blocked the visual image his comment gave me.

"Yes Jenna we have met, his name is Jared Craig and he is a house guest of William's."

"Actually it's Dr. Jared Craig but you can call me Jared, Jenna."

"Oh Dr. Craig huh? Even better. Well, shall we sit?"

He purposely sat between us knowing I would want to talk to Jenna about him. I had to bite my tongue, it was all I could do to hold the words in. Where was William? Why had he let him leave the grounds? He wouldn't let him, he had to be searching for him. I started to worry that Jared had done something to William. I couldn't leave Jenna to go find out, that would be leaving the lamb with the hungry butcher.

I had to be smart, I needed to get us far from Jared and let William know where he was, it is un-telling what he will do if he is allowed to run free.

I discreetly looked for my cell phone thinking I could call William and tell him where I was without Jared knowing. I pretended to be looking for gum. He sat with a smug look on his face. I left the phone in my purse I was careful to open it quietly my heart fell I had no bars, I couldn't get a signal. I felt my breathing getting erratic, I needed to stop and think. I needed an excuse to leave and make Jenna go with me. Playing sick was too obvious, he would definitely have the upper hand as he is a doctor. My mind began to play out different scenarios all of which didn't end well for Jenna or me. The movie was ending and there would be an intermission between maybe we could lose him at the bathrooms. I just had to think of how I would explain to Jenna her dream man was a psycho drug addict, who for all intensive purposes wanted to kill me. I jumped as I felt Jenna tap me and grab my arm leaning in to whisper.

"So? How adorable is he? I told you he was perfect. Is it okay if I invite him back to your place for some drinks?"

My look of horror must have been evident.

"Is something wrong Zoe? I don't have to ask him back, you don't like him do you?"

That was stating it a little mild.

"Why don't you call William and he can meet us there we can all have a night cap."

If I weren't positive that he was crazy, I would feel badly not letting her see him, she really liked him. I leaned in trying not to make eye contact with Jared.

"Let's keep that a secret for now until I find out if he can come. I wouldn't want to make Jared feel badly if William can't make it. I will call him and ask him to come but let's go to the bathroom first."

At least I would have her away from Jared and maybe I would have the chance to call William and let him know where he is. He never took his eyes off me the whole movie, but not in a good way, his eyes were so intense it sent a shiver to my very core. The movie ended as we stood he kept Jenna very close to him always making sure he was between us as we walked toward the exit. I tried to make eye contact with Jenna before we passed the restrooms. I wanted her to suggest to use them so it would sound less conspicuous but I couldn't get her attention she was rambling to him about work.

"Ah Jenna didn't you say you needed to visit the ladies room?"

My heart was pounding in my chest as I spoke waiting for him to decide to go postal grab Jenna and snap her neck right in front of me.

"Sure yah wow, we almost passed them huh? We will be right back don't go anywhere."

I pulled at her arm to hurry her along. Trying to think of what to do, my mind was going in a million directions.

There was a line inside waiting for the stalls I told her to go ahead and I would try to call William. I flipped my phone, this time I had a signal. I quickly located him in my contacts and waited for him to answer. I felt tears welling up in my throat I chocked them back as best I could.

"Zoe?"

His voice was almost frantic.

"William I so glad you answered, he's here with Jenna and me. What do I do?"

I tried to keep my voice as low and calm as possible.

"Where are you?"

"In the village at the Town Hall Movie. What do I do? What should I tell Jenna she thinks this is a date?"

"Stay put I'll be right there."

"No William, she wants to have him back to my house for drinks should I take him there away from all these people?"

"I wouldn't mention that I'm meeting you there and don't let him see you scared he lives for that. Just pretend everything is okay. I don't know what he is up to but he's behaving very erratic."

"William what are you going to do?"

"Let me worry about that just get here safe if he stops at all or goes somewhere else you and Jenna don't follow him just come here."

"Okay, William he won't do anything in public will he?"

"I don't think so Zoe, just try and get there as quickly as possible. I'll be waiting for you."

The phone began to crackle and I dropped the call. I took a deep breath and closed my eyes as if when I opened them I would realize this was just one of my twisted dreams.

I saw Jenna washing her hands and realized I needed to pull myself together and do this.

"Well I spoke with William and he say's he will try to make it. I think William and Jared are having a difference of opinion right now maybe they can patch things up at the house so let's not let Jared know William's coming we will all act surprised if he comes. That way Jared will still come over and not feel badly if William can't make it."

"Sure, Sure I wouldn't want Jared going home just yet. How do I look?"

I wanted to grab the older woman's coat standing in line to put on Jenna she looked a little too good. I was concerned that Jared didn't have the same restraint that William did. As we walked out of the restroom my eyes searched for Jared in the crowd.

"There you are, were we to long? Sorry the line was crazy."

"No problem, where did you park?"

His hand around her waist made me cringe he was too close I didn't feel comfortable having him that close to her.

"Jared, Zoe has invited us over to her house for some drinks would you like to come?"

His eyes popped on me as if to search for an ulterior motive I kept a straight face and tried not to show how frightened I was by the thought of having to be with him another second.

"Sure I guess no harm in some drinks."

Pulling her closer as he finished his sentence but never taking his eyes off me.

"I did have an idea if you don't mind Zoe, I thought maybe you could drive my car back to your house and I could drive with Jared that way we have a little time to get to know each other."

His grin climbed one side of his face as if he was the puppeteer and her the puppet.

"I don't know Jenna I'm not used to your car isn't it a stick?"

"No silly and it's just a car."

She mouthed PLEASE... to me.

"Can I follow you back to the house then in case I have trouble?"

It's all I could think of I was quickly losing control over the situation but there was nothing I could do.

"We will walk you to the car and meet you at the light in front of Hannaford's Grocery store, you know where that's at right?"

"Yes, I think so."

They laughed and chatted back to the car Jenna doing all of the talking of course, every few minutes I could feel him staring again. I tried to ignore it and get my mind on what needed to be done. Once I got in the car I quickly adjusted my seat and mirrors and tried to watch them as they walked away to see what direction they were headed in.

Once they were out of sight I headed for Hannaford's, I knew exactly where it was. I searched for my phone and dialed William. The call wouldn't go through. I sat in front of the store waiting for them still trying to get my call to go through to William. The thought of never seeing Jenna again or having to explain to the Randall family that I am the reason she's dead was not something I was going to let happen. I was about to have a complete break down and then I saw headlights as it slowed and pulled beside me, I recognized the car it was William's Maserati and for a moment I felt relief until I saw Jared driving. He was really pulling out all the stops Jenna's face was lit up like a Christmas tree as she mouthed "OH MY GOD LOOK AT THIS CAR!"

I nodded for them to pull ahead so I could follow them. At least this way I would be able to go where ever he decided to take her. He drove fast and I had to push Jenna's car to keep up. He wasn't trying to lose me though because he could have if he really wanted to.

We pulled into my driveway and my heart fell there was no car parked. I got out and walked to the door. I didn't see Bailey normally he would be going crazy at the sound of a car in the driveway. I unlocked the door and invited them in. They followed slowly I called out to Bailey and went to peek around the corner bumping my head on William's chest. I looked up taking a deep breath he looked down and seeming as relieved to see me, as I was to see him.

"Are you okay?"

His voice low and concerned. I nodded and grabbed his hand squeezing it tightly

"I am now. Where is Bailey?"

"Andoe took him for a walk. Jared, I'm surprised to see you out with all the work you have."

Jared's face was smug and unaffected by William's presence.

"Wish I could say I was surprised William, but that would be a lie. You see Jenna, William considers himself well, my keeper."

Jenna smiled not knowing what to make of the conversation.

"I see you found the keys to the car."

"Well I have to admit it was a little more tempting than I could stand. Hope you don't mind I know how much your things mean to you. Sometimes you just need to push the throttle down and open it up, maybe even let off some steam."

"How about that drink? Jenna and I will get some glasses out of the kitchen and you gentlemen can have a seat in the living room."

The conversation was beginning to try William's patience, I could see the veins in his neck bulging.

I thought maybe if they were alone William could talk him into leaving with him and I could talk to Jenna. I was shocked that they walked towards the living room.

"Well what do you think? He's great right? What's going on with William he's a real buzz kill."

"Jenna there is a lot about Jared you don't know."

Her cell phone began to ring and she held her finger up for a moment.

"Mom? What's wrong?"

There was a long pause and she went to her knees. The phone still in her hand she stared straight ahead. I took the phone from her it was Justin's Mom on the other end.

"Mrs. Randall its Zoe? Is everything okay?"

Her voice was rough and broken with sobs.

"There's been a terrible accident Zoe, can you bring Jenna home?"

"Yes right now, we'll leave right now."

My heart was in my feet. I didn't want to know what happened, I wasn't ready to lose someone else but I knew I had to think about Jenna right now it didn't matter how I felt. I picked Jenna up and hugged her she wept in my arms. The sound of sobbing was more than familiar. I felt a hand on my arm as I turned I saw William standing there with Jared standing behind him looking confused. William shook his head as if to question the tears.

"I need to get Jenna home. There has been an accident and her mother needs her." "Do you need us to drive you?"

I was shocked that Jared would think of offering to drive. I briefly wondered what his ulterior motive was but quickly dismissed it.

"No, I think it's best if we go alone you both have a lot to work out. Please make sure Bailey is okay for me."

"I'll take care of everything Zoe, call if you need me."

As we walked to the door Jared leaned in and whispered into Jenna's ear. She nodded her head and began to sob again.

"I'll call you and let you know how it's going William."

Looking past Jared trying to disconnect from the emotion I was feeling. Even Jared as heartless as he was, he was able to feel compassion for Jenna. I helped her into the car and ran around to get in my side.

"You will need a ride home, Call me and I will come for you."

I shook my head and climbed in the car. Something in my chest felt heavy with guilt. I couldn't think about that right now I couldn't let my mind begin to wonder what happened and to who, I would know soon enough.

I would have normally felt comforted by William's words that he would come for me but they only made me feel more guilt. Jenna was in a ball in the front seat her legs drawn up into her chest. She was staring out the window, tears flowing down her face. I took her hand and held it in mine, completely knowing the empty feeling she was experiencing. All the things running through her head unfinished conversations, things unsaid, wishing it was you instead.

Chapter Thirteen:
Lost and Found

***

As we pulled into her driveway I took in a deep breath wishing I could escape from the days ahead. Walking into the kitchen with Jenna beside me I saw Maggie and Tiffany both sitting at the table with another woman. I imagined it was Taylor, Lucas's wife. She was clutching a coffee cup tightly and looking into it. Maggie had her arm around Tiffany comforting her as she rang a piece of torn Kleenex in her hands. Rebecca Randall was at the sink with her back to us as we entered the room she turned and ran to Jenna grabbing her and holding her they both began to sob again. I felt someone standing behind me it was Maggie, she took my arm and walked me to the living room.

"What happened Maggie? Rebecca couldn't talk on the phone and I couldn't get anything out of Jenna."

"The guys sent a may-day 8 hours ago. Their ship had lost both engines and was dead in the water, there was a nasty storm front coming through and they couldn't get her going. The last transmission from them came over 6 hours ago saying she was taking on a lot of water. The swells were 40 - 60 feet and she was getting rolled. There is a search party out right now but we haven't heard anything yet. Rebecca was trying to reach Jenna earlier when we first found out but she couldn't get through."

"Yes there was no signal, we were at the movie in town."

I had almost forgotten the entire Jared scenario until that moment, it was like a dull blur. I needed to hear Justin's voice to know he was okay. I felt terrible for everything.

He had been so nice to me and I had completely discarded everything. On top of that I couldn't believe I almost got Jenna killed tonight after everything they are going through. We sat for what seemed like an eternity waiting, Jenna pacing the floor, Tiffany had moved on to shredding the paper towel roll and Maggie and Taylor were sitting on the floor in the kitchen. Taylor was silent and still staring off into space. Rebecca was washing the counter tops for the hundredth time trying to keep busy. The phone rang and we all jumped Jenna started to answer it but looked at her mom and began to weep. Rebecca took the phone from her.

"Hello, Yes this is,"

There was silence and then she handed the phone to me. As I listened to the coast guard officer on the other end I felt my legs getting weak. I tried to focus so I could get the information for the family.

"We have found four of the nine so far. We did find a survival suit with no one in it but we are still looking. We will keep you a breast of the situation as we get the information."

"Where are the four being taken?"

“There are only three survivors so far Ma'am. They will be taken to Coast Memorial Hospital. I am sorry but the fourth was deceased when we found them."

I thought for a moment whether or not I should ask who they found. Who were the three alive and who was the fourth.

"Can you tell me the names of the men? Do you know who they are and their condition?"

"Well ma'am, at this time they are all in serious condition. The doctors at Memorial Hospital will know more. As far as identity, I know the three survivors are brothers, the deceased is an older gentleman we haven't had a positive ID on him yet."

I gave him my cell number to contact me as soon as he received word of the others, knowing that Rebecca and the girls would be wanting to head to the hospital as soon as I got off the phone. I wouldn't let myself think about who out of the four brothers had made it so far. I turned to hang up the phone and realized they were all standing behind me looking, waiting for me to tell them what I knew. As I looked at them each in the face I dreaded everything for them. I needed to protect them as much as I could as long as I could.

"They found Survivors, three so far and he said they are still looking. We need to get to Coast Memorial Hospital that is where they are being taken."

"Who did they find?"

I looked to see who it was speaking in such a small quiet voice, it was Taylor her eyes glazed and wide with tears pooling in the corners as if she really didn't want to know.

"They said it was three brothers, that's all he knew about the identity. They are still looking, they are searching in the right area at least and we should know soon. Let's get everything we need and head to the hospital to be with them, okay? What do we need to do? And what can I help with?"

Rebecca drew in a deep breath I'm sure she was torn as to how to feel, knowing that three of her five boys were found and two more still lost, possibly dead. I helped Jenna go upstairs and get dressed while Maggie made calls to take care of her girls. Tiffany and Taylor rode together to pack and meet us back at the house in an hour. I did a Map Quest search to find the hospital. It was about an hour and a half away, I decided to drive to the house and pick up some clothes and my SUV.
It would have more room than Jenna's car and I felt more comfortable driving it.

I made sure they were all okay before I left, their minds busy with getting packed. I waited until I got in the car to call William. I would need him to take care of Bailey for me and watch the house while I was away. He awkwardly asked if they told us who they had found, I am sure he wanted to know if they found Justin yet. When I told him I was on my way to the house he told me to wait, he needed to speak to me. I needed to see him, as guilty as I was feeling, my heart desired to be with him still. I drove trying not to dwell on the situation. I had so many feelings about the last month of my life that literally, I felt like if one more thing happened I would implode from the shear emotional overload. I pulled into the driveway and saw a large black escalade parked, William was getting out of the drivers side.

"Exactly how many cars do you have? No wait, don't answer."

"You look tired are you sure you are up to driving to the hospital? I could have Andoe drive you, I would drive you but I don't think it would be the right thing under the circumstances."

"No William really, you are doing me a huge favor just taking care of Bailey, I know you'll take good care of him for me. Besides you have your hands full with our beloved Dr. Jared. Speaking of him, where is your car?"

"Oh yes, I brought the SUV for you to take it will have more room for everyone than yours will. It also has GPS in case you forget how to get back to me."

He attempted a smile.

"Will you come in while I pack, we can talk more inside."

He nodded and we headed for the house. We went in and he let Bailey out for me while I went upstairs to find some clothes.

I quickly grabbed a couple pair of P.J.'s, socks underwear and the bare necessities. I just grabbed jeans and t-shirts and tossed them in as well. I was looking under my bed for my running shoes when he knocked.

"Almost ready?"

I looked down at my watch I had about 20 more minutes before I needed to leave.

"Yah, I think so."

He helped me to my feet holding me close to him.

"You will be careful won't you?"

"Yes of course I will, I wish I didn't have to do this. I wish it hadn't happened, this family doesn't deserve this."

"It's not about who deserves it Zoe, it's an accident no one can control these things. That is why life is so special you can't take anything for granted."

His hand brushed my cheek and he pulled me closer holding me into his chest I felt myself start to lose it and pulled back. His face looked surprised for a moment.

"I can't do this right now if I start I won't be able to stop. I have to think about them right now. I'm sorry I hope you understand, I appreciate what you are trying to do but I can't William. My only defense right now is to stay closed off with what is happening and focus on what I am doing."

"I'll be here when you get back Zoe, if you need me you know you need only call."

"Thank you, I will call and keep you posted. I love you William."

This time I stepped in and hugged him. His body drew in a deep breath the sound of his chest beating made me want to climb into his arms and close everything else off. There was silence for a moment.

"What's wrong?"

"You shouldn't."

"I shouldn't what?"

"Love me, I'm not what you need."

"It's okay if you don't love me back William just don't give me the, 'I'm not good for you speech.'"

"I love you Zoe, too much to be doing this to you. But I can't help it."

The thought of being so far from him was already difficult to deal with.

"I need to get going. We will discuss this when I get back."

I squeezed him harder. He lifted my face with his hand and looked at me, his eyes so dark but somehow softer than usual.

"Go take care of what you need to, we will be fine here until you get back."

I leaned up on my tiptoes to kiss him, as he leaned in to meet me. It was the feeling I felt when I was in his arms I was going to miss most. That safe feeling like nothing could ever hurt me. His kiss was gentle, more of a caress than an actual kiss, making me want more. This time it was William who pushed away.

"You need to get going, besides, anymore and you won't be leaving."

I wondered if by you won't be leaving he meant because he wouldn't be able to say goodbye or he would lose control and kill me. He picked up my duffle bag and I grabbed my pillow and makeup case and we walked out to the car.

"Please if you have any questions about Bailey or anything Text me, I won't be able to get calls at the hospital."

His face was confused for a moment.

"What, what's wrong now?"

His face was turning a rosy red color.

"I don't text."

"What do you mean you don't text?"

"I don't know how, I've never had to before I just call."

I couldn't help but chuckle under my breath.

"You keep forgetting deep down I'm an old man."

"Stop it, I'll show you here."

Reaching for his phone.

"Never mind, I'll figure it out. I do read, I'll work it out. You need to go."

"Yes I know, take care."

I hugged Bailey and patted his head.

"You take care of him keep him out of trouble Bailey!"

He loaded my things into the large SUV and opened my door for me.

"I hope I can drive this thing it's huge."

"You will do fine. Call when you get there."

He closed the door and called Bailey over to him. They stood in the drive as I pulled away. I had a pit in my stomach, it was building steam to be a full on ache. My trip seemed quicker on the way back to the Randall house. They were waiting on the porch for me when I pulled up. I jumped out and started loading their things in the back.

"Who's Cadillac Zoe?"

I turned to see Jenna on the driveway.

"Oh, William loaned it to us to use it's larger than my Range Rover."

Rebecca walked around her and placed her bags in the vehicle patting my shoulder.

"Well it's a lovely vehicle, who ever this William is, you thank him for us."

Rebecca's voice sincere as usual. Jenna gave me a look I wasn't quite sure how to take I didn't know if she was upset about the fact that the vehicle belonged to William, or just complete exhaustion.

"Jenna why don't you ride up front with me and keep me awake."

I thought I would test the waters to see if she was upset with me.

"I'll ride up front with you but you should know I get lost going to Bangor."

"Where is Tiffany? We are going to pick her up on our way out. She's just down the road from us, she needed some extra time to pull it together."

Tiffany was a mess when we picked her up. You could tell she had been crying, her round eyes were puffy, red and swollen from her tears. I turned the radio on easy listening to break the silence. Jenna stared out her window occasionally looking back to check on her mom. After 15 minutes the car was completely silent almost everyone with the exception of Rebecca was asleep. I saw her looking at me in the mirror and she smiled a loving smile that made me miss my mom. She had such a sincere face, like she could never say a mean word. She leaned up and patted me on the shoulders.

"I don't know what we would have done with out you Zoe honey you have been a tremendous help. So strong for your age."

She obviously had not heard of the numerous meltdowns I had on poor Justin.

"Well, I can't imagine what you must be going through right now but I want to do anything I can to help. You have all been so wonderful to me."

I was hoping the whole Justin and me relationship wouldn't come into the conversation but I should have known better than that.

"I know how much Justin cares for you. I've never seen him like this. That's how it is when you find the one."

I now had a huge burning hole in my stomach where the small pit was. I didn't know what to say to her. I couldn't be honest like I so desperately wanted to be, because I knew it would hurt her.

"Justin is very special Rebecca. He is an amazing person with an amazing family.
I'm just glad I was lucky enough to meet you all."

"The feeling is mutual dear."

She patted me again and returned to her seat. It was starting to get light out as I turned off on our exit. Jenna popped her head up to see why the car had slowed

"Where are we?"

"About 15 minutes from the Hospital I think"

"Is anyone hungry or does anyone need me to stop?"

I guess in hindsight that was a stupid question everyone in the car had only one thing on their mind and that was to see who was waiting for them at the hospital.

"No thank you Zoe, let's just get to the hospital."

Rebecca again was polite and caring in her reply to me. I felt torn and guilty, on one hand I wanted to know that Justin was okay and that they had found the others. But I wasn't ready to face him, not like this. I wish I were back at the house with William, lying on my bed in his arms. That's selfish I know but I had had all the death I could stand for one lifetime. As we entered the parking lot of the hospital I dropped everyone off except for Jenna. She had decided to walk in with me. The car was silent while I was finding the parking spot and parking, it wasn't until we left the structure that she broke the silence.

"Zoe, I was hoping you would do me a favor?"

"Sure Jenna, anything, what is it?"

"If Justin is in there and he's okay, please can you wait to tell him about you and William until after this whole mess is over? I just think it would be a lot right now for him to handle with this."

"Of course Jenna, I would never put that on him right now. I'll wait until he is ready."

She smiled and I put my arm around her as we walked in.

"They are on the third floor ICU, we wanted to all go up together."

Taylor's voice was barely able to keep its composure. I took a deep breath and we headed for the main elevators.

As they opened a flood of memories came back from when Mom was in the ICU right before she passed. The smell and noises where so familiar it hit me like a wall when I stepped out into the hall. The double doors looked monstrous to me, I had to fight to walk through them. Everything in me wanted to run back to the elevator. I kept my hand on Jenna's shoulder and followed her staying in the back. As we got to the nurses' station I heard Rebecca speaking low to the nurse asking to see the survivors found. Rebecca's voice perked up as the nurse told her they have found another survivor. And they are bringing him in right now. The nurse pointed to the glass row of windows on the opposite side of the hall. I could make out what looked like the top of Masons head. Taylor, Maggie and Tiffany ran to the other side, Jenna looked at me as if she didn't know if she should go with them. I pressed into her back and walked with her. I heard Maggie sobbing and saw her enter in the first room, Tiffany was standing outside the next room looking through the glass with a dazed look on her face. It was Mason, he was alive, I patted her on the back and motioned for her to go in

"He needs you now Tiffany. He can hear you talk to him, let him know you are here." Taylor was standing outside the door to the next room shaking her head

"It's Aaron not Lucas, it's Aaron."

"Taylor they found another, they can find them all just don't loose hope now. Let's help the ones we have."

I wanted to feel the same way she did. My heart sank when I saw that Justin was not occupying one of the rooms. Rebecca was probably feeling overwhelmed by the emotions of being thankful her sons were here but that she was still missing three more including her husband.

I felt as though I would pass out. Jenna ran into Aaron's room and hugged him. With no response, she looked up bewildered the nurse standing in the doorway of his room was who was watching her.
"They have all been through a lot and it's not over yet for them. They will need lots of love and prayers to get them through this, it's a miracle they even survived."
Rebecca asked her about the other survivor found she said they would be bringing him in within the next 20 minutes. I got Rebecca and Jenna chairs

"Taylor let's take a walk."

We walked out of the ICU and ended up near the chapel. We sat just outside, I took her hand in mine and held it.

"I didn't get to tell him."

"You didn't get to tell him what Taylor?"

"I didn't get to tell him I was sorry for losing our baby."

"Taylor I don't think you had anything to do with that and I'm sure Lucas knows. He loves you and you have each other that's all that matters."

" But family is so important to them and he has always wanted a big family at least if I was still pregnant I would have a piece of him."

"You can't give up yet he's just missing, not gone. We don't know but you can't blame yourself for any of this. Let's get you some coffee, you're going to need it to take care of Lucas."

I had a sick feeling raising her hopes, when deep down I was hoping they would be bringing Justin back. There was a thought plaguing my mind I kept dismissing, I had to keep it buried.
A voice kept saying it would be easier for him if he were gone then you wouldn't have to break his heart. But who would it be easier for him or me? We got some coffees and headed back up to the ICU. Taylor had decided to sit in with Tiffany.

Rebecca was in with Maggie so I sat in the room with Aaron and Jenna. The clock dragged by, I was surprised that I wasn't even tired it must be the adrenaline still in my system. I heard a buzzing sound coming from the nurses' station and saw two of them quickly walk out of the ICU through the staff doors. I stood up and walked out Jenna stayed not even acknowledging that I was up. I walked to the door where they had left. At first there was nothing but doors at the end and an empty hallway I waited anticipating their return. My heart was in my mouth that now felt like a desert. The double doors opened and they wheeled in a gurney. I could see blonde thick hair, I strained to make out who it was my heart was pounding with so many emotions, I heard Taylor's sobs.

"No, no, no, Oh God."

I turned back to see what she was looking at. It was Justin, he was so pale not his usual tan sun kissed body but a gray blue. There was a large gash over his left eye that had bled down the side of his face. He turned as they passed me, his eyes looking even bluer if possible, his face usually so masculine looked like a young boys. He reached out grabbing my hand,

"Tell them Lucas was with me, he was with me, tell them to go back! He was holding onto me Zoe!"

Taylor's sobs grew louder. I saw Rebecca wrap her arm around her and help her sit on the chairs in the hall.

"I'll tell them Justin don't worry they'll find him, just rest."

He held tight to my hand, I let my hand slip through his so they could take him to his room. I felt as though the room was whirling around me, I tried taking in deep slow breathes to get refocused. I ran to the nurse's desk.

"Where can I get a hold of the Coast Guard that brought him in? I need to speak with them."

"The pilots are leaving that just flew him in, but if you hurry you might be able to catch them."

She looked at the orderly standing next to me.

"Take her to the helli pad and hurry."

"Thank you."

I looked at Rebecca to get her attention.

"Tell him I'll be right back."

"I will Zoe, just hurry go, go."

Her voice was urgent and desperate. We ran through the halls taking a freight elevator to the roof. As we reached the Helicopter pad I could hear the noise from the chopper. I ran through the doors and into a tall gentleman dressed in an orange jumpsuit standing near the door.

"Hey you okay little lady?"

"Yes are you part of the Coast Guard?"

He looked down at his orange jumpsuit that had Coast Guard in big letters everywhere and then back up at me. I rolled my eyes feeling unobservant.

"Are you going back out to look for survivors?"

"Not sure yet but we probably will be as soon as we get fueled back up."

"The gentleman you brought in, are they still looking where they found him?" "Well, we were the ones who found him. I am sure they are covering that area very carefully."

"He says his brother was with him. He said he was holding onto him."

The man looked puzzled for a moment.

"There was no one else with him but we are still searching for the others. No one else was near him when we found him, but with what he's been through it's no wonder he would think he saw his brother.

For a while they might have been with each other but there are 20 – 30 foot waves out there and the currents are so strong it would be hard to hold onto anything. We aren't giving up if they are out there we will find them."

I felt my wall I had so carefully kept in tact since Jenna received the news beginning to crumble.

"Please... please, go back and look,"

My voice was breaking into a pleading sob.

"We'll do our best miss now go take care of your family let us get back in the air."

The orderly that had brought me guided me with his arm back to the door leading to the stairs. I suddenly felt a terrible feeling of hopelessness like it was already over. I sat on the top of the stairs not able to take another step. I motioned the orderly to go ahead, he paused for a second then descended the steps. I sat breathing so hard I felt like a pride of lions had just chased me. My brain was searching for something to lock onto. I felt waves of guilt wash over me, I felt so responsible for everything. As if some how, my love for William had caused a huge rift and turned everyone's life around me upside down. I couldn't bear to see Taylor's face again, that look of disappointment.

I imagined how I would have felt if they told me I would never see William again. I couldn't even let myself think it. I needed to get back to Justin, to make sure he's okay. I felt a strange vibrating sensation in my side I reached down to see what was causing it.

It was my Cell, I forgot I put it on vibrate. It was William he sent me a text. I sat looking at my phone, all I wanted was to be away from all of this and to be with him.

How could I be so selfish to care only for myself?

That was not normal for me I wasn't usually a selfish person. That in itself made me feel even worse.

I clicked on view wondering how long it took him to find someone to show him how to text.

From: William Madison
Sept. 02, 12:45am

Zoe, not really sure I'm doing this right, I hope you get it. I wanted to make sure you arrived and get an update on the Randall family's men. Please remember to take care of yourself .The Randall's are very lucky to have such a caring person like you with them. Don't worry about anything here Bailey is fine. Let me know when you receive this and if you need anything. I could be there in less than an hour.

Love William.

I took a deep breath. I can do this, pull it together Zoe! I text him back wondering if he would know how to open it.

To: William Madison

Sept. 02 12:55am

William, you did a wonderful job texting you'll be a pro by the time I return. They found Justin, his brother Lucas and his dad are still missing though. I wish I was with you, missing you tremendously. I'll call you when I can, I need to hear your voice.

Love, Zoe

I dreaded going back down to the ICU I didn't know how to face them all. Justin would be thinking everything was still the same as before, and poor Taylor and Rebecca. How does ones' life become so overwhelming and upside down so quickly? A year ago my biggest concern was getting home in time to make dinner for Dad and now I had to give up my pity party for the moment and focus.

I walked back down to the ICU floor taking in a deep breath before pushing the double doors open. Everything was quiet, I looked for Jenna she was in with Aaron still.

"Hey Jenna, I let them know about Lucas being with Justin he promised they would not give up yet."

"Thanks Zoe."

Her face looking worn she managed a half smile.

"How is he?"

"Aaron, he's okay, just a bump on the head and sore. They said he would make a full recovery after they get his body temp up."

"Have you seen Justin yet?"

"No, they took him down for x-rays as soon as he got here."

"Everyone else? Where are they?"

"Well, Maggie and Tiff are in with Colton and Mason, and mom took Taylor to get rooms for us all, they have a hotel attached to the hospital. I think mom just wanted to get Taylor some air."

"I have some medicine in my bag I brought in case someone needed it, it's to help you sleep. Maybe I should take it to her later so she can rest."

"She is going to need something Zoe, she won't recover if they don't find Lucas. I have never seen two people the way they are about each other. They are running out of time aren't they Zoe? I mean there is a time line isn't there?"

Her face was searching for something in mine. Hope maybe, but I was struggling to hang on to the last shred of it I had.

"Jenna, I believe there is a perfect reason for everything. I want desperately for them to be found and I believe that they will be. We all have to realize how lucky we are they found the four they did, and focus on being strong for your Mom and Taylor if they don't succeed.

Losing family is the hardest thing I have ever had happen to me but at least you are still surrounded by people that love you. You will never be alone."

"I know this must be hard for you Zoe and I am so glad you are here. You have become a dear friend in a short time. My family is very lucky to have you. Truth be told it makes me really not like this Uncle William guy a lot!"

She smiled and hugged me.

"I care deeply for you all and that will never change."

Chapter Fourteen: Answered Prayers

***

I leaned my head on my hands that were resting on my knees, trying to rest my eyes. As I woke I found myself in a darkened room that seemed familiar to me. I sat up and walked to the end of the bed, there stood a full-length mirror, ornate and huge. I strained to see myself in it, walking closer the dim light reflecting from the moon through the window, it illuminated my silhouette. The sheer white night gown glowed, the tiny straps held the silk fabric on my shoulders. I felt the tips of his fingers slide up my arms, making their way to my neck and tracing my shoulder blades. I closed my eyes feeling his hot breath on my neck. My heartbeat grew fast, I drew in deep breaths as if to slow it. Everything in my body craved his touch, his hands now moved forward tracing my hips and ribs carefully maneuvering around more sensitive areas. I felt his lips on my neck following the curve of my collar until I felt a sharp sensation, not unpleasant but unusual. His breathing became faster, deeper his hands less careful to avoid me. His hand wrapped around and grasped my neck I opened my eyes to see him, his dark eyes sparkled wildly in the moonlight, like a Jaguar making a kill.

His other hand grasping my abdomen as he smiled he revealed his stark white teeth they seemed to glisten, again I felt his warm kiss followed by the sharp sensation this time accompanied by a warm wet feeling as his head moved to the other side I saw the dark trickle of garnet spill down my chest, staining the white silk and spreading. Fear and excitement washed over me.

I knew I needed to stop him but I couldn't, I wanted him, needed him, the feeling was so strong it over ruled everything my mind was telling me. My William, my love, I would rather die by his hand than without him.

He whispered into my ear an inhuman growl, a purr almost like a large cat would make, as if to soothe me, his lips red with my blood. I tried to turn to face him but he turned me back to face the mirror, wanting me to see what he was doing. His touch was firmer now, no remnant of the gentle touch remained I felt him firm behind me. His hands pulling at my gown stripping it off until it dropped to the floor, I tried to look away not feeling comfortable seeing my naked body as he ravaged it. His eyes widened wildly at the sight of my exposed body. His hand held my face forward watching his movements in the mirror as I began to cry, not from pain but from such a strong emotion, I can't explain it. I have never felt it before in my life. My self-preservation mode had been switched off. I had no control over what happened nor did I want control, I just wanted him. There was a loud noise and I jumped.

"It's okay Zoe just a cart going by."

I looked around and grabbed my neck feeling for the bite marks.

"Wow, were you dreaming?"

I realized I was still in Aaron's room.

"Yah, I was dreaming why?" My voice was rough.

"You where twitching and breathing hard.
Jeez Zoe, you look like a ghost. Are you feeling alright?"

"Yah just light headed I'll be fine."

We both stood up, when we heard a nurse asking for the Randall family. I stepped out of the door.

"Here, we're here."

"We are putting Justin in his room now if you would like to see him. They had to do surgery he broke both legs the right in two places and the left well lets just say
he could be the bionic man now. They had to place a lot of pins and a rod."

We both followed her around the corner. I was having trouble feeling awake. The dream was so real and this so dreamlike.

"Here he is ladies try and keep him quiet if you can. He will probably be a bit groggy. The doctor will be in a little while to update you and check on him."

She smiled and left.

"Hey little bro you're supposed to stay in the boat right?"

His eyes opened as he heard Jenna's voice. He looked searching around her to me, his legs were in some type of traction device.

"I told them, I made him promise me he would go back, he said they would not give up Justin."

Tears ran down his face and his voice crackled and was rough.

"I got tangled in the rigging when she rolled, he cut me free. We both went in the water but I couldn't use my legs. He wouldn't let go of me, he held on so tight." "And dad Justin, what about Dad?"

"They didn't find dad yet?"

Jenna looked at me as if to ask me to break the news to him.

"No Justin, he and Lucas are still missing. Just try and rest you've been through a lot."

"Who else did they find?"

"Colton, Mason & Aaron are all okay and resting."

Jenna took his hand.

"They found Jack Kennedy but he didn't make it. Mom has contacted the family for him."

"Poor old Jack he was one of the last off. You know how he was always at dad's side."

He put his arm over his face to cover the tears. Jenna was doing her best to choke back crying.

"Jenna you can go back and stay with Aaron in case he needs you, I'll stay with Justin, he'll be okay. I'll come get you if anything changes."

She patted Justin's hand and hugged him.

"I'll be just down the hall with Aaron if you need me Justin, Zoe will come get me."

He nodded still keeping his hand over his face. I sat beside him rubbing his arm trying to comfort him. I had what I suspected to be the same feeling he had, running through my mind if they found Jack dead and he was with his dad the likely hood that they would find his dad alive was poor at best. That along with the guilt he was feeling that he could possibly be the reason his brother didn't make it, I imagined, was more than he could bear. I laid my head on his shoulder and held his hand. He lay there silent with tears flowing, his body would tremor intermittently for breath between tears until finally he drifted off. I woke up to the sound of Rebecca's voice in the hall speaking to a man. I stood and walked towards the door.

"What do you mean they are calling off the search?"

I froze, my mind trying to figure out what I had missed.

"Mrs. Randall they have been looking for over 10 hours in 55 degree water temperatures. I am sorry to have to say it but at this point we are looking for bodies. "

I stepped out into the hall,

"Rebecca, What happened?"

Her face blank and worn she fell to her knees, her hands on her face.

"It just hit me."

"What just hit you Rebecca?"

"This is really happening."

The nurse and I pulled her onto the bench against the wall and held her.

As I looked up I recognized the gentleman she was talking to, it was the coastguard I had spoken with earlier.

"You promised you wouldn't give up! You promised me you would keep looking!"

"Look Miss, I don't make the rules the storm is getting worse and as I said, we are at this point, looking for bodies, it isn't worth risking more men. I am sorry. "

I held her tightly.

"Where are the girls Rebecca?"

"I sent Jenna, Tiffany and Maggie back to the room to be with Taylor and I was on my way to get you when they came and got me."

"I am sorry you were by yourself Rebecca."

"But I wasn't Zoe, God brought me you. There are no coincidences. He brought you into our lives for a purpose. We will get through this. It will be hard for us all but we will get through it. He would want us to be strong my J.J. he never liked weakness. Taylor will take this very hard, we will need the doctor to prescribe her something."

"I will take care of that Rebecca. Why don't you go have a seat in Justin's room for me and let's let the girls get some rest before we break the news to them okay? I will go talk to the nurse about something for Taylor and make some arrangements."

"I will do that, I need to see him anyway. It will make me feel better to be with him."

I quickly left the room and headed for the roof.

"God I need you now for this family. They need a miracle they have been so good to me. Please show me favor with this man and soften his heart. They could still be alive, you could do that for them."

I pushed open the door to the Helli pad, they were already in the chopper. I ran over half bending, the sound was deafening. I banged on the door, the man opened it.

"I need to talk to you, please?"

He looked at me doubting and then signaled for the other man to hand him something. It was a headset and mic piece. He motioned for me to put it on.

"You have 5 minutes, go!"

"You can't stop searching, Lucas is still alive I feel it. They could both still be alive, they were both wearing survival suits that extends their survival time right there and they are both excellent swimmers. 55 degrees is not as bad as the Bearing Sea and they look for survivors for 6-8 hours there."

"And you know this how?"

"My dad, He loved to watch deadliest catch, but that doesn't matter right now. Please did you check where I told you his brother was?"

"We made several sweeps Miss, this isn't our first day at the rodeo you know."

He looked at me for a moment.

"Wait for a minute Okay?"

I nodded.

"Dispatch this is red bird two requesting an extend on the search for East Girl over."

He winked at me and smiled.

"We may have missed something in the storm and we would like to make one more sweep?"

"Roger that."

"Well you have yourself one more hour miss."

"Thank you, thank you so much."

"Now can I have my headset back so we can go find your men?"

I handed them back the headset and backed up.

"Okay God it's all you now."

I went back to Justin's room, I had made up my mind I wasn't going to say a word to Rebecca about the extra hour no use in getting her hopes up also. I would wait and let God be God. Last time I had prayed was when my mom got sick. She was the spiritual one in our house. She told me if God didn't heal her that it was her appointed time to go and that I shouldn't be angry with God. That was easier said than done. I wasn't exactly mad at God more or less mad at myself for lacking the faith required to get the job done. I sat quietly in the corner of Justin's room and watched, the time seem to fly by on the clock above his door. I listened to Rebecca hum a slow melody. At ten minutes to the hour I stood and walked to the door.

"Where are you going Zoe?"

"Just to stretch my legs I'll be right here."

Twenty minutes rolled by then another twenty minutes. I couldn't stand it why would they not be at least telling me they were done. What could be keeping them? As I walked back toward the room I heard a shuffling of feet and two nurses ran by me. I went straight to the nurse's station.

"What is going on?"

"They are bringing in two more."

She looked up at me in amazement and repeated it to me. I grabbed my mouth and jumped up and down, I ran to Justin's room.

"Rebecca, come quick."

She stood and looked at me tears in her eyes.

"They found them didn't they?"

"Yes, but how did you know?"

"I just saw them both when I closed my eyes before you came in, I saw them both safe."

Justin was still out from his pain meds. I took her hand and walked over to the nurse's station.

"I will call the girls and let them know. I'll be right back."

I left her and walked to the lounge were the courtesy phones where. Jenna answered,

"You need to get everyone and come down here."

"What's wrong Zoe?"

"They found two more Jenna, they found them!"

I heard her screaming and laughing and she hung up the phone. We all waited for what seemed like forever and then the doors opened and we caught the first glimpse of our two miracles. As they wheeled Lucas by his face blue and he was unconscious but breathing. Taylor grabbed his hand and followed them into the room. J.J.'s face was bandaged he was on a ventilator and in a lot worse condition than the others. Rebecca and Jenna hugged each other and held on to his gurney as they wheeled him to the room closest to the nurses' station. I felt an overwhelming sense of peace wash over me. I walked back to Justin's room the excitement of the last two days was beginning to show effects. I slid into the hard recliner/rocker beside his bed and let my eyes close. Thank you, was all I could say.

Chapter 15:
How to Break a Heart

***

It was hard to believe two weeks had past. Maggie and Colton had taken Aaron, Tiffany, Mason, Jenna, Lucas and Taylor home three days ago. They rented a van so they could ride together. I would be remaining with Rebecca, Justin and J.J. until they were ready to leave. Justin had another week of Physical Therapy before he could leave. The good news was J.J. would be able to leave in a few days. I didn't want to leave them alone and after Thursday Rebecca would be taking J.J. home. Justin would have been by himself. It was becoming more and more difficult to skate around Justin's advances. I had to change the subject of marriage and children numerous times. I would have to tell him soon. I missed William so badly, I felt like it had been a year since I last saw him and our late night phone calls just didn't cut it. It made me miss him even more, his silken deep voice so soothing and reassuring. The guilt was the worst though. I hated pretending everything was okay to Justin, when I desired William so badly. I had been thinking about my dream. I had been dreaming every night since I was away, always about Him. None as disturbing as the one I had my first night here, it made me blush to think of it. I walked faster careful not to spill the coffees I had stopped and got for Justin, Rebecca and I. Rebecca had taken up sleeping in J.J.'s room and refused to leave. Justin was going crazy not being able to walk or get out of bed. I was running out of ideas to occupy him that didn't involve getting physical. I had played the sore throat thing as long as I could. I was going to have to tell him soon.

I had a foreboding feeling every time I spoke with William lately I felt like there was something he wasn't telling me. He seemed sad, I don't think it was just me being gone that was bothering him. I desperately wanted to see and hold him. I snapped out of my daydreaming as the Elevator doors opened.

"Good Morning J.J. sure you don't want a Coffee this morning?"

"Nope, gave it up! Promised God if he saw fit to save my boys I'd give up all my vises."

Rebecca thanked me.

"Zoe we got some good news this morning they are releasing J.J. tomorrow morning. Are you sure you will be able to stay here with Justin for a few more days?"

"Sure I will, you need to go home and get some rest."

"Well, I thought if you wanted to take the afternoon off to take care of some things that I would keep an eye on the both of them."

As tempting as that was I would only spend the day alone thinking of William.

"No Rebecca, really I don't mind, I have some editing I am working on my laptop and I can do that here. I'm fine really."

"Well if you change your mind let me know."

"I will, I'll be back in a few to see if you need anything."

I met the doctor coming out of Justin's room.

"Miss Dossin good morning. We are going to miss you when you leave I think you missed your calling your a natural around here."

I wondered if my dad was smiling over that comment.

"Oh no I didn't, it takes a special breed of person to do this for a lifetime." "Well the only reason I'm letting him leave early is because he has promised me you would be taking care of him."

"Leaving early?"

"Yes, we just thought since his father was being released tomorrow that rather than have to have you stay here alone, well what's a few days, you practically do his PT with him anyway. I'll see you tomorrow when I release him."

I didn't know whether to be excited because I would be going home tomorrow or nervous. I hadn't gotten to tell Justin about William yet. I was planning on telling him on the ride home, when we were alone. I put on my happy face and went in.

"Well did you hear the good news? I am breaking outta here tomorrow morning." "Yah that's great Justin, I will call and get some PT set up close to home so you can continue to get those legs stronger."

"Yah, yah that's a great idea, but you will still be able to help me right?"

His face like a boys face would look his first day of school.

"Of course you're not getting rid of me that easy, I do have a lot of work to catch up on though. So you might have to settle for Jenna once and a while."

"Oh, yah sure of course, of course, I just thought..."

"What Justin? Oh see playing coy doesn't suit you at all. Just spit it out for goodness sake."

I had a feeling I would regret pulling his next words out of him.

"Well before I left I was...well staying with you, I just thought it might be nice to hangout with each other more. Maybe I would stay with you instead of home since there are so many at my house and I won't be able to drive for at least another month."

Yep, regret was defiantly the word that fits this situation best.

I was trying not to act out or show how I felt inside but I was screaming great and how do I explain to William that I have a guy living with me who is in love with me.

"And what do you think your mother will think about that? I don't think Jenna can cover that long for you."

"You don't want me to come?"

His face was more than pitiful I couldn't tell him no,

"Yah no what, let's cross that bridge tomorrow. Don't worry I'm not going to abandon you but I won't have your Mom mad at me either!"

"Doc says I can walk some today. He thinks it would be good practice to walk around the hospital maybe even outside."

"Well only if you promise to put something on that doesn't show your underwear."

"You don't like my stylish gowns? I was thinking of swiping a few for home. Seriously you girls got it made there is a certain freedom that comes with the whole gown thing."

"Justin I think they have you on to many medications!"

"It's good to hear you laugh Zoe. I haven't heard you laugh since you got here." "I'm sorry, I didn't mean to be so serious. It's just I was so worried about your family."

"I know it had to be hard to come here after losing your dad. I am glad you came and stayed."

"Justin of course I would come, your family means a lot to me you have all been so wonderful."

"My family means a lot to you as a whole? So what do I mean to you Zoe?"

"Justin, we can have this conversation later, lets get you dressed while it's warmer out."

"See you keep doing that to me Zoe, you keep blowing me off when I try to talk to you about us, why? What's going on with you? You seem so different with me."

"Justin a lot is going on actually and I would rather wait until we get home to discuss it. This is not the place for that discussion. You have a long road ahead of you to recover and you don't need to be exhausting yourself with this, I'm here now isn't that enough?"

"What the heck does that mean exactly Zoe? I'm here now."

His voice was raising and the machine monitoring his heart rate began to ping louder.

"Justin, you're getting yourself upset. Please calm down,"

"No, you're upsetting me because you aren't telling me something, I can tell Zoe, for God sake what is the matter with you? You're acting like I'm your brother, I wasn't your brother 2 months ago."

I felt myself tearing up, I was not going to tell him about William not here and not now.

"Justin I care about you or I wouldn't be here and I understand how stressful this has been but this conversation you are wanting to have right now is not going to happen. I am not ready to have it with you and you aren't ready either."

"You don't know what I'm ready for Zoe, after you almost die and lose your whole family you start to put things into prospective and I know what I want. I want you, I want you and me and a family of my own."

The lump that had been in the pit of my stomach was now in my throat and I felt like I wanted to run.

"Zoe I know this is fast and I know you have been through a lot but you should be able to see where I am coming from. I don't want to wait for my life to start. I want it to start now, with you."

I couldn't do this not now. I felt myself give in to my desire for self-preservation and before I knew it all I could hear was Justin calling my name. I was in the stairwell two flights down before I took a breath. I didn't stop until I was out past the courtyard, near the park, adjacent to the hospital. I followed the path down past the swings into a sunny spot, it was getting cooler out and I was wishing I had my warmer sweat jacket on. I had a miserable feeling inside, I hated what had just happened and I felt awful for walking out knowing he couldn't chase me. But I couldn't hurt him not now and not like that. Now more than ever I knew it wasn't meant to be. He wanted a family, a family I would never be able to give him. I needed William and he could never be that for me, as much as I cared about him my heart belonged to William and deep down I knew it always had.

I wanted to try and figure out what to do about Justin but my mind was on William. He had sounded distant last night when we spoke like he was sad. I couldn't put my finger on it maybe he just missed me. When I asked him about Jared he just said he was dealing with him and he would be leaving soon.

I couldn't wait to see him again. How was I going to deal with Justin? What do I tell him about staying with me? When he found out I was with William he would be so hurt and he was liable to go ballistic. How the heck was I going to explain to William that I had Justin staying with me? I didn't want to hurt him either, he had been so nice through everything. I started to walk back toward the hospital I would be able to think clearer if my teeth weren't chattering. I would try and keep Justin off the subject of staying with me until I could think of how I was going to handle it.

I made it back up to Justin's room only to find him standing on his own in the corner trying to put on his shorts over his casts.

"Hey need some help?"

I walked over to him and put my shoulder underneath his arm to support him. He hugged me tightly.

"I am so sorry I did that, I don't know what's wrong with me lately that's not me I mean normally. I just don't feel like myself right now. Please don't be mad."

"What do you think you were doing getting dressed by yourself?"

"I wanted to find you and tell you I was sorry. I didn't realize what a cripple I am. No wonder you don't want me."

"Justin I swear, you are acting like a girl right now. That whole feeling sorry for yourself thing, not attractive!"

He smiled and we both laughed. I helped him finish getting dressed and we walked to the cafeteria to have some lunch we sat and talked about everything but what I know he really wanted to.

I was glad he had let it go for now. I had decided while we were talking to let him come stay for a while. I owed him that much and maybe the time would help him see how not meant for each other we are. That was my plan anyway. The day flew by and after I left his room for the night I practically ran back to my room, I couldn't wait to talk to William. I quickly changed into my Pajamas before I could call him my phone rang.

"William, I was getting ready to call you."

There was a long pause

"Zoe? "

"Yes, William can you hear me?"

"It's a bad connection."

"Where are you? You sound like you're in a wind tunnel."

"No I am getting on a plane, I had to leave for a while to take care of something that came up. Don't worry about Bailey he is at your house with Darlei."

"When will you be back? I'm coming home tomorrow."

"I'll be back soon as I can probably won't be able to reach me on my cell phone so I will call you when I can-"

"William, is everything okay? William?"

There was another long pause and then static. My heart sank he was being so secretive. I can't believe I'm not getting to see him tomorrow.

I tried to call him back several times but it just went to a message that said his number was out of range. I flopped down on the bed and buried my face in the pillow. My mind retracing the conversation we had just had.Why was he being so cold his voice not warm like before. Was he mad at me for being gone so long? Maybe he was jealous because I was with Justin?

I spent the next 8 hours trying to figure it out.

I hoped it wasn't Jared, I hoped that he hadn't been forced to do anything extreme with Jared. It was 4am the last time I looked at the clock. I woke to the alarm on my phone going off. It was 7 am they would be releasing Justin and J.J. early they said so I needed to get myself together. I took a quick shower and put on my jeans and sweatshirt no need to get dressed up now I wouldn't be seeing William for a while.

I checked out of my room, gassed up the SUV, picked up some snacks for the ride home and headed back to the hospital. I was still cloudy about what had happened with William last night but I kept telling myself it would only be a couple of days and he would be back, maybe a week.

The doctor was in with Justin when I arrived to his room.

"Well he's all yours they will bring up a chair to take him down and then you're free.

Now Justin has promised me he would continue with his PT another 3 – 4 months at least. I gave him the number and name of a doctor closer to where you live for his post-op check in 2 weeks."

"Thank you doctor, I'll make sure he does everything he is supposed to."

I looked past the doctor to Justin smiling from ear to ear.

"I guess someone is happy to be going home huh?"

"Can't wait to get going."

"I can see you already got dressed."

"Yep but I had help my mom came in earlier and gave me a hand getting my stuff for my shower together and then helping me get dressed. They brought me a walker instead of crutches though so now I look like an old fart."

"You could never look like an old fart. Besides we can have that pimped out for you when we get back home."

"Ha, ha very funny, this has been really hard on a guys ego yah know."

"Oh yah, especially the part where the cute blonde nurse comes in and gives you a sponge bath and changes your sheets?"

"It's hard to be reliant on other people."

He was barely able to keep a straight face.

"Did you eat breakfast this morning? If not I can stop and get something for you on our way home. I gassed up the car and got you some snacks for the ride back."

I suddenly realized I sounded like I was talking to a kid.

"Sorry the mom in me is on overload lately."

"See you would make a great mom."

"Yah until I told you it was bedtime."

It came out before I thought and completely wrong.

"I would never get mad if you told me it was bedtime."

He batted his eyes at me.

"Okay Sparky, as you can see I'm not on my game today so cut me some slack."

I gathered his bags and placed them near the door. Thinking about what he said about me being a good mom, it never bothered me that I couldn't have children until I met Justin. Not that I want his children, but his family makes it seem so different than I always thought it was. I could hear J.J. and Rebecca's voices in the hall

"Are you ready to break out kiddo?"

J.J. peeked his head around the corner startled to see us standing there.

"Waiting for my chariot dad."

The cute little blonde nurse came from behind J.J. how fitting that she would take Justin down. I looked at them thinking what a perfect pair, both of them beautiful, perfect hair, teeth and I bet she can have children. But she was too ditsy, not smart enough for him. He deserved the entire package.

Now I sound like William. I offered the front seat to J.J. but he insisted on sitting in the back with Rebecca, Justin had a little trouble at first getting into the SUV but we managed.

"Hey nice rental."

"Oh it's no rental Justin, Zoe's uncle let us borrow this lovely vehicle."

"Uncle? What Uncle is that?"

I loved Rebecca more than anything but I suddenly wanted to kill her.

"Not really my uncle just a family friend. Okay, everyone belted in?"

I was avoiding his look because I could feel it burning into the side of my face. I searched for my seatbelt to make the annoying dinging sound in the car stop. I felt his hand grasp mine and gently guide it to the latch. I had a brief flash back of the night William told me who he was. It made me miss him even worse.

"Thanks I've been having problems with those lately."

I tried to half smile still not making full eye contact. Justin reached over straining to turn on the radio and find a station. He scanned through checking each station stopping on an oldies station.

"Rebecca likes oldies."

He whispered, I nodded in agreement with his choice.

"So Justin, I was thinking dear, we are going to have to move your room down to the den, because you shouldn't be having to go up and down those stairs all the time, they are to steep."

"Well actually Rebecca, I was thinking that Justin should come stay with me. You will have your hands full with J.J. and Aaron there and I work out of my house so I will be home all day if Justin needs anything. I spoke with Jenna and she said she would come stay in the evening and at night with us to help. He would still have to go up stairs but they aren't quite as steep as yours and not as many."

"Zoe, you have done so much already, are you sure he wouldn't be a burden?" "Ah hello I'm right here, adult able to make up my own mind. You are both acting like I'm not in the car or like I'm a little kid."

"Well someone took they're crabby pills today."

"Mom please,"

"Really Rebecca, leave the boy alone he can decide for himself and if he doesn't go stay over there maybe I will to get away from Aaron and Jenna fighting all the time."

I could see Rebecca rolling her eyes in the rear view mirror.

"Rebecca, I am sure he won't be a burden but it is up to you Justin, whatever you chose is fine. And J.J. you are always welcome to come stay with me if Justin chooses to stay home."

I looked over to see if he was still listening, he was facing the window looking out.

"Justin? So what do you think?"

"You called Jenna? Why?"

His voice was quiet and stern.

"I thought it would be better because of your mom. Are you mad?"

Making sure to speak softly so as not to be over heard.

"It doesn't matter, I should probably just go home anyway, she's right I will just be in your way."

"Justin seriously, are you having another girl moment? Are you enjoying that pity party all by yourself? I've got some chips if you want food at your party."

I could see him grinning in his reflection in the side mirror.

"No, but I am hungry."

After a 20 minute deliberation on where to go to they agreed on fast food. The ride home was quiet, they all slept occasionally Rebecca would ask If I wanted her to drive. I was trying not to think about not getting to see William, and wondering if I did the right thing by letting Justin stay. Would William be hurt or mad? And the worst thing, when would I see him or speak to him again?

The ride back seemed to go a lot faster than the ride going there. As soon as I exited the expressway they all woke up.

"I'll drop you and J.J. off first and Jenna can bring Justin some of his things he will need. So he doesn't have to try and get out of the car twice. If that's okay with everyone?"

Turning to look at Justin I could see he was more than okay with that which worried me a little but we did need to discuss our relationship and the sooner the better.

"Yah I'm a little tired and I just feel like crashing."

I helped them with their things and met Jenna at the door.

"You gonna be alright until I come over later?"

"Yes we will be fine, really."

"Call me if you need me to come sooner, you sure this is a good idea? You have done a lot already Zoe don't you want to go see William?"

"I won't be seeing him tonight. Long story I'll fill you in later I promise."

"I'll see you around eight then? Let me know if you need me to bring anything."

She hugged my neck Rebecca came out to the porch and hugged me as well.

"You take care of yourself now dear don't run yourself down."

"I won't Rebecca, I will call if he gets out of hand."

We all laughed at the thought.

As I walked back to the vehicle I could see Justin's face, something was wrong. I opened the door and looked at him to see if he was in pain.

"What's wrong is something bothering you? Do you need your pain meds?"

He just shook his head no.

"I'm fine I just need to lay down I think."

"Okay it's been a long ride, I'll get you home and get you comfortable."

Bailey ran out to meet us Darlei followed and helped us in to the living room. After I got the bags in and Justin comfortable on the couch I walked into the kitchen to get him some water to take his pain meds.

"Master William told me to stay here while he was away."

"That's fine Darlei but I have a friend coming to help take care of Mr. Randall so I won't need you after all. But thank you for staying with Bailey for me."

"But Master William says I am supposed to stay."

"It's fine Darlei, I'll tell him I asked you to go when I speak to him. You won't get into trouble I promise. You can go ahead and send for the car to come and get you, I will be fine. You understand what I am saying right?"

"Yes, but Master William will be very angry."

"No, no he will be fine, he just didn't want me staying here by myself but I have friends staying with me now so I'm fine."

She looked at me for a minute and I handed her the cordless phone. She dialed it and spoke quietly in Haitian. I needed to make a mental note to learn how to understand it because it was annoying not knowing what she was saying. The refrigerator had been completely stocked and so had my pantry. I smiled knowing he had been thinking of me. I poured Justin some juice and grabbed an assortment of snacks and placed them on a tray with his medicine and water. Darlei had gone upstairs to pack I assumed. I walked in with the tray and placed it on the coffee table. He was standing staring out the window.

"You should have called me to help you get up Justin."

"I was just a little stiff and needed to walk around a bit. Besides I have this."

He patted his walker.

"Sexy isn't it?"

His voice was sarcastic and his face looked angry.

"Well alright, yes extremely hot Justin, now why don't you come have a seat and eat something so you can take your pain meds. You've had a long day."

"You know what, I'm not really in the mood to eat right now, and actually I don't want to sit either okay mom?"

"Justin what the heck is wrong with you? You are acting like a spoiled child.

Just sit down and relax you have been through a lot and it's emotional coming back I am sure you just need some rest."

He walked towards me his face still angry.

"No, what I need is for you to quit treating me like a child. And quit lying to me." "What do you mean lying to you? What am I lying to you about?"

"Who is William Zoe? Who is he because I know he's not your Uncle unless you're into that whole incest thing."

My heart was in my throat. I didn't want it to be like this, I didn't want him to find out this way.

"What are you talking about Justin?"

"Don't lie to me Zoe, just tell me who he is? When did you meet him? I was only gone a few weeks."

"I won't lie to you Justin just tell me what you are talking about so I can tell you what you want to know."

"Why would you text him you love him and miss him? When did this happen Zoe?"

"How did you see my texts Justin?"

As I said it I realized when I came back to the car why he was angry. I had left my phone on the console of the car.

"Did you read my text while I was helping your mom?"

"Yes but it was an accident I was trying to call Jenna and have her give you my pillow and I hit the view button. It was an accident."

"Justin, I wanted to tell you but not like this. I am so sorry, I know I hurt you and I never meant for you to see that. I was waiting for you to come back before I told you but then the accident happened and I couldn't do that to you."

"Oh yes, let's not hurt the handicap's feelings. Let's wait until he makes a bigger idiot of himself and then drop it on him. Just tell me the truth Zoe, who is he and when did you meet him?"

His voice was full of hurt. I hated the way he was looking at me as if I just pulled out a dagger from his chest.

"Justin his name is William Madison, I fell walking Bailey there was a storm and the rocks were slick. I slipped. I was hurt pretty bad and he took me in and fixed me up. I didn't mean to lie to you about the accident or William but I know how you feel about the Madison family and I didn't want to worry you. I didn't mean for it to happen, it just did."

"Wait you lied about that whole accident story? William Madison? No, William Madison, seriously? The one who lives in that creepy old museum? The place I told you to stay away from? Seriously? Unbelievable, unbelievable Zoe! Honestly I could have probably understood anyone else but you go find some creepy rich guy to fall for?"

"Justin he is not creepy, it's not how you think. He's not what you think."

I wanted to defend William but the guilt I felt over the situation was making it difficult to do.

"How is it then Zoe? I mean I know I just met you but I didn't realize that's how it is for you with every guy you meet."

"That was mean Justin, you know that's not how I am. I know you are hurt but you have no right to talk to me like that. I told you I needed some time before we got serious. I can't help that I love him, I didn't purposely do that, it just happened."

"I was giving you time, maybe that's what I did wrong if I had jumped you the first night maybe then I would have stood a chance, huh? Sorry that was awful. You love him really, just like that? You can't love him Zoe, you can't because I know how we are together and it's not just me who feels that way.

I can't be that wrong, you didn't even give me a chance. What a disappointment it must have been for you when they found me alive. It would have much easier on both of us if they hadn't."

"Justin stop it! I would never think that! I care so deeply for you and your whole family, I would never want to lose you. We don't choose who we fall in love with Justin it just happens. It would have been much easier for me to pick you trust me, you are perfect. But I could never let you settle for someone who doesn't love you as much as you love them. You deserve much, much more than that."

"Why did you let me come here, why would you do that to me? To make an even bigger fool of me? Oh wait let me guess to help with your guilt? God Zoe I never have ever let myself go like that. I can't believe you did this."

So many feelings were going through my head. I wanted to console him, make this go away for him but nothing I said would ever take the hurt away. I sat looking at the floor at the end of the sofa. I wanted to cry desperately but I felt numb, like all my emotion had been drained from my body.

"Are you just going to sit there? Zoe I wont except this, I can't, your wrong he has done something to you. I noticed right away there was something different about you. It's not like you to sit so obtuse and not even show any emotion. What did he do to you Zoe?"

I felt anger building up inside of me. I tried to make it go away but he wouldn't let it go he wouldn't stop.

"Is that it Justin? I can't just be in love with another man? It has to be something he did. I have never felt like this about anyone not even my parents.

Trust me when I say he has tried to keep me from wanting to be with him. I have to be with him Justin, I can't explain it. Not in words, I am so sorry you were hurt, I am sorry I hurt you. I would rather have been hurt myself ten times over than hurt you. You can't know how awful I feel, and if I had any control over how I feel I would have picked you. Please, I know you are hurting right now but don't hate me Justin, I couldn't bear it. You deserve someone who can give you everything you want. There is a person for you but it's not me. You would just end up regretting your decision if we were to be together, trust me."

He was standing in front of me now. I looked up to see his blue eyes glistening with tears.

"Not him Zoe, anyone, anyone else but him. He's evil, that house is evil, I won't let you do this. You don't know what he is, you're too trusting and too good to even begin to know how dark that whole family is."

I wanted to explain exactly how much I did know but I would never tell anyone about who or what William really was.

"Justin listen to yourself, William is secretive and he is reclusive but with good reason. He is a very caring person and not at all how you are making him out to be. You think I am honestly that naive? Look I don't want to fight anymore, I don't want to say hurtful things or have you say them because you're hurting. I wanted you to stay with me because I care about you and I want to make sure you understand that.

I will be here for you always but I can't be there in the capacity you are wanting. Please just let this all sink in Justin, you have been through so much and I never wanted you to find out like that."

"It was his Escalade that you brought us home in, wasn't it? Does he know I'm here? You both must have been laughing at me while I was spilling my heart out to you in the hospital. Must have been a real ego boost for him to know he beat a cripple out of having you. Don't do this Zoe, don't let him do this to you."

"Justin what are you talking about? He has been nothing but supportive and understanding about this whole ordeal. And you are not a cripple I really can't bear to hear you say it again. You might walk with a slight limp I really don't think that categorizes you as a disabled person. You are being so self righteous right now it makes me sick to hear you talk like this."

"You were seeing him when I was in last weren't you? I can't stand to think about him touching you or putting his creepy hands on you."

"I am not having this conversation until you get a grip on yourself."

I stood and pushed past him.

"Don't let me stand in your way Zoe, I hope I don't see him."

I turned quickly back at him

"Or what Justin? This is my house and he is as welcome in it as you are. So don't you throw your threats around here Justin Randall."

I turned again before he could rebuttal I could hear him mumbling in the living room. I went into my workroom and closed the door. I had just sat down when I heard a tap on the door.

"Justin I need some time to think, please?"

"It's Darlei miss,"

"Come in,"

Her face was red and she looked like she was uncomfortable.

"What's wrong Darlei? Is it William?"

"Yes and no miss, he tells me to look over you while he is gone, but you send me away and I cannot look after you. I don't want to make you mad but I don't want him to be mad either and this young man who stays, he is angry at you I don't think I should go."

"No, no really Darlei I will be fine, Mr. Randall is just feeling poorly right now he means me no harm. Do you know where Master William is?"

"Yes he had to go with Dr. Craig back to Haiti something is very wrong down there, they were in a hurry when they left. Master William, he made me promise to not leave your side and watch over you."

"Yes I got that part but what is wrong Darlei, do you know? Was Dr. Craig
behaving badly again?"

"I don't know miss, all I know is Master William seemed very sad when he left."

"Thank you Darlei, If you could go back to the house and find out what is going on for me you can come back later this evening okay? I just want to know that he is okay so find out what you can, see if he has contacted anyone and let me know."

She reluctantly nodded and I walked her to the door where the car was waiting.

"Is that his spy, so I don't try anything while I'm here?"

"No Justin, not that it is any of your business but she was nice enough to stay here with Bailey while I was helping your family. Now why don't you sit yourself down and remember who you are and stop feeling so sorry for yourself. Nobody is spying on you or me!"

I walked towards the kitchen looking out over the gloomy autumn day wishing he were here with me sitting on the porch watching the waves pound against the rocks. We never really had a day together, not really, I just want that.

Why is it that I feel guilty for wanting that? Everyone has the right to be happy, why do I care what everyone thinks? I looked at my phone and tried to text him I knew it wouldn't go through but I so desperately needed to speak with him to know he was okay.

The next few weeks went by slowly, each day Darlei would go back to the
house to see if they had heard from William and each day nothing. Justin's sulking had turned into something a little more tolerable. At least he stopped staring at me like I was the devil. As much as I was missing William, I don't know what I would have done without Jenna and Justin distracting me, the only alone time I really had was at night and my dreams kept me company in their absence. We had been playing every board game in the house and because of the cheating on Justin's behalf Jenna and I had all but become his servants.

We didn't mention William's name we just kept our conversation away from anything that might bring it up again, thankfully. It was hard to believe September was gone and October was almost at an end. I had forgotten how quickly it turns cold here. Jenna and I had spent an entire day packing up all the summer stuff. Justin only had one more week until he would be able to drive. He was already cheating and going up & down the stairs 50 times a day when he thought we weren't looking. We were getting ready for a bad storm front coming through it was supposed to be a nasty one with sleet and freezing rain, unusual so early even for Maine. We had wood on the porch and in the house. Jenna had brought over lanterns and some candles in case we lost our power. We had decided on an early dinner just in case, which I have been told happens often in cold weather here. I was worried about Darlei usually she was back before now. I tried to call the house but there was no answer.

"Hey Jenna,"

Speaking quietly so Justin wouldn't hear.

She turned and faced me.

"I think I am going to go check on Darlei I'm worried about her she should have been back by now."

"Are you sure you should do that its already starting to look pretty bad out Zoe. Maybe she just decided to stay there."

"No, I thought about that but I tried to call and no answer, and besides when I mentioned that to her earlier she was adamant that she was coming back. I'll be back in like 20 minutes tops I promise. Just cover for me okay."

She gave me her playing dumb look.

"Please Jenna you know darn good and well what I am talking about!"

"Fine but if you are gone more than 40 minutes I am throwing you under the bus!"

"Thanks, a lot!"

"You should probably wear your parka it's really cold out there. Where exactly should I tell him you are going?"

"Tell him I had to get some woman things from the store or something he won't ask a lot of questions about."

"You really don't know my brother do you?"

"Really Jenna? I don't have time for your antics right now just do it."

"Alright, alright, go out the back I'll wait a while before I go in there that way he won't know when you left."

"That's my girl. Thanks I'll be right back."

Chapter Sixteen: Cannibals and Blowfish

***

I grabbed my boots and Parka and put them on, I felt in my pocket for my gloves. I was already shivering and I wasn't even outside yet. I took Williams SUV it would look less conspicuous pulling into the driveway at his house. I began to think of what could be keeping Darlei. The roads were getting icy but still drivable, maybe Jenna was right she just decided to stay there but something deep inside didn't agree with that at all. It only took me about 10 minutes to get to his driveway. As I pulled in I noticed large trucks parked in the rear behind the breezeway. I pulled to the front of the house and went to the front door. I knocked and rang the doorbell but no one came. I gently pushed on the door trying to keep the sleet that had started from hitting my face, my hood was almost completely covering my face. I pushed harder and turned the doorknob and it was open. I stepped in and quickly closed it behind me. There was no one in sight. There was a slight humming sound resonating from below the house maybe generators. I looked both ways to see if I saw anyone or anything moving.

"Hello? Hello is anyone here? Darlei?"

I followed the humming sound down to the left of the stairs towards the back of the house. My boots made a squeaking sound on the polished marble. As I reached out to grab the doorknob to what I thought might be a stairway I heard a scream but not like a woman screaming it was horrific like a large animal was being killed or tortured.

I instinctively covered my ears with my hands to buffer the awful noise. I forced myself to place my hand on the door knob trying to figure out if I should open it.

My breathing was out of control, I had to slow it down or I was going to pass out. All the while the screaming was relentless, it was hauntingly sorrowful. I pulled the door open to expose a dimly lit staircase extremely narrow for a house this size. I began to follow it down, it curved around until I saw the light getting slightly brighter. It was a blue colored light like an ultraviolet light or a black light. The screaming had stopped and I could just hear deep crying or whimpering. There was another door, it was cracked a little and I tried to peek in. I could see a metal table. There was someone in a white coat standing in front of it. And someone was lying on the table. All I could see was bare feet and jeans the man in the coat was blocking the other person's body. Suddenly the screaming started again, it was coming from the one on the table. I put my hands over my ears, it was awful I couldn't bear to hear it. The man in the coat moved away.

"William?"

I pressed through the door my hands now covering my mouth.

"What have you done to him!"

It was William on the table, his olive skin was red and his veins were protruding every muscle in his body shook. I started to run to him, to remove his restraints and get him away from whatever was hurting him.

"I wouldn't do that if I were you Miss Dossin."

I knew that voice, it still made my skin crawl.

"What are you doing to him?"

William heard my voice and looked at me his face streaked red with pain.

"Don't see me like this, please Zoe go you're not safe!"

His voice was rough and like a growl not human.

"Answer me! What have you done to him? I will kill you! So help me if you touch him one more time."

I now stood between William and Jared slowly backing up to William.

"Really Miss Dossin, I must advise you to stop, He's right you're not safe."

He nodded behind me I turned to look, the vessels in William's eyes began to turn red as tears rolled down them.

"Run Zoe, Get out! You're not safe."

His voice more menacing now, he began to pull at his restraints and screaming again. I had to cover my ears.

"Jared what is wrong with him?"

My voice was straining to be heard over the screams. He stepped closer and pulled me away quickly as William broke one of his restraints. Andoe stepped out from the other side of the room and held him while Jared adjusted the straps.

"Let me deal with him and I will answer your questions."

"No, no you get her away from here! Zoe go!"

William was fighting them to get free as if he was not in control of his own body. He was in so much pain, I had never seen anyone in so much agony. I could do nothing but watch. Jared started an IV of what looked like some kind of blood transfusion. There was another injection he gave him and he fell asleep but he was even groaning in his sleep. Jared motioned for me to follow him. I gave no thought to what he might do, I didn't care I only cared that William was in pain.

"Jared what is going on here? What did you do to him?"

"I have done nothing but what he wished. I administered the new dose of serum two nights ago usually it's a one time dose once a month, when the moon is at it's fullest I don't know how much that really effects it but it's become tradition.

The crops were raided again in Haiti and this time we lost everything but a few hundred plants. William decided to test the new dosing out on himself as we usually do, you see He can't die and I on the other hand am mortal and something like what he is going through right now would kill a normal human. I told him the first dose was to low it took six of us to strap him down. I have been trying to get the dose leveled off so we can keep him from hurting himself or anyone else. He has been rationing himself with the scrum lower and lower doses to see if he can get to where he doesn't use as much. But since you have been in the picture his testosterone levels are through the roof. He has been taking twice the normal dose to get it under control. Altering the dosage like that is insanity but he insists, all so he can be around his beautiful little red head. I've got to say I can't see why he would do it. I myself would just have you and then eat you. But that's just me being well, me."

His smile was cynical and disturbing. I moved back against the seat I was sitting in.

"Now is that any way to treat me? He almost got a little taste, you should be thanking me."

"William would never hurt me Jared, never."

"If that's what makes you sleep better sweetheart but I know how bad the cravings are, and I'm not the one who's dead."

"Is he running out of serum? I mean why is he taking half the dose?"

"Because he doesn't want to ever run out completely. He thinks by tapering off the serum we won't be as dependent on it. He loves to be in control Zoe, it's his way or nothing. And this discipline thing, well, he loves to torture himself. Some kind of penance I guess.

Never the less, he is trying to mix half of the pure mixture with half the synthetic we derived to, shall we say dilute the serum. Problem is it dilutes the effect and we can't seem to figure out what we are missing. We have tried everything. I know he thinks I hate him and sometimes I do but more than anything I want to protect him because if he dies so does my chance of ever finding a true cure."

"Cure for what Jared? And you are killing him every time you let him do this, he can't live like this."

"It's his choice not mine, you should know by now you can't make him do anything he doesn't want to."

I shook my head agreeing with his last statement. I did know how stubborn he could be, he was ridiculous.

"Will he be okay again after this dose?"

"I have no idea his levels are completely off the chart. It's like starting from scratch he hasn't been this bad well I would presume since the beginning."

"What did they do to level him off in the beginning?"

He gave me a bewildered gaze as if he didn't understand my question

"William mentioned a poison from fish they used for the first serum."

He rolled his eyes looking at me as if I was out of my league and I was, but more than that I felt desperate. I was not going to watch another person I cared about so much suffer.

"Yes, I know but it's not stable enough to use with the plant material, we have tried it trust me. It makes the hunger worse."

"I am no biochemist but have you tried it with the synthetic serum removing the natural plant material?"

The saying and the light bulb was turned on would have fit perfectly here. He sat as if conversing with himself in his own head.

"No, no that wouldn't work, but if I modified the synthetic material of the first serum and combine it with the natural Tetrodotoxin and plant material extract it might be enough of a difference."

"Yah, you lost me but it sounds like you're inspired."

"Yes actually, I can't believe it's so simple, so obvious!"

"So obvious even I thought of it?"

I would have been offended if I had thought about it.

"It makes perfect sense, I just have to find a puffer fish."

The frown on my face must have given away the fact that I had no idea what he was talking about. The sentence I need a Puffer fish was right up there with the one that had Cannibal in it, two sentences I never thought I would hear in my life time.

" I need the Tetrodotoxin from it. It causes paralysis in its victims but it has quiet another affect when used in combination with the serum. This might work but you need to leave now and let me do what I need to."

I stood for a moment not sure I trusted him.

"Personally I could care less if he eats you but it would cause him to lose focus and for now that supersedes my desire to kill you."

His remarks that once cause fear to stir inside me now only enraged me.

"Honestly, I have never met anyone with such a cut and dry case of Bi-polar disorder in my life. I am not going anywhere. I don't trust you anymore with William than I would a fifteen year old virgin."

"Ouch that hurt sweetheart, but you see the boys have work to do and you'll just get in my way, so shove off!

I'll make sure he calls you when he's all better or well let's just say, either way I am sure he will be paying you a visit. We will let that be his little surprise."

"I have never despised anyone like I loathe you Jared Craig. So help me you'll be in need of a Shaman to perform a ritual on your dead body if you let anything happen to him, do you understand me? You might crave flesh and lust women but something tells me a bullet right between the two little black dots on your face would put you out of your misery. Let me simplify it for you, I love him and if you screw up and anything happens to him make no mistake, I will kill you."

I walked back to the room where William was he was still half in and half out of it. I was careful not to touch him, I remembered him telling me it was painful after he took the serum to be touched. His body shook with every breath he took, every muscle twitching. I should be afraid but I wasn't. I bent down as close as I could out of arms reach and whispered softly as I could.

"I can't get close my love, I don't want you to hurt yourself. Jared is going to help you, I promise and I will be back to check on you. I love you William don't give up. I'm here don't give up."

Andoe led me out of the room and up the stairway. I felt a numbness wash over me, I desperately wanted to cry, scream, something but nothing came it was like I was empty. How much can I lose in a lifetime before I shut down? Is there a number of how much each person has to take before the hopelessness completely washes over you until there is nothing remaining of who you are? I can't lose him! I would not lose him, how could I? He is my breath, without him... I shivered not allowing myself to go to that place.

"Darlei and I will take you home Miss Dossin."

"No Andoe, I mean yes you can take me home but can I please speak with Darlei?"

"Yes, I will get her."

I looked out the window the weather was really kicking up. I was missing the Arizona weather right now, the view of the mountains from our living room and the beautiful dessert sunset. This was a far cry from the always-warm glow of the sun.

"Miss, you wanted to speak with me?"

She was holding her travel bag and had her coat on.

"Darlei I want to ask you a favor. I know you care about Master William."

"Yes Miss very much so."

"Yes I know you do, I can't stay here Dr. Craig wishes me to leave, but I can't leave William here alone will you stay here with him and call me if anything is happening that is not good for William? Could you do that for me?"

"But Master William he says I am not to leave you for nothing."

"Yes I know but he is very sick and he needs you more than I do. Please Darlei will you do this for me?"

She shook her head and patted my hand.

"Good, Good, thank you."

I wrote down my cell number and folded it in her hand.

"Call me if there is any news, I will be back tomorrow to check on him I promise."

I walked into the foyer.

"Lets go Andoe,"

"Where is Darlei?"

"She is staying here to help you look after William."

"Master William is not going to like this Miss Zoe."

"Not you too Andoe, he needs you more than I do right now.

Please don't let Dr. Craig hurt him Andoe, William trusts you, watch his every move let me know if there is anything that seems wrong. I will be back in the morning to see that everything is alright."

"As you wish Miss Dossin."

I pulled my hood up and headed for the car. The driveway was slick and it took some doing for Andoe and I to even get to the SUV. He had warmed the vehicle and it felt wonderful, I was going to have to get used to this weather something told me this was just the beginning of it. My phone was buzzing I looked knowing who it was. Jenna had texted me 15 times last text read,

"You have 10 minutes to call back or my crazy brother is coming after you."

I quickly texted her back,

"On my way."

The roads were terrible but Andoe was an excellent driver. Pulling up in the driveway I had forgotten about having to come up with a reason for taking so long. I had been gone over an hour and it does not take that long to get to town and back. I was not good at this lying thing, where was William when I needed him.

"This is fine right here Andoe, you don't have to pull all the way up."

I was concerned that Justin would come out thinking it was William and cause a scene.

"I will do everything I can to help make him well Miss Dossin."

"Thank you Andoe I know you will, he is lucky to have you. Please be careful going back."

He nodded and I held my breath as I stepped down and tried to slide my way across the driveway into the house. Justin was at the door with Jenna behind him and Bailey was at the window.

"For goodness sake people I am fine, it's not that bad out there."

"Who brought you home Zoe? Was it him?"

Jenna was standing behind him shaking her head, as if she didn't know what I should tell him.

"No Justin, his driver dropped me off that's what took so long. I decided to drop off the SUV and check on Darlei to see why she was taking so long to come back, if you must know. Now if you will excuse me, I am going to go take a hot bath unless you have something to say about that Justin?"

He opened his mouth ready to come back at me but before he could Jenna stepped in front of him grabbing his arm.

"No Zoe, he doesn't I will make sure little brother behaves himself down here. Go on he will be just fine."

Justin pulled away from her and walked into the kitchen.

"Zoe I'll come up in a bit and check on you and you can fill me in."

"Thanks Jenna."

A hot bath sounded good right about now but the only tub in the house was in my parents bathroom. I passed my bedroom door and went straight to the end of the hall into their old room. I closed my eyes taking in the smell of it. Even after all the cleaning and dusting it still smelled like them. I noticed Justin's empty suitcase was sitting in the corner. He had been sleeping in here because it was easier to get around.

He was extremely tidy, the room didn't look like anyone had been in there, except for the suitcase I would never have known. I started the water and went back to my room to get some clothes. I grabbed my robe, slippers, underwear and IPOD and headed back into the other room. I needed to relax and think about nothing for right now. The water had steamed the entire room and I dimmed the lights and got undressed. My mind was trying to replay everything that had happened but all I could think about was him.

I stepped into the tub and sank in it up to my neck, the bubbles smelled of lavender and vanilla my mother's favorite bubble bath to take. I adjusted myself with a towel under my head and put on my headset. I lay back trying to clear my mind I was having trouble getting the desperate sound of his voice out of my head begging me to leave. I could feel my muscles relaxing no matter how my mind was reeling, it was no match for the hot water. I closed my eyes trying to imagine him holding me feeling his warm breath on my face. Would I ever be with him again? We had only kissed twice but it was like I had never kissed anyone else. Like it was the only kiss I have ever known. The dream I had had in the hospital was emerging I kept feeling his kiss on the back of my neck. The euphoric feeling I felt, not caring what happened to me as long as he was with me. I sensed another presence in the room, I didn't want to open my eyes. I wanted to stay where I was it was probably just Jenna she would see I was relaxing and go away. I jumped when I felt the tap on my shoulder. I quickly looked up startled and removed my headphones.

"Sorry."

"Sorry? Justin Randall what are you doing? "

"I need to talk to you,"

"And you couldn't wait until I was through? Where's Jenna?"

"She fell asleep you've been up here a long time. I waited but since Jenna fell asleep and I figured you can't walk away if you're in the bathtub."

"Justin you can't be in here you need to go."

"Just listen to me Zoe please, I know I've been a jerk, and I know I have said some pretty mean things I can't take back, I wish I could."

"Justin we can talk but let me get out and get dressed and then we will talk. Please I'm freezing."

"Okay I'll go wait in your room. I'm sorry Zoe."

"It's fine I'll be right there just close the door behind you."

My heart was pounding still as I got out of the tub, I dried off taking my time hoping Jenna would wake up and save me. I let my hair down so it would dry and slipped my panties and robe on. I hadn't taken the time to grab my pajamas or a bra. I put on my slippers and began the dreaded trip to my room. The door was open and he was standing in front of the window. It made me think of William the night he stayed with me he stood in that very spot. I couldn't get him out of my mind I should have stayed there. I shouldn't have left him this was the last thing I wanted to do right now. I sat on the end of my bed toweling my hair dry.

"You wanted to talk Justin?"

"Come on Zoe don't be like that, I said I'm sorry, you don't understand what this is doing to me. I want you to feel like that about me and you did before he came around. I guess what I am trying to say and I keep screwing it up, help me understand. What changed? What did I do to make you not want me?"

"It's nothing you did Justin and it's nothing he did there was no drugging involved, no voodoo spell. I feel like he has been with me my whole life, I know him like I know myself. I can't explain it. I know it hurts you just to talk about it so why are you doing this to yourself? He is not better than you Justin, he's not smarter or better looking he's just, just, the one."

He was looking out the window now, I walked over to him and put my hand on his back.

"If this is too much to be here Justin, if it's too painful maybe you should leave. I feel like every time you look at me I'm hurting you."

He shook his head his fists clenched.

"Maybe I'm not ready to lay down and except defeat just yet. Maybe I should do what he does and just take what I want, is that it Zoe? Poor Justin he's so polite, but that's not what you're into is it Zoe?"

He turned, his eyes dark and wild no blue remained. Taking my arms in his hands he held me.

"Justin stop it, this isn't who you are."

"Really Zoe? Well good because you don't like who I am so maybe I need to let more of the monster in me out."

He pressed his lips on my neck holding my arms to my side. I pulled from him he grabbed onto my robe to pull me closer to him. I pulled away leaving my robe in his hands.

"Don't fight it Zoe you do love me, I know you do."

I wanted to scream but nothing would come out.

"Justin don't do this, please don't do this."

I grabbed the towel off the floor and covered myself he shook his head as he crossed the room. As I turned he grabbed me holding me to him again kissing my neck and shoulders. All I could do is cry as he held me. As he pulled the towel away I managed to scream his name.

"Justin!"

I jumped and slid under the tepid water as I woke up. I gasped as I realized I had fallen asleep. I heard heavy footsteps coming up the stairs. I could hear panic in his voice, getting louder the closer he got.

"Zoe where are you, are you okay? You screamed my name, is everything alright?"

"I'm in here."

I quickly grabbed my robe and threw it on before he came in.

"I'm fine Justin, I just fell asleep and slid under the water."

"Here let me get you a towel you're drenched."

I flinched as he came near me.

"Easy Zoe, I'm just reaching for the towel you sure you're okay?"

"Yes, I'm sorry I had a bad dream and I'm just a little shaken that's all."

"A dream about me? You did call my name, actually screamed my name. I would never hurt you Zoe."

"I know Justin, it's just been a long night. I'm fine now. Where's Jenna?"

"Oh she fell asleep on the couch watching her shows. She's a really sound sleeper."

"Well you shouldn't be running up those steps like that."

"Oh I just mostly used my arms on the railing I really didn't use my legs that much."

He struck a muscle pose for me.

"Very cute, thanks Justin I needed to laugh."

"Ouch, I was being serious don't make fun of the gun show."

"Ah yah, okay well I'm going to put some clothes on and I'll be down in a minute, okay? Really, I'm fine. Make yourself useful and get us some Oreo's and milk."

"Sure, sure got it, and Zoe,"

"Yeah?"

"It's good to hear you laugh."

"Go."

I hadn't realized that it had been such a long time since I laughed. I got dressed and went down stairs Jenna was still asleep on the couch. I turned and went into the kitchen. Justin had a plate of Oreo's and two glasses of milk on the Island.

"Hey you didn't have to get dressed up to have a snack with me."

"Ha, ha."

I assumed by the tone in his voice he was being sarcastic.

"What you don't like the torn sweatpants and old sweatshirt look?"

"On the contrary it's my favorite look any girl that can still look hot wearing torn sweats and a baggy sweatshirt well, enough said."

"Oreo's? My favorite how ever did you know?"

I said trying to change the subject.

"Wild guess, yah know one of these days you're going to turn into an Oreo or a peanut butter and jelly sandwich. You always take such good care of the people around you Zoe but you need to be selfish once and a while."

"Thanks, now who's being the parent?"

"Right touché, you seem sad since you came back from well you know, is everything alright? I know I have been a real jerk and I haven't been very appreciative of everything you've been doing but something tells me it's more than that. I can't say I'll understand but I will listen if you need to talk."

"Thanks Justin, I don't mean to mope but well I'm not sure I can do this, it feels a little awkward talking to you about this."

"Zoe, just shoot I'll let you know if I am having trouble with what you are saying."

I took a deep breath and blew it out. I needed to talk to someone and Jenna as much as I love her can be a bit ditsy. I debated about talking to Justin but maybe if I treated him like my friend he would understand that's what he was.

"I don't know where to start, I know you hate William and considering everything I understand. But when I went to check on Darlei tonight I found out he wasn't out of town as I had thought he was actually there at his home,"

"Was he with another woman? What a jerk!"

"No Justin, let me finish."

He really was usually better at this.

"As I was saying, I thought he was gone but when I got there I found out he was very ill. There was a Dr. Craig there Jenna knows him, anyway I'm just worried about him."

"Wow, I'm surprised you didn't stay Zoe. What happened?"

"It's a long story Justin, he wasn't well enough for company and actually didn't want me to see him in his condition."

"Well that I understand, I hated letting you see me like I was."

"Yes, I know as I remember you referred to yourself as 'The Cripple'. "

"What? I was feeling a little sorry for myself, okay a lot sorry for myself. So what's wrong with this guy is he dying?"

I wanted to laugh at the irony of what he just said.

"No not dying, just in a lot of pain and I hate seeing him like that."

"What's the story with him Zoe? I mean why all the mystery? Is he an eccentric, a recluse what?"

"Eccentric no, Reclusive a little but with good reason. I mean this town has pretty much written them off as Creepy right."

"Well Zoe the stuff that has been said goes on there..."

"Like what Justin, what have you heard?"

I wanted to see how far away from the truth the stories were.

"Like the fact that old Capt. Madison's nephew looks a whole lot like him. That there is some kind of cloning experiments going on there."

"Is that why you thought I was different? You thought he cloned me Justin?"

I had to laugh I couldn't help, it if only they knew. And I thought the real story was far fetched.

"Well did he? I mean you are different."

"No he didn't clone me, are you nuts! They don't clone people besides it takes years to grown a clone. Come on Justin."
"Okay well what is it then? If he's not a clone how can he be the spitting image of his uncle right down to the scare on his chin? They say it happened right before Capt. Madison died. He and his old man got into it and his father struck him with the hand he wore his ring on making that scar. That's why his dad went so crazy after he died, he never got to tell him he was sorry or so the story goes."
"I never noticed a scar on his chin, are you sure about that Justin?"
"You're asking me? I've never seen him you're the one in love, with him haven't you ever noticed. Maybe they are wrong."
"Well I know for a fact he was not cloned. They do look a lot alike but you look a lot like your grandpa."
"Yah Zoe but not identical and why does he only come out at night?"
"I can't answer everything Justin he is into research and is out of the country a lot. He is a decent person and I think you would like him if you knew him."
"I wish I could say I would Zoe, but something tells me no.
No one will ever be good enough for you creep or no creep. When we first got back and you told me how you meet you said he found you after you fell and fixed you up? He didn't take you to the hospital?"
"No he had his Doctor, Dr. Craig help him tend to my injuries."
"How could they possibly do that Zoe? What, they have an x-ray machine in his house? I mean that was crazy, most people would call 911 right?"

"I know it sounds crazy but like I said he does research he has a full staff and actually he does have a portable x-ray unit. He has a small clinic for his research in the basement of the house. Don't ask me Justin he just does. And no I'm not a clone, He is looking for a cure for his illness."

"And exactly what is his illness? Cancer, HIV what? I mean it's not something that would put you at risk is it?"

Wow, how to answer this one without having to lie.

"It's an uncommon illness I'm not sure what it's called but the medicine available right now for it makes him very sick. And no it's not contagious."

"Well now I really feel depressed. I thought maybe you liked him more because I was all gimpy and would have a slight limp the rest of my life but now I know I just needed a more serious injury."

"You are wrong, you know that? I didn't realize how twisted you are, that is not why I love him. And not why I chose him over you freak."

"You know I was just having some fun with you."

I felt better even though I felt like I hadn't really told him anything, at least he would maybe be able to be more understanding.

"Hey, you guys are having a party without me?"

I turned to see Jenna standing in the hall her hair was sticking out on one side where she had laid and she was stretching. I looked at Justin and we both laughed.

"What are you both laughing at? And who ate all the Oreos?"

"Sorry Zo, gotta throw you under the bus."

"What's with you two and throwing people under the bus, is it a family thing you do? And there are more just open the pantry."

We stayed up until about 3am talking about things we did as kids growing up, an only child compared to being the youngest of six. Jenna insisted that she would have been the perfect only child. It helped to keep my mind off of William and what he must be going through. I decided to turn in so I would be able to get over to William's early. I desperately wanted to see him, I needed to know he was out of pain. Jenna was off tomorrow so she would be able to take Justin to his Physical therapy and I could spend the day with William, hopefully.

Chapter Seventeen:
My beloved

***

The alarm on my phone seemed to go off minutes after I lay down. I jumped up to get ready. I decided to wear a thick cable turtleneck and jeans trying to cover up as much as possible. I pulled my hair up and put on minimal make up trying to down play my appearance as much as I could and still look alive. If I was able to see him I didn't want to make him uncomfortable. Bailey was scratching at my door to get out when I opened it he bolted down the stairs. I looked to see both Jenna and Justin's bedroom doors were closed. I was glad they were still asleep. I wanted to let Bailey out to take care of business and leave. I poured Bailey his food and headed out the door careful not to make to much noise. I started my Range Rover, it turned right over amazing seeing as I had not driven it in over a month. I scrapped the ice off of the window and took a look across the water. The view was breath taking every branch heavy with ice and dripping. Good thing I had decided to wear my hair up it would have been a mess from this cold damp weather. The road crews must have been at it all night because the roads were salted and in much better condition today. As I pulled into the long drive I noticed all the large trucks were gone, someone had salted William's driveway because last night it was like a skating rink. I knocked at the front door and waited. Andoe greeted me at the door.

"Come in Miss Dossin, he has been asking for you." He led me up the stairs to the large double doors at the end of the hall where I had stayed. Darlei was standing outside the door, I handed her my coat and tried to fix myself before we entered. Andoe went in first and I waited out in the hall until he came back to get me.

I didn't know what to expect. I prepared myself for the worst, what exactly would be the worst?

I peeked around Andoe to see William sitting in a chair near an enormous window that over looked the water. His room was twice the size of the one I had stayed in.

"William?"

"It's okay Andoe, she's fine you may go."

I walked closer to where he was sitting. It was unusual for him to not stand he must be extremely weak. His olive skin had returned to its proper color and his dark hair was still wet from what I assumed was a shower. He was wearing a white cotton shirt unbuttoned exposing his chest not as formal as he usually dressed and I had never seen him in jeans. As sick as he had been last night I could hardly tell he was under the weather.

"How is your pain level? I was so worried for you."

"I am feeling much better now that you are here. Andoe told me about what you did last night, I am sorry you had to see me like that. Jared tells me you are the one who came up with the idea to use the Tetrodotoxin & the Synthetic serum together. I can't believe we never thought to do it. Your father was right you did miss your calling."

"No, necessity is the mother of invention. I was just desperate. I don't ever want you to feel like that again."

"Well unfortunately that is unavoidable but it usually isn't quite so bad and since you have figured out a way for me to not have to be dependant on the plant extract as much I will be able to take the proper dosage."

"William, Jared told me you have had to take double your normal amount to be near me. Is that true?"

His jaw clenched and I could tell he was not happy that he had shared that with me.

"Jared talks too much. I am fine, I am just being cautious I will never take a chance on putting you in danger.

I want to make sure I am as careful as possible."
His brows furrowed and he had a half grin on his face suddenly.

"Am I to understand you threatened him last night?"

I felt my face turn red and felt ashamed that he knew.

"It's alright I have wanted to kill him myself several times. Although, I don't think I have ever threatened to shoot him between the two black dots on his head. He was a little thrown that you stood up to him. I on the other hand, don't ever want you to have a conversation like that with him again. He could have killed you or worse. I can take care of myself, I don't need you putting yourself in danger. I would never forgive myself if something happened to you especially if I were the cause. You're being quiet are you alright? You haven't said a full sentence since you came in."

I felt tears spilling from my eyes it was all catching up with me. I hadn't seen him since before I left which felt like an eternity. I felt stupid to cry, dumb tears.

"Zoe what did I say? I'm sorry,"

He stood and held to the chair.

"No William, I'm fine. I was just so worried and all I want to do right now is hold you and make sure you are okay. I've missed you so much, I don't ever want to be away from you that long again."

I took a few steps forward, stopped and looked at him questioning his acceptance of my close proximity. He nodded to me as if he understood my question without a word spoken.

"Zoe I wouldn't have you here if I didn't think it was safe for you."

"I didn't mean it like that, I meant will it cause you pain to be near me?"

He reached out to me and I flung myself into him. I drew in a deep breath, I felt his lips on my head.

"I missed you, I wanted to tell you to come home every night that we spoke. I wanted to tell you to let that Randall boy have his family take care of him and selfishly have you all to myself. I guess I should ask how he and his family are."

"They are fine, he and Jenna, are staying with me until next week when he can get around better."

"I assume you haven't told him about me then?"

His chest drew in deeper breaths now.

"Yes actually, I assumed Darlei would have told you about our argument we had."

"No, she didn't mention it. Argument you said? Did he act inappropriately towards you?"

"William he was upset how do you think he would act? I told him I was in love with you."

"It doesn't sound like he took it too badly. He is still staying with you. "

"Are you jealous of him?"

"To say I'm jealous of him would be an understatement Zoe. He has so much more to offer you than I can. If I weren't so jealous I would step out of the picture and let him have you. But I can't even stand to think of him sleeping in the same house as you."

"Jenna, his sister, is staying there also he will be gone this week. Besides Justin has always behaved like a gentleman to me, and I'm here aren't I? I'm not going anywhere until you are better."

He pushed me back and placed his hand under my chin.

"Let me look at you. Something is different, your skin is lighter,"

"Yes, that's because it hasn't seen the sun in over a month. You are used to seeing me tan. I know I'm very pale."

I turned my face away wishing I had put a little more makeup on.

"No you misunderstand, I like it better it brings out the green in your eyes. You're wearing a little more clothing also. I must have scared you terribly last night."

"Yes you did but not like that, I just don't want you to have to send me away."

He staggered a little and sat back in his chair.

"William are you okay? Have you eaten anything yet?"

"I'm fine, I am still weak it takes a few days before I am 100% again, and last night took a lot out of me."

He pulled me onto his lap and I laid my head on his shoulder we sat staring out the window as I listened to him breathing in and out.

"I wish I were different Zoe, I wish I was the man that you deserve. I want so much to be that for you."

"You are William, you are my beloved, one whom I could not live without and when I'm not with you I can't breathe."

I placed my hand on his bare chest his skin was soft. I looked up to see his expression he was looking back at me. His hands tracing my features, he leaned in and kissed me gently starting on my forehead, then my nose, avoiding my lips he tipped my head back exposing my neck. He kissed down my neck, his lips gentle and warm and then back up pausing for a moment looking into my eyes.

"You are my beloved and I will never live without you."

He held me in that embrace, I wrapped my arms around his neck kissing his neck and chest.

" Is this okay? William, are you feeling okay"

His hand pulled my face to his.

" I am now."

I wanted him with everything in me, I have never wanted anything as much as I wanted him. I could feel him, his body temperature was rising, his blood pumping, his olive skin blushed pink.

"Easy Zoe,"

He whispered in my ear.

"I'm not superman you know."

I looked at his dark eyes and smiled at him.

"What are you looking at?"

He said in his amazingly sexy voice.

"At you, I can't stop looking at you, I missed you so much. Does this have to end? Can we just stay right here and never leave this moment."

"I will stay as long as I am able to."

"How is it that you are able to kiss me and not be like before?"

"It's usually better when I have first taken the serum but never like this. I think it's the new combination. Don't get me wrong I really have to concentrate to remain a gentleman but it's much better."

"Well I'm glad I wore this sweater instead of that dress then."

He looked off for a moment as if to ponder the dress.

"Do you need me to get off your lap? I'm probably crushing you."

"No! - I mean please stay I want you here, I'm not ready for you to go anywhere." "Are you sure? Please don't push yourself William I couldn't bear it if I caused you to have to go through that again."

"Just stay put and let me look at you, I thought about you every waking moment since you left. I haven't been able to do anything else. I think that's why Jared is so put off right now. I have been thinking about you and I and how much I love you. But I don't know what I can offer you. If you stay with me you will never have a normal life."

"William, without you I will never have a normal life. I don't want anything else. I am twenty eight years old and I have dated enough men to know what I want." "And?"

"William I want you, forever, if that means giving up what you consider a normal life so be it, as long as we are together. Hopefully you will feel the same when I am in my seventies and you still look amazing."

"Zoe, you will always look beautiful to me. I don't want you to stay with me because you pity me. I know you, you would sacrifice yourself to make everyone else happy."

"William..."

I kissed him again this time I turned around kneeling over him. I repositioned myself to face him. He looked at me for a moment.

"Zoe I don't know about this-"

I kissed him again.

"William just say the word and we can stop."

"Yes, but I might not be able to stop."

"Well you said yourself this was the best time to test the waters."

"No, I did not say that. Besides this isn't proper, I shouldn't take advantage of you like this. You have saved yourself for your husband it would be wrong of me to take that from you until you decide who you will marry."

"Wait, how is it exactly that you know I am a virgin or are you making an assumption?"

He swallowed hard and ran his hands through his dark hair.

"I'm not being dramatic Zoe, there is real danger."

"William?"

"I may have browsed through your journal, just a few pages."

"You what!

"You have to understand Zoe, I was desperate to know you, and I never thought I would even meet you. The smallest bits of information made me feel like I had a piece of you."

"That is not a small piece of information William, that's huge! I don't know what to say, if I weren't so turned on by you right now, I would leave right this very minute. That is unacceptable, you need to promise me right now no more stalking or invading of my privacy."

He started to object but after a few moments of silent deliberation he conceded.

"And for your information I wrote that in my journal Three years ago."

He looked suddenly disappointed.

"That is no longer the truth then?"

"That sir, is none of your business."

"I beg to differ I have a right to know if I need to hunt the lad down and kill him for steeling your virtue."

I stared at him allowing him to mull it over for a moment. It was cruel but he deserved it for spying on me. I leaned in toward his face.

"I assure you my virtue is intact and waiting."

I caught a glimpse of a relieved smile and then he put his game face back on.

"Are you sure you wish to go through with this once you give me that I can never give it back."

"William, who do you think I was saving it for? You ruined me for any other man years ago."

I kissed him again. He hesitated for a moment and then this time he kissed me back.

"Wait, Zoe are you sure?"

He looked into my eyes so deeply I caught my breath.

"Yes, I am so sure about this."

He stood up slowly at first as if to test his legs. He stepped back a little and turned away from me.

I knew he was trying to back out of this moment, find a reason to deny my request.

"William please don't, it's never going to make sense, being rational you will always find a reason to stop yourself from feeling happy."

He turned slowly and walked back over to where I stood. He looked at me again as if he was sentencing me to death. His face seemed worried, I took his hand and looked at it in mine so much larger so much stronger but just as vulnerable to love as I was.

"I won't do anything you don't want me to Zoe, I'm still not sure about this, we will have to take it slow."

"Yes slow."

I agreed looking up at him through my eyelashes.

"I promise I will follow your lead now just stop thinking so much and kiss me."

He shook his head and smiled, at me his hands gentle on my face, outlined every part. He turned me around and kissed my neck as I opened my eyes I realized I was standing in front of an ornately carved wooden full-length mirror. I tried to dismiss the thoughts of my dream as quickly as they came but the overwhelming feeling of complete euphoria was sweeping over my body. The feeling of not caring about the danger for your safety but the complete and total submission of your will to his was flooding my senses. His kisses burned into me, I felt each one deep inside wanting more of him with every touch.

My breath became faster his hands reached up and released the clip holding back my hair. He moved my head gently to the other side exposing my neck his hands hesitating for a moment, slid underneath my sweater as he looked at me in the mirror, his dark eyes full of desire. I lifted my arms as he pulled the sweater over my head and placed it on the chair. He looked back to the mirror his eyes devoured me.

I could feel his warm breath on my neck and shoulders his lips tracing the line of my neck and collarbone. His breathes becoming more erratic but no more than mine. He turned me to him and kissed me this time more intense than before.

"Is this alright?"

His deep silken voice whispered in my ear. I looked at him unbuttoning his shirt and pulling it away from him. His muscles tensed as I touched him, letting my fingers trace the outline of his perfectly chiseled body.

We walked together backwards still kissing until I felt the post of his bed at my back. He pressed against me kissing me, his hands still avoiding my sensitive areas. He traced the outline of my bra watching as if to make sure not to miss a spot. He kissed my neck and collar again slowly moving down. I gripped his thick waves of dark hair between my fingers, the heat from his body radiating like a furnace. He stopped and looked at me for a moment as if searching for any sign of protest. I felt the intensity in his eyes and hoped he could feel the same in mine. He scooped me up and carried me to his bed and laid me on it, never taking his eyes off mine, carefully he slid his hands down my side. Our eyes locked for a moment I assume he was making sure I wasn't having second thoughts.

"Are you still okay?"

I nodded and reached up grabbing him by his jeans and pulled him onto me.

His body was hot to the touch like someone who had a fever and I could feel his hardened length pressing against me. His hand released my bra and I pulled my arms from it. He closed his eyes for a moment. I felt him slowing his breathing.

"Sorry, I told you I wasn't superman."

He smiled revealing his stark white teeth and dimples. Looking like a cross between an angel and the devil.

I felt a rush of excitement and fear run through me at the same time. Was I ready for this moment with him? I had in fact wanted this moment to happen since the first time I heard his voice. And now I was scared, not for safety but what if I was not what he wanted, what if I was simply a mortal woman to him after this?

"Do you need to stop? This doesn't have to go any further."

His voice was rough with desire, I let out a nervous giggle.

"No, not unless you need to."

I pulled him to me before my stage fright became more evident. His hands freely explored me. I unbuttoned his jeans one at a time he grabbed my hand and held it. Looking at me.

"We really shouldn't do this."

I looked at him getting frustrated with his cautiousness.

"William."

Sounding a little more childlike than I meant to.

"You deserve to be treated with more respect than this. I'm letting myself take to many liberties."

I couldn't help it, before I could stop it I felt my eyes roll.

"I'm not the first woman you've been with am I?"

"Zoe, I don't want you to think this is all you mean to me, because we don't ever have to do this. It's not what I expect from you."

He completely avoided my question.

"William, I'm a grown woman not a child, you are not taking anything from me I don't want to give you. But if it's too much for you too soon, we can stop I understand whatever you can do is fine. We will take it slow."

He looked at me with a questioned look on his face.

"What are you thinking about my beloved?"

I said in my most persuasive voice. I began kissing his arms and chest pushing him onto his side. He lay there his eyes closed deliberating, I am sure. I let my tongue trace his neck down to his chest. His heart was pounding wildly within it. I could feel him tensing and then relaxing with my touch allowing himself to enjoy the moment. I traced the waist of his jeans sliding my hand beneath them. His body tensed and his fists clenched his eyes flew open and he drew in a deep breath. With one sudden motion he threw me over and ripped the zipper off my jeans pulling them off with one hand.

I scooted back looking at him to make sure he was still alright his eyes a little wilder than before. He reached with the other hand and pulled me beneath him holding me with one hand suspending me above the mattress as if I was a doll, weightless. He stepped backwards off the bed and removed his jeans. I couldn't stop staring at him, he was perfect. I felt the slightest bit of fear creep in as I looked at his size. It has to fit right? How bad could it hurt? I dismissed the thought feeling my skin blush as I stared taking him in he was amazing in everyway, the thrill of adrenaline in my body only added to my excitement. His mouth trailed kisses up my thighs nipping and biting gently making my already heated body hotter. He carefully traced the line of my panties with his tongue making my body tighten in response. He allowed his fingers to trace where his lips had been and then sliding his fingers beneath my panties. Electricity shot through me as he revealed my excitement, his other hand removing my panties effortlessly.

> "Did I hurt you beloved? I have to make sure you are ready for me so I don't hurt you any more than I have to."

He answered my question without meaning to. He had been with other women, only an experienced man would know that. He pulled me to him still standing as I lay on the bed. I sat up and kissed him he wrapped my legs around him and lifted me onto him.

"This will only sting for a moment Zoe, then it will feel better once you adjust to me."

I gasped as I felt him press into me, there was a sharp burning sensation as I felt him fully inside, filling me. He stilled allowing me time to adapt. My body and his fitting like they were made for each other. His body was tight, rigid and every muscle locked. He kissed me deeper, his lips lingering as they caressed my skin, his hands holding me to him. My body bent backwards onto the bed as he knelt over me. He bent down placing his face next to mine. I felt his breath in my ear.

"Mon bien-aimé, my beloved, Mon Soufflé, my breath ,Mon bien–aimé my breath, my beloved."

He spoke French? Of course, his father was a French aristocrat. He spoke it beautifully, his voice was rough and sensual, melting me. Every word struck into my chest making me feel as if I would not be able to catch my breath. I closed my eyes to regain what composure I could. He slid his hand under me raising me to him again. I held on to him as we moved together. Any fear I had was now gone, I was lost in him. If he had asked me to drive a dagger through my chest I would have, he owned me now I was no longer my own. I had never felt so alive as I did right now so sure of this moment. Our breathing and movement became one as he spoke softly to me, assuring me.

His voice was like the rain. It was mesmerizing, his touch was gentle but firm.

I felt wave after wave of pleasure wash over me as we worshiped each other, everything I wanted everything I had ever imagined was right here, right now, in this moment he was my perfect match. It was as if he could anticipate every pleasure point, every climax.

I loved him. I loved him more than my life. My mind and body were filled with such emotion I felt myself holding back tears of complete joy. He held me against him tightly as if I might slip from his grasp, still kissing me and caressing my skin. We lay together, not a word was spoken.

I didn't want it to end I prayed he would lay here with me and not move. As his breathing returned to normal, he lovingly kissed my forehead.

"Are you okay? Do you need anything?"

"I'm perfect."

"I wasn't too rough with you was I?"

"No you were..."

I paused looking for a word that best fit the description.

"Are you hurt? Did I hurt you Zoe?"

He sat up and looked at me.

"William do I look hurt? No bite marks, no flesh missing."

I lifted the covers he smiled again this time more boyish as if he had conquered something.

"You are so beautiful, Mon bien-aimé."

His hands tracing the inside of my arm sent electricity through my body.

"Don't blush, you are and I don't deserve to have you. I should make an honest woman of you. Will you forgive me for being weak?"

"Weak, what do you mean weak?"

"I should have waited until we are married that would have been the gentlemanly thing to do."

"William, first of all, can you be married technically your dead. So would that make me a widow with benefits?"

"Technically half dead, and the second reason?"

"Who said I would have let you wait? Was it very difficult for you? To hold back I mean."

"Zoe, I think any normal man would have trouble holding back with you. Whenever I felt like I might lose it I would just look at you and I was able to control it for the most part. Sorry about your jeans and panties. I'll have Darlei get you something to wear. Or maybe not, this is definitely a good look for you. Maybe I'll just keep you locked up in here with no clothes. I rather like that, then no one else could look at you like I look at you."

The picture ran through my mind of being trapped in his room at his beckon call.

"Hmm... Is there a bathroom close to your room."

"It's right there."

He pointed to the door beside the bed.

"It's attached to my room. Are you terribly sore? I tried to be as gentle as I could."

I did feel a little soreness but nothing a hot shower wouldn't help.

"I'm fine William, better than fine. I am a little sore but I would assume that is to be expected. I am under the impression I had an experienced teacher and I was in good hands."

He looked at me regretfully,

"I wish I could have given you the gift you bestowed upon me, I told you I was not worthy of you."

"You gave me everything I could have ask for and more. I love you William."

I kissed his hand and caressed it gently. He pulled me tighter to him as if he would never let go. I lay with him as long as possible before my bladder screamed to be relieved.

"I think I'll slip into the shower if that's okay?"

"Yes, I have a robe on the back of the door and I'll have Darlei bring up some food for us what would you like?"

I smiled and looked at him.

"Haven't you played with fire enough for today?"

I stood up and walked to the bathroom door still naked, turning to see him climbing after me. After our shower Darlei brought us some lunch if you want to call it lunch I think he must have had her bring every kind of food they had. I confiscated a pair of William's pajama bottoms and spent the afternoon in his room talking and laughing. I called and left Jenna a message that I would be home tomorrow, I was taking care of William and in a way I was taking care of him. We sat together looking out over the water talking about mostly me but he told me about his mother and how much he loved her. He talked very little about his father. He got quiet and I could tell he was thinking about something. I stood and walked to the window.

"You know Zoe, there really is no need for you to have to go home. We can be married and live here. That is what you want, isn't it?"

I hadn't thought about it, yesterday I was worried I would never see him again.

"What about Jared?"

"The closer I keep you to me the safer you will be from him, besides once Jared perfects the serum. He will be leaving and we'll be alone."

"Does he know that?"

"There would be no reason for him to stay. I have given him a very comfortable trust fund he can still do his research here but under constant supervision."

His face was searching for an expression from me.

"Don't answer me right now I want to do this properly. Just stay with me tonight."

He could see my hesitation it's not that I didn't want to spend the rest of my life with him, I just never thought it would happen so fast. I wouldn't be returning home and getting married, I would have to tell Aunt Kate, Jenna, Justin and his family. It was like part of me wanted to never leave and the other part would miss my old life. The life where I wasn't in constant danger. But I love him and I will let this play out because ultimately all I wanted was to be with him. I loved to hear him talk his voice relaxed me, made me feel safe and protected. He showed me every part of the house with the exception of the basement. I assumed Jared was down there working. He was like a little kid, I had never seen him so open and unguarded. We would stop and take breaks allowing him to rest. He was still very weak and the day had been a strain on his reserves I am sure. He never let go of my hand the entire day, like if he did I would vanish.

My favorite part of the house was the library where all his mother's paintings were hung. It was the most peaceful room in the house. We were sitting in what he called the parlor it just looked like another big room but in contrast to the other rooms it was the most intimate. I felt my cell phone vibrate in my pocket and I answered it thinking it was Jenna.

"Hey Jenna,"

"Guess again,"

"Justin?"

Williams face turned and looked at me.

"Yah is everything alright with you? Jenna said you wouldn't be home until morning?"

"Yes that's right, I'm going to stay and make sure William is okay."

"Is he making you stay there because you sound funny."

"No Justin, everything is just fine, I'll be home tomorrow okay. Will you take care of Bailey for me?"

"Yah, yah sure but if he lays a finger on you Zoe so help me."

"I'll talk to you tomorrow Justin, goodbye."

I tried to cut it short I could see Williams face getting red and his veins in his neck starting to bulge slightly.

"What did he mean, 'am I making you stay here'? And why is he so concerned with why you are here?"

I can't believe he heard that. His voice had changed his tone was protective border lining on jealousy.

"He is just worried because all he knows about you or this house is what he grew up hearing. He thinks you are doing some kind of cloning experiment."

I giggled trying to lighten things up.

"He didn't mean anything by it, well you know what I mean. He doesn't know you the way I do."

"I should hope not. I don't like this Justin Randall."

"That's fine, I think the feeling is mutual for right now. Besides cut him some slack he is hurting still about you and I. He is a little jealous because I'm with you and not him."

His face softened slightly and he stepped closer standing directly in front of me.

"I am so very lucky that I am the one you love. I will never forget that. But I don't like his tone with you. He shouldn't address you in such a casual manor. How long have you known him?"

"About two weeks longer than you."

I said it without thinking. I could see him thinking about what I had said.

"William, I didn't mean it like that."

"Well enough about young Mr. Randall for now, lets not let that spoil our evening."

Darlei walked into the room and whispered to him. He shook his head and turned to me.

"Zoe, if you'll excuse me for just a moment I need to check on something."

He smiled at me and winked. I shrugged my shoulders and nodded. It couldn't be Jared he was in too good of a mood for that. I grabbed my phone and quickly texted Jenna asking her to do some damage control for me with Justin from the way he sounded he was on the verge coming over here. I was looking at the grand piano in the corner of the room when he came back.

"Do you play?" His voice startled me a little.

"Not really, well a little, my mother played she loved music. I had piano lessons when I was younger but I was never very diligent with the practicing. You?"

"No, it was my mother's she also loved music."

"Is everything alright?"

I noticed he was holding something behind his back.

"What do you have?"

"Oh, this?"

He pulled out a large beautifully wrapped box all pink with a pink satin bow. I smiled like any girl would who was just given a gorgeous present.

"William what is it?"

"Well, I guess you will have to open it to find out."

I let the box rest on the end of the piano and untied the beautiful bow.

"It's such a pretty package I almost hate to open it."

"Almost?"

He smiled he seemed so happy. I lifted the lid and on top of the tissue was a note:

I would like to request the privilege of your company tonight for dinner.

Love,

William

I looked up at him and he pointed down to the package, I pulled back the tissue. It was a beautiful pale blue silk dress.

"William it's beautiful, when did you do this?"

"I had Darlei send for it. I told her the color I wanted and asked them to find the most beautiful dress they had. I sent her earlier after lunch."

"I love it, but what's the occasion?"

"What? I have to have an occasion to buy you beautiful things besides I owe you some clothing remember?"

"Yes, jeans and a pair of panties."

I said in a low voice.

"Well, you didn't answer my note."

"Yes, I would love to have dinner with you, my beloved."

He pulled me to him.

"You should be careful when you call me that,"

"And why is that?" He bent down and kissed me.

"Because I am starting to get used to it and I won't be able to let you go."

"I'll try and remember that. What time is dinner?"

"Whenever you wish, you must be getting hungry?"

"Actually I am, how about an hour that will give us time to change."

"I'll let Darlei know."

"Is it okay if I get ready in the room I stayed in before? I want to surprise you."

"Darlei has already put some things you might need in there for you."

"So smart, I should have known you would attend to every detail. You should really be careful doing that."

"And why is that?"

"Because I could get used to it and never leave."

I walked by him to leave the room his hand still holding mine.

"William, I'll see you in a few minutes I promise, but I have to take my hand with me."

"Yes, yes I know. If you don't need anything else then Darlei will escort you to the room and show you where she left the items she purchased for you."

He reluctantly let go of my hand slowly. I was so excited to know I wouldn't have to leave him tonight. Excited that if for only one night we could both pretend this was a fairy tale and it would be happily ever after. Darlei took my hand and patted it. She had such a sweet disposition about her. She was very motherly, I know why William keeps her close to him. I can tell he still misses his mother greatly. She seemed almost as excited as William to show me what she had purchased for me. As we entered the room it smelled of lilacs; there were bouquets of them everywhere. The dressing table had everything I could imagine needing down to the makeup I used and my favorite perfume.

"Darlei, you cheated you've been spying on me for him haven't you?"

She covered her mouth to hide her smile and turned her head away looking guilty. She had laid out on the bed beautiful pale blue satin panties with lace.

There was also a square flat wrapped package on the bed wrapped like the other package he had given me.

"What's this?"

I asked her, her eyes sparkled and she shrugged her shoulders.

"Master William says for you to open it when you are finished getting dressed, before you come down."

"Of course,"

She turned and left me to get ready. I sat down at the dressing table looking at myself dressed in his pajama bottoms and one of his sweaters, my hair pulled back and no make up.

I remembered the first time I sat at this table, how unsure I was of him. I felt so happy now, I have never been so happy as I was right now. Could it always be like this or did it have to end? I had to stop before I ruined my perfect mood. I took my time getting ready and putting on my make up, the panties fit perfect and they also matched the dress exact. He must have paid a fortune for them, the tag was in French but I could make out pure silk, I was a little surprised that there was no bra. As I slipped into the dress it felt like butter on my skin. It was vintage looking, like something Jean Harlow would have worn from the 1930's.

The front draped just below my collarbone, a halter style top and was A-line cut in the front very conservative but elegant. The back on the other hand was plunging below my waist into a slight peak, with a tiny crystal strap connecting each side at my shoulder blades. That would explain why there was no bra.

The shoes were also stunning; 4-inch heels with silver straps that were lined with crystals. I stood in front of the full-length mirror looking at the dress thinking how much my dad would have loved the color it was his favorite on me.

I asked Darlei if she would help me put my hair up I couldn't bear to hide any of this gorgeous dress. I touched up my lipstick and checked the time. I had a few more minutes until I needed to head down stairs Darlei handed me the package. I looked down feeling myself tearing up. I tried to fight it back, I didn't want to ruin my make up or the dress. I carefully unwrapped it, the beautiful velvet box was a dead give away that it was jewelry. Inside was a pair of white gold earring's and a matching bracelet studded with blue stones. I had never seen anything like it.

"They are Blue Diamonds." She said in a low voice. "Very rare."

I put them on and went back over to the mirror. They were breathtaking! How could he know me so well? I couldn't have picked out anything more beautiful.

"We should go now Miss."

"Yes, I don't want him to have to wait."

He was standing at the bottom of the stairs pacing in his black perfectly tailored tuxedo. He looked up when he heard me coming down. He walked halfway up to meet me. His eyes never leaving me as he approached. I stopped and posed for him.

"Is everything to your liking?"

"Very much so, you, - you look exquisite."

I turned around on the step, holding the strap to the train of the dress in my hand.

"I have never seen anything more beautiful. Do you like the jewelry?"

"Yes William, it's lovely. I love it."

He offered me his arm still never taking his eyes off me. He led me into the room where we first had dinner together. It was candlelit with soft instrumental music playing and again the Lilacs were everywhere. Their fragrance was sweet and light.

"How did you know I liked Lilacs?"

"Earlier you said you loved picking them from the backyard with your mother."

"Yes I did how did you get them this time of year? You know what forget it I don't need to know. They are beautiful thank you."

"I wanted everything to be perfect for you."

"I love it William but what can I do for you? You are much better at this than I am."

"Zoe, you have already given me everything I want, you gave yourself to me.

That is all I want. You saved me in so many ways, before I met you I was ready to give up. I had nothing to live for, from the first moment I saw you

I felt hope again, there is a peace I feel when I am around you. I have never had that feeling before even when I was alive. I could never repay you for that; I could never find a gift worthy of that to give you. These are just things, if I had nothing but you it would be perfect."

I felt the tears pooling in my eyes.

"I'm sorry."

He handed me his handkerchief.

"I'm sorry I have upset you?"

"No, William I have never been this happy. I have never felt this way about anyone. If I died tonight I would die fulfilled."

He took my hand and led me to the table he pulled my chair out and we sat. The weather had subsided for now and it was a clear night sky. The ice laced the tree line and the waters edge making it look like a fairytale outside. We enjoyed our dinner and continued to talk long after it was over. Moving on to the sofa on the other side of the room. He added some wood to the fire and brought me a wrap. We sat together, he played with my hands as we talked he seemed a little more nervous. Suddenly I felt his breathing get a little more rapid.

"Are you really happy Zoe? Is it possible that I make you happy?"

He sat up turning to me.

"Yes William, I have never been so happy."

He knelt in front of me taking my hand.

"I should have never let you see me, I should have never let you get this close to me."

I started to speak and he gently placed his finger over my mouth.

"I was selfish to do so, but I couldn't help myself I could have cut my arms off easier than deny myself of being near you.

If you had not fallen in love with me it would have been enough to just be close to you to stand in the shadows watching you. You have become my breath, my only happiness, Mon bien-aimé, my beloved, Mon soufflé, my breath. I wish I could say I regret what happened between us today but I can't, I could never regret it. I never want to be away from you again. That being said, if you don't want this, if you don't feel the same way I understand. you would be wise to leave and never look back. I love you with all my being as much or as little as I have is yours. Will you marry me Zoe Dossin?"

He held in his hand a small box the size that would hold a ring.

"William?"

My chest pumped trying to get air to my lungs.

"This was my mother's. I will buy you a new one if you don't like it."

I couldn't speak, he opened the box revealing a white gold setting. The band was ornate scrolled with a floral pattern and a looping design, the center blue diamond was a princess cut and lay flush with the rest of the setting. I looked up at him his face worried, searching for my expression.

"It's beautiful William."

The tears I had held back poured down my face,

"I love it, it's perfect,"

"Does that mean yes?"

I shook my head and he placed the ring on my finger, which fit like it was made for me. I wrapped my arms around him as he stood and twirled me around the room kissing me. I could not have denied him anymore than I could have denied breathing; he was my breath now.

I could never be who I once was. Who was she anyway? Alone and afraid, mourning the loss I had suffered.

I would never have to watch death take him. We would face this together and make it work. I had worried about what others might think but it didn't matter when I was with him. I would never have been strong enough to deny him. No matter what consequences my actions caused. Was it wrong to think only of myself? Probably, but I was his in someway, I always have been as he is mine.

Chapter Eighteen:
Calm Before the Storm

***

I woke to the sun peaking through the window. I took a deep breath in feeling to see if he was beside me. I looked to make sure I was feeling in the right place he must have already gotten up. I pulled his pillow to my face breathing him in. I lay there trying to make sure I hadn't been dreaming. I felt a little more soreness today than yesterday and wondered if it was because it had been my first time or because of the frequency.

The thought of him made me smile and the pain seemed to lesson. My mind wanted to go over everything that could go wrong but my heart was strong today and it wasn't going to let my useless worry ruin this wonderful morning. I sat up and threw back the covers getting up I walked to the window and opened the curtains. The sun was bright reflecting off the melting ice. It would be a beautiful day to shoot some of that lighthouse William took me to. I hadn't worked in two months I really needed to try while my head was clear. I grabbed the jeans and sweater along with the other items Darlei had brought me and went into the bathroom to change. I was surprised that William was nowhere to be found when I got down stairs.

I grabbed some paper and a pen out of my purse and jotted down a note for him to let him know I was running home to get everything settled there; then to the lighthouse to get some shots. I asked him to meet me if he had time and we could spend some time together. I left the note on the large table in the middle of the foyer. I let Darlei know I was leaving and she said William had some business this morning and he would be back soon. I asked her to make sure William knew I left him the note. The weather was a little deceiving as I stepped out I realized I would need a warmer outfit before I went to the lighthouse.

I hoped that Justin would be receptive to everything and I wasn't sure I even wanted to tell him yet. I'm sure Jenna would say I was being a chicken but it bothered me to think how upset he would be. I looked down again at the beautiful ring on my finger watching the light refract off of it.

Jenna's car was gone when I arrived home. Could I be lucky enough that they had decided to go out for a while? Bailey met me at the door happy to see me. Poor guy I hadn't been home very much lately and he wasn't used to that. I patted his head and ran upstairs to grab some warmer cloths. I got my smaller suitcase and packed some necessities that I thought I would need for a few days. I still couldn't think about being away from William right now.

I made a stop in my workroom and packed my things I would need for my shoot. I glanced at the painting I had started of William before, it was such a dark contrast to the person he really was. There were two sides to him as is the case with everyone, I would be naive not to understand that. His was just a little darker than most. I re-adjusted the cover on it and went to the kitchen to get myself something to eat and to feed Bailey. I sat on the stool at the bar looking out over the yard and water enjoying the moment of silence that would have been painful two months ago. I grabbed my note pad and wrote Jenna & Justin a note letting them know where I was headed and that I would be taking Bailey with me. I figured he needed to get out and spend some alone time with me. I took a quick look around making sure I hadn't forgotten anything and we headed out. Bailey was happy when I opened the door for him to leave with me. It had warmed up a little thankfully, I had to try and remember where the turn in was for the lighthouse.

It only took me having to turn around twice to find it. I had been gone from William's house almost three hours, I was surprised he hadn't called me yet.

I quickly let it leave me and decided a little separation was good. I walked around the area deciding what I wanted to shoot first. The water was rough although it was cold with large chunks of pale blue jagged ice floating in it. It would make for some great pictures. Bailey was at my heels for the most part never going more than a few feet from me. I think it was the water making him nervous. It felt good to just be able to get into my work and not have to be anywhere. It was getting kind of chilly and I know Bailey was getting cold so I let him in the car taking a second to check my phone I had left charging. There was 1 voicemail and 2 missed text messages. I read the texts the first one was Justin: 'which lighthouse Zoe? There are over 20 in the area.' And the second message was from William: 'Stay put I'm coming to pick you up. I'll explain later.' It was sent 2 minutes ago. I was replying to William's text when I heard Bailey bark. The noise made me jump I turned to see Justin standing there.

"Hey, I was just getting ready to send you a message."

I closed the door locking Bailey in the car and turned to talk to him.

"Yah well, you should keep that thing on you I've been trying to get a hold of you for the past hour. It took me three lighthouses to find you."

"Sorry, I would have been home eventually. Hey you're driving! "

"Yah they told me today at therapy I can resume all activities except I have to go easy on the stair climbing and uneven surfaces. What ever that means."

I started thinking that William would be here soon and wondered what they would do when they finally met each other. We walked towards the entrance of the lighthouse.

"So what are you doing out here?"

“I have wanted to get some shots of this place for a while and today seemed perfect. I would really love to get a shot from up there but I can’t get in it’s locked.”

“Hold on let me show you something.”

He reached from behind the electrical box near the door of the lighthouse and removed a key.

“How did you know about that?”

“High school, we used to come up here and hang out.”

“Right!”

He opened the door and let me in.

“It’s been unmanned for years they do tours in the summer here.”

“I’ll be right back.”

I reached for the banister to start my climb and he grabbed my left hand.

“What the heck is this Zoe?”

My heart sank I was not prepared for this right now.

“What does it look like Justin?”

“It looks like a ring, an engagement ring.”

“Well that’s what it is. Justin I keep doing everything wrong with you and I’m sorry. Please don’t be mad at me just let it go for now. William will be coming here soon and I don’t want you two to get into it.”

He shook his head and looked down. I didn’t hear the door open until I saw Justin go down to his knees and then the floor. I looked up and saw Jared with a large board in his hands. His eyes wild, I backed up the winding staircase.

“You think you’re so smart don’t you? You think you can ruin everything I have given up my life for?”

“Jared calm down!”

I backed up slowly trying to keep him talking until William got here.

"Whore! You and I had a deal and you broke it."

"What deal was that Jared?"

He stepped through the door completely now and closed it behind him.

"The one where you promised not to stick your nose in where it didn't belong, you think him sending me away will get rid of the monster? You have no idea, I'm not going anywhere you are!"

His eyes where crazed and wild I turned and ran up the stairs he stepped over Justin's lifeless body and followed dragging the board making a banging sound as he came up. I reached the top out of breath and pushed hard on the door to the outside.

I climbed out onto the catwalk and closed the door wedging some cinderblocks over it. I had a lump in my throat thinking about poor Justin, I prayed he was alive. I made myself move, walking pressed against the lighthouse leaning forward every two feet looking over the edge for a way to climb down. Not realizing that the railing had a service latch that I must have accidentally pressed when I leaned in. I almost went over, I pulled it back struggling to catch my breath. I made the mistake of looking down it was much higher than it looked from the ground. Okay Zoe breathe, I told myself. I just needed to stall, William would be here soon and he would take care of Jared. The waves crashed below and the sound was deafening. The dream I had had of the lighthouse was now front and center in my mind.

I heard the blocks fall over and the door swing open, hitting the side of the lighthouse and closing back with a loud crash. My heart raced, the cold air was sharp on my face and hands I grabbed my gloves out of my pocket and put them on, my hands already numb from the cold air.

I noticed a pipe against the side of the wall and grabbed it holding it tightly in my hands. He approached me smiling.

"I knew you wouldn't make this easy, you are all about complicating things aren't you? Well we will be putting an end to that right now."

He raised the board.

"What do you mean Jared? I don't understand what you are talking about. Why are you doing this?"

"You pretend to not know, honestly? And I thought we had come to an understanding, remember that night in my room? I was very clear, I wouldn't tolerate you getting in the way of things. He is marring you, he's moving his little whore in and I who have done nothing but be at his beckon call my whole life, out. You must be really something special."

"Jared, I told him I wouldn't marry him, I said no."

I hated lying but at this point I was desperate.

"He's all yours I could never be with him, as his wife, you know that."

He looked confused his face uncertain.

"Who told you we were to be married? Would I be here with another man if I was going to marry William?"

I could tell he was thinking now.

"It doesn't matter if he is or not, you need to go, he will just keep looking for you unless there is nothing left to look for."

He raised the board higher this time swinging it. He missed and hit the rail.

"Whoops, wow that was really hard, that looks like it would hurt."

His face consumed with madness. He swung again this time striking my left knee and forcing me to fall forward onto all fours. The pain shot up my leg. He raised it again this time I came up with the pipe and struck him in his groin.

He bent over in pain, and I pushed back trying to stand back up. I heard gravel from a car and William's voice yell. I screamed but it seemed to be stifled by the sound of the turbulent water. Jared's eyes glared when he heard William.

"Enough playing with my food! Fortunately for you I'll have to get this over with quickly."

He stood and swung again this time losing his balance he hit the rail with his body where the service access was. He slipped grabbing onto the rail and my jacket. We both went down him over the edge and me on the rail holding on to the side. I wedged myself across the opening as best I could.

"Let go of the board Jared and take my hand."

His face was surprised that I wasn't struggling to get loose from him.

"No, you ruined everything you have to die."

He pulled harder and swung the board again.

"Jared you'll kill us both, let go of the board and take my hand please!"

I grabbed his jacket sleeve with my free hand my other shoulder burning with pain where he was holding on to me. He began to cry, shaking his head back and forth. I heard William say my name we both looked up. Justin was right behind him.

"Don't come any closer William, or so help me I'll pull her off here."

"Jared you're a fool let me help you. It doesn't have to be this way."

William's voice was desperate.

"Yes it does, you know it does, I have nothing now she took everything away from me. She's a whore William, can't you see that she's just a whore!"

My arm was slipping and we both slid closer to the end.

"Let go of him Zoe, just let go!"

I heard Justin pleading. I looked down at him, his face pitiful I couldn't just let go.

As crazy as it sounds he was sick and hurting. Letting him go would make me the monster.
He dropped the board and looked up at me and smiled. I couldn't just let go, I looked back at William telling him I loved him. I pulled hard wedging my foot into the rail. As I did I felt myself slip over the edge, the rail had given way. I heard Jared screaming and then nothing. My shoulder was dislocated; I could feel the hot pain in it as it swung in the air. I looked up to see what was holding me; William had me by my glove. I felt like I was being torn in half Jared's weight had pulled against my arm and dislocated it. William pulled at my other arm.

"Hold on Zoe, give me your other hand. I can't it's broken I can't raise it."

My body was swinging making it hard to hold on, he had only my fingertips. I heard Justin behind him.

"Hold on Zoe we'll get someone."

William was trying to squeeze thru the rail to get a better grip.

"William don't you'll fall!"

I could hear Justin on his cell phone calling 911. I looked back at William tears in his eyes.

"I won't let go, I'll get you, I won't let go."

And I knew he wouldn't.

"We'll both fall you can't pull me up you don't have a good grip the rail is blocking you."

My glove began to slip, Justin was on the other side of the rail trying to grab onto my jacket. When the rail broke it twisted back making it impossible to reach through the railing.

"Damn it Zoe, don't you let go! Don't you give up. Hold on the fire department and EMS are on their way."

Justin's voice breaking as he shouted, I looked down to the water and rocks below.

“Don’t look down Zoe, look at me, just look at me, they’ll be here soon and they’ll help us get you down.”

“William!”

I let out a cry as the wind pulled at me every movement felt like hot pokers stabbing my shoulder.

“I love you, William.”

My glove was slipping more now as I felt my hand going numb. I looked at Justin and then back at William, I could see the fear in their eyes and how much they both cared for me. I thought how lucky I was to have them in my life. Then everything was quiet. I felt the wind blowing my hair upwards. I watched Williams face as I fell into the icy water. I wanted him to know how much I loved him but there was not enough air in my lungs to say it again. My body was instantly numb I could feel the freezing water all around me smashing me into the rocks and ice and pulling me back out. The water burned in my lungs, I grabbed my chest fighting the water from coming in at first but gradually letting it take me. I felt a sharp pain then heard a snap.

Justin Randall:

I couldn’t believe it, he just jumped off after her! At first I thought he was overcome with his loss and jumped. I realized he did it to get to her, I ran as fast as I was able to get down to the waters edge sliding on the rails with my hands most of the way down ignoring the horrible pain in my head and leg. As I reached the bottom he was fishing her out on to the rocks. He carried her to the flat ground and began CPR on her, tearing away her coat and top like it was paper. I wanted to do something I didn’t want him near her. He had already done enough putting her in this danger.

"I can’t get her, how long did they say? Justin?”

His voice barking at me, I couldn't think it all happened so fast.

"15 minutes. Should be about 15 minutes."

"We need a defibrillator now, we are losing her. Zoe stay with me my beloved."

His voice calling her that made me sick. If she survived this I was getting her far away from here and him whether she liked it or not.

"The EMS is here."

I heard my sister say. I had called her as soon as we found Zoe.

"William let them in, they can help her now."

I looked at Jenna surprised she knew who he was. I hated him with everything in me. There was something unnatural about him that was more than just creepy. The fire department medic was checking my head while they tried to get her stable enough to move. I watched as they loaded her in the ambulance after they got her stable enough. They motioned for me to get in I couldn't see his face but I'm sure it burned him up knowing I would be in there with her instead of him. They worked on her the whole ride there. I couldn't believe it was Zoe I was looking at. It looked like someone had thrown her into a meat grinder. There was blood everywhere. I kept turning away, I couldn't stand to think of the pain she had been in. He was already there when they were unloading her following the gurney as they wheeled her in. They tried putting me in a wheel chair but I walked past them following behind her.

"What relation to the patient are you sir?"

"Her fiancé"

The words made my skin crawl, I felt the anger building.

"And you sir?"

"A friend."

"I'm sorry we'll have to ask you to stay here. Both of you, for now."

We looked at each other staring as if to see who would turn away first.

"This, everything, it's all your fault! You know that right?"

I couldn't hold it in any longer and who was that guy? Why would anyone ever want to kill Zoe?

"This is not the time or place for this Randall."

He started to walk away. I grabbed him and spun him around wanting and fully intending on beating him until he looked like poor Zoe did.

"Don't walk away from me Madison, we aren't finished and your money isn't going to absolve you of this."

"Justin calm down, not here."

Jenna positioned herself between us making sure I made eye contact with her.

"He's not going anywhere. Think of Zoe Justin, she wouldn't want this. Please let's try and make sense of this. Later you two can go out and have a ball killing each other after we find out about her. Besides mom and dad are on their way up here you want them to see this mess?"

"Did you call Zoe's Aunt Kate?"

His voice lacked expression.

"No William, I thought I would wait until we find something out, no need to worry her until we have some news."

He nodded and walked out into the large hallway sitting across from the nurse's station. Every time the doors opened we all jumped looking to see if it was news about her. Forty-five minutes had gone by and no word. They had just moved us into a large family waiting room when the doctor came in. We all stood holding our breath.

"Are you the Fiancé? "

"Yes, How is she?"

Both my parents and Jenna popped their eyes on me and then back at William. I struggled to let it go.

"I can't explain how she is alive but she is. She just came out of surgery, there was internal bleeding, and we had to remove her spleen. She has sustained three broken ribs on her right side, four ribs on her left. Her left lung was punctured, her left collarbone was broken, and she has a dislocated kneecap and shoulder on her left side. Her back was fractured in two spots and she has some head injuries we are watching. There is slight swelling of the brain, which is normal for a head injury but considering her other injuries it's not our biggest concern right now. We think we have the bleeding stopped but I am concerned about some swelling around her heart, caused from the trauma to the left side. Her heart was almost punctured along with the lung, it missed by centimeters. We have her on life support right now and we are monitoring her, it's a waiting game at this point. Her body has been through a lot and has a lot more healing to do before she will be out of the woods. I'm sorry I don't have better news for you, we have done everything we can do. Now we wait."

"When can I see her?"

"Let's give her a little bit to get settled up there and then you can go in, one at a time."

He shook the doctors hand and walked out into the hallway. I felt my dad's hand on my shoulder. His voice quiet but stern in my ear.

"Calm it down boy, don't let it get the best of you. She's got a long hall ahead of her as you well know and she'll need all of us just like we needed her."

My mom hugged me. I needed to get away from this place and punch something. I was so angry with her. How could she do this? If she had just stayed away from there, she's so stubborn.

She's the kind of person who brings every stray dog in the neighborhood home with her. It had been hours since we heard any more news. William had not come back in the room, he stayed out in the hallway. I could tell Jenna was chomping at the bit to say something to me but she was waiting, waiting for what though? I got my answer soon enough when my mom and dad decided to go have some coffee and a bite to eat. She could hardly wait for them to leave.

"Okay little brother spill when did he become her Fiancé? And you knew about this when? Because I know you and if you had just found out like us he would be on the floor."

"Jeez Jenna, give me a little credit would yah?"

She stood looking at me her hands on her hips.

"Really Justin? It's me Jenna."

"Okay she told me right before the accident. I don't really want to think about it right now."

"Next question, what happened up there Justin? Did she jump or did he push her? What?"

"Some guy creepier than William, ah his name was Jared I think. He hit me with a board and knocked me to the floor and then chased Zoe up the stairs. He kept saying she ruined everything for him, and calling her a whore."

"Jared Craig? Justin, was his name Jared Craig? Brown hair medium build good looking?"

Her face was desperate, she was on the verge of freaking out.

"Yah Jenna, Pretty sure that was his name. You know him too? I was gone like 3 weeks what did you two do hit the streets looking for freak guys the minute I left?"

"Was? What do you mean, was his name?"

"He attacked Zoe with a board and slid off the edge, that's how she fell trying to hold onto him, he wouldn't give her his hand. How do you know him anyway?"

"We went out once..."

I could tell it was more than that, she looked like she just got punched in the gut.

"Did they look for him at all? I'm sure they did Jenna I told them he fell first.

Besides Jenna the guy was a total nut, He tried to kill her. "

"He seemed so normal."

"Yah, about as normal as the one out there in the hall way? What is with you two thinking that is normal?"

"Okay, I don't want to fight or get you upset. Do you think I should call Zoe's Aunt Kate? I mean it's her only family Justin."

I didn't know how to answer. I could hear Zoe's voice in my head saying don't tell her you'll only worry her but if there were any decisions to be made I didn't want creep boy making them.

"Yah, maybe we should but I wouldn't tell her how it happened Jenna, she'll just freak out and it's a long trip here."

"Okay, you alright to stay by yourself for a few minutes?"

"Yes I'll be fine, and Jenna stay away from him."

She gave me a puzzled look.

"You know who I mean!"

She nodded and left the room. I had paced the entire room a few hundred times before anyone came back in, the last person I expected was him. He walked over looking straight at me as if to see if I would be opposed to talking.

"I just wanted to let you know the nurse told me we can go see her now. I would like to go in for a moment alone first, I talked her into letting us go two at a time so you would have some of your family with you, if that is alright?"

"Why so nice? Don't do this on my account I can take care of myself and my family without your help. Don't think you can change anything by trying to be nice."

"I was thinking of what Zoe would want, but as you have said you are capable of taking care of yourself. So I will be going in for a moment and then you can have your turn when I am through."

I pushed my way past him and walked down the hall where Jenna met me.

"What's wrong Justin, is it Zoe?"

"That guy he's ah!! Trying to be nice now like that will make up for the fact that he almost got her killed. Where does he get off treating me like a little kid?"

"I have no idea."

Her voice had an overwhelming sarcastic tone.

"Look at you Justin it's like someone took your ball so now you won't play anymore. We need to all have some patience with each other. Oh by the way did you know Zoe had a cousin?"

"Yah she has a few, she said her Aunt Kate's kids. She said they were like her brothers and sisters growing up. Why?"

"Well I just spoke with Abbey, her younger cousin, and her mom is recovering from the pneumonia and can't really go anywhere so she is coming out tonight as soon as she can get a flight. I'll have Mason or one of the boys pick her up from the airport.

On second thought maybe you should Justin, you could fill her in on what she needs to know and the boys don't know Zoe as well as you and I do. I would go but it's a long ride to Bangor and well I think you need some alone time to process this whole mess. There I said it, you need to come to terms with the idea that Zoe picked him Justin. She didn't do it to hurt you and he didn't do it because he wanted to win. It just happens, we don't get to pick who we fall in love with. You unfortunately don't either. It will get better little brother I promise! You have all of us here for you. Just know that even though she picked him, she still cares very much for you and she's been a great friend."

I hate her when she's right or thinks she's right. She is so trusting just like Zoe, they don't know who he really is. I can see it in him there's something not right. No one is that perfect. I might not get to have Zoe but he sure as hell was not going to get her.

"I'll think about it."

"Well she's calling me back in a few minutes to let me know what flight she got. Mom and dad left, dad needed to rest. Mom was having Mason and Tiffany get some groceries for Zoe's house and let Bailey out. I'm sure Abbey will want to stay at Zoe's instead of a hotel. You and I can stay there with her so she's not alone and it will be closer to go back and forth to the hospital."

"Sounds like you have it all worked out then Jenna."

"Don't get your tone with me Justin Randall. She's my friend too. You're not the only one upset."

She walked away I was batting a thousand. Guess I'm destined to tick off everyone today.

I took a deep breath and closed my eyes for a second to try and regain some composure. I opened my eyes, looking at the doors to ICU made me angry to think he was in there with her alone. Jenna was right about one thing I needed to get a hold of myself before I do something really stupid. I decided that if Zoe were stable I would go get Abbey from the airport. That way I could clear my head and fill her in on mister wonderful. I stood by the door to ICU and saw him in her room. I felt a tap on my shoulder and turned,

"Hey we need to stick together not fight okay?"

I shook my head and turned back around taking one more look at him with her. It felt like a hot blade was being shoved into my throat going all the way down into my stomach.

"I really thought we had something yah know?"

"So did I Justin but you need to give yourself some space, and time to let it all sink in you've been through a lot in the past few months. It's hard on all of us watching her go through this and have no family. My heart goes out to her but she's a strong person and she has us."

"And him?"

"Yes and him, for now anyway. Oh before I forget Abbey's flight will be in around 10:30pm what should we do?"

I took another deep breath and turned back around to her.

"I'll do it, I'll leave in about 45 minutes. After I see her."

"Great Justin that's good, I'm sure Zoe would want you to do that for her."

I pushed through the door and walked into her room. He didn't even look up, I stopped at the foot of her bed. Her face was badly bruised, on her left side was a large bandage that covered part of the deep scraps and abrasions.

Her once beautiful Auburn red hair, dark with what I imagined to be dried blood. She looked so frail like if you touched her she would break into pieces. There were monitors everywhere. His face looked worried, and worn. I was glad, I hope he was suffering as much as she was having to because of him.

"Was your sister able to get in touch with Zoe's Aunt?"

His face was still looking ahead.

"Yes, her cousin Abbey is coming out instead. Her Aunt Kate is recovering from Pneumonia and can't make it."

He nodded still never looking directly at me.

"Did you need me to send someone to get her from the airport?"

"No, I think Zoe would want one of us to go so I am going to pick her up tonight at 10:30."

"That will put you back at around 1:30am then."

"Yes, your point?"

"No point just an observation."

His voice was steady, smooth never changing tone, unnerving. I had tried to ruffle his feathers since we got here so I'd have an excuse to hit him, but nothing. It was becoming annoying.

"Have the doctors been in anymore?"

"Yes, I need to talk to you about that. There is more swelling around her heart if it gets any worse they will have to drain it."

"That's bad right?"

"Yes, her heart rate is slowing the fluid around it is keeping it from pumping. Even if the drain works there are no guarantees she will be able to come off life support. If that was the only injury she had that would be different but with other complications it makes recovery less likely. He also suspects more internal bleeding because of her blood count."

His eyes never left her face the entire time he spoke.

"I have a favor to ask you."

I could only imagine what the heck he could possibly have the nerve to ask me.

"I have to go home and take care of some things. Will you be able to stay here with her?"

I knew it the first sign of trouble and he bails.

"Of course but I won't be back until midnight from the airport, Jenna will be here until I get back."

"You can't let them do anything until I return. Please, this is very important Justin."

He looked at me his eyes darkened if that is even possible.

"What if they don't do something she'll die right?"

"Not necessarily, please I know you dislike me, okay you hate me. But we both care about her, I want her to have a fighting chance. Please promise me you won't let them do it. I just need a few hours Justin, can you buy me some time?"

I had no idea what he was talking about he sounded crazy his eyes were desperate but for some reason I trusted him about this.

"Do you think your sister could stay with her and not let them do anything until we both get back? The sooner I get started the better."

"William, I understand that the whole mysterious thing is hot for the girls but I'm going to need a little more than you're telling me here, because I gotta tell yah it sounds like your cooking something up and I'm not comfortable with chancing Zoe's life on your hunches."

"There's no time, I know Zoe told you a little about what I have been working on, with Dr. Craig for my illness, but it's more than that, I could save her if I can finish it, reduce the risks. Look Justin let me tell you what the Doctors aren't letting us know yet because they figure it's not going to come to that. Why make us worry about everything else.

If she recovers from the Pericardial- her heart problem there's, the chance of infection, and there is the fact that she will probably be paralyzed from the fractures in her spine. I've been looking over her chart. She would be a paraplegic at best with the diagnosis they have suggested. She wouldn't be able to walk or run ever. She is so weak, if she does make it through the first part she still has all those obstacles. If she doesn't what I have won't help her, She deserves a better chance. And you're right it is my fault I put her at risk stupidly thinking I could protect her. I was blinded by what I wanted don't be blinded by jealousy right now let me make it up to her give me that chance to give Zoe her life back Justin, all I'm asking for is a few hours."

"Fine you have until morning I would stay here regardless but I will do as you have asked for Zoe, not for you. I can't speak for her cousin though you will have to explain this to her when she gets here. Give me your cell number if anything happens while your gone I'll call you. And don't worry about my sister if I tell her not to let them touch her she won't let them near her."

He looked back at her whispered something in her ear and kissed her face, then looked up at me and reached out for my hand to shake it. I noticed her locket necklace wrapped around his wrist.

"Your word you'll keep her safe?"

"My word, nothing else will happen to her while I am here."

He wrote his cell number on a paper towel and placed it in my hand. He looked back at her and left. Everything he had told me, all that information, was somehow scattered in my head. I struggled to understand how two days ago she was laughing, talking to us and eating Oreos. I can't process this it doesn't make any sense.

My heart wanted her back, well like she was, but my mind was telling me to do the responsible thing and listen to the doctors. Why trust him? What if he made her some freak like he was or worse?

"Hey, how you holding up bro?"

It was Aaron, Jenna was behind him.

"Not good man but here."

"We saw William leave he sent us in, what's going on he left?"

"Yah Jenna I have to talk to you about that."

As I explained it to them I realized I now sounded crazy.

"Justin these are doctors, they know what's best for Zoe. He's not a doctor, are you sure about this?"

"No Jenna, I'm not sure of anything but if you would have seen him, I don't know something about what he was saying felt right. I am going to keep my word and give him until morning. By then her cousin will be here and it will be out of our hands. I just want what's best for Zoe."

"Us to bro and we have your back. Jenna and I will keep her safe. If you want I'll go get her cousin."

I debated for a minute whether or not to stay I really need to stay but maybe if Jenna stayed she would make the better decision.

"Justin she'll be okay for now go get your head straight. You'll be gone a couple of hours and a phone call away."

I could tell she wanted me out of the hospital, maybe to spare me from the pain of making that decision. I looked at her lying there but hearing her voice in my head so clear.

"Trust him Justin."

I didn't want to, with everything in me I hated him but I couldn't not listen to that voice.

"No I'll go but Jenna let's give him until morning okay? Zoe would want that." "Wow, someone put his big boy pants on."

"Aaron! I'm proud of you Justin. She is gonna make it Justin, she's too stubborn not to."

"You got your cell Jenna?"

She held it up in her hand.

"Use it if you hear anything and don't leave her alone until I get back."

"I promise, we'll stay right here."

"Hey, do you know what this cousin looks like?"

"All I know is she said she would be wearing a red sweater and when I spoke to her mom she said you would know they were related."

She gave me the gate and flight number and I looked back once more, I walked over to Zoe leaned in and whispered to her.

"Don't quit yet Zoe, give him a chance to make this right."

I hugged Jenna and left. It was the hardest thing I think I've ever done. I felt like I was betraying myself. Why should I make him look good to her? I didn't owe him anything.

Chapter Nineteen:
A Slight Resemblance

***

I don't remember the walk out to my truck or the 40-minute ride to the expressway. Why did she have to love him, I could have accepted anyone else but him. I cranked up my music and let my mind take a much-needed break. I must have been a million miles away because I made it to Bangor airport in less than three hours.

I found a parking spot easily that time of night the airport is pretty quiet. I stood at the gate not really knowing who I was looking for. There must have been ten women in red jackets none of them under 40. I saw the second wave of people coming down the escalator and her. Her auburn hair was a dead give away, it was long, same color as Zoe's but straight and angled more towards her face. As she got closer I waved so she would see me. She had a thin red jacket that said Nauticuss across the front in gray and yellow.

"You must be the good looking guy Jenna told me to look for. Hi I'm Abbey, Abbey Saunders and you are?"

"Sorry, Justin Randall, and thanks. I don't know about good looking it's been a long day."

"I am sure it has been, thank you so much for picking me up I could have grabbed a shuttle."

"No, No problem. Your bags?"

"Oh just this carry on I travel pretty light."

Beauty definitely ran in their family it was a little unnerving how much she looked and sounded like Zoe except for the eyes she had striking blue eyes, and she was extremely tan. She was built a little more athletic than Zoe, and a little shorter.

"I look a little worse for the wear myself."

We walked towards the parking level.

"Rough flight?"

"Which one I just got in from South America this morning when we got your sisters call about Zoe I had only been home 3 hours."

"That is a long flight."

"Yes it is but my mom was determined to come, I had to promise I would come instead."

"Yes I'm sorry to hear she was ill."

"She will be fine I'm sure but her doctor said travel was not even an option until she was well."

As we exited the building she stopped as if she had hit a clear wall.

"Wow it is seriously cold isn't it?"

"Do you need my coat?"

"No I'll manage as soon as I catch my breath. How do people live like this?"

"We stay inside as much as possible."

"She gave me a glare and smiled."

She had deep dimples when she smiled that made her look even younger than I imagine she was. We came to the car and I helped her in the truck.

"It's about a three hour ride back sorry I know after all that travel you probably don't want to hear that."

"No it's fine you can fill me in on Zoe's condition. How is she? Jenna was a little vague on the phone I assumed it was for the benefit of my mother? She must be pretty bad if Zoe let you call us. She hates to worry my mom always so independent that girl."

"You have no Idea,"

"Yes I do, we grew up together. I haven't been able to correspond with her in about 4 weeks I've been out of signal range."

"You mentioned South America? Did you live there or were you on a vacation?"

"Oh neither, I was on a Marine research vessel for the last month in the Atlantic. South America actually, Paramaribo was just our port."

"Wow, like green peace?"
"No, not exactly, I'm a Marine Biologist, I was lucky enough to get a spot on the Nauticuss. I'm supposed to be going back next month once they get the grant money to fund another trip."
"Are you old enough to be doing that? I mean to be a Marine Biologist?"
"Exactly how old do you think I am?"
"I don't know like 20?"

She laughed but not an amused laugh, more of an insulted laugh.

"They said you were Zoe's younger cousin. How old are you then?"
"I am younger than Zoe by 14 months."
"So I was off by five years. Did you borrow that jacket?"
"No it's mine why?"
"Who's Quinn?"

She laughed and blushed making her blue eyes even bluer.

"No I'm Quinn, well not really, it's just a nick name I got pinned on me. See when I was younger I thought I had to do everything Zoe did she was going to be a doctor so I thought that's what I wanted too. I went into the Peace Corps for a year when I turned eighteen to Honduras, I helped set up all the triage clinics and they called me Dr. Quinn medicine woman. Over the years it got shortened to Quinn. I stopped fighting it about 3 years ago. Besides it's get called Quinn or Saunders. At least with Quinn I don't sound like a football player or a Colonel."

She was shivering I felt bad that she only had a thin jacket on. I turned the heat up.

"Here take this."

I handed her my jacket to put on.

"Thanks, guess I'm not cut out for this cold weather."

"Did you bring anything warmer with you?"

"I live in Arizona and I just got back from South America everything I have is for warm weather."

"Well Jenna can help you find some things at Zoe's place to put on so you don't freeze."

"So enough about me what's going on with our Zoe? Is she in a lot of pain she's probably already wanting to leave."

"Did my sister tell you anything?"

"Just that she had fallen over a rail and was at the hospital being treated."

She looked confused. I wanted to kill Jenna for making me be the bearer of bad news.

"She's not saying anything she's unconscious and on life support."

Her face lost all expression.

"Seriously, she's that bad? I thought a broken leg or arm or a bump on the head but not this. What happened what kind of rail did she fall over?"

I began telling her from the beginning, from her first accident and about William for some reason she didn't seem surprised about William. I wondered if Zoe had mentioned him before. She was quiet facing straight ahead.

"I'm sorry I feel like I just dumped a ton of information on you. I wish I had better news."

"She got engaged? When? God I feel like I've been sleeping for a year and just woke up. This guy William, Zoe told me she had just meet him, when did it get so serious?"

I wanted to ask the same question.

"I don't know but it did. She told me herself they were engaged right before the accident."

"So this guy Jared he goes crazy and tries to throw her off a lighthouse rail? Does this really happen? This is so not Zoe, I couldn't even get her to bungee jump with me when we went on spring break. And she hates heights I can't believe she was that high. She doesn't usually do things without thinking them through. I've always been the impulsive one. She debates for hours over what movie to watch on TV. Maybe it's the loss of her parents she hasn't been the same since she lost her mom. She was in med school when her mom got sick. I think being at the hospital around the clock with her burned her out on being a doctor. Her dad was so upset with her when she quit. If it weren't for her mom stepping in and helping resolve things they would have never started talking again. She can be really stubborn."

"She never told me she was in medical school. I guess it just never came up. How long did she go?"

"She was in her third year when she quit. About 4 months before her mom died. She was always very close with her Mom and dad but she was the apple of his eye. Until she decided to walk away from everything, the guy she had been dating, school, everything."

"This guy who was he? Was she serious about him?"

"No I don't think so, they dated for a while he was an intern. Her dad loved him but she never really fell hard for guys. She was always holding them up to her father, they all paled by comparison I guess. She's going to kill me for being such a blabbermouth. You found my weakness, I talk a lot when I'm tired, sorry."

"No I appreciate your insight she can be guarded sometimes."

"About Zoe, did they say how long her recovery would be?"

I hated to tell her this part I was mixed on whether I should paint William out to be the freak I knew he was or to let her decide for herself.

"She is in pretty bad shape, she got pretty messed up when she fell. They did surgery to stop some internal bleeding but there are some complications with her heart."

"What complications she's only 27 and in great shape what happened to her heart?"

"There was an injury to her lung and ribs and it has caused some swelling near her heart. She has some injury to her spine and knee also."

Her face was stern she had her hand over her mouth. Her fingers pursed her lips, her eyes frowned.

"So your telling me her injuries could be fatal?"

"We are hoping not, but she is in critical condition. See this guy William, Zoe told me he is sick and he has been researching a cure for this illness he has. He has a research clinic set up in his house."

She was looking at me like I was crazy now.

"Wait hold up this William guy has a clinic in his house? Who is this guy? This doesn't sound like Zoe at all."

"He is very wealthy, and his house well it's not your normal house I've never been in it but have you ever seen that movie Grey stoke the legend of Tarzan?"

She shook her head no.

"Well it's a huge state building. Anyway he thinks this cure might be able to help her."

"He wants to test some home spun drug on my cousin?"

"Well yah I guess, It's sounds crazy I know and trust me, nobody dislikes this guy more than me but there's something about what he said that makes me believe him when it comes to Zoe I honestly believe he loves her."

"Okay but is he even a doctor? How do we know this won't kill her, not to mention I think the hospital is going to have a big no for him when he asks if he can give her the drug."

She took a deep breath and held it waiting a long time before she blew it out.

"God Zoe what the heck did you get yourself into? " She spoke under her breath as if speaking it to Zoe. "What are the Hospital doctors saying?"

"They are wanting to do a drain to relieve the pressure around her heart, but even if they do that she still has to have surgery on her back. William says the injuries are in areas where she would probably be paralyzed. That's why he wants to try this drug he has."

What does he think he can re – grow bone and muscle? There is nothing known to man that can be taken orally or injected that could help her with that if it's fractured or crushed. Is this guy there with her now?"

"No he left to go finish working on it to get it ready. My sister and brother are there with her until we get back. I'm not explaining this very well and see there is something different about William and his family they have lived here a long time. He's a bit of a recluse and he's very smart.

Zoe said he has been working on this for a long time with this Doctor the one that tried to kill her. But it was because he felt like Zoe was interfering in their research and he even said now that they found the cure William didn't need him anymore.

That is why he was mad, William was sending him away. I know this sounds crazier every time I open my mouth and please don't get me wrong I think it's crazy too but I don't want her to..."

I felt my eyes started to fill with tears, I tried to choke them back.

"I just want her to have every chance to come back to us."

"I will speak with the doctors when I get there and see what is going on, I can't afford to put Zoe's life in the hands of some love sick nut that thinks he has a magic cure. Please don't get me wrong I appreciate everything you and your family have done for her but if it's this serious and she's that bad we will have to listen to what the experts say. I have learned that when we let our emotions get in the way of our decisions we tend to make bad ones. Wow I really wasn't expecting this."

"I'm really sorry to just dump this on you, I know it's a lot to absorb but one thing to keep in mind and I can't believe I'm telling you this but Zoe trusted him. I know that she does love him and I think he really loves her I honestly believe he has her best interest at heart even if he is strange."

I hated myself right now because everything I said I wanted to take back I didn't
want him near her and I didn't completely trust him but her voice was so strong in my head.

"Did you eat anything or do you want me to run through somewhere and get you something to eat?"

"No I'm good I have some energy bars in my back pack if I get hungry."

It made me laugh she really wasn't like Zoe in that area because Zoe would have had Oreos.

"You are in love with her too aren't you?"

The comment completely caught me off guard.

"What? Where did that come from?"

"I can tell by the way you talk about her, don't get me wrong what's not to love about Zoe? She's wonderful she said she really cared for you. She even said how understanding you were when she first got here. It doesn't make sense."
"What doesn't make sense?"
"Why she would pick him over you?"
"She told you about me? "
"Kind of, we corresponded via emails and texts when we can. She sent me a long email when she first got here letting me know she was alright. She said there was a really hot caretaker that had been really sweet to her. And how great your family was but she barley mentioned him. That seems weird doesn't it?'
"Not really, Zoe keeps a lot to herself it seems like."
"Yah I guess, Thanks for telling me everything. I know it's not easy when you
love someone and they don't love you back the same."
"You sound like you speak from experience."
"That transparent huh? Yah I wish I could say it gets better but I think it's kind of like when someone dies you just learn to pretend it's okay."
"Is this a recent injury?"
"Well if you call two years recent then yes. He's the reason I stay away from home."
"I'm sorry I pried, I tend to just say whatever comes to my mind Zoe says I have no filter."
"You too? Yah I can understand I feel like I have spilled my life story out to you in the last two and half hours. You really should have been a therapist."
"We are close to the house, did you need to stop in before we go to the hospital? "No I really just want to see her and find out what's going on. But thanks."

"So are you an only child? No I have an older sister and a younger brother. You have a large family like 5 or 6 right?"

"Yah there are 6 of us. Are you close with your family?"

"Ah, well I am with my mom and brother, my dad past when I was 15 and my sister is the other reason I stay away from home. She married the cause of my heartache. Did you ever say something that you wish you could take back? I must be really tired. Sorry."

"No it actually makes me feel better your more screwed up than I am."

We both sat quiet for a moment and then laughed the kind of laugh were you could begin to cry easily it could go either way.

"What a pair we are, well I'm here if you need to know how to run from your issues."

"And I'm here if you need to learn how to internalize them and pretend its all going to work out."

"Thanks Justin,"

"For what?"

"Being there for her, you and your family. She needs that, she tries to be so independent and has become so used to relying on herself that she never asks for help. When you grow up with siblings you get accustom to depending on each other, even when they let you down."

"Well she was there for us when we needed her the most and we all care a lot for her."

We pulled into the hospital garage I dropped her off at the door and parked the truck. We walked up to ICU together.

"She looks pretty bad Abbey, I don't want you to be shocked when you go in there."

Jenna and Aaron were standing outside the ICU doors when we stepped out of the elevator.

"What's wrong why are you both here?"

"Relax Justin they took her back down to have another MRI done to see if the swelling in her head has gotten any worse. They will be back in a little while."

"Hi, you must be Abbey?"

"Yes, and you are Jenna, and?"

"Oh this is Aaron my older brother."

They shook her hand and Jenna popped her eye on me mouthing Oh my God,

"Well your mom was right there is definitely a family resemblance, you're the spitting image of Zoe. Except for those eyes, I'm jealous."

"Well thank you Jenna, I will take that as a compliment but there is only one Zoe."

I pulled Aaron over to the side.

"Seriously you need to stow the wolf look."

"What?"

"Close your mouth bro, it's embarrassing."

"Whatever, you do realize she looks just like Zoe, she's totally hot. I call dibs on her after this is over."

"Really? Show some couth she's not meat. You better be a gentleman or I'll tell mom how you're acting."

"Fine, just saying."

"You boys having a private conversation? The nurse just said it would be another thirty minutes before she's back up here. Aaron why don't you go get us some coffee and we will all go sit in the family waiting room. I am sure Abbey is very tired from her trip."

"Yah sure, how do you take it? Oh I'll just have a water thanks."

"You sure you don't want some caffeine?"

"Yes I'm sure I don't drink Caffeine."

"Okay this coming from a girl whose cousin lives on Red bulls?"

Jenna was an avid Caffeine drinker she and Zoe where soul mates about the Red bull.

"Is she still drinking that stuff?"

"Oh yes, and Oreos."

"Let me guess you're a vegan?"

"No, but I try to eat healthy, the things they put in that stuff is terrible for you."

"Well Jenna if eating healthy makes you look like that maybe you should try it."

Jenna shot Aaron a look that sent him into silence

"Wow you guys sound like me and my brother."

"Ah yes brotherly love I have 5 of them want another?"

"No I'll pass but thanks."

We walked over to the waiting room that had completely cleared out. We sat in the corner closest to the door. I felt bad I couldn't stop looking at her, it was hard not to compare the two of them. There were so many similarities between the two of them yet they were so different.

Listening to her, she seemed like quite the adventurer, and a little bit of a daredevil with skydiving or swimming with sharks not your usual roller coaster daredevil. Although Zoe's recent track record didn't make her mother Teresa either. I could tell Jenna was fascinated by her as well there was something about her that made her interesting and easy to talk to. She wasn't the type that bragged about what she did, she seriously wanted to convince you to try it. That was the thing I loved most about Zoe, her ability to make conversation anywhere and make it poignant. Aaron had returned and made it a point to sit right next to her.

He was so overbearing at times which is probably why he was still single.

Jenna had started telling her about our boating accident and how much Zoe helped us through it. I could feel myself intentionally getting pulled into the conversation by Jenna.

"We thought for sure Justin and Lucas were goners. Zoe never gave up though."

Jenna's voice broke as she spoke Zoe's name.

"Justin how long were you missing for?"

"Long enough for them to almost stop looking for us."

I hadn't intended on talking about this but something about her made you want to spill your guts out.

"When did you know she was sinking?"

"About 5 minutes before we all had to jump. We barely had time to get our survival suits on. My legs got caught in the rigging as she pitched and I went over with two broken legs. If it weren't for Lucas hanging on to me for so long I would have drowned."

"I can't imagine how awful it was not knowing who had survived from your family and who hadn't. It must have been unbearable, worse than the freezing water I would imagine."

"Yes, it was the worst thing not knowing if you were the only two and if you would even be found. I don't recommend it."

"Well it sounds like you have all had your share of excitement lately. I am very glad Zoe has had all of you to keep her company. My mother was very upset when she decided to come out here and leave home. But Zoe was soul sick, she was bent on doing it alone. The last time I saw her was right after her father's funeral. She literally went home packed made the arrangements to leave and within two days she was in her car. I offered to come out here with her to get her situated and she wouldn't hear of it.

She said she needed to sort everything out and get some perspective. I don't think she planned on getting it this way. Before I left to come here my mother told me I wasn't to come home without her. She's a very strong and determined person when she wants to be. This William, what do you know about him?"

They all turned and looked at me seeming to have the same question.

"What? Why am I supposed to be the one who knows?"

"He's quite the mystery,"

Aaron's voice was quiet as if he was telling a ghost story.

"It all happened about a hundred years ago, see old man Madison and his son had a huge fight right after the mother had died of like TB or something, anyway they fought and it came to blows, they say he struck his son, leaving a small scar on his chin from a ring the father wore. They never spoke again. About a month after that happened William was on his vessel the Haddy and ended up sinking her after he took out another ship like eighteen people lost their lives there was a huge scandal. William was blamed for the whole thing. Old man Madison went loony after that, he started talking about bringing his son back and making it right with him, he was drinking heavily at the time I'm sure. Anyway the old man dies still grieving for his son. The house stays quiet for like two years until people start to see stuff like weird lights, a lot of foreign people, no one ever goes out during the day the help always goes into town at night. I know this girl in Bangor she says that her dad works at the freight company and they get shipments from Haiti all the time. Huge crates the men who come to pick it up don't speak English."

"So where does this William come into the picture?"

"He is supposed to be the Cousin or Great nephew of the old William Madison." "And you think he's not because?"

We were all leaning in at this point like if anyone over heard the story we would get into trouble for telling it.

"See the really creepy thing is that the old William and this new relative look exactly alike, even down to the scar on their chin from where the dad's ring cut it."

"And you think that the old William is still alive and looks the same?"

"No way that's crazy, it has to be some kind of cloning experiment or something right?"

"And that's not crazy because?"

"Don't listen to them my dad and grandfather, God rest his soul, have always pumped their heads full of this stuff. He is just a really eccentric, wealthy guy who minds his own business and that intimidates the rest of the Yokels around here, gives them all something to talk about around the campfire. Beside Grandpa only made that stuff up to keep you boys away from that place and keep you off the bluff. I've met him he seems very nice a little quiet but nice."

Jenna, she's always playing the advocate. He was nice, too nice, and those eyes, something so empty behind them.

"It's the nice ones you have to watch out for, right Justin? Stepped right in and stole your girl."

"Not now Aaron."

I stood up and walked away. I loved my brothers but the constant pouring of salt on my wounds gets old. I could hear Jenna reprimanding him as I left the room. I was just in time to see them bringing Zoe back up from her test.

If it was possible she actually looked worse or maybe it was because Abbey looked so much like her when she was well I had already forgotten how terrible she really looked. I followed them into her room holding her hand as we walked. It was ice cold and clammy. I was beginning to hear Williams' words in my head. 'She deserves to have a better chance.' What if he was wrong? What if I let him help her and it kills her or worse. As they finished getting her in her room I turn to go get Abbey I completely knocked her down she was coming up behind me, I caught her mid-flight.

"God I'm sorry what a klutz. I totally didn't see you. Are you okay?"

"Yah, I'm fine I should have made more noise I guess, you looked like you were in deep thought so I didn't want to startle you."

She adjusted herself and stepped around me. She clasp her hand over her mouth.

"Oh Zoe, What did she fall into she's bruised from her head to her toes."

"I can't believe it but she looks worse than she did earlier."

"Did her doctor come in yet since they brought her back?"

"No he hasn't been in yet."

"I would like very much to talk to him. Her color is terrible her lips are really blue that can't be normal. What did William say exactly about her heart?"

"Just that they wanted to drain the fluid from around it if it got any worse."

"Have you talked to this William anymore since we got here?"

Her tone was becoming as desperate sounding as I felt.

"Hard to see her like this isn't it? I feel the same way I want her back the way she was. Wanting it so badly you're willing to do something completely insane."

I needed to talk with William again, find out what he was talking about. I needed to know more than what he was telling me.

"Abbey I'm going to step out for a second I'll send Jenna in if you want. I won't be gone long just need to take care of something."

"Sure Justin, She's lucky you know."

"Who's lucky and why?"

"Zoe is lucky, she has the love of two men who are willing to do anything for her. Most women can't find one. This William must be an angel for her to have picked him over you. That's personal I know and from what I gathered relatively fresh but I just wanted you to know I appreciate what you are all doing for her. A lot of guys would have booked it when she picked the other man. I know she would want to tell you how much that means to her."

"I owe her a lot, and she would do it for me and has."

I walked out not knowing whether to feel better or worse. I made it out to the main hall and called the number He had given me. His voice was frantic when he answered.

"What is it, is she okay?"

"She's about the same I guess. They just brought her back from another MRI but she looks awful. Her lips are completely blue and the bruising is worse. We are expecting the doctor in any minute. How are things coming there?"

I am terrible at making small talk especially when it comes to things like this.

"I have everything set that I need and I should be able to be back there in about an hour."

"Yah, I think we need to go over this plan of yours because frankly I don't have a freaking idea what it is and I've got to tell yah the whole trust me thing doesn't work with me.

I need to know the details and I'm sure her cousin Abbey is going to want a complete break down as well."

"She made it in good, is she very young, and how is her personality? This isn't coming out right. I'm sorry do you think she will be willing to discuss an alternative treatment for Zoe? Is she even old enough to make that decision?"

"She's like 25 and she's very bright, you will have to judge the on board thing yourself, I'm not really sure how I feel about it actually."

"We can talk when I get there, I just need you to keep and open mind."

His voice sounded stressed and tired. I tried not to feel sorry for him after all this was entirely his fault. He knew the risk and still put her in danger for his own selfish agenda. I heard Jenna calling for me from down the hall.

"Look William I have to go they are calling me back in, just get here."

I never thought I would be telling him that. I hated him right? Jenna's voice sounded upset. I walked out from the room I was in and saw her face she was white as a sheet.

"Come now Justin, hurry."

I ran down to her we ran together as she tried to explain what had happened.

"Right after you left a nurse came in and then a bunch of monitors went off they made everyone leave the room. Abbey came and got me. They had to revive her twice, Justin they did the drain, they had to, to save her or she would have died they didn't give us the choice. They are still trying to get her stable again, her heart rate is all over the place. She is so weak the doctor is coming in to talk to us as soon as he gets her stable."

I felt the blood run from my face, I wanted to vomit. I saw Abbey in the hall her head in her hands she was leaning with her back to the wall. I felt Aaron step in front of me as I went to go in her room.

"Let them do what they need to Justin, you'll only get in their way bro."

I glared at him all my anger was coming to a head. I felt blood now rushing to my face. I shoved him off me and walked away. I felt bad that I pushed him I knew he was just trying to help but I didn't need that right now what I needed was to punch something. I pushed through the double doors that led out into the main hall I had no idea where I was going. I felt the hatred in me building. Why didn't she just let him fall instead of hanging on to him? He throws her over a rail after pummeling her with a board. And she is risking her life to keep him alive? This whole thing is completely stupid! Creepy men, Psychotic killers, twin cousins, almost girlfriends... I feel like it's all a nightmare. My head kept thinking about what William said

"He put her in danger."

He knew Jared was dangerous and still he let her be around him. He really has her snowed into believing he's harmless. And here I am making it easy for her to just be with him. I knew she needed to stay away from him I felt it in my gut and I stupidly stepped aside being

"The best friend."

I was mad at her for trusting him, for choosing him. I felt a hand on my arm from behind me. I pushed it off of me and turned thinking I was going to let Aaron have it. When I saw her face I immediately felt bad for pushing her hand away.

"I thought you were Aaron again, I shouldn't have done that, I'm sorry. I'm not myself right now."

"I understand how you are feeling right now. Anger is a more comfortable emotion than the feeling of helplessness."

Her voice had an instant calming effect on me, I don't know why but just her tone and demeanor made me relax a little.

"The doctor came in after you left. He said it's a waiting game right now to see how her body heals itself. Not really what I wanted to hear but she is strong and she has a lot to live for, you have a really nice family, they care a lot about you, you know. They asked if we would wait a little bit to go back in until they have her stabilized. I was going to take a walk get some fresh air."

"It's pretty cold out there sure you want fresh air?"

"Fresh air or just a walk around the atrium in the foyer, I just need to take a walk."

I hesitated for a moment,

"You want some company?"

"If you want, sure."

We walked through the hospital and around the front Atrium with it's glass ceiling that had a thin skiff of snow on it. We sat near the huge tree in the middle. We had not spoken since we were up in ICU. Her voice startled me when she finally did speak.

"Are you feeling better now?"

I didn't feel better just not as mad.

"A little, you?"

"Not really, just don't know what I'm going to tell my mom. I have to call her soon I promised once I got here and talked to Zoe I'd let her know how she is."

"Well technically you haven't spoken to her yet."

She gave me the look you give someone when you can't believe they just said something that stupid.

"Sorry I think my brain shut down like five hours ago. I know I'm no help, and your mom she's a worrier isn't she."

"Well that is an understatement. She would be on the first flight if she knew Zoe was this bad. I feel terrible not letting her know what happened."

"You have two choices Abbey,"

I turned to look at her.

"One you lie and tell her they did surgery and she is going to be fine, they just removed her spleen. And then be firm with her and tell her you don't need to take care of two sick people and they won't let her see Zoe anyway if she is sick."

"Okay and two?"

Her eyes probed me for my second suggestion.

"Two? What you didn't like one?"

She hit me and smiled

"You don't have a second choice?"

"Well yah but I personally think one is the way to go."

"Justin,"

She said losing her patients with me.

"Okay two is that you completely lie and tell her everything if fine and that you are staying here to help her once she leaves the hospital."

"So either way I'm lying is what you're saying."

"Sort of but with one you're only keeping information from her not really lying."

She sat chewing her bottom lip for a moment thinking.

"Your right I just have to be firm and tell her to stay home I've got this."

But she didn't look resolved with her decision completely.

"But, there's a but isn't there?"

"Well just what if something happens to her and my mom never gets to see her again."

"Do you seriously want her to remember Zoe like this? Your protecting her why make her go through it now and then later to if something happens."

I shivered even thinking about Zoe not making it. It wasn't something I had allowed myself to think about yet.

"I need to call her while I have the nerve. Do you mind if I leave for a second? "No, I'm gonna head back up."

"Okay then I'll meet you back upstairs when I'm finished."

She was pulling out her cell phone before I even walked away.

"Justin."

She raised her voice over the noise of the fountain beside her. It echoed in the large room. I turned to see what was wrong.

"Thanks, for everything."

She said quieter than before.

"Sure."

I mouthed to her and gave her a thumbs up. Instantly regretting the thumbs up, how dorky, I must be tired. I walked slowly up the stairs I had decided not to take the elevator I wanted time to prepare to see her again. I dreaded seeing him too. My head ached I don't know whether it was from the blow to the head from Jared or the amount of thinking my brain had had to deal with today or possibly a combination of both. I sucked in a deep breath and opened the door to the ICU level.

Chapter Twenty: Choices

***

It was bad enough having to see her like this but him being here made it intolerable. He was standing there beside her looking so frail and broken. Her color was somewhere between gray and blue. Her once silky ivory skin was now bruised and dull. I hated him for what he had allowed to happen to her as much as if he had shoved her over that rail himself. I swallowed hard and sucked it up for her sake.

"William" I said as normal as I could get it out. He turned his head and nodded.

"Your sister told me what happened. I'm sorry I wasn't-"

"Sorry? That's the second time you weren't there when she needed you. Kinda becoming a habit isn't it?"

I cut him off before he could finish. He looked down as if I had said something he was already thinking.

"You are right to be angry at me. I have been selfish, but I want to make it right give her a second chance but for that I have to have your help."

I stared at him feeling so conflicted. Help him that's rich what I wanted was to kill him not help him. I broke my stare to look at Zoe.

"I will do whatever I can to save her, but there are some things we have to discuss if you want my help."

"Things? What would these things be?"

His eyebrows creased deeply somewhere between anger and curiosity.

"First I'll help you as long as I don't think it's going to put her in more danger. Second, you are going to tell me everything about what you are planning.

I don't want you just telling me what I need to know. And third, once she is better you leave, disappear, make her think you're dead or something I don't care but I don't want you anywhere near her."

His hands where in fists now I could see his jaw was clenched and the veins in his temples were bulging.

"That's all?"

He asked sarcastically. His voice was so weird sounding it resonated deeply as if it were multiple voices. I felt the hair on my neck stand up.

"For now? Yah."

I tried to play off the goose bumps that were forming if I wasn't so pissed right now it might be intimidating.

"Now that you have given me your stipulations here are mine. I will tell you everything I feel is related to helping Zoe recover, my personal information is just that, personal. I would never purposely put her in danger contrary to popular belief I love her more than my life and I will do anything and everything within my means to save her and give her the life she deserves even if that means being away from her. And for the record I don't care for you either, but I know how much she cares for you and your family so I will over look your insecurities and immaturity but know this if you get in my way of helping her that I won't over look. Now that we have bared our souls to each other where is her cousin? I wanted to speak with her she will have to be on board as well."

I wanted to lay him out, there was something there in his eyes and voice not human. I didn't want to have to trust him but I knew one thing was true he did love her in his sick inhuman way and at this point he was probably her best chance.

"Abbey is her name, she was calling her mom to try and convince her to stay in Arizona for now. She's coming back here as soon as she's done."

"As soon as who's done?"

We both turned towards the voice. His face had the same expression mine did when I saw her.

"I don't think we've met. I'm Abbey, Zoe's cousin. You must be her mystery man William is it?"

She stepped forward and offered him her hand.

"We were just discussing you, I'm William Madison very nice to meet you Abbey. How is your mother taking this?"

"She is satisfied for now with my explanation. Justin here tells me you are somewhat of a research genius and you think you can help Zoe with her injuries."

"Yes I think it best if we involve as few people as possible but Justin I believe your sister Jenna should hear this as well we will probably need her help also."

"The chapel is two floors down we could leave Aaron up here with Zoe and all go down there it was empty when I passed it."

We both looked at her blankly.

"I got off on the wrong floor. I haven't slept in 24 hours."

Her agitation from the mishap was clear in her voice.

"Okay then Justin if you can arrange for Aaron to keep watch and get Jenna we will meet there."

"Sure, I'll go make it happen and meet you both down there."

I leaned towards Abbey,

"You ok with walking down there with him?"

I saw him shoot me a glare.

"Of course, I'm a big girl Justin."

If I had closed my eyes it would have thought it was Zoe speaking.

So naive, so stupid and trusting. I nodded looking over my shoulder at Zoe again before I left. I wondered if his kind was allowed in the chapel, after all in all the horror movies the monsters can't go on consecrated ground. I explained to Jenna that I needed to talk to her and Aaron agreed to text me if there was any changes in Zoe's condition. As we walked to the chapel I tried to explain as much as I knew to Jenna trying to fill her in. We reached the double stain glass doors to the chapel and went in. They were waiting at the far end past the pews towards the front.

"Okay William we are all ears."

I said in a more than disrespectful tone, Jenna nudged me and mouthed lay off to me. I rolled my eyes and gestured nicely for him to begin.

"I looked over Zoe's chart before I left and then again just now. With everything that is going on with her injuries her best outcome if she is treated here and we do nothing is Quadriplegic, maybe paraplegic. She sustained a spinal chord injury just above her first thoracic vertebra. Any injury above that usually results in a Quadriplegic. That is if they can keep her alive long enough to endure the multiple surgeries it will require to repair her knee, that she will never walk on again, her shoulder and pelvis. They are monitoring the swelling on her brain they think it could be just a contusion or I should say they are hoping but it could be much worse."

"By worse what do you mean brain damage?"

Abbey stayed with her eyes fixed on him as she asked the question no one wanted to think about.

"Yes brain damage, vegetative state or permanent coma."

"Why haven't they told us any of that yet? You're painting a pretty grim scenario for her."

Again she stayed completely focused on him as if trying to read him or his motives.

"They aren't even sure her heart is strong enough to pull through this they are giving us need to know information right now."

"And you know of a way to reverse paralysis and head trauma?"

Her tone was that of disbelief. Jenna and I were still stuck on the initial assessment of Zoe's condition he had described.

"What I am about to tell you can not leave this room for everyone's safety including Zoe. If it fell into the wrong hands it would be catastrophic. I have been involved in research on cell and nerve rejuvenation and reconstruction on a molecular level. I can't explain every detail but basically it re-grows human cells. It is experimental and not completely refined."

"Meaning there are side effects to your drug?"

She said it more like a statement than a question.

"Yes, there are side effects but they can be controlled."

"What are these side effects?"

He looked up as if to figure out where to begin we looked at each other waiting for the explanation.

"There is an extreme amount of pain that comes from the administration of the serum, followed irregular levels of dopamine, serotonin, & testosterone, to name a few. Resulting in temporary tremors, aggression, heightened senses, fatigue, endurance, disorientation, you get the idea. But all of this can be controlled, the Serum has the ability to completely heal the body restoring any damaged or injured cells are restored."

"William, I appreciate the risk you have taken telling us this but if those were the only side effects of this serum you would have gone public."

"Those are the side effects when the drug is closely monitored. When it is abused the drug has more menacing side effects."

"And those would be?"

This time I spoke up I had to hear this it's what I had been waiting for.

"The drug is extremely addictive, once you start taking it you can't stop. There is a limited supply of the plant materials needed to reproduce the drug until now. Thanks to Zoe we have figured out a way to make it synthetically. I have been unsuccessful in being able to taper off the dosage like I said once I administer it to her she will be dependant upon it until I can figure out a way to discontinue the drug."

His face began to look tired, his eyes got darker as he spoke.

"What happens when the drug is not administered? Why would you not be able to stop taking it?"

"I'm not sure on a molecular level why but your body becomes dependant on it to maintain your renewal of cells. Your body begins to break down with out it."

"So let me get this straight, as long as you take it your body stays alive there is no cell degeneration?"

He shook his head.

"None?" She asked

"No none."

"What does that mean exactly?"

Jenna said sounding as lost as I felt in the conversation. Abbey turned to her, her eyes wide with disbelief.

"It means you don't age."

"Well you age but slowly, very slowly."

I swallowed hard as I began to put the pieces together in my head.

"I am sensing that you are holding out on us William, it doesn't make sense.

The side effects you described and the result don't make for a catastrophic outcome if it gets leaked out so what is the other side effect you are conveniently keeping from us?"

She was standing now, Abbey looking so much like Zoe but in so many ways different. There was an insight to her voice, an ability to see through the veil and not trust the unseen. A trait, unfortunately, Zoe did not possess. His eyes looked at her as if she had called him out as I assume she had.

"You are correct in the assumption that immortality comes at a high price. The other side effect or curse to this cure is a desire for human flesh."

He stared blankly at her as if it had taken his last bit of strength to admit to her his secret. I heard Jenna gasp. Abbey sat back quietly in her chair still staring at him as if looking at him would help make what he had just said believable.

"You have been around her and you have these side effects? Are you mad?"

His eyes flashed at me.

"I have been taking the serum a long time and I have learned to adapt to it, become stronger than it."

"Your disease you have is not a disease at all is it?"

He looked hard at me.

"It was death that was your disease. You aren't a clone of William Madison, you are William Madison."

My heart beat loudly making me breath hard. I felt like someone had knocked my feet out from underneath me hearing my own words as I realized what they meant.

"Make whatever assumptions you must. I was not given a choice in my fate.

The bottom line is this, how much are you willing to do to keep her alive? Do you think she deserves to die like this? "

"If we decide to go along with this... plan of yours how do you propose we pull it off."

I looked at her in complete shock.

"Abbey you can't be serious do you think Zoe would want to be like him a monster?"

Jenna looked at me her lips pursed

"Not you to, you are both mad."

She grabbed my arm

"Justin, Zoe loved him you know that, she knew what he was and she didn't care. That has to count for something."

Jenna's eyes filled with tears now. Looking at me waiting for my response I had none. My chest felt hollow like someone had taken everything out of me. Abbey seemed to be driven now, maybe from her lack of sleep but she only briefly paused her conversation with William.

"The plan she prompted him."

"Yes, as I said before the fewer people who know about this the better I'm sure I don't have to explain why?"

He glanced in my direction.

"I need you on board with this to help it go smoother. I think our best route would be to tell the hospital we are bringing her home making it out like we are giving up and bringing her home to well, make her as comfortable as possible. Of course we will wait until they give us the grim news that they will most likely be doing after they do their next rounds."

"Aren't you assuming an awful lot?"

I could feel both Jenna and Abbey staring at me. My tone was sharp but I wasn't holding anything back now.

"How do you know what they are going to say?"

"I have already spoken to her doctor."

We looked at each other and then back to him.

"What doctor did you speak to?"

"Her personal doctor, Dr. Jared Craig."

"You have gone mad, he's dead. You're using a dead man's credentials?"

"Not exactly,"

Abbey looked a little lost now I saw Jenna explaining it to her quietly. He waited as she finished telling her who Jared Craig was.

"I can't explain how but he's not dead. He has agreed to help-"

"Absolutely not this discussion is over, done, I can't believe I let you talk this long."

I felt a hand on my arm. I turned to see her there looking at me so calmly.

"Step back Justin, we need to think clearly. It's not about our feelings right now."

I looked back realizing I was less than 10 inches from his face. I backed away my fists still clenched. They didn't understand who this man was at all. I saw his face as he tried killing her and for all intensive purposes he did.

"Abbey, you don't understand, please William tell her the truth, this is Zoe we are talking about not some experiment. He tried to kill her you were there you saw him he's probably trying to finish the job."

"Justin trust me, I wanted to kill him myself and almost did when I saw him waiting for me at my house. But he couldn't believe she tried to save him after all he had done, she reached him somehow. He is the one who offered to help me, I know what this looks like. I can't believe I am willing to trust him but as crazed as he has been I've never seen him so human as he is right now."

"Wait how is he alive? Didn't you say he went over before Zoe Justin?"

Jenna spoke up for the first time in the conversation. I looked at her waiting for the light to come on. Her eyes opened wide followed by her mouth forming the words.

"Him too? He's one of them?"

I nodded and looked at William.

"Seems our William here likes making these monsters."

It was him that stepped forward this time his eyes dark and crazed.

"I had nothing to do with Jared taking the Serum. It was an accident."

His voice had lost its humanity sounding low and hissing.

"Yah, those happen pretty frequently around you it would seem."

I had finally gotten him, he was starting to crack, and I wasn't backing down now. But in that same moment I saw him look away for a moment and close his eyes. Turning back his demeanor changed partially calm but his voice still inhuman.

"He is the most qualified person to save her. He has been a part of this research since he was a boy with his father. He was top of his class in medical school he is a brilliant doctor that had a terrible moment in his life that altered him. Losing someone you love can do that. You fortunately have never had to deal with that first hand have you Justin?"

I swallowed hard not wanting to lose my anger it's all that was keeping me going now. I looked at her now trying to make her see how wrong this all was.

"You can't make this decision Abbey, because it's not for us to make it was taken out of our hands when she decided to trust him. I care for her too and that's why I can't do this to her, condemn her to a life of being a monster consumed with what they are consumed with."

The words spouted from my mouth as if they tasted like acid and they did. I
wanted a miracle for her I wanted the fairy tale he was apparently living in but there was no fairy tale here only death and denial of what he really was and wanted to make her.

"Are you willing to face her and tell her she'll never feel below her collar bone, she'll never have the ability to walk, run, feed herself, that's if she makes it. Are you ready to say goodbye to her forever?"

What she said hit me like a bus. I couldn't breathe thinking about being the one to make this Zoe's death sentence. Could I let her go if it meant she would be out of pain and not become a monster? I shook my head I wanted off this ride I felt no trace of sanity in anything I was thinking right now. Was it selfish to want her here no matter what her sacrifices would be or selfish to not want him with her because I loved her no matter how she felt. Did I not want this to happen because it was the morally right thing or because I couldn't stand to think of him with her?

"I can't do this right now,"

My voice broke I hadn't cried since I was a young boy and I was trying to choke back the liquid trying to emerge now.

"I'll be back, give me a minute."

I didn't make eye contact I couldn't. I didn't want this right now, my body was rebelling not allowing me to keep my anger or control. I shoved the door open and walked out into a brightly lit hall, too bright.I search for the stairwell and walked quickly to escape the lights.

I made it about six steps down and sat my head in my hands, I let it go sobbing like I had just lost my best friend and I had.

No matter what she was gone forever. She would never be the same again.

We would never be the same again. He would always be in her life if I let this happen, he would be her drug dealer. I heard a voice inside me now clearly say 'stop it, stop being so self absorbed, you're acting like such a baby.' It was her voice, I heard it like a chime in my head. What she would tell me, say to me to make me see it clearer. I stopped the sobs and listened trying to hear again. 'This isn't helping anyone listen to your heart, what is it telling you to do?' Her voice chimed again I kept my eyes closed, I could imagine seeing her more clearly that way. Her Auburn hair, glossy and smelling of strawberries, her green eyes with a hint of gold in them, no gashes or blood. Her lips pink with color not blue, her face ivory instead of sallow and gray. She was as beautiful inside as she was outside. If I let him do this she could never be a monster could she? Not Zoe, she was strong her will was strong she would be able to overcome anything I imagined. I tried to picture her in a wheelchair her body lifeless her eyes pleading for someone to help end her torment of being trapped in that body. An independent spirit trapped by the weight of her broken body depending on everyone around her to help her. That would be a living hell for her. Then the other option I tried visualizing her laying in her coffin her face like a chalk statue completely lifeless empty. I shuttered as I watched them lower her. I pounded my fists against my head trying to get rid of the horrid thoughts invading my mind. I sat in the silence wanting her voice again to calm me. It was gone, I listened intently willing it back but nothing. This is what it would be like, forever without her. I didn't trust Jared or William but I trusted her. I didn't hate him enough to let her be gone forever. I loved her to much for that. I loved her enough to let him have her if it meant I would hear her voice again, see her face, see her happy again, I loved her enough for that. There was an ache in my chest similar to the day I found out about William but somehow more definite now. She wasn't mine, she had already given herself to him and no matter how much I put him through to hurt him, I would only end up hurting her. I couldn't do that to her. I felt her hand on my shoulder and closed my eyes holding it with mine. I even felt her sit next to me and lean into me as she had done that day at my house on the quilt. I drew in a deep breath trying to see if my memory would serve me in remembering how she smelled again but there was a different scent not unpleasant more tropical like coconut. I opened my eyes slowly half squinting her red hair becoming less blurred.

"Abbey?"

"You okay you look like you saw a ghost?"

Her voice made me take a deep breath.

"She's gone."

"Who's gone, Justin are you feeling alright?"

I thought I had said that to myself.

"I'm just tired."

I tried wiping my face and eyes with my sleeve.

"Here,"

She said handing me a tissue.

"Everyone has meltdowns Justin they are how our body responds to distress. It's okay nothing to be ashamed of. That was intense in there and a lot to try and absorb mentally. It's like someone taking your world like a snow globe and shaking it. Everything you thought was stable on the ground is now whirling around you at light speed. It's easy to lose prospective and let your judgment be clouded by our emotions."

"How are you so calm over this? You're so young, it's a little disarming."

"I don't know, it's strange but I almost feel removed a little, emotionally I mean. Like it hasn't registered that it's Zoe in there we are talking about. Maybe it's the place I'm in right now with my life.

I've learned to shut myself off these past few months, I function better that way. Losing my fiancé and then my Uncle Adam dying he was like a father to me, well I just learned facing reality is fine and dandy but to function sometimes you just have to watch it for a while and stop participating."

She stared straight ahead now nodding slightly as if in telling me she had revealed it to herself.

"Yah well that's a nifty trick you'll have to teach it to me someday."

"I know she hurt you Justin, not meaning to doesn't make it any easier it is still hurt. But she thought a lot of you and your family she spoke of your kindness every time we communicated. It meant a lot that you and Jenna understood what she was going through. We have a very big decision to make I don't think I can do this alone. I might appear like a rock but underneath it's shaky. I didn't prepare for something like this. His plan I had no idea it would be so out of the realm of normal but I can't let her go like this. I know if it was me I would want this chance or death but not a life of well what he described. It would be a prison for her in just the short time you have known her you have to know that."

"I do and I wish I felt as resolved as you seem to be. I guess it's what I know about him that makes it harder for me."

I blew out a breath and stood she stood too, looking for a response to my sudden movement. I looked at her trying to absorb her positive attitude into myself as if it would give me the strength to say what I was about to say. Her eyes that should have looked exhausted and weak from the ordeal looked untouched by it.

"I'm not promising I can do this but I will try."

"That's all any of us can do Justin. We have to keep in mind that we have to respect Zoe's wishes, she obviously loves him, and she would never promise to marry if she wasn't absolutely sure that's just not her. I believe she would want him to do this as twisted as it has all become. I can't see another way around it. That being said I have asked him to wait until morning give us all a few hours to get ourselves resolved to the idea and figure out what we will tell everyone, your parents included. And then there is your brother Aaron, I think he's going to know something's up when she is walking around in a few weeks like nothing happened."

"Yah I can deal with them, your mom will never be any the wiser since you didn't tell her how bad she is."

"Yah thanks to you." She half smiled.

"We should probably go get you some food, Jenna said you haven't eaten all day and well you look like hell."

"Wow thanks you will have to teach me how to go thru this and not look like hell sometime then."

"Thanks I think, now we are all going to have to be on our game for the next few days so let's go and get the food out of the way. We can just run down to the vending machines grab some sandwiches and bring them back here for everyone and discuss the actual game plan."

"He's in there with her isn't he?"

She looked at me as if I had foiled her plan to keep us separated.

"Yah, he is."

She looked at me with pity in her eyes. I hated being looked at like that.

"I'm not going to start anything with him in there you don't have to worry."

It came out sounding more like a little kid arguing his case to his mom.

"You're not going to start anything with him period because there is no point to it. It's over and he won Justin, sorry it hurts but it's the truth don't be mad at him, it was her choice not his. He didn't make her have feelings for him."

"I know that, you think I don't know that? It's not that he has her, it's what he is that bothers me."

"Are you sure about that? Because it doesn't seem that way to me."

I wanted to tell her she hardly knows me and she's way off on this but I couldn't. I couldn't because she was right. I was nursing ego wounds. I had definite reasons to hate him as far as putting her in danger with Jared and himself but above that I simply hated him because I was jealous of him. Having someone hold a mirror to your face sucked! I didn't like it one bit but she had nailed it and I couldn't argue with her I didn't have the strength to lose another argument.

"You really should have been a therapist you're pretty good at this, calling people out."

She rolled her eyes.

"Well it's not hard when it's like looking at a mirror image of yourself. We have that in common hating someone for all the wrong reasons. Not that you don't have reason but just the wrong ones."

"Okay sandwiches and then maybe once I've eaten I won't be so crabby. That was your point right?"

"Something like that yes. Jenna and I drew straws on who would come deal with you."

"You lost huh?"

"Nope, I won!"

She walked past me and I stood for a moment processing what she said.

"You coming or what crabby?"

Chapter Twenty-One: The Enemy of my Enemy

***

They all looked at me when I entered her room Aaron, Jenna, and William. I had promised myself not to dwell on what had happened but to focus on the task at hand, making Zoe well again. Jenna hugged me and kissed my cheek whispering how proud she was of me. William just nodded at me.

"I can't promise I'll be okay with everything but I won't be the one to stand in the way either."

Abbey was standing beside me now. It was like she gave off a positive vibe that made me more at ease with my decision.

"Let's do this then."

She said with a sound of dread of what was to come. We were all feeling it even William. It was on every ones face the look of remorse that we had to even put her through this but it was this or the other options, this had been her best chance and so we all stepped into the unknown with her. It went exactly as William said it would the poor prognosis although it took a little longer, two days to be exact, she acquired a severe staff infection from the drain causing more damage to her already weak heart. William was eager to get her out before there was any more brain damage it was a difficult 48 hours for all of us to say the least.

Of course her family doctor stepped in and made all the arrangements to have her brought to his private residence to make her and her family as comfortable as possible at this time, of course having money at your disposal helps with any questions or normal red tape. Jenna and Aaron were waiting for us at William's house. Abbey, William and myself were waiting while Jared got all the paperwork finalized, William and Jared were to ride with Zoe in the ambulance and Abbey and I would follow in the car.

William had promised us he would never leave her alone with Jared. One of the stipulations Abbey had given him as a safety net as if there was any such thing with what we were all doing. Zoe looked inert as they rolled her out into the ambulance. Almost as if she was only a shell, lifeless I couldn't wait for her to be filled with life again.
"We will meet you at the house I will call if there is any change on our way."
He reached out to take my hand, I numbly shook it knowing Abbey was behind me watching, it would be worth it to suck it up now rather than endure the 2 hour lecture from her on our way home. I followed close behind them wanting to hurry. It was difficult to know you were so close to her rescue and still having the possibility of her not making the trip.
Abbey played with her hair nervously, neither of us wanting to talk. These last two days had been hard but she had helped us all keep a good attitude. William had been kind enough to put us all up in his home so we could stay close for the next phase of his plan.
Jenna, Aaron, and I had taken a two week leave of absence from work and Abbey had told her mother she would be helping with Zoe's recovery for a while it was all easy enough to orchestrate easier than I had thought it would be. We had gone over everything we could expect to have happen with Jared.
It was difficult at first to even be near him but we had come to an understanding although there was no love lost between us we had a common enemy DEATH and it had forced us to become allies. Although he did seem different I still did not trust him and I guessed neither did William, he never let him out of his sight.
It was amazing that he had taken the same fall and only had a slight scrape above his left eye that was already healing. William had said it was because of the high level of serum in his system that kept him from being injured more severe.

"You okay over there?"

I must have startled her because she jumped when I spoke.

"Sorry, I didn't mean to scare you."

"Yah, I'm a little jumpy your sister talked me into drinking a Red Bull this morning and I feel like a crack fiend right now I'm a little wired."

Jenna was already trying to win her over to the dark side.

"Well you need to be careful with that stuff if you're not used to it, it will make you wired and then you crash. Hey I'm worried too but we have come this far. We have to have faith it will all work out right?"

"Right, now if I can just get that to register. I know it will work out because it has to, I can't let myself think any other way but it keeps trying to creep in you know?"

"Yah"

I did know exactly what she meant. I had been fighting doubt since I decided to go along with this, everything had gone so smoothly I was worried it was all building for a huge let down. When we arrived at the house everything moved swiftly Aaron, Andoe, William and I quickly got her out of the ambulance, Jared dismissed the drivers and went ahead to get ready for the next part. We had all been shown the room but I still couldn't get used to it. It looked exactly like an operating room you would see on TV with stark white walls, white tile floor and stainless steel everywhere.

It was blindingly bright Jared had brought in extra monitors and equipment they would need. By the time we got her down there he had already changed into scrubs William excused himself so he could change. We helped move her to the other bed I noticed the restraints on the bed those were new not there before on this bed they had been on the other table in the back of the room. I swallowed hard hoping they would not be necessary.

William came back into the room Jared was prepping the IV they would be using to administer the serum.

"You should probably have a seat out in the other room now the less you have to see of this the better."

His voice was quiet and seemed sincere. Abbey was in front of me Aaron and Jenna both walked out.

"I would like to stay if that is okay."

Her voice was calm but firm. He looked at her his brow furrowed and then relaxed,

"If you insist but I don't think it is necessary."

"I'm staying too."

I said not as pleasant as she had stated. He looked at us both not pleased but not ready to argue his point.

"Alright but you must not interfere no matter what you think is happening we have to stay focused for Zoe. It is going to be painful like we said and we will do everything we can for her but I can't help her if we have to deal with you."

"Yes, we understand we will be spectators I promise. I just can't leave her to go through this."

Her eyes filled with tears and he relaxed his expression. We stood near the door as we watched them connect her to the blue colored IV bag. It was only minutes until the tremors started the monitors began to ring loudly. Jared and William strapped her into the restraints carefully. As the tremors became more violent her body arched and convulsed and then stopped suddenly she began to cough and her body arched again Jared ran to her side and began removing the tape form the intubation tube.

"Wait! If you do that she can't breathe."

"She can breathe on her own now. It's causing her to feel like she's suffocating please stand back."

William said his voice sounding aggravated at my questioning.

She coughed as he removed the tube and the monitor flat lined for a moment and I saw Abbey hold her breathe with her hand over her mouth. Then a heartbeat and another, they came quickly now. Both of them focused on her intently, watching as her chest heaved deeply drawing in the air as if she was running. Her color started to change to a red tone almost matching her hair, her hands gripping her straps Abbey and I looked at each other in amazement

"She moved her hand's did you see that?"

She said excited.

Her excitement didn't last long. Zoe let out a scream that sounded gut wrenching and it didn't stop. William's face turned away from her his fists clenched I presumed he understood what was causing the screams having experienced it first hand. Abbey put her hands over her ears, the screams were getting louder as her body began to flail wildly her hands gripping her restraints.

"Is she going to hurt herself?"

Abbey yelled over the screams, Jared looked back at her.

"No she will be okay once it gets into her system her body is fighting it right now we can't touch her. Anything that touches her feels like red-hot razors. Her entire nervous system is on overload right now she is feeling the extent of her injuries multiplied as the serum works to help her body heal her."

I held Abbey to my side hoping to muffle the sound of Zoe's screams, it was like someone was being torn apart or burned alive. It seemed to last for hours. Finally the screaming subsided but her body heaved and wrenched in pain for most of the night.

William and Jared took turns monitoring her progress and we took turns placing cold towels on her head careful not to touch her at all except for the cool towel.

Abbey had fallen asleep on the other table in the back of the room, William and I stood near Zoe watching.

It was amazing her body was healing at such a quick rate her bruises had already started to vanish, he had removed the bandage on her head and the once large gash looked like a small scrape. Her breathing although still faster than normal had slowed and she seemed to be somewhat resting as much as I expected she could.

"She's doing very well." I looked up at him.

"We are about halfway through she will have to have more serum in a few hours but it shouldn't be as bad as the first dose."

"She has to do it again?"

"Yes she will, until her body adjusts to the serum, and then once a month she will have to have it sometimes more often in the beginning depending on her control."

"Is it like this every time?"

He looked up at me searching for a way to tell me what I already knew.

"It hopefully will never be this hard for her again. She was severely injured as her injuries healed she began to feel the pain caused by them and it made it worse for her but there will be pain when she takes the serum."

"When will the other part start?"

He looked at me confused at first and then catching on to my question.

"Right away usually, she will be out of sorts it's a lot for her to get used to the over active senses, increased emotion, and the cravings. We will have to be careful around her until she gets it under control."

"Her skin is so red and hot to the touch, is that normal?"

"Yes, her body temperature is permanently altered and will normally run about 5 degree's hotter than a normal human's.

Her skin will return to its normal color. Her blood vessels have been broken do to the strain put on her body and the increased temperature."

Her eyes flashed open widely making me jump. The green more pronounced because of the broken blood vessels in her eyes.

"Get Jared quickly. Now Justin!"

I moved quickly to the door I could hear him talking to her as I left the room and walked down the hall. Jenna and Aaron were sleeping on the couches in the room across the hall I turned to walk to the next room when I saw him coming towards me moving fast.

"What's wrong?"

He said quietly.

"William needs you, she opened her eyes. "

His face looked alarmed and he moved faster down the hall. I heard screaming and we began to run. She was struggling against the restraints and screaming every time he stepped near her. He was standing back now obviously upset.

"She won't let me near her." He said his voice full of hurt.

"Shhh it's okay Zoe your safe now."

Jared's voice sounding soothing and soft. She calmed a little, Abbey was standing at her side now.

"It's okay Zoe it's Abbey, you're going to be okay."

She looked at Abbey as if she recognized her but couldn't see her.

"Careful Abbey."

Jared said calmly. Zoe breathed in as if to smell something in the air closing her eyes and then opening them quickly and looking wildly in William's direction. She pulled away from him closer to Abbey. William stepped closer as if in disbelief that she was drawing away from him. She let out a scream as inhuman as his voice had been before as he came closer.

"William step back! it's you she's afraid of."
Jared's words were like bullets. William's face looked like he had been mortally wounded.
"Abbey try and talk to her again but stay back don't get too close."
Jared's voice was almost a whisper. William sank behind Jared still staring in disbelief.

"Zoe look at me, its Abbey honey, can you hear me?"

She looked at her inquisitively as if trying to figure out what she was saying. As if she recognized the voice but not the words. She closed her eyes a single tear fell down her cheek, and she squeezes them tightly as if not wanting to see anything. Jared motioned for us to step away with him.

"She is having trouble communicating possibly due to her brain injury still healing and possibly she is overwhelmed with the sensory overload. We expected this William." Jared said looking at William.

"Yes but not this soon how is she already opening her eyes?" He shook his head.

"I don't know, I had hoped she would stay unconscious longer so she would be less stressed by the process but we will have to deal with it now.

"Why is she screaming every time William gets near her?"

William looked away as if re-injured by the words.

"I don't know, possibly her fight or flight response he might smell like danger to her, some memory maybe triggered by his scent or face. It's probably just temporary but for now you should probably stay out of sight William, to cut down on her stress."

William shook his head in agreement.

"Whatever will make this easier for Zoe."

We walked back over to her bedside her eyes still closed but her hands were clenched into fists. William stayed back behind us making sure to stay out of sight.

"It's okay Zoe just rest, you have been through a lot."

Her eyes opened slowly following Abbey's voice this time she seemed to understand what she was saying. Another tear fell from her eyes. Abbey looked up at Jared he shook his head as if he had no explanation for the tears.

"We are all here Zoe all of us, we won't leave you. I'm right here."

Zoe blinked slowly once as if to let her know she understood. Her eyes shifted towards me looking hard as if to try and figure out who was standing there. I stepped slowly closer to her she blinked searching my face.

"Hey Zoe just relax your gonna be fine. Just hang in there."

Her eyes closed again this time staying closed. I looked at Abbey she smiled looking relieved.

"We should let her rest now she has a long couple of days, ahead of her she'll need her rest and so will we. William why don't you and Justin go get some sleep Abbey and I will take the first watch. I'll have Jenna come wake you in a few hours and you can take over."

William looked at Jared hard at first and then nodded knowing what Jared was asking for.

"She's been through a lot William, it will be okay give her time. Andoe is right outside the door, have him come in and stay with us that way he can come get you if she needs you."

Jared reassured him again.

"William we both need some rest, come on Doctor's orders."

I said pulling at his sleeve he looked up at me and slowly looked back at her.

"You'll call me right away?"

"Right away, I promise."

He walked out his head down

"I'll be right there."

I walked over to Abbey.

"You want me to stay with you?"

"No go get some sleep. Really I slept for a few hours I'm good. She'll need us more tomorrow and you look like hell, get some sleep."

"Get Jenna or Andoe to get us if there is any change."

"I will, now go."

She said softly almost mouthing the words she motioned me out with her hands. William was waiting for me out in the hall.

"I had Darlei bring us some blankets down and she is making us some temporary sleeping arrangements in the room just down the hall."

"Thanks William, I didn't want to be too far in case she needs us."

"There are two couches in that room they should be pretty comfortable."

"I could sleep on anything, trust me."

Actually the floor was beginning to look pretty good at this point. He led me to the room were Darlei was putting the blankets on the couches. I slipped off my shoes and let myself sink into the overstuffed couch.

I pulled the cover up and closed my eyes not allowing myself to think about anything. I just shut down my body twitched a little, I guessed in response to the relaxed state it was trying to acquire. I woke to the light of the new day coming through the window. I looked over to the other couch William had slept on, he was gone. I popped up my body protesting by the sudden movement I was stiff from laying in one position. I tried to stretch but it only made it worse. I smelled hot coffee and turned to see William standing there with two cups in his hand.

"Jared will be starting her second treatment soon, I thought we could both use this."

"Thanks" I said scratching my head.

"Is she still resting?"

"They think so she hasn't opened her eyes again since we left. Jared doesn't know if it's because she is having trouble focusing her vision or if she is just overwhelmed." He shook his head, his voice sounded haggard still tired but human at least.

"I knew this would be hard but it's proving more difficult than I had imagined, seeing her like this."

I didn't want to tell him but I had imagined that things would be worse after seeing her the first twenty minutes but she seemed to be doing better now. But then again she wasn't screaming every time she saw me either. I imagine it was hard for him to take terrifying her like that, not being able to be close to her. I should have been happy at his pain but I wasn't. I felt pity for him probably because I was tired or I have been around Abbey too long. We finished our coffee in silence and walked back down to where she was. Jenna and Aaron were having breakfast in the room they had stayed in last night.

"Did either of you eat yet?"

Jenna said in a motherly tone. William shook his head as if not interested in eating.

"No not yet, has Abbey been out yet to eat or sleep?"

"No, she was waiting for you to come back I think."

I grabbed a piece of toast off her plate and stuffed it in my mouth to try and silence my stomach.

"I'll send her back out make sure she eats something and gets some rest. she's been up almost all night."

"I will I promise. How is it in there?"

"She's better but it's going to be a while I think."

I glanced over at William as if to let her know I would fill her in later.

She nodded as if understanding me. That was the good thing about siblings you learn each other's body language and understand without a word being said. Jenna and I were especially good at it. It was a result of years of playing euchre with Aaron and Mason and their cheating. I took a swig of my coffee it burned my lips and tongue. I didn't want to take it in with me though, I didn't want the smell of coffee wafting through the room and Zoe having to smell it. William seemed apprehensive as we got closer to the door.

"Maybe you should go in first." He said his eyes cast down.

"Sure it's a new day Will, and so is tomorrow and she has that because of you so don't get manic just yet Aye?"

I gave him a slap on the back and went in holding the door for him. I figured that would be my good deed for the day. He was just lucky he caught me in a good mood I told myself. Abbey was sitting in a chair near Zoe's bed, Jared was nowhere I could see. I looked at her as we got closer trying to see if her eyes were open.

"Hey."

Abbey said in a low gravely voice.

"Is she resting?"

She just shrugged and shook her head. William went over to her monitors checking them.

"You should go get some thing to eat and rest now while you can. She is going to need you again in a while."

"You look better, must have gotten some beauty sleep, huh?"

"Something like that yah. Where is Jared?"

"Right here."

His voice was louder than I expected. He walked over to William and they both left walking over to the other side of the room were Jared had been when we came in.

"What's up with that?"

Abbey motioned for me to walk with her over to the other side of the room.

"He thinks she is playing possum."

"What? What do you mean?"

"He thinks she is staying still listening and observing what's going on as if to figure out her surroundings. I guess this drug brings out your most basic of instincts. He thinks because of her head injury she can't remember anything possibly she doesn't even know who she is. The serum is still reanimating her damaged brain cells. She could be having random memories, nightmares, anything could be triggering good or bad."

"Yah, but she seemed to recognize your voice."

"Yes and she screamed when she saw William and cried when she saw you. That's why he thinks there are memories being blended with some kind of dreams or nightmares because of her reaction to him and you. She felt extremely guilty, Jenna said, when she thought she was going to have to hurt you. Your voice could be triggering something like that."

"So why would she scream when she saw William?"

"I don't know he was the last one she saw before she fell. Jared thought it might also be that she can smell him kind of like a predator smells another predator and reacting to a basic survival instinct. It's just a theory we have both been up a while without sleep and it was beginning to get a little out there, with our what if's."

She must have seen through my halfhearted attempt to be supportive of their theories.

"So she is keeping her eyes closed so we think she is still out?"

"Yes it's also very confusing coming out of a coma, people react differently and since it was such a violent way that she fell she could still be in a survival mode. He thinks it's hard for her to focus right now also and that could be why she doesn't open her eyes."

"How does he know she's just not really asleep? Maybe she's just resting."

"She has never reached REM sleep. You have to reach that before you go into a deep sleep. You know where your eyes move back and forth under your eye lids, where your subconscious takes over, your dream state."

I had no idea what she was really talking about but I didn't want to seem dumb so I made a mental note to Google it later.

"Right, so what now?"

"Well, we need to keep our distance from her for the time being and don't get too close to her until he is sure she has herself under control. He said she's pretty strong right now and probably scared."

"When are they going to do the next treatment?"

"He was waiting for William before he started it."

She had dread in her voice the same dread I was feeling about it.

"I'll wait until they do it and then I'll go get some rest and eat. I want to be here so if she does recognize my voice she won't be so afraid."

They came back to where we were.

"Did Abbey fill you in Justin?"

"Yah, a little Twilight Zone but at this point nothing surprises me."

I looked down he had the second IV bag full of serum. It was the blue bag like before.

I looked at William, he was staring at me with a strange expression not angry but not endearing either, almost like he was jealous but in a completely humbled way. I looked away to Abbey. His eyes still creeped me out, I shivered a second and regained my composure.

"So what can we expect with this, the same thing?"

"Shouldn't be as bad for her this time but similar she will be in some amount of pain."

I saw Williams jaws tighten as Jared spoke.

"Well are we ready? I would suggest that you all stand here and let me do it alone that way she won't hold any of you accountable for causing her pain."

William was still walking with him.

"You too William, I think it's better if you stay back, for her."

He simply nodded and stepped back. We all seemed to be holding our breath in anticipation of the serum running its course, it didn't let us down. Almost immediately her eyes opened as she shot Jared a glance. Her eyes no longer red but different somehow, wide and then she narrowed them screaming in a voice that I can't even describe. It was as bad as the first time but this time it didn't seem to last as long her body arched as much as her restraints would let it, the thin sheet they had over her seemed as if it burned her every time it rubbed against her. Jared stepped back towards us.

"Her spine must be completely healed now she couldn't bend like that yesterday."

Abbey held her hands over her ears, only occasionally looking away when it got
to be too much for her. I couldn't look away or cover my ears it was horrifying to hear it but it was also a relief to know she was alive. Jared was whispering something to William, there was a snapping sound almost like tearing. One of her restraints ripped on her right hand she grabbed at the other feverishly.

The right foot strap snapped next we ran to her.

"I can't believe it! that's never happened!"

Jared said in a panicked voice.

William went to her right side to take her arm she let out a deep growl and then screamed pulling away from him he stood there dumbfounded. Abbey pleaded with her to try and calm down so we could help her. I pushed William out of the way and took her hand. Her skin was hot. She looked at me starting to pull away and then a puzzled look came over her for a moment. Jared had managed to re-strap her leg restraint I just stood holding her arm she didn't fight me she just stared her eyes widened and a strange grin climbed up one side of her face.

I had never seen that expression on her face before. I could hear Jared saying my name but it all became muffled like the chaos in the room had gone into slow motion. And then I saw her eyes look to my left the smile left her and she closed her eyes and screamed as he pushed me out of the way and grabbed her hand. The sound came back with a vengeance I shook as if coming out of a stupor.

"Fool, back away you want to get hurt?"

Jared's voice was hard. He quickly restrained her as she continued to scream.

"She was fine! She wasn't even struggling with me."

"That's because she was sizing you up."

"Sizing me up?"

I stood looking at William and Jared for a moment Abbey was talking to Zoe trying to get her to calm down. It finally sank in a little. I guess I would smell differently to her I didn't have that same smell they both had. I stepped back a few more feet and stared at her she seemed so vulnerable right now, so not capable of what they accused her of.

"It's a temporary thing Justin, look at William and Jared she will learn to cope with it as they have but we have to give her space and not test her too soon."

I sank into a chair near the door. The screaming again became muffled and my head whirled. It wasn't as clear as it had been this morning when I gave William his pep talk, reality had crept in somewhere between then and the serum being administered. The screaming subsided as quickly as it had started and she rested again panting, her chest heaving and then slowing to it's now normal fast beat. Her skin began to return to its somewhat ivory, pink hue.

"I'm going to go get some rest Justin will you be alright or do you want to come out with me? I can send Jenna in for a while to stay with William."

"No, go I'll be fine. I just need to be here right now."

She searched my face as if to see if I was telling the truth.

"I'm fine really, just having a reality check right now. I'm golden but if it will make you feel better send Aaron or Jenna in they can sit with me. Go!"

This time I gestured her to scram. I felt a strange feeling of sadness come over me like someone had died. I couldn't understand why I would be feeling like this. There was a huge lump in my throat as I sat trying to figure out what was wrong with me.

William paced in the back of the room making me feel like I was watching the wolf exhibit at the Zoo. I felt bad for him, as much as I disliked him but I couldn't shake that feeling I had when I was around him, uneasy and unsettling. I tried to dismiss my depressed mood and just not think about anything. When that failed I started thinking about Bailey of all things, I wondered how she would respond to him, she was always so concerned about him.

It was hard to think about the possibility that she might not recognize him. We had brought him with us at William's request he didn't trust my brothers to take care of him I guessed or maybe he thought she would want Bailey close. Of course if she reacted to Bailey like she did to William that could be bad. Okay I was not making myself feel better, I stood and stretched a little stiff from sitting. I felt air in the room it was Aaron, he stood trying to adjust his eyes to the dim light in the room.
The only light was behind Zoe's bed and it was very dim. Jared had decided the less light the better it would be less stressful for her. Aaron seemed like a fish out of water, which wasn't like him at all. I guessed the screaming would make anyone a little more than apprehensive. I patted the seat next to mine and after a minute of his eyes adjusting he sat.

"Hey bro, how's it going?"

Aaron's voice was low but not quite a whisper.

"It's going, I guess, just wish she didn't have to go through this."

He nodded in agreement still staring towards the dim light.

"Is she in pain right now? I mean she seems like she's resting but she's breathing awfully hard."

I looked at her laying there her breaths deep and fast making her chest heave with every breath.

"I think its normal for right now, the medicine makes her entire body function differently. Jared says it will eventually become less noticeable."

We sat looking at her for a little while in silence. I could tell he was wanting to say something but was too uncomfortable to do it. I couldn't take it anymore.

"Okay Aaron spill it, what's up?"

He looked at me trying to look puzzled at first but then almost relieved that I had noticed.

"Jenna and I were talking and we thought that it would be good for you to go out and get some fresh air. You've been with her not leaving her side since this all happened and it would do you some good to go take walk."

"No way, look I'm not leaving her here alone with Dr. Jeckle and William and anyway Abbey has been here as much as I have."

"Yah well that's the thing, we think you should both take a break and get some air its just that you've been through a lot lately and she is going to need you to be here for the long hall and your no good to her if you're stressed and tired. Think about it, in a little while when Abbey wakes up both of you go get something to eat. Go to Zoe's let Abbey get some fresh cloths and a change of scenery. That's what Jenna and I are here for. Then when you come back you can relieve William he'll probably need some time to rest by then as well. Look this isn't negotiable if I have to I'll send Jenna in here."

The thoughts of leaving her here long enough to go to her house and back being that far away was hard but I did need to get out and get my head straight.

I was no good to her right now and if Jenna and Aaron were here to keep an eye out, I guess it would be alright. Besides Zoe would have wanted me to make sure Abbey was okay. I looked at him for a long time before I spoke.

"Fine but if you let anything happen to her while I'm gone, I'm gonna kill you both!"

It was a few hours later William had taken a seat as close as the shadow of the room would let him get just out of Zoe's sight. It had to be killing him to not be able to be close to her and even have her afraid of him. I should be basking in it, revealing in it even but I couldn't. Seeing him like this no one should have to feel that badly.

I didn't want to go down the 'what if' road, I don't think I wanted to face the answers I might be giving myself right now. I watched a beautiful woman full of life taken and basically had it all stripped away. It seemed like the only choice at the time but now it was starting to creep in. Would Zoe have wanted this? What if she never fully recovered to herself and she stayed like this, what did we condemn her to? I shook at the thought and quickly dismissed it.

There was a change of air in the room again and some additional light that quickly reseeded. It was Abbey she had been gone only about 4 hours.

"How is she?"

Her voice surprisingly bright for someone who had only had at most 3 hours sleep.

"Quiet since you left no movement at all. What are you doing back so fast?
You didn't get much rest."

I said as more of a declaration than a question.

"I'm fine, couldn't really rest."

Aaron stood up and motioned us both out for a moment. As we entered the hall the light caused us all to squint and have to shield our eyes. Daylight, I forgot it was even daytime in that room.

"Ah Abbey I have a little favor to ask you."

I looked at Aaron disapproving of his decision to take it upon himself to make sure I got out.

I knew I was tired because I didn't even have the energy to dispute his blatant and forward pursuance of what we had discussed earlier.

"What he's trying to say Abbey is he and Jenna seem to think we both need a break. To get away from here for a few minutes, go for a ride, get some air let you go to Zoe's and freshen up if you like."
She grinned
"Looking out for little brother huh?"

Her comment was directed towards Aaron but she was looking at me as if to see what my true response was. She cast a glance at the door to Zoe's room and then at the floor as she deliberated her decision.

"Well I really don't like being far from her, I could use a little breather but I don't know."

"Jenna and I will stay right in there with her and won't leave her until you both return I promise."

He made a gesture crossing his heart with his finger, putting on his most charming smile. She still hesitated as if having a private argument with herself.

"And it's not that far to her house?"

"No, it's only 5 minutes but we don't have to if you would rather not, I could have Jenna take you."

Aaron's gaze was sharp and directed at me.

"I think the whole point is to get you some, what looks to be much needed air." "It's fine I have my cell and if it's only 5 minutes we will make it quick, some sun and air will do us more good than sleep right now I think."

Now they were both looking at me.

"Okay, alright I got it I look like crap, a little crabby and need some air I understand. I'll go but I swear if you don't call us immediately if anything changes I'll ... well you don't want to know."

I must be really, really tired I wasn't even making coherent sentences.

After speaking with William, and Jenna we headed for Zoe's house. Jared was still resting I imagine he was worn out he hadn't really rested since we arrived yesterday. It was a little overcast out but the sun tried peeking through in spots. The cold air felt good as I breathed it in. I noticed Abbey grabbing her arms her thin jacket not quite able to shield her from the cold northwest air.

"Want my jacket?"

"No thanks the cars right here, I'll borrow one of Zoe's when we get to the house."

The drive there was short and silent we both just drank in the air and daylight. Pulling in the driveway I felt strange, like something was missing and it was, she was. It was an empty hollow feeling that I prayed would go away.

"Just the way I remember it."

She said quietly as she opened her door. We both hesitated before we walked in.

"I'm just going to go get a shower will you be okay down here for a bit?"

"Sure, just yell if you need me."

I looked at her regretting the way my last comment had come out.

"I know what you meant Justin relax."

I went into the kitchen and searched for something I could quickly fix to eat. The toast I had eaten earlier today was a distant memory. I pulled out the peanut butter and jelly and laughed out loud how ironic that Zoe had lived on these when she first moved here. She loved P.B.J.'s I felt my throat get dry and felt myself building tears. I swallowed hard and made a couple sandwiches I would wait until Abbey was finished before I poured the milk. I heard the shower on upstairs I placed some plastic wrap over my near perfect sandwiches and walked to the living room and plopped on the overstuffed sofa. I must have passed out because the next thing I remember was Abbey's voice singing as she came down the stairs. It was a wonderful sound that made me smile it was Bob Marley's 'Three Little Birds'.

"Hungry?"

I met her at the bottom of the stairs.

"Starving what's on the menu?"

Her hair was silken and the light from the windows made every highlight glow moving as if it were liquid. As she reached the bottom of the staircase there was a waft of Peach and vanilla. I drew in another breath, the smell was familiar but new somehow. She smiled revealing two large dimples I had barely noticed before. She turned and headed into the kitchen her slender body dressed in jeans and a sweater that was also a little familiar.

"I actually feel human again thanks to the shower and Zoe's closet."

She must have noticed my close examination of her apparel. The black sweater was form fitting and showed more of her figure off than her T-shirt and jeans had before.

"Sorry I know I was staring. It's a little unnerving how much of a resemblance there is between you and Zoe."

She turned slowly and looked back at me her eyes looking directly into my eyes.

"And yet, we are nothing alike."

Her smile curved slightly up one side of her mouth exposing only one dimple this time.

Her eyes had a spark to them that was completely different than Zoe's something a little more dangerous and less guarded.

I needed to stop comparing them it wasn't fair to Abbey. I always hated when I got compared to my brothers, I always worked hard at being me and purposely not like my brothers. I grabbed the milk from the refrigerator and some glasses from the cabinet.

"You know your way around here pretty good huh?"

Her voice was searching for a more detailed answer than just yeah.

"Well I did stay here with Jenna and Zoe after my accident."

"That's right I had forgotten about that, how is your leg?"

I had actually forgotten about it as well until she mentioned it.

"Well I still walk with a limp but the doctor says it will slowly become less and less noticeable."

"Well I think it's kind of endearing."

"Endearing? No not endearing! Maybe strapping or mysterious but not endearing."

She grabbed the plate of sandwiches walking to the table.

"Endearing!"

I was confused that she had walked to the table Zoe never ate at that table.

"What's wrong did you forget something?"

"Ah no, no it's just I'm not used to eating at this table."

"Oh I just thought it would be easier for you to sit at this height with your strapping leg."

"Ha ha, make fun of the cripple."

As I said it a flood of memories came back remembering how much Zoe hated when I called myself that.

"Oh my someone has a healthy dose of self pity. Thank you for the sandwich that was nice not very many guys think like that."

"Think like what?" snapping back out of my moment.

"Thinking about someone else other than themselves."

I nodded a you're welcome. It was easy talking to her she is really open and a great listener. I saw her gazing at my watch.

"Oh wow we really lost track of time."

She said as she pushed back her chair. We had talked for over two hours I had almost forgotten about all the craziness that was happening.

"Yah, we should probably get back huh?"

She just shook her head looking out at the water now as if dread was setting in about going back.

"She has a lot to live for you know?"

I looked at her wondering where that thought had come from.

"You mean Zoe?"

"Yes, she's very lucky to have so many people who love her and care about her."

I could tell this was more than an observation.

"Lucky I don't know, I think she deserves it she gives as much as she receives." I watched her swallow hard and she nodded in agreement.

The next two weeks had gone by quickly and things had been progressing quite well with Zoe. she was still not talking but she was more alert and even in her own room. William had made sure everything was perfect for her. He even slept outside her door in a chair every night never leaving her. She didn't scream anymore when she saw him but she was still afraid of him for some unknown reason. She didn't care for Jared all that much either. Jenna and Dr. Jared had become quiet close and Jenna has sworn to reform him. Jenna and Abbey were the only ones besides Darlei that she would let close to her, well, and me, but they didn't want me close to her, she behaved strangely when I was too close. She was able to move her arms and legs with no problem, she could eat on her own also but her appetite was ravenous.

I honestly don't know how she keeps from weighing 500 lbs. but she hasn't gained at all, in fact she has lost a little since her fall.

Jared says it's from her accelerated metabolism that burns three times the calories as before but it will taper off as they reduce the dosage.

I'm not sure if the dosage changes are responsible but she has seemed more dossal if you want to call it that in the last few days.

Aaron went back home yesterday and Jenna is going today but she will be coming back in the evenings to give Darlei and Abbey a break.
We have all been hoping to hear Zoe say something, anything, that would tell us she is still Zoe but nothing yet. Jared insists we be patient and when you consider what she has been through she is probably still in shock. Abbey and I have been going to Zoe's house every evening just to get out of that house, it's so huge it feels like a museum. It's been great having her to talk to I don't now what I would have done if she hadn't been here. Jared is reducing her dosage again this evening with hopes it might make her less on edge.
I really miss her, the old Zoe, she is still Zoe I know but she's different now her eyes more green than before with darker edges, her features seem different as well, hauntingly beautiful instead of just beauty. Behind her eyes there is something that wasn't there before. I feel it when she looks at me as if she is piercing them through me. Abbey says she knows we did the right thing but sometimes it scares, me this decision we have made to cheat death, I just don't know.

Chapter Twenty Two:
E'Veil (Awakening)

***

Zoe Dossin:

I felt my body as if for the first time I had felt gravity. It was heavy and pain was everywhere and spreading, as if someone had set a pile of hot metal chains on my body and was dragging them all over me. The pain was unbearable, thoughts coming in and out of my head, I couldn't think my mind was everywhere trying to make the pain stop. I couldn't understand where I was, the fear was unreal and I couldn't breathe something was choking me. Finally I felt air coming and noises, no voices, calling a name, Zoe and speaking softly in low tones. My hands are held down and I can't see, I can't see where I am or who these people are. I just wanted out to run, get away, his voice it makes me feel strange and makes my chest hurt. I hear sounds, screams, coming from my dry throat. I felt my body jerk as I awoke opening my eyes, I could see dim light. The room was familiar but I wasn't sure if from life or a dream, she's saying that name again Zoe. I know her, I've heard that voice before. Closer... closer... It's so dark, I can't see her, as I struggled to focus in the dim light, I heard another voice saying 'too dark' it was my voice, sounding gravely and course. It hurt to make the words come out. Her eyes became large with surprise making them seem even bluer than they had been. I heard whispering and with a little concentration I was able to hear them

> "She said too dark go get Jared or William, should we open the curtains?"

I was still struggling to see the people attached to the other voices. There was a man's voice but he was farther away from me, I could smell him. He smelled like the woods, cool with a slight hint of musk.

There was another smell coming from him much stronger it made me hungry, I felt my mouth watering making me have to swallow. I breathed in again this time another scent even stronger than the first. It made me shiver and not want to breathe, the smell made fear come over me and I felt myself withdraw into the bed I was in, I scooted backwards farther into the pillows sitting up now. I squinted to make my vision better. I concentrated as hard as I could and was able to make out the figures, there were three of them no, that's not right, I smelled four different scents. Where is the scary one? I couldn't see him but I knew he was there. There was another voice and a sound of a door opening and closing. I could smell another scent. It wasn't as disturbing and not as bad as the other one, just different, it still made me leery of who it belonged to. He came closer, the new smell, and his face somewhat familiar but I wasn't sure.

"Zoe it's me Jared, can you talk to me? Do you know who you are?"

They all moved closer except the one that stayed in the shadows the one that made me feel fear every time I breathed. Of course I know who I am. I thought to myself but then I tried to think, who I am? I felt my eyes searching for something that would help me remember.

"It's Okay Zoe take a moment and just try to say something again."

Her voice was steady and soft as she spoke to me she called me Zoe is that right? Am I Zoe?

"I'mm Zoee?"

It was my voice again gravely and low.

"See? Did you hear it? She said her name."

She was even more excited now I don't think she realized that was a question. I was concentrating all my attention to my words now, why was this so hard?

"Who am I?"

I said it louder this time.

It hurt to make it come out louder and I was unsuccessful in incorporating the emotion with my words, they came out flat. They all looked surprised at me. I closed my eyes and felt warm tears stream down my face feeling confused and frustrated. My body felt foreign and I kept replaying the dream I had had of the pain, the absolute fire I had felt.

"Shhh don't cry sweetie it's okay, your alright we are all here with you. It's me Zoe, it's Abbey. Justin and William are here also."

That name, the last name William, I know that name. It made my chest hurt again. I felt pressure like an elephant was sitting on my chest when I thought of that name. Who was William? which one? I slowly opened my eyes. I took a deep breath and dragged my fingers through my hair it was long and the same color as hers but different it had curls. I laughed to myself for some unknown reason, I found the fact that my hair was curly humorous. I looked down at my body examining it, touching it to make sure it belonged to me.

"Give her time, she has a lot to process."

His voice, this Jared person was talking again. I couldn't tell if I liked him or not yet. I liked the woman, I felt warm inside when she spoke, comforted at the sound of it. There was the other man he was younger, he looked as scared as I felt. His blonde hair and blue eyes where in contrast to his darker skin. He hadn't spoken yet he stood behind her, the one who called herself Abbey. I searched the room for the other one, the one I could still smell but had not seen.

"This is Justin, Zoe, do you remember Justin Randall?"

She pressed the young blonde man forward I drew in a deep breath. I felt my eyes widen and felt my heart accelerate, the smell was making me overwhelmingly hungry it made me have to swallow hard.

Again I closed my eyes to try and control what my mind was thinking. I held my breath and opened my eyes. He was behind her again farther back this time.

"She likes the way you smell I think Justin."

She told him in a whisper.

"Yes a little too much I'd say, I'd keep your distance just a little longer Justin, if I were you."

It was Jared. I could put his voice to his name now. I felt a small surge of satisfaction from that. The other man Justin gave him an unusual look I couldn't figure out. William must be the one in the back of the room. I desperately wanted to see what he looked like. Put a face to that feeling.

"Light."

I got it out a little easier than before.

"Yes Zoe, we'll open the curtains for you."

She turned to walk to the other side of the room.

"Just a little Abbey, her eyes are still sensitive and need to adjust gradually."

I felt a sphere of light blast into the room like an explosion. I held my arm up to block it out, it made my eyes water.

"Sorry is that too much?"

I felt the light withdraw slightly and slowly lowered my arm, my eyes adjusting to the new depth of the expansive room. It was larger than I had imagined, I looked warily over towards the direction of his scent. My eyes took him in he was dark, his eyes met mine in a stare that took my breath away. My breathing became rapid, his scent grew more intense as my breathing multiplied.

I felt my hands grip the bedding beneath me.

I tried to make sense of the thoughts going through my head, they were strange the word run, run, RUN, kept going through it. I wanted to close my eyes, I wanted to break this stare but I couldn't. I was locked into it somehow.

"William."

My voice was a whisper still coarse and graveled. He gasp, his eyes widened he stepped forward slightly and stopped.

"Easy William, take it slowly."

Jared's voice was muffled by the sound my heart was making thud, thud, thud it echoed in my head. I felt my legs draw up underneath my body and I scooted farther against the head of the bed smashing the pillows. He seemed saddened at my retraction.

"William?"

I said, this time it was louder and more assertive.

"Yes Zoe, that's William do you remember him?"

Abbey's voice was elevated slightly but still calm. My body would not listen, all I wanted was to stop breathing so I could think, I couldn't even close my eyes. Concentrate I told myself, I drew in one big breath and held it. I closed my eyes and let out the breath. The scent was gone I could hear muffled talking, I concentrated on listening and could hear them.

"I told you William, give her some time she is working things out."

"You saw her she is terrified of me, I can't put her through that! She's been through enough because of me."

It was Jared's voice and one I hadn't heard earlier, William's voice. Why did I feel fear when I smelled him? Why was I able to smell him? This didn't feel normal to me but it felt right somehow.

"She doesn't even know who she is, it's going to take time."

"I know that, don't you think I know that! She didn't react like that with Justin or Abbey."

"Yes well you and I both know why she doesn't act that way with him. His pheromone signature is different than mine and defiantly different than yours. He isn't a threat to her."

"I'm not a threat to her either, I love her! I know all of this Jared I just, ah... It's killing me I want to touch her, hold her, talk to her, comfort her, not terrify her."

I stopped listening after that I couldn't, how could he love me when I don't know him. What is wrong with me? Everything about him makes me want to scream and run, he makes my chest hurt. I felt the warm wet tears again. I slid down into the bed curling into a ball my face planted into a pillow. I felt like something had been stolen from me my thoughts, someone or something had come in and stolen my very being. I was sobbing now and felt her at my side petting me and trying to sooth me with her soft words. The smell of warm vanilla and peaches entangled my senses and made me feel safe. I felt my body begin to shake and convulse and then darkness.

I saw the light coming through the window, I sat up to see no one there in the room. I slid off the bed toward the window, feeling the cool satin of my gown slide across my skin as I stepped onto the floor. Something was drawing me to the window, I had no choice but to go to it. My eyes adjusted quickly I saw a dark figure below wearing a dark cape. Its hood blocked the face of its owner. I watched as it crept along the stone path as if it were following something as well. There he was just off the path near the water. His hair reflected the moon's light making it look white instead of blonde. I drew in a breath sweet and lovely making my mouth water, I felt my heart beat increase but very controlled. The dark figure crouched, he was unaware of the dark figure still looking out over the water.

As the figure got closer his scent grew stronger in my lungs, my hands were against the window now pressing against it watching excitedly, the dark figure was within three feet of him. My eyes batted quickly as if I were afraid to miss anything.

The dark figure leaped grabbing him and dragging him down as the hood flew back and I looked as the auburn hair glowed like fire in the moonlight. Her head flew back tearing the flesh from his throat silencing his screams. I felt the warm liquid drip down my face and chest. The sweet smell filling my senses, I gasped as I watched the dark figures hand pull the liquid down her throat to her bosom spreading it. I shuddered with excitement. Licking my lips, my throat was no longer dry but filled with the warm sweet taste of him.

As if waking from a dream I stepped back the dark figure looked up at me as I still gazed down at her, she bowed holding her cape out and smiling through the crimson liquid. I saw her teeth, they shown in the large smile as if they were made of white marble. I gasped as I caught my reflection in the mirror I was covered in the dark crimson liquid, my auburn hair looking exactly like the dark figures. I touched my face hoping my reflection was not the one in the mirror but to my horror it was mine. I tried to scream as I watched his lifeless body slump over. The dark figure was gone there was just me. What had I done? It felt right before, I felt the screams coming now easily my voice coarse and low building higher as the screams progressed. I jumped to a standing position in the bed still hearing the screaming everyone in the room jumped as I did. I stood unsteadily on the mattress trying to get my bearings as I wiped the stinging hot tears from my eyes.

"Easy Zoe, it's just a dream."

"No, no..."

I felt myself say in a pleading tone as I ran my hands across my chest to feel if the crimson liquid was still on me. It was dry I looked down my gown was a pale cream silk no crimson liquid. I gasped for breaths now trying to figure out where I was and what had happened. I heard that name, my name.

"Zoe, Zoe it's okay calm down."

I couldn't focus it was as if my senses were not listening to my mind. It was then that I heard the voice that brought me back quickly. His deep, satin voice made me shiver as it spoke my name.

"Zoe, concentrate on my voice. Good now try and sit down."

I felt his hand reach for mine I could sense the heat from it nearing. I wanted to pull away but something deep inside told me to stay and listen. I let him take my hand, I held my breath it was easier that way, the fear didn't make me incoherent.

"Okay that's good, now concentrate on opening your eyes."

I focused on his request and slowly opened my eyes he was close, too close. I had to breathe but I didn't want to. His eyes looked at me, I turned my head and drew in a shallow breath. Turning back to him, his face was searching for something in mine.

"A dream, I dreamed."

My words were not coming out exactly how I wanted, I had planned a much more elaborate sentence but it's all I could get out.

"Yes you dreamed, it's over now it wasn't real."

"But I killed him."

That wasn't supposed to come out. I didn't mean to let it out.

"You killed who Zoe?"

He didn't seem horrified, he didn't even seem surprised. My eyes betrayed me as I caught sight of him, his blonde hair and blue eyes so innocent.

"You killed Justin in your dream?"

He whispered now so only I could hear. I shook my head and lowered it sobbing.

"But you didn't really, it's just a dream." His voice still whispering.

"But I wanted to, very badly."

I whispered back to him through the tears forgetting to hold my breath as his scent slammed into me like a brick wall. I drew back a little, quickly exhaling to get rid of his scent. His hand was still firmly holding mine, it felt warm instead of the cooler hands that had been helping me all day. He sat looking at me it was difficult to focus on anything. I was having to pay to much attention to my breathing. I felt myself getting light headed and realized I wasn't breathing enough. I had to get away from his scent. When I did manage to breathe in it made me shiver, I didn't want to hurt him after what I had heard earlier and he seemed so nice now, my body must be sending me false signals but I couldn't bare it. I tried to look at him and convey my apology as I drew back further from him removing my hand from his touch. I turned and drew in a deep breath.

"William, I think it's your scent."

Jared had come to stand beside him now my lungs burned with both of their scent but it wasn't as bad as it had been when I was so close to him.

"Zoe I know this probably sounds crazy but does the way William or I smell bother you?"

That was an understatement but how was I going to convey to them how I felt? I was having problems making the words come out.

"Hard to talk, say what I feel."

Ahh! It wasn't right, that's not right, I can't stand this I wanted to scream. I was shaking now with frustration.

"You have to be patient and calm down, it will only be worse if you get upset."

Jared's voice meant to be reassuring but it was grating me! I didn't want to be patient there was too many things I needed to say. Against everything my body was telling me I drew in a deep breath and blew it out slowly closing my eyes to focus, I concentrated all my energy to my mouth.

"It's hard to breath when he is close... it hurts my chest... and I - I feel... fear."

I kept my eyes closed, not wanting to see their reaction.

"Amazing, I thought it was something like that."

"Jared I've never felt fear when I breathe your scent."

"Of course you wouldn't William, I have never felt fear of your scent either just the contrary the first few times I was near you after I took the serum it made me angry but she is female we are males different pheromones get released, predatory pheromones."

I opened my eyes what were they talking about what serum?

"What? What have you done to me, What did you give me?"

My voice was shaking with a vast quake of emotions.

"Tell me!"

I looked at him and then at William. His intense gaze was aimed at the floor, my eyes met Jared's.

"See, it's already getting easier to speak isn't it?"

"What have you given me? What have you done?"

My fists were clenched and my chest pounding with a new release of adrenalin, the fear was replaced with anger. My mind was trying to reason with me that I didn't really want to know what they had done.

"Zoe honey it's okay, nobody will hurt you we love you, it's going to be alright."

Her soft voice usually calming to me was interrupted by my fully intense glare. He motioned them both back stepping closer I made no attempt to withdraw this time I didn't care about his scent. My mind was focused on a most definite wrong that had been done to me to my mind and my body.

"We had to give you a medicine or serum to save you. You had an accident and you were in bad shape without it you would have died."

He spoke slowly as if I was a child. It didn't seem real or right, it felt wrong what he was saying. Something in me was repulsed by the thought of what they had done but I couldn't think of why. Every time I tried to process it, It was like a huge white wall went up in my brain and no matter how I tried I couldn't get past it.

"I'm not right, it feels wrong, something is wrong with me."

The words were coming easier now but still took almost all of my concentration to convey or express any emotion with my words. My body, this body who's ever it was, was beginning to feel like all the bones had been removed. I felt my knees bending and weightlessness as the room became a bright white and then black. I could still hear their voices and felt him grab me, his warm hands carefully cradling me. The more I tried to focus and struggle to regain consciousness, the darker it got. I willed myself to completely relax to let my mind go blank, it worked. Their voices that seemed miles from me before were close now and clear.

"She will be alright, it's just too much for her to process, her body went into self preservation mode and just shut off, kind of like a kill switch. She is okay, she can probably even hear us she just needs to relax and rest."

"But Jared does she remember what the serum is? How-"

Her voice abruptly stopped and I felt only one presence close to me now where there had been more at least three other scents just his remained. I felt his warm hand on my face brushing the hair that had fallen across my face back. I tried to breath shallow again at first but I needed air and my lungs had over rode my minds urge to suppress that function.

"I'm so sorry, so very sorry my beloved."

I heard him whispering it, it was almost unbearable for me to hear.

His breathing was labored and deep, it trembled when he spoke resonating in my ear as he still held me. Whenever he spoke the word beloved it was like a blunt object was smashing into my chest. Nothing I was feeling felt right. Why couldn't I speak, or see, or hear normally without having to concentrate? I felt anxiety building in my body again and drew in deep breaths to relax myself, I let a flood of cool white light pour over my mind calming it giving into his arms and relaxing every muscle in my body. It was difficult at first it went against the original urge to flee or to run, but became easier as I felt the wonderful feeling that came with the cool white light.
The heaviness from my sleep was still present as I willed the heavy lids of my eyes to open, my body felt the full force of gravity as if I had been weightless and now was somehow strapped down. I worked my arms free from my covers and stretched as if to release my arms from the heavy force of gravity. I looked around the room, the curtains were drawn and there was only a rose colored dim light coming from the side table. I scanned the room for anyone else, I was alone?
I held my head in my hands for a moment trying to figure out if I was dreaming now or had been dreaming. I meant to turn the covers back and flung them across half the bed, I looked quickly to see if anyone had been watching then remembered I was alone. I stepped lightly off the bed and walked around it to look out the window. I needed to assess what time of day or night it was. It looked to be early morning there was a light fog rolling across a blanket of white snow.
The sun was masked by dull gray clouds. I turned walking towards the door I got halfway across the room when I heard the door opening I stopped and stood still.

"Zoe, what are you doing out of bed? I left for 5 minutes and you try and get up on your own?"

"Abbey?"

"Yes Abbey that's excellent you remember from yesterday. Here let's have a seat here near the window you can look out and we can talk. Are you hungry?"

I grabbed my stomach that flipped when she mentioned food and nodded. She patted the seat next to the window and I stepped back towards it and sat. She walked over and pulled on a tassel near the bed and came back over to sit near me.

It was easy to breathe around her she didn't make my mouth water or make me scared. I felt safe when she was near me.

The smell of vanilla and peaches wafted every time she stirred. A small woman came in and she asked her to bring us some breakfast and to tell the boys not to interrupt our girl talk. She looked at me her eyes a vivid blue and sparkly, her skin was smooth and tan.

"You look so much better today Zoe, if you would like I can pull your hair back before your food comes and we can even get you dressed if you want to get out of that nightgown."

I shook my head in agreement and she walked over to the dressing table and picked up a paddle brush and a hair tie. We will braid this gorgeous, curly, thick hair of yours so it doesn't get in your way today. She quickly and gently brushed the knots from my hair and braided a long thick braid down my back it felt good to have it out of my face. She then grabbed a large black duffle bag from the corner and pulled out a pair of jeans and a sweater and returned stopping just in front of me.

"Here we go, I had Jenna stop at your house last night and get some clothes for you."

"Jenna? I have a house?"

Her smile faded slightly but came back quickly.

"Yes, you have a beautiful house that over looks the water and Jenna is a very dear friend to you.

She is Justin's sister the blonde man who was here last night. They care very much for you and have been here staying and helping to take care of you until you are better."

I tried to process the names and catalog them so I would remember them later on saying them over and over to myself.

"Don't worry Zoe, it will come in time, Jared says you will probably regain most if not all of your memory. You just have to take it really slow your body is still healing. Let's get you dressed and we'll talk."

I had practiced what I wanted to ask her while she was helping me put my clothes on concentrating on the most important questions.

"Abbey, what happened to me? How did I get sick?"

She sat beside me and took my hands in hers they felt cool as if they were chilled.

"Well Zoe, I wasn't there..."

She paused as if to make sure she remembered the story.

"From what I have heard you were at a lighthouse near here taking photos, you're a photographer and you are always out taking pictures of landscapes and scenery. Anyway, you had stopped to get some pictures of the lighthouse. Justin had stopped to see you and he found you and Jared there."

Again she paused as if to figure out how to tell the rest of the story.

"Well I guess there was a damaged railing and Jared fell over it, you tried to save him and fell over the side. Justin's knee was still hurt and he wasn't able to help. William got there a few minutes later to try and help you but they couldn't reach you because of the damaged rail. You fell and got washed into the rocks below."

As she finished the story of paramedics and my head trauma and various life threatening injuries I tried to remember the accident about falling but I couldn't, it was the same white wall in my mind blocking any memories.

"Who are you to me? Are you a friend?"

She smiled deep dimples erupted on either side of her face and she put her arm around me.

"I'd like to think I'm your friend but I also have the great privilege of being your cousin, our moms were sisters."

"Were sisters?"

Her expression changed and I felt her body tense beside me.

"Yes, Zoe they were sisters. I'm sorry I don't know how else to tell you your mom was very sick with cancer and she passed away a few years ago."

I suddenly felt sick and a lump was forming in the back of my throat.

"And my father? I have a father right?"

She shook her head her eyes were pooling with tears.

"Yes, you had a wonderful father the best I have ever known and he loved you very much they both did."

She wiped tears away from her face as new ones replaced them.

"So he is gone also?"

"Yes, he passed last summer. I'm so sorry Zoe I didn't want you to have to go through this again."

"I am alone then?"

"No, not alone, you have us and my mom Kate your Aunt Kate, some cousins and so many people here, friends who love you. You will never be alone Zoe."

I knew there was an appropriate response to the sad news she had given me but I wasn't sure what that was. The reality was I felt very alone everyone was a stranger to me now even myself.

I folded my hands and placed them in my lap, my head down as if waiting for my heart to tell my mind how to respond. We sat still for a long time my thoughts blank as I struggled to feel the loss she had just described. The small woman Darlei returned with food as hungry as I had been I suddenly had lost my appetite and simply pushed the tray aside. After I don't know how long there was a light wrap at the door Abbey got up and opened the door she looked back for a moment.

"Zoe I'll be right back okay?"

I nodded and she slipped out. I could hear muffled voices and concentrated for a moment straining to hear who it was. The voices suddenly became very clear and it was easy to hear as long as I kept my eyes closed and concentrated. It was William, Abbey, and Jared Abbey was upset that she had explained what had happened.

"She wants to know, wouldn't you?"

"Yes of course, Abbey it's only natural that she is questioning her surroundings. It's a hopeful sign that she is having coherent thought."

Jared's voice was distinctive stoic in a way very matter of fact.

"William what do you think? Should we continue to tell her every detail? It seems to upset her more that she doesn't remember not so much what I am telling her."

"She has no memories of people it's like telling her a stranger died. My first thought is to protect her from it all but she would want the truth. We have to pace ourselves, give her time to absorb a little at a time. We could cause a lot of emotional damage, I'm afraid if we go too fast with her. She is in a fragile state right now, the serum causes your emotions to react differently. How is she now? Do you think I could speak with her?"

There was a long pause before she responded.

"I know how much you want to be with her and I know if she even had a vague memory of you wild horses couldn't keep her from you but take it slow just like you said don't push her."

"At this rate taking into consideration her head injury I think within a few days she should be functioning on her own. I'm not saying her memory will be back but as far as reasoning and her cognitive thought process she will be in good shape. I also think that you should speak with her William about the effects the serum is having and what she can expect. The more she knows the less frightened she will be about it. I think it would be good to keep Justin away for a few days, let her get a grip on what she is experiencing, then under strict supervision we will expose her to him. So for now let's limit her visitations to just us let her learn our scents, then slowly expose her to the others."

"Do you really think she would do him harm?" Abbey's voice was strained as she spoke the words that made me afraid of myself, would I do him harm? Would I hurt anyone? I tried quickly to regain my concentration to hear their response.

"If the desire is there and the temptation, most definitely. She is physically twice as strong as he is and absent of the ability to decipher consequence to her actions, she is in a primal mode pure instinct. Do animals feel remorse when they kill or injure another animal? It's because it is their nature she has to go against her nature when she shows restraint in how she reacts. It's an extremely dangerous state to be in but as we level off the serum dosage she will be able to manage it as William does. We also have to make sure she eats, it's much harder to control when there is a natural hunger."

"I am going to call Justin and Jenna and have them hold off coming today to see her as you suggested Jared. William would you stay with her until I have spoken to the Randall's and explained this to them? She should probably not be alone much longer I've been out here a while."

I stopped concentrating on them I didn't want to hear anymore. I felt so many emotions it was hard to sort them out but one was gaining speed and taking over quickly, anger. Comparing me to an animal?

I felt a release of self-control wash over me for a moment, now is not the time to lose control. I had to keep my head on straight, I didn't know these people and I needed to be careful. I wanted some answers, needed answers and I would have them. I stood up and looked in the mirror at the reflection staring back at me lost, pathetic and weak looking.

The blue sweater she had picked out for me was juvenile and prissy. I stepped over to the black bag and riffled through it, ahh yes, perfect. I slid the black cowl neck sweater over my head. It plunged low in the back so the bra she had helped me put on earlier was unnecessary, I quickly removed it. I placed the blue juvenile sweater and the bra neatly into the bag and stood again in front of the mirror still something not right yes the braid it had to go. I looked like a Child's doll dressed in woman's clothing. I pulled at the hair tie and shook the thick braid out and ran my fingers through the loose curls. I could feel something happening, something was changing inside me as if another person was coming to life more confident not scared, not worried. It was as if a cool resolve had washed over me and everything I had been fearful of or apprehensive was lifting.

The door opened and I turned slowly as he entered the room.

His eyes canned my body inconspicuously he moved more fluent than the others he walked slowly to the center of the room. I maintained eye contact with him.

"You look like you are feeling better."

"Better? Yes, much thank you." my voice was smoother now and flowed easily.

"Would it be alright if I come closer?"

"As you wish."

I walked toward the window his eyes followed me intently as if figuring out a puzzle. He stopped about five feet from me.

"Is this okay for you? I don't want you to be uncomfortable."

I admit the scent from him still made my chest hurt and my heart beat quicker but the fear was all but dissolved for now.

"I'm fine."

Again I purposely answered in a smooth flat tone.

"Was there something you wished to speak to me about?"

"Yes actually but first are you sure you are feeling alright you seem different."

"I feel different; as I said I'm better much better don't I look better?"

I held my arms out and pivoted left and then right and then in a full circle my eyes met his as I completed the turn. They were black and the veins on his neck pulsed quickly, I could hear his heart rate accelerate. His scent had become more intense, I swallowed and hid the grin that tried to form from his reaction to me.

"Now that we have established that I'm better, were you going to tell me what your next question was?"

I stepped closer to him this time I could not contain the grin, his heart rate had almost doubled.

"Do I make you nervous?" I asked him.

"Is this too close?"

I was within a few inches of him now pushing myself to ignore what my chest was saying. He looked down at me searching for something. I felt another wave of emotion, I was suddenly very aware of our close proximity. I could feel him, his heart rate accelerate the closer I got. It made something in me feel euphoric to have that kind of control. I purposely allowed my face to get closer he looked into my eyes searching for something.

"I think maybe it was the serum you were going to tell me about is that right? How it will affect me, poor Zoe, turn me into a monster?"

Now his eyes glared he stepped back.

"That's kind of cheating you know, eaves dropping."

I stepped closer again this time our bodies almost touching I could feel the heat from him penetrating my chest. I sensed that he wanted to pull away but at the same time desired to be closer to me. I closed my eyes trying to read him, he was difficult the harder I tried the more he blocked me.

"You mustn't let what was said offend you, it was spoken with concern and love for you."

I held my breath as he spoke trying not to breathe his scent in.

"Ah yes the utmost, I understand what's next let's put her in a barred room so she can't hurt anyone?"

I had to focus with everything to hold back my rage that was building. He had closed his eyes I assumed to gain more composure to his heart rate. He leaned in slightly as if to kiss me I pulled back allowing his lips to brush mine slightly.

"This serum you have pumped into me has made me this way but I'm the monster? Really?"

His eyes shot open realizing that I had pulled back. I felt my blood run hot inside of me. I felt myself changing, my mood shift dramatically.

I desperately tried to hold onto the calm façade just a little longer.

"Zoe you are not a monster! No one thinks you're a monster, we all love you and just want to protect you."

"Yes that's right you love me, you wish to only be close to me? To hold me?"

His expression changed his eyes narrowed.

"Yes that's correct...How long have you been able to hear us?"

"Long enough but before I was weak and scared allowing myself to be fragile, I believe were the words."

"Zoe let me help you, this is a side effect of the serum it makes you paranoid, jealous, angry all of those feelings and more you have to let us help you get through this, it will get better."

"But I told you I am better, much better I don't need anyone to fix me I think you have done enough. You have changed me I don't know how I was before but if I'm different it's because of what you all have done. There are consequences to our actions, I might be different but this animal knows that much."

"Zoe I understand more than you know, I had to deal with these changes like you are right now. I was dead and my father brought me back. I hated everyone and everything about myself what I had become until I learned to adjust, to acclimate myself to my new life. But it wasn't until I met you that I felt like there was purpose to my life. It was selfish of me to put you in danger like I did, I wanted to make it up to you.

I just wanted to give you a second chance with the serum, it doesn't have to stay like this. Zoe you can be you again just give us time to help you.

I never meant to hurt you, you helped me have hope again that I could be different. The way you feel right now betrayed, alone, I have been there where you are, the anger and distrust all of it."

A part of me wanted to listen, to believe his words, truth is I didn't trust him or anyone. Everything in me was in turmoil it churned inside of me, thoughts randomly came and went as I tried to stay clear. I turned towards the window and walked closer to it my heart beating faster now.

"You love me now William but for how long? How will you love me once I slip up, lose control, and hurt or even kill? Will you love me then?"

He started to respond but I couldn't listen anymore I was through listening.

"Did I tell you how hungry I feel right now William? It's almost painful how ravenous I am."

I looked back at him casting a full grin his eyes grew large and then narrowed his voice seemed muffled in my head and he lunged for me.

"Zoe no!"

I felt the wind from his hand swiping my shoulder as I leaped my arms over my head for protection as they erupted through the glass. I felt my stomach lift and then my feet land hard on the cold ground beneath. My mind screamed run! I obeyed this time letting it guide me as I came to the wall I could hear him closing in on me, I leaped grabbing a branch from the tree above me catapulting me upwards. I carefully landed onto the closest limb and then leapt over the iron fencing. I could still hear him pleading for me to come back. I shook my head dismissing his voice. My feet ached with cold as I continued to run, the rocks digging into my slippers.

I didn't know where I was going, I ran towards the south end of the beach first for about 10 minutes but something was drawing me north back the other way.

I turned and headed through the woods this time keeping off the rock shoreline. My muscles felt right running somehow even with the cold moist air it was energizing. My breathing was becoming normal again and I pressed harder to get away from him.

There was a light coming from a house close by I instinctively ran towards it. I stood at a distance watching as they entered into the house all three of them. The girl Abbey, Jared, and William I stayed back not wanting to let them know I was there. They had expected me to come here, this was my house, I felt a pit in my stomach brought on by the realization that this was my house.

I quickly dismissed the thought filed it away to be dealt with later. I watched through the window as they explained to Justin what had happened.

> "She had extensive head trauma with untold brain damage the serum has healed her but there are probably still parts of her brain recovering from that type of emotional and physical damage. Until it has run its course she will be unpredictable, irrational and dangerous."

I was really starting to hate this Jared. I was able to read them all easily now, William was a little more challenging but when he wasn't aware I was there it was easier, his feeling of guilt was beyond help. I read their thoughts as they discussed how to handle this situation not being able to call the police and report me missing as Justin had originally suggested because what would happen when they found me. I was growing aggravated with their conversation it wasn't helping that it was cold and I had started to shiver or that a deep burning had begun in my stomach and was getting worse. They had decided to leave Justin there to wait for Jenna, who would be there in a few hours after she had finished with some business and the rest would start a sweep of the area.

Abbey would wait back at William's house in case I decided to come back there. I watched them leave and in particular I watched them together Abbey and Justin to say it bothered me was an understatement. I don't understand why it bothered me, I had no feelings for this man, I didn't know either of them really yet something made me feel angry at their extended gaze and lengthy hug followed by a kiss. My blood felt hot beneath my skin as I watched so perfect so enamored of each other and then a random thought of me in the back of his thoughts kept surfacing. What a bad boy kissing one and thinking of another? The shame he felt after was priceless, I waited impatiently for them to finish and for her to finally leave.

I stepped back onto the slate path making sure they had left. I looked upwards towards the house my mind flashed and I closed my eyes. I heard laughter and a voice saying 'let's go in Zoe before you freeze to death' and then I saw him, tall with dark hair wearing a denim jacket. My chest hurt as if being crushed. I loved this man? He turned and motioned me closer I watched as a young girl clasped his hand she was happy smiling and he took her under his arm.

I watched her looking at him 'sorry dad,' she mouthed and I felt another crushing blow in my chest. I fell to my knees as I watched them disappear into the house. I felt myself becoming weak again like I was losing my newfound confidence. I shook my head clearing the thoughts that had emerged but the lump was still there in the back of my throat. I swallowed hard to get rid of it but it wasn't going anywhere. I took in some deep breaths and the damp cold closed back in and it was gone. I stood up and followed where they had disappeared. I looked cautiously through the window of the faded red house trying to see where he was. I heard footsteps, I slid back hiding myself out of plain sight.

He walked through the house wearily pacing. My mouth began to water as I drew in deep breaths why was he so appealing to me? Making me feel so, so hungry. I closed my eyes imagining how he would taste, his warm flesh. I shook inside with excitement. I stepped back looking up above me a new urgency to get in the house swam inside of me.

There was a large tree its branches were very low I pulled myself up and climbed to the light coming from the upstairs window. I pressed hard on the wooden frame and it slid easily open. I climbed into the room it was pale blue and the dim light reflected off of white washed furniture.

I tip toed towards the door stopping for a moment to see my reflection in the full-length mirror. I stood staring at the image in the mirror it was a little unnerving how dark I looked. I had made a mess of my clothes. My jeans were torn as was my sweater there was dark liquid like mud everywhere but my eyes were the unnerving part. Bright green with dark circles around the pupil and outer edge of the Iris.

My skin had an eerie glow cast by the moonlight from the window I slid the slippers off and ran my hands through my hair tussling it a bit trying to release some of the tangles to no avail. I turned my head back and forth making sure I had control of the creature in front of me. Maybe they were right to be afraid, maybe I was a monster this image was me but felt foreign and dangerous. I shivered but not from the icy cold temperature I had been exposed to it was something else. I wanted to not look anymore but it was hard to break my gaze, I marveled at how completely wrecked I was but still something alluring about this creature something unnatural. I traced the large gashes in my sweater across my chest and stomach. They were deep but I felt only moderate pain.

I closed my eyes to break the gaze and took a deep breath my mouth immediately watered and I quickly snapped out of the trance I was in. I felt a deep instinctive need to go downstairs my breathing began to speed up, I fought to steady it.
I walked out into the hall seeing the amber glow of the warm light below I slinked down the steps partially crouched the house had no familiarity to it. I was thinking I had misunderstood what they meant when they said it was my house. It felt wrong making me on edge. The feeling of hunger was more than I could stand but I was very focused as I neared the bottom I drew in another breath my jaws clenched to help me swallow.
I stood watching him, his reflection in the window he was working on what looked like a puzzle on the table. I noticed him freeze and stop in mid-motion. I looked up to see him looking back at me through the reflection in the glass. We stood staring at each other for a moment, I was taking shallow breaths to accommodate my rapid heart beat. I took a deeper breath trying to slow down my breathing again this time as quickly as it started my heart beat steadied I felt my eyes widen.

"Zoe? It's okay everything is going to be alright just don't go anywhere."

He moved slowly turning to face me I stepped back a little at first my mind trying to process the information my senses were sending to my brain. It was confusing, part of me was trying to be rational and deny my body of the horrendous urge to fulfill its needs. He stepped towards me again.

"Stop! No closer."

I held my hand up for a moment holding my breath. I don't want to do this I repeated to myself over and over my body shook as I fought it.

"I don't want to do this."

"Do what Zoe?"

I said it not meaning it to be audible. He stepped closer again.

"I said stay back!"

I pushed him backwards he stumbled back hard into the table knocking puzzle pieces everywhere. His eyes were large and full of surprise.

"Zoe easy, I just want to help you."

His mind was racing torn between the love he felt for me and the natural fear his body was telling him to feel. It was annoying me reading his thoughts it was easier when he was just scared he smelled better but when he started thinking about her and myself it was difficult.

"I wish things could be different I do, I wish I didn't want to rip the flesh from you right now but I do and I am really trying to figure out a way that will hurt the least so please stop thinking and shut up!"

His mouth dropped open and he stared at me silent.

"And stop thinking of her it's really annoying me."

"Abbey? But how did you know?"

Now I was the one pacing he sat in the chair I had thrown him against. He was still staring at me watching me pace the floor. I needed to do this because they would be back soon to stop me, and I would miss my opportunity. This stupid voice in my head will not let up begging and pleading to me, I wanted her to shut up go away. 'You don't have to do this, you will regret it, Listen to him.' Ahhh!

"Shut up, shut up, shut up!"

He jumped as my voice growled out the command.

I grabbed my head I was going insane, I don't remember who I was but I know this is not normal hearing voices.

"Zoe?" his voice was soft and broken.

"What, what do you want from me now? Want to beg me to not do this too?"

"Not beg, I don't want to die don't get me wrong, and I don't want to hurt you, I will do whatever it takes to help you. You're hurt and need a doctor, let me call William and Jared they can make you better."

I was letting the sap in me have to much rope she would hang us both. Besides with every breath I drew in the hunger called to me to do its bidding. I felt that calm feeling again I adjusted my neck hearing my spine crackle with the twists. I was starting to feel a little stiff and the wounds on my legs had begun to pulse with every heartbeat. I walked closer to him feeling his breathing get quicker.

"Help me? Help me like before Justin? Make me better or fix your mistake?" "That's not it at all Zoe look at you, you're bleeding everywhere you need help please."

"Anything you would like to say before?"

"You mean before you kill me?"

"Something like that."

"Zoe, I don't want you to get hurt, but I won't let you do this."

"I'll tell you what Justin"

I looked towards the large glass door.

"I'll give you a head start, I'll even count to 20 before I start that seems fair right?"

He moved circling the table his mind playing out different scenarios none of which were feasible. I saw a coat hanging on the hook near the door I walked over and grabbed it off the hook "Here we wouldn't want you to get chilled.

"Zoe, wait-"

"One, two, three-"

He grabbed the coat on and scrambled out the back door towards the water.

Not because he was afraid of me so much because he was still viewing me as a girl weak and fragile, his weak emotions playing with his survival instincts. He was still trying to save me. I stood still counting out loud while I listened to him. He was looking for his cell phone as he ran down the slate path. This reading peoples thoughts came in handy it was proving to be a two edged sword.

"Twenty"

I said louder, I could hear her in my head again

"Why are you doing this to him?"

I not so politely told her to SHUT UP! I stepped out into the damp night air breathing in his scent deeply. It wasn't hard to follow his clumsy footsteps but his scent made it even easier. He would be calling them buy now and it would even out his chances if they found him before me. Somehow that seemed more sportsmen like.

I ran after him, he had crossed over the road around the front of the house and began running south, I imagined towards William's.

I had to give it to him he was pretty fast the ground was slightly frozen and hard to get traction I was beginning to miss my slippers I had taken off up stairs my feet were covered with only thin footie socks little to no cover on my frozen feet but it didn't matter I was in a different mode now I only felt raw adrenaline from the chase. The moon cast an icy, blue glow over the road and the huge pine trees lining it making his tracks easy to see. My chest and stomach were beginning to protest the running and I needed to catch him quickly before they got here. I pressed harder to gain some ground on him, my body ignoring the pain, as the scent grew stronger. I followed him into a narrow path that went into the pines and came out the other side into and opening. There was an old building some sort of old boathouse that was built over the water, I could hear him telling them to hurry. He didn't want to have to defend himself and hurt me, how sweet.

I slowed as I approached the old shack looking for possible ways he could escape. I felt his thoughts scattered thinking of what he could grab to defend himself what would do the least damage, his mind whirled making me feel dizzy.

"You really out did yourself running. I almost had a hard time keeping up but then again you're lucky I'm injured. I would have been much faster if not."

I saw a long board near the side and slid it over the wooden handles of the rusted metal door locking it into place and crept around the back of the building.

"I know your in here Justin, aren't you tired, tired of running, feeling frightened, of hurting me to protect yourself? It would be easier for me if you would just come out we played the game and now it's over. Why drag this out?"

I slipped around the back of the shack towards the water there was a large opening where part of the building had fallen away.

"What if she does get here and she gets hurt? Aren't you worried about her safety?"

"Stop it Zoe, just stop it! You are going to wait until they get here and get some help damn it!"

"There you are."

He walked around the other side of the opening in the floor where they stored the boats the water was black looking similar to black oil. There was no boat now though this building was decrepit and falling apart. I circled the opposite direction I was salivating now my mouth moist awaiting the first bite the warm liquid I had dreamed of spilling over my lips. My muscles tightened and I leapt over the eight-foot opening landing on him and knocking us both into the tarps and old gas cans. As I landed I struck the side rail used for bumpers and floats. It broke and tore at my side and arm, I landed half crouching half standing.

He was underneath me half knocked out I stumbled backward catching my balance before I fell in the black water. He shook his head and scrambled to his feet grabbing the board that had broken my fall and holding it like a bat.

I suddenly had a flash in my mind seeing the same image and feeling pain in my knee and leg I had the sense of being high above water and cold. I saw him, Jared, but this was Justin, I clasped my eyes tight opening them again trying to relieve myself of the images. I saw Justin again as I opened my eyes trying to stand, scared, trying to wake up from this nightmare. I could hear his voice muffled but becoming clearer. I saw tears in his eyes forming

> "Zoe I love you, no matter what you do, I will love you. I know we did this to you; look at what we have done to you!"

He grabbed his hair with his fingers pulling it back out of his face tightly staring at me.

"This is what you wanted wasn't it Justin?"

I looked down my sweater torn into shreds baring half of my bare chest and midriff smeared with deep crimson and deep gashes of flesh.

"To get me naked, I have seen it in your thoughts. Being with me how it would have been to hold me for me to be all yours, not having to share me with him. Here I am Justin and you're running from me."

> "You're right I did want that but not like this we caused you to feel like this. I loved you so much I couldn't let you go, none of us could. It's the serum Zoe it's not your fault. Remember this isn't your fault I know your in there somewhere, I know it I'm so sorry for what you have gone through. Please try and hold on I know you're in there, hang on just a little bit longer fight it!"

The words burned in me like hot daggers each word penetrating my flesh and scorching it.

I tried to not listen but it was no use I had to do this she was becoming stronger every time he spoke emerging from within her stupid pity, and remorse flooding my thoughts memories beginning to bombard me with weakness and emotion.
I heard the car pull up outside and spun listening as the doors opened. I turned back looking fondly at him, I would allow her that much. I looked over my shoulder as they tried the doors pulling the heavy board from the handles I gazed back at him the grin I felt inside emerging up one side of my face. I heard him gasp and he dropped the board holding his arms out. I felt my muscles tighten and burn from my torn flesh as I leapt at him this time landing on him successfully.

"Zoe stop, stop!"

His voice muffled again and then silence I felt heat through my body and then a cool white light. I saw him there in the sunlight laughing, his blonde hair and tan skin, smiling looking at me so lovingly, I felt warm again my chest feeling the extent of the heat. The sound of their voices and screaming pierced my vision of him.

"What have you done Zoe Dossin?"

Her voice was frantic and angry. She clasped her hand over her mouth her face horrified. I looked down his limp body beneath mine there was blood everywhere, I couldn't remember what had happened. I fell backwards into a crouching position steadying myself from falling with my hands. My legs trembled from the adrenaline retreating out of my body.

"Abbey wait!"

William interrupted her stepping in front of her.

"Zoe just be still I'm coming over."

"NO! stay, stay."

I felt tears pour down my face as a flood of emotion wafted over me.

"Pleaseeee stay, stay there."

I looked at him feeling sorrow for what I had done, for what I had felt.

"Zoe we can help you let me come over to you, we need to check on Justin."

I stood stumbling slightly I moved opposite of them away from Justin towards the opening of the dingy shack. Jared and Abbey raced to Justin's side checking on him his body still lifeless. William followed my steps from the opposite side. I stood staring at the black abyss wishing I could disappear into it.

"I am a monster, I deserve to be dead, this serum, this cure you have given me has damned me, Cursed me, to this sickness and I can't fight it, I'm dead in every meaning of the word except I draw breath. I am no one, I have memories of someone else who loved you all and you loved her but I'm not her, I just look like her. What have I done?"

I looked over at him laying there as they feverishly worked on him.

"Do you still love me now William? How many will it take before you stop loving me?"

"Zoe-"

I held up my hand to him to stop.

"Don't, don't answer me. I understand you can't bear to let me go no matter how great a monster I am. But I can't live like that, not knowing who I am, who you are and why you all love me. I keep seeing visions, dreams of people I don't know but I love, it's ripping me apart. I can't live knowing I am capable of doing this."

He looked at me puzzled for a moment.

"Please let me go."

I whispered.

"Let me go if you love me."

New tears spilled over the old ones still saturating my face.

"Zoe don't, don't you do it!"

I looked back at them feeling my strength leaving me. It was like slow motion as I fell into the blackness calming and something almost familiar about it.

The cool water felt good on my hot skin as the darkness covered me. I wished I could stay here in the cool, white light no noise just quiet everywhere.

He was beautiful standing there I couldn't see his face but I could sense his beauty his desire for me. I ran to him as he scooped me up and held me. I felt his warm kisses everywhere and his smooth warm skin. I tried to see his face to imprint it into memory this one I loved more than life. I had misplaced his image but his memory was there in tact. Our bodies seemed to fit perfectly together I never wanted to leave this place. I suddenly felt a burning sensation on my stomach and chest and a tugging feeling. I resisted opening my eyes I wanted to stay here.

"Zoe can you hear me?"

The voice was distant and sounded muffled like I was in a tunnel.

"Zoe can you open your eyes?"

His voice called me out from the white light from my Eden.

"Open your eyes it's okay your safe."

I struggled to hold on to this utopia I desperately needed to stay here where I was truly safe.

"Zoe, Justin is going to be fine he's just a little beat up. Zoe honey open your eyes if you can hear me."

I slowly opened them the white light was all around him behind him making it hard to see his face but I knew that voice.

"Beloved?"

My voice was groggy as I spoke.

"Yes I'm here."

My eyes focused on his dark eyes I felt warm tears spill on my face as they dripped from his eyes.

"You remember?"

"Of course."
I felt my finger and looked down at it.
"Where's my ring?"
Wondering why he had taken it off me? had I lost it? And why wouldn't Justin be okay? What had happened? He reached into his pocket and pulled out the silver band dotted with beautiful sparkles and placed it back on my hand. Bending down to kiss it and then kissing me deeply. I whispered in his ear.

"I've been sleeping a long time haven't I?"

"Yes my beloved you have but now you're awake."

COMING SOON

***

The Madison Curse Series
Vol. 2

Le Maudit

Also check out allie fishers new book

Maybe I do?

Visit allie's website @
www.alliefisher-author.vpweb.com